The Ares Virus

By

A P Bateman

Text © Anthony Paul Bateman

2015

All rights reserved


No part of this book may be reproduced, or stored
in a retrieval system, or transmitted in any form
or by any means, electronic, mechanical,
photocopying, printing or otherwise, without
written permission of the author.


Author contact: anthonybateman1@gmail.com

For my wife Clair
For putting up with all my silliness

To Summer and Lewis
For keeping me silly

**ONE**

The air was crisp and clean. Little wind. Fall was finally edging through after a balmy summer. The forest felt alive with movement and noise as he listened to the night sounds, his senses slowly becoming in tune with his surroundings. Nocturnal creatures were foraging for food, occasional screeches piercing the night. Some hunting, the others hunted.

His feet crunched on the stony ground, popping seed pods and the first of the brittle fall leaves as he walked around the vehicle and opened the trunk. He caught hold of the corpse under its ankles and heaved it out towards the opening. He allowed the feet to drop to the ground then got a good hold under its arm pits, dropped his own weight and pulled the torso over his shoulder like a slaughter man carrying a quarter of beef. The cadaver was heavy. The dead man had been two hundred and thirty pounds in life. Still was. The body was fat and gelatinous. Rigor mortise had subsided and the form was cumbersome. But the man was six four and two hundred and fifty pounds of muscle and bone and he easily lifted the corpse out and around the vehicle and to the open driver's door. He dropped the body as well as he could into the seat. It was a big vehicle, a Chevy Tahoe. The body slid a little on the leather seat but the man heaved it back up and got the seatbelt around and buckled up. It was difficult using the gloves. But they were necessary. He had worn them the whole time he drove the big SUV up the mountain road and he had worn them whilst he had pinched the dead man's nose shut, clamped the other over his mouth and straddled him, holding him still with his two hundred and fifty pounds of muscle until the man beneath him ceased struggling and accepted death.

He switched the vehicle's ignition on and the V8 rumbled into life. He wound down the driver's window and then took a tool out from his jacket pocket. It was a spike on a handle. A honed screwdriver filed down to a dart's tip. He got down on to his back and wriggled his frame under the vehicle and put the tip on the bottom of the fuel tank. Holding it in place, he drove the palm of his gloved right hand onto the pommel of the tool's handle and the tip ruptured the tank spilling out a small but consistent trickle of fuel onto the ground. The flow of fuel was satisfactory. The engine was running and sucking petrol steadily. It was similar to plumbing whereby there was now a free flow effect. He got back up brushing the debris of leaves and earth off his back and returned to the driver's window. He reached in and turned the lights on. The beams cut a swathe of light through the darkness into a void of nothing beyond. The patch of ground was fifty yards off a track which in turn ran a half mile from the road. It was a mountain road and the road in question wound a ribbon both a half mile behind the Tahoe and forty yards and two hundred feet below out in front of the dazzling beams. The site had been chosen well. Another hundred feet below the road was the next section of black top. With enough momentum the Tahoe would hit the first section of road, crash through the barrier and carry on below. The leaking fuel tank should emit enough fuel and the impact should create enough sparks as the two tons of metal smashed into the asphalt and rocks and metal crash barrier below. It was the fuel vapor that mattered most and the small puncture in the fuel tank would guarantee a steady amount.

The man reached in through the window past the cadaver's shoulder and he picked up the length of stick he had earlier trimmed and tested as he had waited for darkness to fall. It was similar in dimension to a walking cane. He used it to press down on the footbrake and then with his right hand he shifted the automatic selector into drive. He took the stick off the footbrake and the vehicle eased forward so slowly that he did not even have to move. Positive creep, the manufacturers called it and it enabled perfect hill starts. He positioned the wooden stick over the throttle and then pressed down hard all the way to the floor. The V8 growled and the big Chevy shot forward throwing debris up with all four wheels. The man twisted away, keeping a firm grip on the stick and the SUV immediately started to slow but not enough before it reached the edge of the precipice and disappeared from view. A full two seconds later there was an almighty crash of two tons of metal impacting on the asphalt like cannon fire. A tearing, screeching sound and silence once more, before a second shattering impact on the meandering section of road further below. The man could hear a faint whoosh and almost immediately the night gave way to a warm yellow glow.

He stood at the edge and watched. The flames grew and licked gently at the night sky. They didn't rush, simply enveloped the vehicle and teased at the gas tank heating the metal and waiting patiently for the tank to split and release the rest of the gasoline. He took off the gloves and tucked them inside his coat.

The eventual explosion was bright, but not loud, and surged high into the air. Flames imploded on themselves, turned a tight circle then threw themselves full force towards the sky. There was enough light from the flame to see a large smoke pyre in the shape of a giant mushroom billowing skywards.

He was satisfied with the effect although outwardly he showed no sign of emotion. He did not smile, nor allow himself any sense of relief at the completion of the task. The efforts of the exertion had left him breathless and hot, but the sensation was subsiding and the distinct chill in the air was enough for him to raise the collar of his jacket. He casually tossed the stick into the fringe of the forest as he turned around and walked back into the night.

## TWO

She had heard the expression before. Only now she knew what it really meant. An 'air of tension' had taken hold of the entire facility. It had moved through the building like a thick fog, enveloping all in its path and consuming relentlessly. For some, the tension was euphoric. What had been achieved in the past four months of the five year project was illuminating. The anticipation of what now lay ahead had even the most senior staff acting like children at the end of semester. They were looking ahead, some realizing that their career paths may have dramatically widened with the culmination of the project. Others, like her were unable to process recent events. It would appear that many though had not given it a second thought. She knew that none of this project, and nothing that was about happen today would have been possible without one man. Her mentor, her boss. The man who had found the few breadcrumbs that Mother Nature had left for them to follow. The man who had put the pieces together in the right order and found the picture staring back at him.

She tidied her workstation and put the computer on stand-by and switched off the monitor. There was little clutter at her desk. She liked it that way. No clutter in her work life, no clutter in her home life and certainly no clutter in her love life. Although she would have to agree that the latter was not by choice, merely circumstance born of fourteen hour days and little hope to change that just yet.

She felt the tension like everybody else, and had it not been for yesterday's tragic announcement she would quite possibly have joined in on today's mood within the facility. Only now she was far from happy. A momentous occasion such as this should have been something to savor, something to treasure for the rest of her career. Yet now she was left with the feeling of emptiness which had somehow avoided her senior colleagues. On the surface at least.

She slipped off the white technicians coat and smoothed down her skirt. It was part of the suit she had bought for the interview five years ago. She had thought it smart and sophisticated at the time and had thought how it would also be suitable attire for possible dates in expensive restaurants, weddings of her colleagues or friends and smart social gatherings. It was her only suit and quite possibly the third time she had worn it. On the plus side her figure hadn't changed over the five years, but on the minus side it said a hell of a lot about her life. A quick glance in her compact told her she was passable and then she picked up the folder and her note cards and walked to the door.

She was nervous as she climbed the few steps to the stage and walked to the lectern. She remembered the old cliché about speech making and that was to picture the audience in their underwear. One glance was enough to make her want to pack up and go home right now. Mostly a collection of middle-aged men or older still, with muscles running to fat, long since softened by polishing a seat with their backsides for too many years. There was also a scattering of sour-faced women who had been hardened forever, the price paid for fighting their way to the top in the last bastion of a man's world.

There was a dazzle from the lights in the auditorium. Her podium was a little too high and the microphone seemed too far away. But it hadn't been set for her and the realization suddenly added to the stress, making her sad for the department's recent loss. Her boss was tall and would have set up the microphone as he practiced his speech most of this past week.

Much was riding on this project and the recent developments meant selling something altogether different from the initial brief.

"GOOD ..." The sound made her jump. Several people in the front row jumped or flinched along with her. A technician dutifully trotted out across the stage and finely tuned the volume adjustment on the microphone. He smiled briefly and mouthed a good luck to her. She smiled back. She liked him. They had both been tearful at the recent news.

She took a deep breath. She could see the look of amusement on the faces in the audience and she felt frustrated that she was losing them at the start.

"Good morning ladies and gentlemen," she paused, relieved that the microphone was now on her side. "My name is Isobel Bartlett and I am Senior Consultant, and acting Head of Technical Advancement in Bioresearch. Before I start today's presentation, I would like to express my deepest sorrow for the recent loss of our esteemed colleague, and creator of the project, Professor Joseph Leipzig. Without him, I know, as do my colleagues that ARES would not have got off the ground. And our greatest technical achievement would not have been announced today," she said. "As you are no doubt aware in your briefs, ARES is our name for bio-formulae Xarianchloro 47B. A project initially started in the late sixties as a weapon to hold in the Cold War. To keep it in layman's terms, although it is described in further detail in your briefs, this is fundamentally a virus with similar genetic structure to Spanish Influenza. The project was soon shelved following more sophisticated development of nuclear weapons including ICBM's. However, we have developed the project in such a manner that we have been able to tap into its potential in ways not thought possible. Ares, the ancient Greek god of war was our name for possibly the most audacious weapon of modern warfare. We chose this name because in Greek mythology Ares himself was a god of great flaws. He was a blunt instrument, and although other war gods used strategies and guile, Ares himself was a god of domineering, overwhelming force. He had an affair with Aphrodite, the goddess of love, and was left ridiculed and embarrassed by her husband. However, Ares was the greatest warrior in ancient Greek history and subsequently the most feared and revered," she paused. Her lips were dry and she took a quick sip of the glass of water in front of her. She put the glass back down and noticed she was shaking a little. "As was our brief, we achieved an accumulative virus closely representing the symptoms of flu. What differs, in fact is ARES' destructive spread through the nervous system, culminating in severe spasmodic episodes. After initial contact the flu symptoms develop over a period of between three and eight hours. The virus is airborne and spread through spores as well as hand contact, body and sexual contact. However, this is not just a common cold. This is aching, agonizing muscle fatigue combined with respiratory discomfort, headaches and aversion to light. After twenty-four hours the virus really begins to catch hold of the subject," she paused. "Or I should say, victim."

There were a few hushed tones in the audience. But this was what they were here for.
"It paralyses them, rushes through their body like napalm through their veins, agonizing convulsions occur which will last another twenty four hours. The skin will delaminate from the muscle making voluntary movement impossible. Internal organs virtually rot away. Convulsions and spasms are so violent that they can practically snap the subject's own spin. Death in any case comes at approximately forty-eight hours after initial contact with the virus. This latter stage pulls upon the worst case scenario of a virus like Ebola."
She felt the speech lacked the dramatic impact that her audience were craving. She hoped that she wasn't like a performer dying mid-way through their act. But she had only cobbled together what she could from Leipzig's notes, and the man had been a natural orator. She bent down and ran her finger on the mouse pad of the laptop

on the small table beside her. The large screen behind her came into life and the moving icon, the symbol of the government research facility moved in small semi-circles across the screen. She clicked the icon in the bottom left of the screen and the large screen behind her continued with the display.

"What you are looking at now is the genetic structure of common flu. To the right," she paused while the next diagram whirled downwards from the top of the screen and rested still, a comparison beside the flu structure. "Is the genetic makeup of ARES." Two more genetic structures dropped down on the screen. "And here we have Bird Flu and the common cold."

All of the structures then moved across the screen and rested on ARES which was highlighted in red. All the structure combinations fitted completely. The audience looked unimpressed, they wanted pictures of victims. A video clip of an entire city rendered moribund by a killer virus. Perhaps in time, the video clips would come for real. She hoped not.

"There can be no doubt as to the destructive capabilities of ARES. Though, if you look at the similarities between our virus and that of common flu, you cannot fail to see that many of the traits and idiosyncrasies are the same. That is because common flu is still one of the world's largest killers. It may also be worth noting that the common cold claims many lives each year, costs industry billions of dollars worldwide in lost production and that there is still no known cure for the common cold." She moved the mouse and the screen changed once more. Two new genetic structures appeared. "Until now, that is."

There were a few mumbles and hushed tones from within the crowd. Somewhere from the back a man cleared his throat and whispered to the man next to him.

"With our development of ARES we had to create an anti-virus. An antidote. This of course, is common practice. We cannot stare into the mouth of Hell without the knowledge that there is a heaven above us. APHRODITE is the answer to ARES. As ARES was the god of war, APHRODITE was the ancient Greek goddess of love. From our antidote came far more beneficial research than ever could have from ARES ..." she was cut short by a muffled gasp from somebody within the audience. There was no follow-up, the audience clearly wanted to see where she was going next. "APHRODITE could well be the answer to our prayers. The antidote has been experimented with exhaustedly and we feel that there is much to be gained from further research and development. We have gained great advances in creating strains to counter many immune-system attacking viruses. A strain from APHRODITE has been proven to eliminate flu symptoms in trials as well as mere cold symptoms. We believe that not only does APHRODITE contain the secrets of fighting immune-system attacking viruses, but what we may have here is not merely a cure for the common cold, but one which with further research, we believe can be the biggest advancement in fighting HIV and AIDS. We have great confidence that APHRODITE is merely months away from a strain which will counter Ebola," she paused. There was emotion in her voice. Here was research worth working towards. Here was what her department had felt so happy about. And who really could blame them? Professor Leipzig was dead, but the door for so many opportunities was open. "I will take some questions now." There was a hand in the air immediately. It belonged to a large man in full military uniform. She looked at the man and smiled. "Yes, Sir?"

The man stood up and cleared his throat. He was a four star general. "General Chuck Howard, Ma'am. Tell me, with the greatest respect, what has all this talk and speculation about AIDS and a cure for a God damn cold got to do with my weapon? We're not the World Health Organization; we don't give a rat's ass about some shanty town in Africa being struck down with AIDS. Hell, a bunch of pop stars can sing a song for them and celebrities can launch a new range of peace chips. Organic ones flavored with sea salt and wasabi," he smirked. "You want a result for world freedom from strife and disease; you go work for the World Health Organization. You want to keep everybody in this room happy, you talk about our new weapon and what it could do for us logistically on a global scale." He sat back down and folded his arms across his chest. He looked pleased with himself. So did half the audience.

Isobel Bartlett looked shaken. She looked down at one of the hard faced women in the front row.

"Karen Somerton, Department of Defense. What testing was carried out with ARES? Were human subjects involved?"

Bartlett shook her head. "No. We tested ARES on both primates and swine. Both closely resemble human organs and respiratory systems. Computer simulation and genetic block building was brought in to get a clearer picture. Believe me when I say ARES is an effective killer. What we did test on volunteer subjects was APHRODITE and her, sorry *its* ability to break the flu viruses and offer more towards other viruses. In later trials both myself and Professor Leipzig volunteered for infection with common flu. Both of us were cured within twenty-four hours. Professor Leipzig went further and infected himself with strain one avian flu and was cleared healthy within forty-eight hours of the administering of APHRODITE."

"So it's all hypothetical? We don't know if ARES actually works the way you say it will," Somerton scorned. "What we have here is speculation. Your antidote is all well and good, but we're here for ARES"

Bartlett shook her head. "No. The antidote is always more important. You always need a method of containment," she paused. "As for ARES, think of it like this; we invent a new type of gun. The powder is different, the shell casing is made of composite, not brass. The bullet is made of a new blend of alloy. Would you doubt its ability to fire by placing the barrel against your own head? No. The facts are there."

"But unproven."

"You could volunteer," Isobel had said it before she could help herself. There was a murmur of laughter. Karen Somerton look displeased. "Look, we are experts in our field and we have done all the testing possible at this stage. But what we have found that is really to be celebrated is the cure, the antidote to the most terrible of the world's diseases. I have no doubt ARES would work out of the bottle tomorrow, but who knows how quickly it could spread? We've used the best simulations designed by the best analysts and statisticians the US government has to offer. If deployed in a major capital city ARES could reach a billion people within a month. Given airline travel, train stations, bus stations and the speed at which ARES works..." She trailed off, feeling suddenly very hot under her collar. "It's unthinkable. After time governments would find methods to contain the virus, mainly because infrastructure would start to fail. But by then it may even be too late. Containment is the biggest factor with ARES. Hence the need for APHRODITE. ARES could be for us what the asteroid was for the dinosaurs; a total species eliminator."

## THREE

"Tough break, eh?" McCray sat down, perching himself on the edge of her desk. He was smart forty year old who had probably always looked preppy. For a while Isobel and he had held the same status but he was higher up now. He oversaw each project and was the administrative link between them. He often met with White House representatives and personnel from the pentagon. She had never shown any resentment at his promotion, it took him to a desk and she preferred the research. She considered him a friend. "Come on Isobel, what did you expect? Bunch of warmongers and desk warriors, they don't want to hear you gush about the possibility for a cure for AIDS."

"The possibilities of APHRODITE have barely been tapped into. It's the building blocks to the unknown. Specialists in other fields could find its application used towards a cure for cancer. If what we have discovered with the

21

development of both ARES and APHRODITE were to be made common knowledge, for free, then who knows where research could take us. We're at the world's biggest crossroads and it could not matter more which way we turn."

"Honey, I've been in the same meetings," McCray smiled. "I know."

"Well what more do they want?"

"Their weapon," McCray paused. "And the world can never know about ARES. The US government sanctioning a potential global killer. A new WMD for a new world order? What would our enemies make of that? What might they do to pre-empt any potential deployment? North Korea are twitchy enough as it is. And Russia has been flexing its muscles for years."

"They can't even have their weapon," she said, wiping her eyes as she leaned back in her chair. She had been crying. McCray could see this and it annoyed her. It had been a combination of emotion, of Professor Leipzig's death of the reception to her speech, of the fact she knew APHRODITE had not been appreciated. "ARES is a concept, a think tank's invention, produced by us to be applauded by the men in grey suits and starched uniforms. When would ARES be deployed? And against whom? What we got with APHRODITE is something tangible from a whole load of evil. We've pushed the boundaries in what's achievable and in doing so we have created one of the most important discoveries in medical history. It's a eureka moment as important as the discovery of penicillin. Professor Leipzig knew this, that's why he called the conference," Isobel paused. "Only..."

"Yeah, tough breaks all round," McCray said. "One minute you're breaking through the barriers of science, the next you're breaking through the barriers of a road and off a cliff." It sounded flippant, but he genuinely looked like he hadn't meant it to. "I'm sorry I mean ..."

She shrugged. "I know. I just can't believe it. It hasn't quite sunk in yet. He was a good driver and I'm sure he wouldn't drink and drive. The police said a toxicology report is unlikely, due to..." she paused, shuddering involuntarily at the thought of her friend and mentor's charred remains at the wheel of a burned out wreck. "He was ever so tired though. Perhaps he just nodded off for a moment."

There was a rap on the door and woman peered around the doorjamb. It was Mary Long, a senior lab technician who was also helping out with guided tours for some of the visitors today. Isobel hadn't seen her so happy in months. The atmosphere must have been as infectious as the testing samples she normally worked on. "Your public awaits you Isobel," she smiled amiably. "A few more questions, it won't take long. A few of us are having drinks at Landon's afterwards. If you fancy coming along?"

Finally the suit gets some use. She shook her head. It just didn't seem right somehow.

The function room had been built during a previous administration back when the American government had more money. They don't come as standard in government facilities any longer. The walls were wood paneled on two sides, the other two sides were glass and looked down over the lake. It was a corner room and the architect had made good use of it. Ducks and swans swam not far from the shore of the lake and a large water fountain sprayed an enormous plume of water at the middle. The lake was purpose built and artificial. Lakes don't come as standard in Government facilities anymore either.

There were buffet tables along one wall of the gallery room and it was always an in-house joke that you could gauge the importance of the visitors by the quality of the menu. Department briefings and brainstorming exercises were followed by coffee and donuts. If you were lucky you got glazed Danish pastries with a cherry on top. Interdepartmental briefings were usually followed by a selection of open sandwiches, a Danish or jelly donut and a fruit cup if you didn't care for coffee. This briefing, however, was a pretty good gauge of the demographic. Sushi and sashimi, a selection of savory pastry cases with various fillings, two dressed salmon with cucumber slices for scales and aspic jelly as a glaze. There was a whole table devoted to freshly carved roast meats including some very rare roast rump, a honey glazed ham with cloves, tempura battered shrimps with a variety of dips, as well as a whole table of fruit pastries, mini pavlovas and chocolate desserts with whipped cream. Wine replaced coffee, and the room was humming with attentive chatter as the people mingled and swapped their views on the presentation.

The project PR woman greeted Isobel at the door and led her through the room to a group of men who were standing by the buffet table and doing their best to cope with large slices of roast meat as they ate and juggled a plate in their other hand. The kitchen had tried to impress, but had ignored the brief of a finger buffet. But they didn't get to cater like this often and probably relished cooking for White House and Pentagon elite.

"Ah, Florence Nightingale herself!" The big four star general smiled. "Loved the talk, little lady. Hope I didn't upset you, but I could see you were well off track." The voice was southern, Georgian she reckoned. No, North Carolina.

"No," she lied. "We have simply developed more than our brief. Professor Leipzig decided to push efforts towards the antidote. Once he realized the true worth of APHRODITE's applications he maintained that it would be criminal not to. I believe Professor Leipzig to have been a true humanitarian."

"God damn irony, right?" General Harris smiled. He forked a huge piece of bloody beef into his mouth and chewed slowly. "Leipzig created some serious shit. I mean, you're too young to know, but the man was a genius in his field. He was around during the Cold War. We poached him from the Brits. He came up with stuff at their facility in Porton Down," he paused long enough to swallow. "That was their chemical and biological facility. They tested the stuff on their own soldiers. But hey, they didn't get to rule the world for so long by being nice."

"Yeah, but we rule it now." The voice belonged to a man in his mid to late fifties. He wore a shabby cheap looking suit and his laminated ID badge read: Tom Hardy, and underneath: Strategic Security. Isobel had never heard of it, but for the entire world he looked like CIA. She had been briefed that nobody would be as they seemed today. "This guy Leipzig, he died recently, right?"

"Yes, two days ago in a car accident."

"Too bad." The man stuffed a large piece of wet sushi into his mouth. He chewed, leaving a little kelp on his lip. "This time of year, wet roads, fall leaves. It happens. Good speech though, I guess it was short notice."

"I'm David Law." A smart-looking man in his mid-thirties held out his hand. Isobel shook it. His hand was cool and firm. She looked him in the eyes as he spoke. "I'm with the National Security Agency. Tell me, what would be the dispersal rate of the virus?"

"Well, as I said it works fast. Symptoms as early as three hours," she paused, realizing she was still holding his hand. She let go and picked a glass of fruit juice up off the table. "The victim dies after approximately forty eight hours."

"Forgive me, I was listening in there," he smiled. "What about conditions? Are there factors to consider?"

"Yes, a number of factors," Isobel said. "Weather conditions."

"Such as?" The NSA representative cut in.

Unperturbed, she looked at him. He seemed alert, confident. His eyes were cold though. Glacier blue and hard. "Temperature is key, as with all flu like viruses. Wet and warm is ideal. Viruses always favor humid conditions. Wind speed plays a factor as it's an airborne virus. And then there's population density. If the population is dense and transient, we could be talking about thousands every day," she paused. "But it becomes exponential. Like grains of rice on a chessboard. This is why we do not favor ARES as an effective weapon. It is accumulative and extremely unstable. It could come back and bite you on the ass," she smiled. "Excuse me. But in order to be an effective weapon you need control of the parameters within which it is deployed. Leipzig realized this, but ARES was merely guided into shape. Mother Nature controls a piece of it too."

"With all due respect, little lady," the general smirked. "We are the military experts, not you or your department. If we see ARES as a viable military application then we may have ideas for it that you guys might not comprehend."

"And with the greatest respect, general, we are the biochemical experts, not you or your associates. If Professor Leipzig felt that ARES was not an effectively controlled weapon, then I am sure he speaks not only for the entire department but the US government." She steadied herself. "What Leipzig and his team discovered was a cure, potentially, for some of our most hideous viruses and diseases. Surely that deserves funding and developmental time within the program budget?"

"Not in this company, no." Tom Hardy stared at her, the kelp still attached to his lip. He had also managed a sizable stain down his ten-dollar shirt.

Wasabi was Isobel's guess. "The WHO would welcome this development with open arms. However, Ms..." he paused glancing at her left hand for confirmation. She felt like she wanted to flinch at the intrusion. "... Ms. Bartlett, the WHO will never hear of this development, because the WHO does not work for the United States government, and the WHO is not part of the Government Strategic Defense Program."

Bartlett did not know this man, nor had she ever heard of his agency, but she recognized the talk and she recognized the feeling of her own helplessness; being talked down to by a bureaucrat with a lot of power behind them. She looked at this man Hardy, but he was already working his way through another piece of sushi and had turned his attention towards the smart young NSA representative.

After an hour of mingling and repeating much of her speech Isobel left the room and headed down stairs to the restrooms on the third floor. They were not the closest, but that meant she would have less chance of being interrupted.

The walls were white porcelain tiles with mint green plaster away from the sinks. The floors were black marble. Again, from a time with more budget and less red tape. She stared at her reflection in the wall mirror. It took up the entire length of the bathroom. The faucets were polished stainless steel and she looked down, her face distorted in the metal. The sinks were standard porcelain with black marble surrounds there were twelve of them in a row. Behind her were twelve cubicles, each with a foot and a half of space between the door and the floor. It was an executive restroom and it was fashionably mixed sex. This was fine for most instances, but there had been discrepancies, a couple caught *debriefing* each other for one, but that was something now laughed about. No, the thing with mixed sex bathrooms was the fact that a girl couldn't have a cry without it becoming a major incident. Shed a tear and the next male in the bathroom would either run a mile for fear of accusations or would come over all brotherly and try and offer a shoulder to cry on. A girl couldn't simply let out a PMS induced sob without either having modern new man invade her space, or the missing link crashing down the door to get out. Isobel Bartlett felt no such hormone imbalance, simply the fact that a shitty couple of days just got a whole lot shittier. She pushed the spring-loaded door open and locked it closed behind her. She then put the toilet seat lid down and sat heavily. She was quiet for a second, checked nobody had come in, then felt the tears well within and started to cry softly. Partly was for the loss of her friend and colleague for which she had found no time to grieve, and partly was for her own misery at the briefing and presentation. APHRODITE was something to celebrate. ARES was something to put back in Pandora's Box and shut the lid. Then throw the thing in the damn ocean.

The bathroom door crashed open and she stopped sobbing with a start.

"What the fuck was that about?" The voice was angry. It was as loud as the crashing door. "Fucking bleeding heart!"

Instinctively, Isobel listened. She raised her legs high, not wanting to be seen and risk ending the conversation. She tucked her feet in under herself, coiled like a cat, tears still on her cheeks. In truth she was scared. Something about the tone of the man's voice unnerved her.

"Listen, it can still go ahead," a second man said. "The virus…"

"Sshh," the first man stopped him. "Are we clear?"

There was a scrabble and the sound of a belt buckle on the marble floor. Isobel imagined a faceless man holding a push-up as he checked for an occupied cubicle.

"It's OK," the first man replied. "Go on."

"The virus has been destroyed."

"What!"

"Relax. It's standard procedure. It's too

hazardous to keep here in its mature state. Atlanta has the storage facilities, but they're out of the loop." Isobel thought the two voices were familiar but the echo in the restroom distorted everything. She concentrated but she thought the man was also chewing gum or something. Then she smelled it, he was lighting a cigarette. "ARES is stored on two flash drives, in two halves. So is APHRODITE. Leipzig thought it too dangerous to keep ARES in its live state. Simpler and safer to make it to order, so to speak. However, APHRODITE is also held in animated state in ready to inject ampules. A safety measure during the testing of ARES and further antivirus research."

"Our investors can't have one without the other. What about production?"

"Just need a couple of decent graduates and a place to work."

Isobel concentrated hard. There were footsteps, then the sound of a faucet running. A splash of water, probably on a face. The towel rail rattled and then there were more footsteps.

"Morgan-Klein's stock will go through the fucking roof if they have the only antidote for what will be forever referred to as Chinese flu," a man laughed. Isobel couldn't tell which through the cavernous echo. "Our investors have been buying stock steadily for months. And shortening stock held in Chinese companies."

"When China is on its ass, we'll buy them back up. US productivity will rise, as will the rest of the west. Factories will relocate, commerce will build and the natural order will be restored once more," he paused and exhaled a lungful of smoke. Isobel could hear the faucet again he was most probably disposing of the cigarette down the drain. "Our investors are true patriots."

"As are we. And between us we'll have personal wealth more than some European countries," he chuckled. "What about bleeding heart? Where does she figure?"

"She'll carry on working on projects here, most probably continue working under Leipzig's replacement. She won't get his job. She'll finish out her twenty and retire an old maid, probably with lots of cats." The voice mumbled. "Leipzig has, or had the two flash drives in his safe. The other two we have access to. By the end of this charade today, we'll have both sets and things will never be the same again. Thousands infected daily, world-wide threat of a pandemic and countries that will be willing to pay Morgan-Klein billions for the antidote."

Isobel tensed, it was all she could do to remain quiet.

"She had better stay out of the way. Leipzig was one problem too many. He was too long in the tooth to develop a conscience," there

33

was a pause. "Besides, it would be a shame to waste such a nice piece of ass."

She heard the door open harshly and hit the rubber stopper on the wall and then it sprang to with a loud thud. The echo it made around the room made her flinch. And then the room was silent once more.

## FOUR

She had moved fast. There was no point in doing it any other way. The conference was in full swing. It was not often that the CIA could talk to the NSA over sushi. It was not often that Air Force Intelligence could mingle with their Army or Naval counterparts whilst swilling down free Californian chardonnay. In all there were nine US intelligence agencies in attendance, denoted by forty-two representatives. By now the talk had probably moved on from the concept of ARES, and the occasion had become a chance for shoulders to be rubbed, and no end of promises and favors to be made.

In the bathroom she had looked at her watch. It was three-forty. She had waited ten whole agonizing minutes and then had cautiously made her way out. At three fifty-five she was inside her office and had taken her security pass, handbag and her document folder. At four-ten she was inside the late professor Leipzig's office and opening the overt wall safe. This was a stainless steel cabinet used for the storage of various project related information. The facility was deemed secure by government contracted security operatives, searches were held on entry and exit, otherwise personnel had roaming access within their own departments. It was common practice for senior level personnel to have access to secure documents within their project.

The formula and genetic map of ARES and APHRODITE was held on two separate flash drives. Half the information was here, the other half was held securely in McCray's office, which was a separate department within the administration wing of the building. As second in command of the research and development, Isobel Bartlett had access to Leipzig's office and safe cabinet. She had access to his files in the admin library and she had access to his login files on the mainframe computer. They had worked together like that in case of illness or what little vacation they could take. The project never stalled because of a person's absence.

She took the two flash drives. She knew she had to move fast. She felt alone, trapped. She wanted to call security, but to tell them what? That she had heard two people talking in the bathroom? The nation's top security and espionage personnel were in the building. Nobody would take her seriously. She had no visual identification, wasn't even sure about the voices, although one had sounded vaguely familiar. Besides, as the facility was full of intelligence agencies what would be so strange about a hypothetical conversation by two colleagues taking about an application or deployment of ARES? But she knew this was no hypothesis. She knew that the two men had been deadly serious, and she knew that Professor Leipzig's death had been no accident. She felt she had to act, and act proactively. She could always bring the drives back to security later. Right now she wanted to warn McCray of what she had heard. She dropped both flash drives into her leather handbag and made her way towards the administration wing.

The offices were empty. There was little work to do on these occasions. Research and development were buzzing around the conference, so admin had nobody to answer questions or take suggestions. The office services girls had packed up and gone home before the kitchen had served lunch, and the research center was empty. This cavernous room was nothing more than a library really, with every scientific publication in the field of viral infection, genetics and medicine ever written in either book form or increasingly available on the database as e-book format. It was also a room that many of the senior staff relaxed in under the guise of research. The facility commanded long hours and human nature what it is, the room had been a sanctuary to many. Isobel continued walking down the sanitized corridor. McCray's office was at the end boasting similar views to the function room, with a panorama over the manmade lake and its fountain. His office suite was entered via an outer office, which was manned by McCray's personal assistant, Agnes Dempsey. A severe woman in her fifties little was known about Agnes, who was something of an enigma. However, she got things done like no other and much of the push for the ARES program was driven by her. It was Agnes Dempsey who devised the scheduling for the project and not, as everyone thought, McCray. Professor Leipzig had once told Isobel in strict confidence of Agnes Dempsey's husband who had acute bowel and colon cancer. It was APHRODITE that Dempsey was driving forward in the vain hope that their discovery could be applied to medicine in time. Isobel's opinion of the severe and motivated woman in her fifties, who was feared by people with slipping deadlines or poor accounting of personal budget, completely changed. She knew nothing much of her colleague's personal lives, but you never could tell what people were living through.

The door was ajar and she could hear the soft mumbling of voices from within. She entered discreetly. Agnes was not at her desk, but the door to McCray's office was open and there were voices, louder now, coming from inside.

She froze. Rigid, like ice. The same voices she had heard not half an hour previous, only this time, without the echo from the marbled bathroom, she recognized the voice of one of the men.

"Power," the man chuckled. "Power and money."

"Just get it, we don't have much time." There was the sound of a heavy metal door on a tight, secure hinge. "Right here, both of them together."

"Zeus."

"What?"

"Zeus," he paused. "Ares was the god of war. Aphrodite was the goddess of love," he laughed loudly. "Pretty corny really. But scientists aren't blessed with lateral imagination." The heavy safe door closed and locked. "But Zeus was the God of Gods in ancient Greek mythology. And with both of these, that's what we'll be. Fucking God!"

"Here, just take these and watch the door. I want to make sure that everything in the office is as it was left."

Isobel had to will her legs to move. She glanced around for somewhere to hide, but the office was small and there was nothing but

Agnes Dempsey's empty desk. She threw herself down and curled up beneath the desk, her legs tucked up tight to her chest in the fetal position. She heard the door swing wide and two legs paced over the floor and stopped in front of her. They were unstill and restless. The toes of the shoes were slightly scuffed, the sort of shoe leather that was used every day and had done a bit of mileage.

The door to McCray's office closed. The other set of legs joined the first. The shoes were immaculately polished. These shoes had seen little mileage. They had a range of stable mates at home some place. Probably mostly Italian for the spring or summer months or British for fall and winter.

"You done?" It was the owner of the high-mileage shoes who spoke, his manner gruff.

"Finished. Just need Leipzig's set and we're through for the day."

Isobel felt that should her heart beat any louder, the two men would surely hear. She kept as still as she could but her legs were shaking uncontrollably. The edge of her shoe clipped the hard floor and her heart felt like it had stopped. She held her breath, willing the two men not to have heard.

They hadn't and as they walked out of the office and their footfalls carried down the corridor, she let out a steady stream of breath and started to feel light headed as the rush of adrenalin coursing through her veins subsided.

She was back in the bathroom now. In a cubicle, her feet tucked up onto the seat. There was little time to lose. She had to get out of the facility quickly. To do this she had to get past the security with the two flash drives. It should be easy enough. It was a rare event for a strip search and that would also be governed by the presence of a female security officer. There were a few but they did not cover every shift.

She estimated that she had no more than fifteen minutes to get away. Any longer, and she was sure that the two men would discover that the drives had been taken. With Leipzig out of the equation it wouldn't take anyone too long to discover who else had access. And that could only lead back to her or McCray.

She opened her leather hand bag and removed the items, placing them in her lap. There was her purse, hairbrush an old, small can of Mace an ex-boyfriend had once given her, a very sparse cosmetics bag – the mere essentials, and likewise, an emergency feminine hygiene pocket which consisted of a couple of sanitary towels and a couple of tampons. There was also a packet of scented wet-wipes. She quickly slipped the two flash drives out of their clear plastic cases and dropped them into the bottom of the soft leather bag, then discarded the cases in the bin beside the toilet. She opened up the cosmetics bag and dropped the contents on top. To this she added the contents of the hygiene pocket, opened a sanitary towel, rolled it up and wrapped it loosely in the wrapper as if used, pulled out a scented wipe, crumpled it up and poked into the sanitary towel parcel, then placed it carefully on top of the loose contents. The can of mace slotted down the side of the contents, along with the hairbrush. She took a deep breath and opened the cubicle door.

The exit to the facility was empty. Unusually quiet. However, that was not necessarily a good sign. Security checks become more perfunctory when crowds are thicker. And the facility had many VIP's today so the guards should be switched on and operating on a higher than usual security condition. She walked at a quick pace, her hand bag in her right hand, the document folder squeezed under her right arm. With her left hand she cupped her stomach as she walked.

The team of security covering the entrance and exit consisted of four men from a contracted private company called SECURE-EXCEL. Two men operated the foyer and two wearing thick military style jackets stood outside just visible through the opaque glass. They wore uniforms similar to riot police with dark navy combat trousers and calf-high boots. Heavy utility belts at the waist that housed tactical batons and handcuffs, large metal torches and holstered 9mm Berettas. The two security officers were standing by the security check desk, chatting casually yet occasionally glancing over each other's shoulders. Like they were relaying dirty jokes and keeping a lookout not to get caught. One of the men turned towards Isobel and smiled. He wore seventies style mirrored sunglasses. His name was probably Buck or Hank.

She rubbed her stomach gently, pushing out her posture to form a small pot. She was slim but managed a fine swollen-looking belly. She walked on to the check desk and stopped beside them.

"Miss Bartlett." The man with sunglasses nodded and smiled. Then held out a hand for her security pass, which he checked quickly and handed back to her. "How are you today ma'am? Leaving early for a change?" It wasn't so much as an interrogation, merely an effort at small talk. He seemed friendly and had made the effort to remember her name. She felt bad for not having bothered to learn his.

The telephone rang at the check desk and the second security officer picked it up and listened, answering questions. The first security officer checked Isobel's name off his log sheet. The second security officer put down the telephone and held out his hand for her bag. "Mind if I have a quick search?" he asked. "Just routine."

"Sure," she replied casually. She passed the bag to him and waited. "But if you could hurry, I don't feel so good." She rubbed her stomach gently and grimaced. The guard unzipped the bag and held it open. "You know, time of the month. I'm really heavy and need to get to a drugstore."

The guard stared down at the loosely wrapped sanitary towel which unfixed had naturally started to unravel. His eyes flickered for a moment, and he suddenly lost interest in his search. Regaining a little composure he closed the bag tightly and gave it back to her. "You have a nice day, ma'am."

She was in her car heading north on 129. Off at the bridge, then across the Potomac to Georgetown. Past the university and north towards Westchester where she lived in a quiet suburb near Glover Park. The car was a ten-year-old BMW 3 series coupe, but it was well serviced and maintained and with a three liter six-cylinder engine it managed a good turn of speed. Not that Washington offered much in the way of fast motoring, but the traffic was light and she made good progress along the well-travelled route.

Her mind swam with what had happened. Technically she was a fugitive. No technically about it. She was a fugitive. She had stolen classified government information and was on the run. But she had had no choice. Could she have gone to security? The hell she could have. A privately owned security company who had won the contract by being the lowest bid. The byproduct of ongoing government cutbacks. Buck or Hank, or whatever the hell his name was with the mirrored sunglasses, and his partner who had baulked at a sanitary towel wrapper. The outfit were hardly cutting edge. They would merely do what the most senior person in the place told them. And then who else was there to go to? She knew what she had heard, both in the bathroom and in McCray's office. McCray's set of drives had already been taken, and the only other person high enough up to go to was Agnes Dempsey who hadn't been at her desk. Or maybe she had. Maybe they had killed her and dragged her into one of the other offices? The place had been empty throughout. She tried to concentrate on her driving, tried to concentrate on what to do next.

Should she go to the police? And tell them what? *"Hey, I work for a government research and development agency and we've just created a virus that could wipe out the entire eastern seaboard in four to five days. I think rogue CIA agents want to get the information held of drives that I stole and attempt to play god and ransom the anti-virus, which we called Aphrodite. You know, after the ancient Greek goddess of love.*

*Hey, I think they even killed my boss and made it look like an accident."*

She could just hear the reply. *"You stole what, lady? Hey, why don't you wait there while I give your employer a call? Say, what's their name? The Pentagon you say? And let me get this straight, you stole what exactly? Aphrodite? And where was she from? From Greece, you say? Perhaps we should call the Greek embassy and get them involved..."*

There was nothing else for it. She could not attempt going to anyone inside the facility and she could not go to the police. That did not seem to leave her many options. But right there in the car she could think of at least one.

**FIVE**

Their lovemaking had been frantic. There were no strings attached to their relationship and it had been an act of mutual pleasure and convenience. Now, warm and snug in the afterglow, their legs entwined their skin still moist, she half dozed and thought of warm, snug thoughts. She could feel his heartbeat against her left breast as he rested heavily on his chest, his head turned away from her into his pillow. He slept heavily, drained. She was at that particular stage of sleep where you can design your own dreams and she was putting the scene together like a film set. There was a large bay window; beyond which, the sea tossed up white horses and the cold wind blew salt air onto the window pain. Outside was cold and severe, inside was warm and cozy and safe. There was a log fire in the corner of the room and the light outside was fading.

The telephone woke her with a start. Beside her, her lover barely sensed the intrusion and shrugged a little, before settling back down into his pillow. She was awake now, and looking around at the stark contrast to her dreaming. The walls were whitewashed and the furniture in the bedroom was modern and featureless without either character or soul. They had been self-assembly pieces like you buy when you're starting out or starting over. The telephone continued to ring, and was just about having an effect on the man beside her who was starting to roll over onto his back. She fumbled for the receiver, a small cordless thing that looked more like a cell phone. "Delaney here," she said.

"Elizabeth, is that you?"

"Who is this?" She reached for a packet of cigarettes and a small gold lighter, fumbled a flame and blew out a thin plume of smoke from the side of her mouth. "Hey, that's not you, is it Isobel?"

"Yes, it is," Isobel Bartlett paused nervously. "I haven't spoken to you in a while. How are you?"

"Fine." She spoke with a cigarette from the comer of her mouth, flicked the wheel of her lighter almost continuously out of habit and exhaled the smoke from the corner of her mouth. "How are you? What's it been, three, four years?" She glanced down and shrugged at the man beside her who was now firmly awake and looking bored. "What can I do for you? You sound a bit upset, if you don't mind me saying." She didn't mean to sound so business like, it was just one of those awkward situations and her work made her cut to the chase.

"I've got a bit of a problem ... With work." Isobel paused. "Look, you're still with the bureau, right?"

"Of course," she snapped, not meaning to. The last time they had spoken it had been because of Elizabeth's promotion. She had become 2IC in the New Jersey counter terrorism field office. To ask if she was still with the bureau was strange. She knew something was amiss; the tone of Isobel's voice was odd. Not sassy and confident like she always remembered her fondly as. She sat up in bed, pulled the sheets over her waist. She slapped her lover's attentive, inquisitive hand away from her breast. "What's wrong honey?"

"I really need to talk to you," she paused. "I see you're listed in Brooklyn, I called your folks for your new number. It was good to speak with your mum again, but she wouldn't talk about your work."

Elizabeth felt a pang of guilt. She hadn't forwarded the number to any of her old friends since she moved from New Jersey. Isobel had been the last of her high school friends to break contact with. Now she was running her own desk in Brooklyn there seemed to be no time for her old life. "I'm sorry Izzy, I've been real busy with work and I never went through my address book after I moved." She took a deep drag on the cigarette and slapped her lover's hand away again. It annoyed the hell out of her. He could hear that something was wrong, but still he tried for a handful of breast. She got out of bed and walked over to the couch. She was still naked and felt the slight chill from a draft. She felt she could talk more openly now, give her old friend some attention. "Come on girl, speak to me. What's wrong?"

"I'm in deep trouble Liz, deep shit. I know somebody who was killed in an accident. Only, it *wasn't* an accident. I've taken something from work that I shouldn't have, but I was only trying to *save* it." There was anxiety in her voice. A feeling of helplessness. "Oh Christ, Liz. I'm in deep shit. I need to come to New York and speak to you. I don't even know if it's safe for me to talk on the phone."

Delaney thought for a moment. She sounded scared, sure enough. But should she suggest that she go to the police, or even a closer office of the FBI? She sounded as if she was about to lose it emotionally. She knew that Isobel's work was highly sensitive, in previous conversations Isobel had skipped over most of what the facility did, and as Elizabeth was with the FBI, she knew not to press her, and respected her friend's position.

"Liz, are you still there?"

"Yeah, I'm here honey. Look don't panic. Whatever it is, we can work it out."

"I'm coming tonight. I'm going to get a night train. I'll get a hotel someplace and call you in the morning," she paused. "Please meet with me, I don't know who else to turn to." The voice was near frantic, more intense with each moment that passed.

"OK, don't panic. Listen, why don't you come stay with me?"

"No, I'd feel better in a hotel I don't want to put you to any more trouble. Besides, I'll be getting in real late."

"Ok, babe,"Delaney agreed amiably. "Here, let me give you the number to my cell phone. Ring it when you get in, let me know you're OK and where you're staying."

"Thanks." Isobel keyed the number straight into her cell and suddenly felt a little better. At least she had a plan now. "Hey, I mean it, thank you."

"No sweat honey," Delaney paused to draw on her cigarette. "Hey, we'll even have a drink and talk about old times. Take care now." She cut the connection and turned around to look at her lover on the bed. "High school friends, what can you do? Who said there had to be a rule you stay friends with your childhood best friends forever?"

"Beats the hell out of me." He stretched his shoulders, yawned and patted the empty space on the bed beside him. "Not too tired, if you know what I mean."

Delaney smiled. She picked a towel off the back of the couch and wrapped it around her, covering her breasts and most of her backside. "Not now, lover." She picked up his shirt and pants and tossed them across the bed at him. His gun, cuffs and wallet were on the bedside table. She picked them up and they followed the clothes. The .40 Sig Sauer pistol was nudging two pounds loaded and holstered. It landed in his crotch. He cupped his hands over his manhood and let out a deep breath, his body contorted and his eyes widened as he grimaced. "Now shake your ass back to your wife," she paused, on her way to the shower. "You're making the place look untidy."

## SIX

The fall leaves swirled and pirouetted in the wind gaining height slowly, gradually and then dropping suddenly to the wet ground, as if the wind had become bored, then changed its mind and lifted them off the ground again. An empty drinks can scraped along the ground, caught in the gutter. The wind blew it along the edge of the platform keeping it at pace with her footsteps.

She had arrived at the station a little after seven, but had not had enough time to make the seven-ten Amtrak to New York. The next was at eight and would get her into New York at eleven.

The station was emptying steadily. The commuters had long since left Washington DC, the weekend commutes started a little after lunchtime on a Friday and by seven the platform was left with the stragglers. She looked at her watch and then made her way over to a vending machine for a soda. She needed the caffeine. And the sugar. Hell, if they vended alcohol she'd have gone for a Long Island Iced Tea. With full measures.

She had arrived home at five-thirty, called Elizabeth Delaney soon after and had then packed quickly, just the essentials. She had fastened the two flash drives to her key bunch and placed the key bunch in a secure pocket in her hand bag. She had then picked up another two flash drives she kept by her own lap top, and dropped them into her handbag. One was empty and the other held photos, some music and some back up files she'd made over the years. With just this and a well-packed sports bag containing her clothes and toiletries she got on to Amtrak online and got the combined schedules for New York. She tried to think as straight as she could and kept getting a feeling of despair. Was she doing the right thing, should she not simply go to the police? Each time she thought of this, and with the minutes that passed, she kept finding reasons not to go, to simply get hold of the police and return to the bioresearch facility. But she knew what she had heard, knew what had been implied and she knew there was no other choice. She had made up her mind back in the facility. Instinct had taken over, and instinct was going to take her away from here.

She dropped two dollars into the machine and got out a can of cola and some change. She pulled the tab and drank thirstily. She willed the caffeine to take effect. It was going to be a long night and she didn't want to fall asleep on the train. She wanted her wits about her and she wanted to approach Elizabeth Delaney with a sound case. She wanted to be taken seriously and the only way to do that was to be out of the panic that she had been on the phone and delivering her story with conviction. Her friend was a professional and would be looking at every possible angle. If Delaney decided Isobel was wrong to have taken the flash drives and left DC, then she was sure her old friend would help here with some much needed damage control later. But for now, she would hold on to her convictions. She needed to sit back and go over every detail until she was fluent in time and events and could recall every word that had been said. She had bought a pen and notepad with her and as soon as she was underway she would start recording the facts.

She swilled the remainder of the cola down and looked for a trashcan. She stopped suddenly. A man at the end of the platform seemed to be watching her. He was tall and business suited and carried a brown leather briefcase, and he didn't seem to be looking, but *watching*. There was a difference, like when you could feel someone's gaze undressing you. Only this man didn't seem to be looking at her in that way. There was something sinister about the way he had looked. She stopped herself suddenly. She was being ridiculous. Perhaps the guy *was* just eying her. She suddenly felt paranoid. She dropped the can into a nearby trashcan and strolled down the platform for about fifty yards. She turned around casually, but the man had disappeared. She relaxed a little, but still felt uneasy. His stare had been intense and if he were catching a train, then why had he left the platform?

She clutched her bag tighter in her right hand; the tight grip making her feel more secure. There was a woman on the platform now, right where the man had been. The woman glanced across and then looked back at her timetable. She seemed uninterested in everything around her.

Isobel studied the woman. She was in her thirties. Fit, or at least slim. She presumed both. Her hair was scraped back in a ponytail and she wore little or no makeup. After closer inspection the woman looked plain and unattractive.

She stopped watching and felt foolish and paranoid. There was nothing to suggest she was in immediate danger, and the man had proved to be a false alarm. She looked around for a seat, dropped the bags on the ground beside her and sat down. She reached into her small shoulder bag and took out her cellphone. She kept a large selection of music on it perhaps some of her favorite tunes would calm her nerves a little.

After another ten minutes the music had done its trick and Isobel was a little less tense when the huge silver Amtrak crept into the station, its heavy steel wheels squealing on the iron track as the brakes bought the leviathan to a gradual halt. There were about twenty people on the platform now and the majority seemed in a hurry, picking up their luggage and advancing towards the edge of the platform before the train had come to a halt. There was a guard on the platform. He stood in the center of a thick yellow line and blew a whistle and motioned people away when anyone got too close.

A girl in her late twenties rushed across the platform, holding the hand of a young man, almost pulling him along. She was pretty and fresh-faced, wore little make-up and wore her long, dark hair in a ponytail. She was dressed casually in fitted jeans, delicate leather ankle boots and a short black leather jacket. The man was more *street,* and wore baggy jeans with a lot of underwear on show and a tattered skate shirt. His hair was spiked, his lip was pierced and his forearms were almost completely tattooed. They stopped at the yellow line and embraced frantically, lips locked in a searching kiss. It was a platform good-bye. Rushed *I Love Yous* and hurried assurances to call later. There were tears in the girl's eyes. The young man seemed indifferent.

The train drew to a halt and the automatic doors parted. Nobody disembarked. Isobel looked up and saw the man in the suit again. He was only interested in getting on the empty train and finding a good seat for the duration of the journey. He launched himself forwards and disappeared for a few moments and then she saw him through the glass, backlit from the carriage lights. He had settled into a seat and was reading a newspaper that had been left behind. The woman she had caught watching her was nowhere to be seen.

Isobel found a backwards facing seat and dropped the two bags on the seat beside her. The carriage was all but empty, save for an old couple who were shedding layers of clothing and folding them into neat bundles. They carried a lot of luggage and had opted for a seat near the luggage rack beside the carriage door. It was also near the lavatory, which seemed mandatory for old folk on long journeys.

She craned her neck to look further down the aisle and caught sight of the plain looking woman who had been watching her on the platform. She was slouched back in a seat, her eyes scanning the pages of a magazine. Isobel tried to see what she was reading, but couldn't make out the title. She settled back in her seat and put the earphones of her cellphone back into place. The pretty girl was kneeling on a nearby seat, her hands touching the pane of the window, tracing the shape of her partner's hand through the glass. She was mouthing something to him, and he was calling something silently back above the train's engine as it increased in revs. Isobel had said rushed good-byes and she had had known what it was to leave a loved one alone on the platform or watch them drive away from her college dormitory. She turned away, feeling as if she were intruding on the couple's moment of intimacy.

She felt a little easier now, more at ease than she had been for many hours. The drives were safe, and her friend was expecting her in the city tonight. She may not have a job after today, but at this moment she at least had piece of mind that she had made the right decision.

**SEVEN**

He stepped out of the shower and toweled himself down vigorously. He caught sight of his profile in the mirror. His jaw was square and jutted. Some would say it made him look arrogant. He didn't think so. There was a thin scar running down most of his left cheek. It showed more when he was tanned and showed little with a days' stubble. He was dry and dumped the towel in the laundry basket, walked out of the bathroom and into the bedroom.

The mirrored wardrobe caught his reflection. He was toned and muscular. He stood six foot four and weighed two hundred and fifty pounds. He could have been an NFL linebacker. There were more scars on his body. A long thin line on his right side just below his ribcage. He took comfort knowing that the man who gave him the scar died that same night. There was a cluster of shiny dimples to the left of his navel. These were bullet groupings from an FBI special agent. It had been good marksmanship, but not as good as his own. He had only needed the one shot as he had lain on the ground bleeding. He looked at the bullet scars daily and they acted as a constant reminder not to get sloppy. Not to be overconfident. His shirt was white, well starched and crisp. His suit was immaculate and free from creases. He dressed quickly and put on a pair of clean, black leather shoes. They were polished to a shine. His wallet was on the dresser and thick with high denomination bills. He checked it quickly and slipped it into his back pocket. He picked up a compact pistol. It was a Glock model 19. The weapon was light due to its polymer construction. He checked the magazine then inserted it into the butt of the pistol and racked the slide chambering the first 9mm round. They were Black Talon dumdum rounds that would mushroom and then fragment upon impact creating a devastating injury. He tucked the weapon into the discreet soft leather belt holster behind his right hip. Next to the holster was a thin black canvas sheath, from which protruded the thin steel handle of a flat throwing knife. He slipped his suit jacket over his shoulders and checked himself in the mirror, before walking purposefully to the door.

Outside the house, the street was quiet. There were rows of trees down each side of the road and they were fast losing their leaves. Fall had come quickly this year. The wet leaves swirled gently in the wind, glistening in the orange glow of the streetlamps.

He unlocked the car with the remote. It was a new Mercedes E63. He opened the trunk and dropped a small leather travel bag inside. Next to the travel bag was a carpeted panel difficult to notice in the dull light of the streetlamps. He lifted the panel to reveal a purpose-built rack, fixed tightly so it would not move. The Colt M4 assault rifle that nestled in the rack differed from other M16 variants. It was a completely custom-built special. The carry handle and open sight furniture had been removed and fitted with a Leopold 5.7 x 70 low-light sniper scope. A suppressor had been fitted to the muzzle to be used with subsonic ammunition making it virtually silent to anybody standing a hundred feet away. The trigger had been lightened as had the cocking lever and the ejection port opened up. Instead of standard thirty round magazines he used sixty round double stacked box magazines. They were filled with match grade Swedish soft-nosed hunting .223 ammunition, precision made and more powerful than standard military 5.56mm. Every fifth bullet was a phosphorus tracer round for marking the target. Next to the compact rifle was a Remington pump-action .12 gauge shotgun. The barrel had been shortened to just twenty inches, and the stock cut down just a little to make the weapon less cumbersome to wield, without drastically affecting performance. The last of the weapons was an old but restored Ingram .45 caliber machine pistol with a retractable shoulder stock. The weapon was capable of spitting out thirteen .45 bullets every second and accurate up to two hundred feet. It was a spray gun for keeping people's heads down. Or knocking down walls.

He replaced the carpeted panel and slammed the lid down. The weapons never really impressed him. He had picked as a good a selection as he thought possible and felt he had about every situation covered up to about five hundred yards. He didn't really feel anything for them like a civilian hobby shooter would. He looked after them well because it was essential for reliability and accuracy. They were merely the tools of his trade. And he was about to go to work.

**EIGHT**

The train was fast and smooth. The seats were comfortable and thick on fabric. She hadn't realized it at first, but she was seated in business class. The train was quiet, nobody seemed to mind. The old couple were still fussing with their clothing arrangements; they appeared to have entirely too many coats. The old man was finally seated, but his companion now found that she needed something in one of their many bags and was making a big effort to coax him to go and get it. He was reluctant and looked displeased. Grudgingly, he got up from his seat and walked unsteadily with the sway of the carriage.

Isobel had watched them for some while and didn't know what was worse  the fact that she had no partner and could not visualize herself with someone else at that age, or the fact that the two old souls were still together after god only knew how many years and seemed to be making each other's life a misery. She watched as the old man shuffled back to his seat and passed his wife her book. She took it without a word, and then rested her head lovingly on the man's shoulder. He wrapped an arm around her and looked to settle down to sleep. They now looked contented and happy, far removed from the harassed couple who had entered the carriage and fussed and griped for the first fifty miles of their journey. First appearances could be deceptive. She supposed it was a familiarity which grew through both age and time spent together. She guessed she would have to first get past four dates to even think about that.

The train had swept through New Carrollton and BWI, stopping for only a matter of minutes and was rocketing towards the city of Baltimore. There were a few more passengers after the initial few stops, but she didn't expect any heavy boarding until Baltimore. Although there were fifteen stops between DC and the New York, she did not suspect the train to fill considerably other than in Baltimore and Philadelphia and she imagined being able to keep her luggage on the seat beside her and remain relatively un-cramped all the way.

Baltimore came and went, and the train was still less than a quarter full. They stopped for approximately ten minutes in Wilmington, probably allowing space to free up on the track ahead. The plain-looking woman that she had noticed earlier got off the train, her cell phone against her ear. Isobel noticed that there was a quiet understated beauty behind her initial judgment of plainness. The woman strode along the platform towards the front of the train and out of sight.

Isobel felt foolish. She was being paranoid. She knew what she had heard and she knew that Dr. McCray's files were out of the facility. But did they know that she had taken Professor Leipzig's drives? Would they know that she knew about them, and knew about their plans?

By now, yes. She was sure of it. But how should she separate paranoia with fact? She was sure that they would have her marked and she was sure that they would do everything within their power to get the information about ARES and APHRODITE back. But how quickly could they move, and what was more, who in Hell's name were *they?* Paranoia had taken her over earlier, and paranoia could force her into making a mistake. She needed rational thought and sound convictions if she were to make it.

She sat back in her seat and thought about professor Leipzig. They had killed him. They had murdered him and then made it look like an accident. But why? Was it because Leipzig stood in their way, or was it because Leipzig planned to eradicate ARES and concentrate on more beneficial science? Developing a multi-antidote or anti-virus to the world's most hideous viruses and diseases. Or was Leipzig in on it with them? By taking him out of the equation, did they stand to gain more money? Certainly. But surely there would have been enough to go round. Billions as opposed to millions. The questions swirled round her head and left her feeling giddy, her accusations were capricious. She was convinced that Professor Leipzig was a good man. He had merely been an obstacle to them. And they had coldly, calculatingly taken him out of the way.

Philadelphia came and went, and with it about another sixty people filed into the train. Even so, the Silver Amtrak was still under half full and nobody had come through and told Isobel she was in the wrong carriage. Or maybe they knew most were in the wrong seats and simply didn't bother because of the train's capacity. Either way, she was grateful for the legroom and grateful that she didn't have to share her seat. She looked at her watch. It was a little after nine. She decided that she could do with stretching her legs and slipped the rucksack over her right shoulder as she got up from her seat. She walked down the aisle and past the old couple, who were now both sound asleep. After three carriages she came to the small buffet cart, which was closed. It would seem that it had been open for business until Philadelphia, but would be closed now until

Trenton. She guessed that the guy had needed a break and had taken off because of the lack of trade. She went to turn around, but someone caught her eye in the next carriage. She leaned against the wall of the carriage and studied the woman, who was approximately thirty yards further down the train. She was reading a magazine and Isobel knew she had seen her before. She felt the pang of excitement, of shock all at once. It was the plain-looking, yet understatedly attractive woman from the station back in DC and she had watched her leave the train at Wilmington. She was positive it was the same woman, but how could it be? The woman had left the train, walked in animated telephone conversation along the platform and straight towards the exit. At least that's what she thought she had seen. Why had the woman boarded the train again and when? She had watched from the window, but she had lost interest once the woman had disappeared from view. Could she have simply made a mistake and got off at the wrong stop? The train had remained in Wilmington for around ten minutes to allow the track time to clear ahead. She could simply have got back on in another carriage. Isobel tried her very best to be rational, but there were too many questions to be asked. You don't start an almost four-hour train journey and get off after ninety minutes. And even if you were not going all the way to New York, you still wouldn't make such a silly mistake so soon. And besides, Wilmington station has a huge sign declaring the destination spread across half the platform. If you're in Wilmington, you *know* you're in Wilmington. A train out of Wilmington is about the best thing the damn town's got.

The woman glanced up. Isobel froze. The woman tried her best to look through her but failed. Isobel turned around and walked quickly back to her seat. The train rushed through North Philadelphia station. There was no scheduled stop.

Her heart pumped, blood surged around her veins. She had caught the woman out. It was quite possible that she could have made a mistake at Wilmington, but the woman's reaction to seeing her had told a different story. Isobel dropped back in her seat, the rucksack clutched firmly in her hand. She tried to think, but was failing to concentrate. For the first time since she had left the facility she was actually scared. Not uneasy, not paranoid but actually scared rigid. She knew that she had caught the woman out, but what was more, she knew that the woman knew it too. Her mind started to race. There was no scheduled stop at Cornwells Heights. The next time the train came to rest would be in Trenton. She had no idea of what to expect in Trenton. She needed the police, or at the very least she needed a crowd. Then she needed a way into

New York and a quick way of getting to Elizabeth Delaney. Newark International Airport was going to be her safest bet, for the crowds at least. Hell, from there she could just bite the bullet and get a taxi the forty minutes or so into the city.

She craned her neck to see down the aisle, but from where she was seated she couldn't see very far. The train started to slow, at first slight, but increasingly until they travelled at approximately half speed. Trenton was nearing and several passengers started to gather up their belongings and start the disembarkation shuffle. Edging their way closer and closer towards the doors. The train surged a whole lot slower again and continued to break. The railway sidings became more built up, and there were the shells and wrecks of old decommissioned trains alongside the track.

Isobel got out of her seat and picked up the sports bag and kept the small rucksack handbag over her right shoulder. She joined the shuffle and edged towards the door, standing in line as they waited to leave. A guard, the first she had seen since DC walked slowly past, easing himself politely through the blockade of passengers. Perhaps he was the buffet cart steward returning from his impromptu break.

"How long does the train stop in Trenton?" she asked, beaming the man a smile.

The guard looked puzzled for a moment, then shrugged. "Two and a half minutes, tops."

She nodded a curt thank you and braced herself while the train drew into the station and came to a halt. She left with the throng of passengers and walked calmly towards the exit. The platform was colder than in DC. The night air dropping a few degrees along the way. She pulled the collar of her coat up around her neck. She glanced out of the corner of her eye, straining her peripheral vision to the maximum. It hurt her eye and she could feel the start of a headache but she strained to see as much as she could. The plain-looking woman stepped out of the furthermost carriage and walked casually amongst a group of foreign students. She looked out of place. And she looked uncomfortable. Isobel knew the woman had not intended to get off at Trenton. That was obvious. She had left her carry-on bag on the train.

Isobel disappeared through the exit, then immediately stepped into the men's lavatory on her right. It was empty and she went straight into a cubicle and locked the door. It felt frighteningly familiar. She breathed deeply and looked at her watch, counting down the seconds. She made a full two minutes and opened the door. Another deep breath and she charged towards the door, pulled it towards her and stepped out into the crowd. She kept her head down and pushed through, using her elbows to barge the unsuspecting people out of the way. She was out on the platform and running for the train. There was a shout from behind her. It belonged to a man. She thought it was a warning from a station guard, telling her that she was too late. She ran on regardless. The doors were starting to close and she leapt into the carriage, making it by less than an inch. The door impacted shut behind her and the sounds of the platform were instantly shut out. She steadied her footing as the train started to move away and walked through into the carriage. She dropped into the nearest seat and stared out of the window, breathless.

The plain-looking woman was back on the platform. She looked troubled, distraught. And she was talking animatedly into a cell phone.

**NINE**

The man stood in the shadows and watched the passengers intently. His mind worked quickly, like a computer software package processing figures. It was a mechanical process, subhuman. He had the carriage number and the thorough description of the target locked in his mind. He scanned the crowd, hastily looking for resemblances to what he had conjured within his mind. It was like an Internet search, using key words to get closer to the end result. Height and weight, hair color, prominent features, color and style of clothing, a description of how the person moved. All this was in his mind as he scanned the crowd and rejected the possibilities and focused on a match. His eyes locked on to one woman in particular. The description raced in his mind and he finally had the crucial result. Confident it was her he took the cell phone out of his pocket and checked the woman on the train station platform against the grainy photographed which had been messaged to him earlier. The hair color and style were right, the face was the same. In person she looked a little younger but photographs were never exactly the same in his experience. He walked casually across the platform and joined the crowd heading for the exit.

The crowd started to thin as soon as they were through the main gates. Some went straight to the ticket sales and information booths. Others were simply changing platforms to connecting routes.

The taxi rank outside was sparse but as the crowds waited car upon car drove into the line and switched on their for hire signs. The procession was continuous and the crowd on the sidewalk were soon thinning in numbers.

His eyes stayed on the target. He didn't lose sight of her for a second, not even as he crossed the street and got into his vehicle, parked in the twenty-minute wait spaces across the road.

Isobel was in the taxi and had started to relax. She was sure she had not been followed from the station, and had sat back in the seat and was taking in the sights as best she could. There was always much to see in New York and at this time of night on a Friday, the city was only starting to liven up. Everywhere she looked there were couples or groups of people on their way back from restaurants, or on their way out to clubs. She wished she were here under different circumstances, wished she could join in on the fun. But even more, she longed for the relative safety of a hotel room and to talk with Elizabeth Delaney.

The taxi pulled up by the curb outside the Amsterdam Court Hotel on 226 west 50th Street. She paid the fare and left the six dollars change as a tip. She was tired and hungry and was pleased with the taxi driver's recommendation as she climbed the steps to the entrance and walked into the vestibule.

He had kept a lot of distance on the short journey and had watched intently as the taxi dropped the target off outside the hotel. He had watched her pay and had waited for the taxi to move away, before he parked in a nearby space and got out. He fed two dollars and a handful of quarters into the parking meter and walked round to the trunk. He organized what he needed and placed the items in the hold all.

As he climbed the steps and walked into the lobby, he watched the woman at the desk. She was signing the register as the concierge placed a key with a large brass effect tag on the desk beside her. He walked towards the desk and looked at the number.

The concierge was young and arrogant looking. He ignored the man as he dealt with the woman's details, then as she thanked him and walked towards the elevator, he looked up expectantly.

"I'd like a room please," he paused. "Just for the one night." There was no trace of an accent, no telltale pronunciations or idiosyncrasies. He didn't sound southern or mid-western. There was nothing to place him anywhere, but faintly in the United States. "I'll be paying cash, and checking out early."

The concierge smiled. "That'll be one-fifty, mister...?"

"Keel." He dropped three fifty-dollar bills on the desk and wasn't surprised when he was given the key without being asked to sign the register. He knew the bills would end up in the concierge's top pocket as soon as his back was turned. This was New York and everybody had a scam going somewhere.

"Room two one three."

"Is there anyone available to show me to the room?"

The young man shrugged. "I'm sorry, pal. Just myself on duty tonight, the graveyard shift. It's difficult to leave the desk."

The man took another fifty-dollar bill out from his wallet. "Not too difficult to drop a couple of sandwiches and a can of soda up to me in about twenty minutes?" He waved the note in front of the young man and smiled. "Been a long day and I'm kind of tired and hungry."

The concierge took the bill without hesitation and smiled. "Of course. I'll see what I can do."

"Ham and cheese, and no diet sodas." He turned his back on the concierge and walked to the elevator. He had travelled around the world many times and he knew that cash called for no questions, at least nine times out of ten. He also knew that at this time of night and with no other staff on duty the concierge would not only make the sandwiches himself and forget to register the transaction, but would also personally make up the room tomorrow morning. Leaving housekeeping none the wiser, with no trace of a man named Keel having ever stayed at the hotel.

Isobel relaxed on the bed. The room was quiet and functional and offered all she needed. She had switched on the television set and was staring up at the ceiling listening to the background sound as she gathered her thoughts and planned what to do next. It was late, almost midnight. She would call Elizabeth Delaney and arrange to meet over breakfast. Then, she would take a long hot bath and try to get a good sleep. She seriously doubted the latter and realized that she would probably see-in every hour on the luminous hands of the bedside alarm clock.

The sandwiches had been delivered in less than fifteen minutes. The concierge's neck had been broken in less than three seconds. His body lay still on the floor of room two one three. Prone and lifeless. The money had been retrieved from his pocket and his bunch of keys were now in the man's hands as he searched for the master key. He found it, marked with MK in crudely stamped letters. He slipped it off the fob and set about wiping the other keys free from prints using a clean cotton handkerchief. He repeated the process with the room key and left it neatly beside the key bunch on the bed. He ate a sandwich and chewed deliberately whilst staring at the cadaver on the floor. It was a good sandwich with Virginian ham and Monterey Jack cheese. The eyes of the corpse were lifeless, drained of life like liquid spilt from a vessel. It fascinated him. He wanted to touch the body and feel the heat leave forever. Feel the permanence of death on his hand.

He opened the door and stopped momentarily to wipe the handles free from prints. He took one last look of the serenity, the all-encompassing peacefulness of the body, and then closed the door.

The key slipped easily into the door of two one seven. There was the sound of a television from behind the door.

He gripped the silenced machine pistol tightly in his right hand, then eased the key clockwise and pushed the door inwards with the toe of his highly polished shoe.

There was a large space, a mini vestibule area inside the door where the wardrobe and luggage racks were situated. He stood inside and quietly closed the door, keeping his back to it as he surveyed the room. He could hear the sound of water splashing as she bathed. The door to the bathroom was slightly ajar. He stepped past it and into the bedroom. Her bags were on the floor beside the bed. He searched them quickly with his left hand, his right remained on the butt of the machine pistol, his finger resting lightly alongside the trigger. The sights of the weapon held firm on the bathroom doorway.

The woman continued to splash in the bath. She was happily humming a tune to herself. He didn't recognize it. But he never listened to music. Didn't see the point of it.

He slipped his suit jacket off and hung it carefully over the back of the chair. He then unbuttoned his sleeves and rolled them up to his elbows. Loosened his tie and the neck of his shirt and carefully tucked the tail of his tie into his shirt, between the buttons on his chest. He casually opened the door to the bathroom and lunged towards the woman. His movements were swift and decisive. She looked up in terror, but was plunged down into the water before she could truly register what was happening to her.

She splashed and he cursed inwardly as the soapy water rushed over the edge of the bath and onto his clothes. He pressed hard into her throat with his left hand and pushed with all his strength down onto her stomach with his right. He counted off thirty seconds and brought her back to the surface. She gasped and coughed and her body shook uncontrollably as she searched for precious air. She couldn't talk, she was paralyzed with fear.

"Tell me where the flash drives are." His voice was calm. It had been a great effort to hold her down, despite both his height and weight advantage, but he was breathing easily. "Now!"

She coughed and swallowed. Her eyes were wide and her naked breasts heaved as her lungs worked to breathe. He dunked her again. Her legs kicked out wildly, her hands clawed madly at his face. He brushed them away with his elbows and waited for the seconds to pass. He dragged her back up and waited for her to stop coughing. She panted and moaned and looked at him despairingly.

"Please... Please don't kill me... I'll do anything you want..."

"Where are the drives you stole?"

"I... I don't know what you're talking about!" She screamed.

He held a finger to his lips. "Sshh, quietly please. You are Isobel Bartlett. You stole two flash drives that do not belong to you." He was quite patient, as if it were a minor misunderstanding. "My employers want them back."

"My name's Kathy Anderson ... I don't know what you're talking about." She was shaking, her eyes pleading. "My purse ... Check my purse, it's got my ID in there!" She was almost jubilant.

He frowned at her. He was sure it was her. Same train, same carriage, same description. And there had been nobody else of that description get off at the station. He had followed her all the way and he had checked the room number on the tag. He couldn't have made an error. He released his grip and took the cell phone out of his trouser pocket. He thumbed the screen and looked at the image. He stared between the naked woman in the bath and the image on the smartphone's screen. They were almost identical. Almost. Only now, in the light of the bathroom and with her make-up washed off he could see there were a few differences. It was not the same woman.

She stared up at him. She was shaking a little less now, sensing his mistake. But she still looked terrified and her eyes pleaded silently with him.

He looked down at her and smiled.

"Sorry..."

He plunged her back under the water and held her down with all his might. Her legs and arms flayed wildly as she ran out of breath and she started to take huge amounts of hot, soapy water into her lungs. The water splashed his clothes, and he pressed down harder with annoyance. Eventually her legs dropped down onto the faucets and her arms fell lifelessly across her breasts, covering her nakedness. A few last air bubbles drifted to the surface and broke with a soft pop. Then there was nothing more, no movement as the water became still.

He knew about drowning and knew that she had slipped into unconsciousness. There was a sudden surge of her body as the nervous system frantically reminded her to breathe and fight for life, and then her body went completely limp.

The towel was warm and dry from the heated rail and was soft in his hands. He liked the feel of it as he used it to dry himself off. It was soothing on his skin and he wiped it over his face as he looked down at the body in the water.

It had taken just under three minutes for her to die. It usually did. Three weeks without food. Three days without water. Three minutes without air. And when a bullet rips through the heart or brain, or a knife slices through the veins and arteries in the throat, three seconds to die and bleed out and for the central nervous system to shut down. He saw the number three as scholars saw a Fibonacci number. It always intrigued him.

## TEN

Isobel Bartlett sat on the edge of the bed with her cell phone in her hand, waiting for the call to be answered at the other end. It was late and she realized that Elizabeth Delaney might be annoyed, but she hadn't wanted to ring on the journey. She had wanted to be safe and secure in her own room. It was like setting herself a base.

The bathwater was draining in the bathroom and the water was still hot. Steam drifted out through the bathroom where every surface was wet. It looked like a sauna from the bedroom. At this time of night there hadn't been a great demand on the Hotel's hot water reserves. She had used the complimentary bath salts and was refreshed after her long day. As she looked back on the day's events, it seemed a world away. It was hard to believe that she had been in Washington giving an impromptu speech to the intelligence agencies and military establishment at lunchtime.

She got off the bed and dropped the towel to the floor. She was dry enough to put on the robe which hung on the outside of the wardrobe door. The call tone stopped abruptly and her friend was on the line. "Delaney here."

"Liz, it's me... Isobel."

"Hi girl," she paused. "You OK?"

"I'm fine." She was relieved to speak to the FBI agent. It made her feel secure. "I'm at the Amsterdam Court Hotel. Do you know it?"

"No. You got an address?"

"Hang on." Isobel walked into the bedroom and looked at the hotel's welcome pack on the dresser. She muddled through then noticed the complimentary set of headed stationary. "Yeah, two twenty six, on west fiftieth street."

"Got it. You want to meet for breakfast? I'll be over at eight o'clock and we can talk then."

"OK," Isobel paused. "Listen Liz, I think I was followed on the train."

"You sure?" There was surprise in the agent's voice.

"Yes. As sure as I can be. This woman was watching me at the station in Washington. She got off the train in Wilmington, but I saw her again later in the journey. I got off at Trenton, but doubled back and saw her on the station as the train pulled away. She looked real pissed, she was

85

talking into her cell phone."

"What happened after that?" The voice was calm but concerned. "Did you keep watching out for a tail?"

"A tail? Oh yes, I see. Yes I did, but I didn't notice anybody else. I got off at Newark International Airport and rode a taxi into the city from there. Nobody was following... Or at least I'm sure there wasn't."

"Look Isobel, try not to worry too much," she paused. "I know you're frightened, but we're going to sort this thing out. I'm sure the woman was just a coincidence, that's all. Dumb ass probably got off at the wrong station again and lost it when she realized she missed the damn train. Maybe she was a foreigner and couldn't read the schedule. These things happen."

Isobel felt a little easier at the thought o f that prospect. "Yeah, maybe. Listen Liz; I'm indebted to you for this, thanks for agreeing to see me at such short notice. I didn't know who else to turn to. I'll see you at eight down in the foyer. Good night." She cut the connection and tossed the tiny cell phone onto the bed. As she walked toward the window she tightened the robe around her. She glanced out into the street below. There was no other traffic except for a large Mercedes sedan driving swiftly past.

Inside the Mercedes the man's hands gripped the wheel tightly in frustration. He turned right and headed through a suburban street. As was the way of New York, a turn off the main thoroughfare would often be met by near total darkness and the feeling that you were the only person in the city. There were few lights on from inside the buildings. He hung another right and was deep inside a warren of darkened buildings.

His mind raced. He couldn't get the thought out of his head. It was like an annoying song or tune, rhythmically pulsing between his ears. There was not even the briefest respite from it. Where had he gone wrong? He had followed the only possible woman to fit the description that he had been given, and he had made sure that he stayed in sight of the taxi at all times. He had not lost sight of it once. And he was positive that the woman he had killed in the bath was the same woman whom he had followed across the platform at the station. He would not make such a mistake because he was a professional. He was good at what he did and these things just simply didn't happen. Had never happened.

His success rate was total. Nobody who hired him could doubt that, because nobody who had hired him had been left anything but satisfied with the service he had provided.

After he had killed the woman in the bath he

had ripped the room apart from floor to ceiling and had come up with nothing. There were no flash drives hidden and the woman hadn't been Isobel Bartlett. She had been telling the truth. The frustration welled within him as he drove. It started in his chest; a palpitation at first and then a driving shudder through his entire body as the blood pulsed rapidly through his veins. His hands trembled on the wheel. He looked at them and felt disgusted with himself for the sign of weakness. His life was one of staunch control and self-discipline. There was nothing random left in his life, not a single element that was out of place, or out of his control. The feeling of anger and despair became more acute. He wanted to scream and shout and pound his fists against something and release the rage from within.

He screamed at the top of his voice. It was a deep resonance. A growl that came from the pit of his stomach and wore on lasciviously until he was completely hoarse. It released the pressure from within, but he was left with a sour feeling of failure. And he had never felt it before, because he had never failed before.

Ahead of him a down and out ambled slowly across the deserted road pushing a shopping cart full of empty drinks cans and plastic bottles. He was using the cart as much to hold himself up as to transport his precious cargo. The man was either blissfully unaware that he had become an obstruction, or was arrogantly expressing his pedestrian rights. Either way, the silver Mercedes had to slow down to a crawl. The homeless guy slowed his pace and shouted something towards the car.

The car stopped. The drivers' door opened and the immaculately dressed man stepped out and walked round to the trunk. He made an impressive figure in the well-tailored suit and looked like a linebacker or heavyweight boxer at a charity event. The down and out guy was mumbling something and his voice rose until he was shouting animatedly at the vehicle. He was drunk and he half swaggered half staggered to the sidewalk, struggling with his cart as he tried to mount the curb with the tiny wheels.

The man stepped out from behind the raised lid of the trunk and aimed the machine pistol at the drunk's chest. There was an eruption of different sounds all at once, which when combined, sounded nothing like an identifiable sound. There was the coughing of the silenced muzzle as it spat out thirteen bullets every second, the impacting of hot copper coated lead into the drunk's body, the sound of empty brass cases spilling twenty feet out onto the sidewalk and rolling into the gutter, and the sound of the spent bullets as they ripped out through his back and slammed into the side of a building some fifty feet further down the street.

Then came an eerie silence as the man stood over the corpse, the pungent smell of burnt powder and hot oil in the air. The cadaver's eyes stared lifelessly into space and the man felt a little better in relation to all that had happened earlier. He was calmer now, and felt more positive. Death had brought him peace once more.

As he casually studied the body on the ground he decided what he should do next.

He would call his employers, and offer the contract for free. His reputation as a professional was paramount, and this was merely a temporary hitch. He would achieve his objective and this act of good will would allow his reputation for professionalism to remain unblemished. He would find the woman Bartlett, and he would retrieve the disks intact. He would take her life, watch it ebb from her like a falling tide. And he would feel the peace around him as she took her last few breaths and entered her eternal journey. He would feel great pride at giving her what would last forever. It would be an honor, as it always was. To be there ... at the very end.

## ELEVEN

The waitress brought the coffee over to the table and poured. The coffee smelled good. Arabica beans, apparently. Isobel didn't care, as long as it wasn't the instant sachet type that was in her room. The silence was total. The waitress felt awkward, sensed that there was no point attempting to make small talk and walked away to the next table, where she poured, smiled and received a more welcome reception.

Isobel buttered a piece of toast and took a bite. She was ravenous. She had not bothered to eat so late in the evening, but wished she had. Before she knew it the toast had gone and she was buttering another slice. She watched her friend. She was drinking the coffee. Strong, unsweetened and black. Isobel had always joked that that was how Elizabeth liked her men. She in turn always joked that once you went black, you never went back. But that wasn't true. Delaney just took what she could get. And if they were married, then that at least made it far less complicated.

Elizabeth Delaney had arrived a little before eight, but it hadn't mattered because Isobel had been waiting in the foyer from seven-thirty. They had greeted each other warmly, hugging and kissing cheeks. Not in a chic fashionable air kiss, but in an affectionate and meaningful embrace. It had been a long time since they had last seen one another, and seeing each other again brought back a wealth of good memories.

They had taken a quiet table in the window and had drunk the complimentary orange juice, which had been freshly squeezed with a little pith left in it and a few pips dotted on top for good measure. Proof it wasn't out of a carton. It was bittersweet, like Florida oranges at that time of year. They had ordered breakfast, Isobel choosing eggs benedict and a side of crispy bacon. Delaney opted for scrambled eggs, bacon, sausage links, hash browns, sausage pates and fried potatoes. She chose a side of pancakes and maple syrup. She then felt she had to justify her order by explaining that she seldom did lunch and breakfast had to take her through the rest of the day.

They had not broached the reason for their meeting and were just about to when the waitress brought along the refill of coffee.

"So tell me everything," Delaney paused.

"From the beginning, and try not to miss anything out."

So she did. She told of Professor Leipzig's work on the virus and the antidote, and she told of his accident in Vermont. She told her about the presentation to the security agencies and combined military intelligence representatives. As she told her about the incident in both the bathroom and McCray's outer office, she felt her heart beat faster and her cheeks flush. The memory brought fear to her.

She told her everything, and when she had finished she sat back in the chair and took a sip of coffee. The breakfasts arrived and the waitress dropped them silently in front of them. She sensed they were remaining silent for her benefit again.

"So..." Delaney looked thoughtful for a moment, and then looked up at her friend. "You genuinely felt that your life was in danger, and that you couldn't trust the security?"

Isobel shook her head. "I thought my life was in danger if I got caught in between the information and whoever was planning to take it. I *would* trust security, but not the establishment. These were government people planning this... I had no idea how deep it would go." She pushed her untouched plate in front of her. She had suddenly lost her appetite. "I thought I knew one of the voices, but..." She trailed off, thoughtfully looking into the cup of coffee in front of her.

"But what?"

"But it just doesn't work out."

"Let me be the judge of that. Tell me."

"McCray was the project manager, the administration manager. He handled the budget. He was always at loggerheads with Leipzig until we got about two-thirds of the way through the project. They became firm friends. Everyone within the department was talking about it. It seemed so strange."

"You suspect McCray?"

She nodded. "It sounded a little *like* him, but both times I was just too panicked to pay attention to the details. And that executive bathroom really echoes. In the outer office my heart was pounding so hard and all I could hear was a pulsing in my ears."

"Adrenalin, it can be a real bitch," Delaney mused. "So what's so strange about McCray being in on it?"

"Well, they *really* looked like friends. For the past year and a half, at least," she paused. "Prior to his turning point he saw ARES as a waste of the department's time, money and resources. Another bastard lovechild, from another government think tank. But he really got onside when APHRODITE was born. It was almost overnight. Suddenly, he couldn't do enough for the project or the people involved."

"Sounds about right. Maybe he suddenly had some motivation?" Delaney paused and took a forkful of scrambled egg. She chewed quickly and spoke with her mouth full. "He sees it as another waste of time and research and it eats right into his budget. But he also sees the possibilities behind the antidote, this anti-virus. Unleash ARES and sell APHRODITE. He stands to make millions of dollars. Or even more. Honey, if he is the sort of person willing to kill and infect hundreds of thousands of people indiscriminately, then he isn't going to worry about faking a friendship and getting this Leipzig guy out of the way later. Besides, nothing easier than breaking in to your own safe, is there?"

"I suppose," Isobel conceded. "But the strangest thing was Leipzig reciprocated the friendship, and that was what really took everyone by surprise. Leipzig couldn't so much as tolerate McCray before."

"Maybe they back scratched," Delaney paused. "Maybe McCray promised Leipzig more funding, more resources. He held the purse strings after all. McCray had an agenda and knew the best way forward was to have the professor onside. Maybe Leipzig was just gullible and walked right into the trap. Probably shared more information than he normally would have. Maybe he unwittingly helped McCray closer. Only to be killed by him. Or someone sent by him."

"You don't think McCray killed him personally do you?"

"Honey, I don't know Jack-shit. All I'm doing is surmising. Hypothetically looking at the possibilities. You're not even sure it *was* McCray, are you?"

"I don't know, but it sure sounded *like* him. The more I've thought about it, the more it made sense." Isobel looked up, there were the beginnings of tears in her eyes. They were moist and glistened in the morning sun. She took a tissue out of her shoulder bag and dabbed her eyes gently. "But what are we going to do about it. The FBI will get involved, right?"

Delaney remained impassive. "Tell me about this CIA guy at the conference. And the general. What was his name? Chuck..."

"Howard. General Chuck Howard. He was a typical gung-ho general in his late fifties. A relic too highly decorated to be cut loose and too old to walk the walk anymore. The military's full of old warhorses like him. He seemed to think of ARES as *his* weapon and probably couldn't wait to unleash it on some small aggressor they could probably take out in their sleep. The CIA guy was called Tom Hardy and was really low rent, if you know what I mean?"

Delaney shook her head.

"Just shabby. Mid to late fifties. Cheap suit, cheap look. Couldn't even get his food in his mouth without a scene. He looked more like a divorced car salesman than a CIA operative."

"Cheap suit could come from paying too much alimony. Cheap look could come from living alone at that age in life. Too many TV dinners. Might have made a mess of things because he was eager to get some good buffet down his throat. Besides, CIA guys are pretty plain. Not all tailored suits and designer shoes."

"The other guy was though, the NSA representative. David Law, I think his name was."

"You didn't mention anyone from the NSA."

"It was just some guy. He was clean-cut and tidy, pretty smart. Handsome, I guess. He asked about the dispersal rate of the virus and then looked uninterested. I think he was there for the free sushi and chardonnay as well." She looked at Delaney. "Do you think they're all in on it?"

"Lord, no. But there *is* someone else, and it's someone you've met. They wouldn't have mentioned you in the bathroom if they hadn't of already met you. Does anyone else's voice sound like that of the two men you heard? Think about it, and try to imagine it muffled or echoed around a room."

"You think it's McCray, don't you?"

"Well, you said it sounded *like* him. And that's enough for me to go on. The guy is an insider, has keys to his own safe, naturally, and is abreast of all information concerning the project. He is also in a position to have put certain pressures on professor Leipzig."

"Why didn't you answer me when I asked if the FBI will get involved?" She stared at her and held her gaze. "I *need* your help Liz, I'm scared for my life."

"Hey kid, I didn't say they wouldn't get involved. *I'm* already involved."

"What then?"

"It's just all this talk of military intelligence, the CIA. NSA for Christ's sake! The fucking National Security Agency are heavy shit. They are almost unaccountable. Forget what you hear about the CIA. NSA is where it's at. Nobody really knows what they do, they don't even ask. The FBI will get involved, but it will need a hell of a lot more intelligence to lock horns with this lot. Some will think you are mistaken, others will think you are just some stupid bitch who got paranoid. Some will think you should have gone to your own security, and others will suspect you as the traitor. They will open up, and thoroughly explore every possible avenue before they take you seriously. Then, and only then, will they listen to what you have to say." She looked at her friend, who suddenly looked destroyed, her hopes sunken. "But *I'm* here honey, and I'm not going anywhere."

Isobel smiled at Delaney. It was a great relief to have her friend take her seriously. "What do we do then?"

Delaney took a mouthful of food and chewed thoughtfully. "Where are the flash drives at?"

"Hidden. In my hotel room."

"Where?"

Isobel hesitated. She couldn't explain why she had lied to her friend. "Under an edge of carpet, under the dresser."

She trusted Elizabeth Delaney, but she had suddenly felt the realization of what holding the information on the drives meant. Being in possession of them made them as much her lifeline as her death warrant. No harm could come to her for as long as she held them and as long as she kept others from knowing where thcy really were.

"That's good thinking." Delaney pushed away her empty plate and took a sip of coffee. "Keep them there for the moment. I'm going to get some advice on this and get back to you. I can reach you on the number you called me from last night, right?"

"Sure."

"OK. What I'm going to do is this - I'm

99

going to talk to a bureau friend of mine, a man named David Stein. He has a lot of experience in witness protection and worked in anti-terrorism for a long time."

"What does he do now?"

"Field agent, just like me. I dropped a paygrade recently to join a division with better prospects. Our division investigates any crime covering more than one state, serial offenders or anything remotely politically sensitive," she paused. "He'll help us get on the right track and together we can find the right approach to make. If we bring you in now, we could end up in a world of red tape and bureaucracy. If the information on those drives gets out of our hands and into the system..."

"You're not filling me with confidence, Liz."

"Hey kid, trust me. I know how it works. We need to be so righteous, so goddamn full of ourselves and clear on the facts that we walk on in and bowl the whole establishment over. If these drives are paired with the other set, and if ARES is as lethal as you say, then we're all in deep shit. Why in God's name would anybody come up with such evil crap?" She looked at Isobel, and then sensed she had said too much.

"It doesn't always start out that way. Government-funded research facilities come up with the cures or breakthroughs for illnesses all the time. However, you find yourself going for promotion, or being transferred or sidelined to other facilities. Pretty soon you're a world away from what you trained so hard for and what you spent your whole life wanting to achieve."

"I'm sorry."

Isobel shrugged like it hadn't mattered and took a sip of coffee. "Do you trust him? This Stein guy."

"Absolutely."

"But I need to know, can *I* trust him?" She stared into her friend's eyes, her look intense. "I need to trust this man with my life. He may well talk, he may well hand the whole thing over to the FBI, officially. The drives may walk. Somebody may simply walk on in and kill me. These are government agents of some kind and they may well be able to grease the wheels of the FBI, for all I know."

Delaney shook her head. "Not a chance."

"You'd be so sure with your *own* life, would you?"

Delaney smiled. "I know you're out on a limb here, but trust me. Trust me with your life and you'll be OK. We'll get through it together. The FBI will be involved in all its force, but we just have to think our approach through and get it right. Afterwards, we'll have all the support we need."

Isobel nodded. "So tell me about Stein. He's a good lay, right?"

"How did you guess?" She beamed a devilish grin. "And yes, you'd better believe it."

"Elizabeth Delaney ..." She scorned her mockingly. "You never change!"

It lightened the mood and they talked for a while about their own lives and how they had differed to what they had imagined in high school and college. They drank more coffee and this time the waitress felt less intimidated when she came around to pour. She asked them if they had enjoyed their breakfasts, and they both agreed they were excellent, even if Isobel's was hardly touched. The waitress looked at the untouched plate and seemed unsure whether to clear, so left them to go and tend another table.

After half an hour of talking Delaney had stood up and unhooked her shoulder bag from the back of the chair. "I'll get this," she said looking at the remnants of service on the table.

Isobel shook her head. "Not a chance. It's already on my room bill, I arranged it earlier." She stood up and picked up the small rucksack. The disks were stored inside a small internal pocket. She would have to find another place to store them. She still felt guilt at deceiving her friend, but could still not explain why she had.

"What happens now?"

"I'll go and speak to David. You sit tight and wait for me to call."

"I feel like a prisoner."

"Come on, it's a nice hotel, there must be plenty to do." She was completely serious, but it sounded condescending nonetheless. "Try and get some sleep or relax and read a book in the bar. There's a sign for a spa at reception. Get a treatment."

"Great," she said flatly. "Can't I just come with you?"

"Better not, not just yet at least." She put a hand on her shoulder and squeezed tightly, reassuringly. "Don't worry. You're safe here. But I wouldn't go and see the sights just yet."

## TWELVE

All contact was made through multimedia. There were five e-mail accounts and text messaging on one of three cell phones he used under different network providers. This also enabled him to have near complete coverage across the country. He also managed a Facebook page complete with over four hundred friends whom he had never met. He had cultivated the legend of a divorced thirty year old mother of two. Guys liked to friend single moms. Especially married guys. However, the more friends he had, the more communication traffic went through and the more it appeared unnoticed. Like hiding a needle in a box of needles. He could also use the personal messaging for coded messages. More discreet postings could be shared on particular timelines with the privacy settings keeping it from view to all but certain people. It was simply another medium through which clients could communicate. The more methods there were, the less chance there was of something becoming flagged.

All payments were made through offshore accounts. He was as faceless as his employers. It was the only way. There was an element of mutual trust. There had to be. Half the payment had been made. It was a deposit. Once the assignment had been completed, the remainder of the funds would be processed. There was always the nagging doubt that they would not pay, but likewise, there was always the nagging doubt at the client's end that if they backed out of the deal, they would be next on his list. It seemed to work. Nobody had previously been disappointed with his work, and nobody had ever avoided the second payment.

He paced slowly around the room as he waited for the reply. It would take time, but all his e-mail and Facebook notifications would sound on one of the three cellphones. Once he had this, he would know where to log in to.

He was naked. His toned body glistened with sweat from his workout and he liked to cool off in the cold air before taking an icy shower. His workout was a twice daily routine. He had reached the rank of black belt in a style of traditional karate made up from Wado Ryu and Gojo Ryu. He had touched on karate and judo whilst serving in the Airborne Rangers. Later, as a civilian, he had trained for three years in a Dojo in California. Later, he was told this was an incredibly short time to reach black belt. But he was a perfectionist in everything he did. And an obsessive. He would start with Taikyoku and then the five Pinan katas. Each would take between forty five seconds and a minute. Each would work every part of his body. Then the Seinshin kata. A powerful display with deep breathing techniques, followed by Saipai – a fast, fluid form that no matter how fit he was always left him breathless. Lastly he would perform full speed techniques for three whole minutes. It was an easily managed work out that he could perform anywhere that worked all of his muscles and kept muscle memory for unarmed combat. In addition to this twice a week he would swim a mile in the pool and three times a week he would run between three and five miles. He also lifted weights every other day.

The house was a Georgian style terraced town house and situated in a desirable part of town. His neighbors were doctors, IT consultants, lawyers and accountants. The entire street was made up of working professionals. He saw himself as the same. He certainly approached his work with the same degree of professionalism, probably more so. His work was important to him; it was his life. He put a great deal of time and effort into his preparation. There was the physical fitness, of which he performed dutifully regardless of his workload or location.

His marksmanship skills were important and he was a member of several exclusive shooting clubs, just to keep his eye in twice a week using either legally held weapons for practice or the vast array of club-owned guns. For his more specialist training he would take off to the Appalachians or Vermont and test himself in the forest and mountains. He would hunt deer, elk, bear or boar and he would test his various types of ammunition from different distances. This gave him the opportunity to test his home loads. Different configurations of bullet weight and shape or grains of powder. Hollow tipped bullets with mercury or magnesium sealed with plastic or wax. Or carefully notched soft lead bullets that mushroomed upon impact. Powdered glass poured into a hollow point cavity then topped with melted wax was his newest invention. It was a fire and forget delivery method. Even fired into an elk's leg brought on a cardiac arrest within minutes as the glass violated the bloodstream. It was this sort of testing he enjoyed most. Occasionally he would wound the animal purposely, and then hone his skills with a blade. Knives were important tools in his line of work and often overlooked in favor of firearms by other so-called professionals. Anatomically, the large animals were different from humans, but arteries and internal organs still cut the same. Still bled the same. The animals still struggled the same as humans as they died, and had the same look of fear in their eyes. They were more dangerous too.

His anger was starting to get the better of him lately, and it troubled him deeply. He saw it as a weakness and he despised weakness in every way. He attended anger management classes from time to time and even integrated himself into the support network. Occasionally he would see the irony of city executives calling an accomplished and working assassin for anger management counselling from a contemporary when they felt stressed-out. However, he saw his work as a viable and highly skillful profession and did not look upon it any other way. Granted, for security and operational reasons, he never told a living soul what he did, but he felt no shame and he felt no regret. He loved his work.

A black iPhone chimed indicating an incoming message. He thumbed the screen, then put the phone down and scrolled a silver Sony laptop to the email home page. It was easier to look at the message on a larger screen. He read the short, concise e-mail and smiled. He had been thanked and congratulated upon his professionalism. His offer of returning the deposit and completing the assignment free of charge was denied. He would be awarded a substantial bonus upon completion. New intelligence would soon be on forwarded to him. He was to standby and await further instructions.

## THIRTEEN

There was more to procuring a safety deposit box than Isobel Bartlett had previously realized. There had been her proof of address, two forms of identification, a contact or next of kin and a thick pile of papers to check through and sign. It didn't sound much in this world of ever increasing bureaucracy, but it was enough for her in her fragile state of mind and her patience had long since started to ebb. She was glad when it was done.

She had been escorted to the safety deposit vault of the bank and given instructions on how the double key lock worked, how the inner drawer was removed, and that she should deposit and retrieve items in the privacy of the booths at the far end of the vault which were secreted by thick red velvet curtains. At the end of the talk the teller had reminded her that security cameras operated throughout. It had seemed like a guarded warning at the time and she wondered how many illicit items were held within the bank's walls. It seemed like a no man's land, a DMZ between the establishment and the last bastion of a willful nation. A place where drug lords could deposit ill-gotten gains alongside wealthy dowagers, putting diamond encrusted necklaces to rest until the next ball or society banquette. A place where the two ends of culture and society place their faith in one resource. The bank stood alone. It seemed to say - *place your faith in us, you are all equal in our eyes.*

The booths were approximately the same size as your average department store changing room, but fitted with a table on which was placed a selection of stationary and a pen held on a thin gold-colored chain. Next to the table was a wastebasket with a mailbox style slot. Once something was discarded into the basket, only bank staff could retrieve it. Beside this was a paper shredder. Across the entrance to the booth the dark red, velvet curtain blocked off the vault room and allowed the client all the privacy they could possibly need. She placed the two flash drives in the inner tray. She could not believe it had come to this. She looked at them and thought about the project. There had been so much work, so much time money and effort spent on creating a destructive killer. But from this had come

APHRODITE. That was why she was here in New York and that was why she was in the booth locking away the two flash drives. ARES needed to be kept from misuse, but APHRODITE needed to be kept safe to use for all mankind.

## FOURTEEN

The town of Deal had very little going for it. Or quite a lot. It kind of depended on your point of view. If one horse towns tucked away in the hills, with two bars, a diner, an old fashioned boarding house, a general store and deli, a small pharmacy and an even smaller sheriff's department were your thing, then the town of Deal would be your home from home.

To most, Deal was neither here nor there. It was too low in the hills to be a ski resort and was not on the route to any of the ski resorts further north. It wasn't on any major roads or routes and wasn't even geared up for summer tourism. It offered the locals a rural, unsophisticated way of life, and that was exactly what they wanted. The spring, summer and early fall offered good trout fishing in the many tributaries which flowed through to Burlington, or down to New Hampshire, but Deal missed out on the vast river flows which offered so much to the extreme sports and thrill seekers who frequented other areas in the vicinity. In fact, if you could come up with something other than hunting and trout fishing, it would be pretty good odds that the town of Deal missed out completely.

Rob Stone liked the town of Deal a lot. He liked the quiet, unhurried and uncomplicated aura that the town gave off. It was almost a reversed snobbery. A boast that only the free spirited could understand. He didn't mind that *Sally's Diner* didn't offer eggs benedict or cream cheese and lox bagels at breakfast. He didn't mind that his eggs were a little too over easy and he liked the fact that most people ordered the porterhouse steak for breakfast, himself included. Men sat at the counter and ate their fill, whilst talking about local issues and the people they knew mutually. Their pickups were parked outside with no risk of being towed, and the keys were most probably still in the ignition without the risk of being stolen.

He drank down the remnants of coffee and pushed his empty plate away, giving himself enough room to look at the folder in front of him. He opened it and started to shuffle through the mounting material. He had been investigating for a little over four months with little to go on. He likened any investigation to a magic eye picture, those annoying patterns of squiggles and colors, which suddenly leapt out at you to reveal stampeding horses or cascading waterfalls, just when you least expected it, or had almost given up completely. An investigation needed to be looked at in various ways, with an open mind. It was suddenly starting to open up, but there was still little he could see. All he knew that when a guy named Leipzig went over a ravine in his truck there was a glimmer of light in the darkness.

He glanced up and watched the cruiser as it pulled alongside the sheriff department building. A large man in his late forties got out and walked into the front entrance. Stone new him to be Sheriff Harper. He had acquired a short, concise file on him as well. He knew that the man had been the Sheriff for eight years, and had served for twelve years as an officer on the NYPD. Retiring early at the rank of sergeant. He knew the man had been the epitome of a professional police officer, but had moved suddenly with his wife after their eight-year old son had died tragically in a school bus accident.

Stone gathered up the papers and placed them back in the file. He could understand why a man like Harper had moved to a place like Deal. It was unpretentious and not judgmental in any way. It was the perfect place for people with a lot of baggage to start over again. He dropped a twenty and a ten on the table and walked out of the

115

door. He checked the traffic, but there was none and walked across the road and into the Sheriff's department.

The sheriff was seated at his desk and looking at what appeared to be an empty diary. He looked up and studied Stone for a moment as if deciding whether to offer him coffee and a warm good morning, or take out his gun and shoot him. He kept his gun where it was and gave a glimmer of a smile.

"Help you?"

"Special Agent Stone... United States Secret Service," he paused. "We spoke on the phone two days ago."

Sheriff Harper looked at him for a short while. Stone wondered how many Secret Service agents the man had talked with lately.

"Sure," he said, as if it had taken a while to get his week straight. "How can I help you? You want some coffee?"

"I haven't driven up from Washington for coffee, Sheriff." He walked up to his desk and sat down at the empty chair. He dropped the file on the desk and loosened the button on his jacket. He had been abrupt and he knew it. He looked at the police chief and smiled. "Just had a damn fine breakfast over the road. Steak and eggs and plenty of coffee."

"Let's cut straight to the chase then. You're

here because I disagreed with the coroner from Montpelier."

"Yes." He decided that he liked Harper. "Why, exactly?"

"Smart ass just wouldn't listen to me. The damned truck went off the hill at *Sauer's Lookout*. Sort of place where the younger folks go to make out. Not just the young either. Couple having an affair around Deal, sure thing that they go up to *Sauer's Lookout* and get the springs moving, if you get what I mean..." He smiled and gave a little knowing wink. "Just didn't figure, that's all. The coroner maintained that he simply skidded off the road. To me, it's plain and simple he went over the edge of *Sauer's Lookout* and smashed on through the barrier and on to the road below."

"Like I said. Why?"

"You got an hour?"

"Sure."

Sheriff Harper drove through the mountain roads with what appeared to be wild and reckless abandon. Stone held on to the armrest and tried to keep his eyes from fixating on the drop. He preferred to drive whenever he could.

The trees and escarpments were impressive. The morning light reflected off the yellows and reds of the fall leaves, painting a blanket of color away towards the horizon. Stone used the view to take his mind off the road. Each turn took them higher and further into the mountains. They passed through a small tunnel etched into the cliff and out into a sort of plateau of granite rock and young trees. To their left, the thick forest spread upwards as far as he could see. To his right, the bank of the verge narrowed quickly and became the cliff edge. The tarmac of the road almost ran straight off the edge.

"Fire took this lot down." The sheriff explained. "Those trees behind us on the right are only about three years old. Deal and a couple of other nearby towns got together and planted them. The road stopped the fire from spreading any further."

They continued to wind their way along the road, then turned onto a sharp switchback with an absurdly steep gradient. After approximately a mile the road surfaced worsened until it was merely hardcore and gravel.

"Here we are." The cruiser lunged to a halt and Sheriff Harper opened his door. He walked towards the cliff edge and stood precariously close to the edge.

"Guy drove right off the damn edge, in my opinion. The coroner said there were too many tire tracks to get an identification. Everyone's come up here at some time and rocked the springs at some time or another. Those who weren't old enough, and those who were but shouldn't have. I don't have a

CSI unit, but I suppose he's right. Tracks are everywhere."

Stone looked at the ground and saw the tire tracks. The edge of the precipice was solid rock and he couldn't tell if it was marked by a vehicle's tires. He peered over the edge and studied the view ahead of him. There was a long drop to the road below, but with the road snaking its way down the mountain before him, the overall effect was that of a huge precipice into oblivion. The road spiraled out of sight and was swallowed up by the trees over a thousand feet beneath them.

"Quite a drop," he commented. His legs felt a little unsteady. He wasn't really keen on heights, but hadn't noticed how much until now. "How far did he go?"

The sheriff spat on the ground and pointed to the road below. "Right down onto the road, then off the edge and down onto the road below that. Probably a hundred feet in all, maybe one-twenty."

Stone looked back at the road and followed it towards the drop. A segmented barrier was to one side with hairpin bend chevrons to act as a warning. From the direction they had come it was completely safe, a large rugged outcrop of rocks would act as a barrier from the cliff edge. But coming the other way would be another matter entirely. Stone had read the coroner's report which had been emailed to him. Imagined the man rounding the mountain corner, getting his positioning wrong, standing on his brakes, a look of fear on his face as he knew what was about to happen, then...

"You see it yet?" The sheriff spat on the ground again and looked at him.

Stone looked at the road below, then smiled. "No skid marks."

"Not a damn one. Now look at it a while longer, Mister Stone. You're an educated man, I can see that." He pointed down the road in the direction they had travelled. "You get it wrong here and you nudge into the barrier. It throws you back into the road, or if you're unlucky, you hit that outcrop of rocks. That would probably kill you anyways. On the other hand, if you come the other way, you break hard and go straight into the barrier. Might not stop you, but you sure hit it nevertheless. The road people use the metal barriers sparingly. They may not use much of it, but they sure put it in the right place. For the guy to go over the edge, he would have had to be going real slow. Real slow, then across the road, turning hard to the left, and over the edge. You agree?"

Stone looked at the road in both directions and nodded. "That's the only way, yes, I agree. The only way he could possibly go over the edge would be to go across the road and over at low speed. That would explain the lack of skid marks." He looked at Harper and frowned. "So why did you disagree with the coroner?"

The sheriff spat on the ground again and looked up at him. "Because the guy was travelling in the other direction. He was heading back to Washington from his weekend retreat. To broach the barrier he would have to have been heading in the other direction. And then he wouldn't be going fast enough to break through the barrier. Nope, up here is the only way he would do that. Speed and gravity. Hell, you can see the impact marks on the asphalt. So why didn't the coroner take any notice of it? There's no way he'd drive through that barrier and onto the road below. Not a damn way in the world ..."

## FIFTEEN

The traffic was thick and heavy, and the sound of the street was lying dense in the air. Distant sirens echoed off the buildings, drowned occasionally by the intermittence of vehicle horns. On the sidewalk the pedestrian traffic was just as intense and she was hustled along, caught in the throng of people moving down the avenue. The city was all around her, touching her, enveloping her into mere insignificance. It caught hold of her and thrust her into a distinct anonymity.

After she had finished her breakfast with Elizabeth Delaney, Isobel had taken a short walk outside the hotel to clear her head as much as to obtain a safety deposit box at the nearest bank. As it turned out, not every bank carried the facility and she had walked for more than thirty minutes, taking her down towards Greenwich Village.

She saw the sign for the coffee house, high above her as she walked. She figured Delaney would be some while talking things through with David Stein, so decided to grab a cup of coffee before walking the rest of the way back to the hotel. She knew Delaney would not have liked her leaving the hotel, but for some reason she actually felt safer on the street. The anonymity of being in the city was a comforting sensation.

The coffee house was finished with the ubiquitous wooden floor and deep red or brown distressed leather couches around the edge of the room. The counter had six high barstools and a brass foot rail ran along the bottom of the counter. Old monochrome photographs of a bygone, much romanticized era donned the walls with everything from pictures of boxers such as Jack Dempsey and Rocky Marciano squaring to the camera with boxing gloves ready and cold hard stares, to World Series victories for the Yankees.

The coffee was freshly ground on the premises of course and offered a more thorough selection than even the purest of connoisseurs could wish for. Isobel opted for a cappuccino with extra cream and chocolate shavings and took a small table directly in front of the counter. The coffee arrived quickly and the waitress dropped the check down beside it. They were obviously accustomed to a rapid turnaround in customers and she already felt hurried for the table. The place was filling up and there were only the stools left at the counter.

She sipped the coffee, feeling the odd sensation of the cold cream and then the seeping of the hot, strong coffee from beneath. It was almost sensual. The bitter chocolate contrasted the sweetened cream beautifully. It came as a harsh reality as she suddenly remembered why she was there, and that she was not just another person on vacation, or going about her day-to-day business. She put the cup back down on the saucer and glanced around the room. People were merely going about their day as they always did. It felt voyeuristic as she watched, almost an out-of-body experience. Normality was all around her, the clock was ticking and the world was turning for these people. To her right, a couple were talking, flirting intimately with one another over giant lattes. To the other side of her, two women were looking over papers together and discussing their business schedules. All around her people were simply going about their day. She only wished she could do the same. Only she had no idea of what that day might entail and no idea when it would end.

As a brief distraction she took another sip of her cappuccino, then tried to discreetly dab some whipped cream from the end of her nose with the paper napkin. She felt she managed it subtly enough and glanced up to the television behind the counter. One of the baristas was flicking through the channels with the remote. It looked like a montage to poor quality viewing. He was obviously searching for something in particular because he did not let the channel rest for more than a second. She took another sip from the cup, this time managing to avoid any potentially embarrassing incidents with the three-inch layer of whipped cream. She looked back to the television screen and something caught her eye. It was like subliminal advertising. She had seen something significant but in the same instant it was gone. Another five or six channels had swept by, but it was no use trying to recall what she had seen. Just a face for a split second, like a snapshot through the turning pages of an album. A memory partially reacquainted, then lost again in the chasms of your mind. The tender settled on a roundup of the week's sporting news and returned to taking orders at the counter.

She was trying to recall what had snatched her attention, but it was useless. The cappuccino had not cooled much, so she stirred it up with the spoon, infusing the mix into a thick, tan colored mess with flecks of melting chocolate. It didn't look half as appealing, but she was able to drink it down in a couple of gulps. She stood up, dropped a five-dollar bill on top of the check and made her way to the door.

She opted out of walking back and took a Yellow Cab. The driver was called Juan, spoke great Spanish but little English and took her on an interesting journey back to the hotel. She did not know the city, but she knew that she hadn't been driven back in many straight lines, and that it may well have been quicker to walk. However, she enjoyed the opportunity to see more of the city and it also helped to clear her head a little. She paid outside her hotel, but didn't tip feeling that failing to put up an objection to the route was kind of a tip in itself.

Back inside her room, she felt more secure than she had last night. Her confidence was growing, now that Elizabeth Delaney was involved and officiating the matter. It would only be a matter of time before the FBI was involved in force and the bioresearch facility was under proper investigation and the likes of McCray, General Harris and Tom Hardy were either cleared or arrested. This thought filled her with confidence and she realized that she had made the right move in taking the flash drives and involving Elizabeth Delaney.

With her spirits lifted a little, she switched on the television and flicked her way through channels.

She froze.

It was like looking into the mirror. The

reporter's voice was talking, but she couldn't hear the words above her own heartbeat. The blood pulsed through her ears and she felt faint, queasy. Her legs started to buckle.

The photograph was of the young woman at the train station back in Washington. The photograph had been bordered in red and was in the top left hand side of the picture with the name underneath, taking up about one-sixth of the screen. The moving footage was of a gurney handled down the steps of an unnamed hotel by two city coroner workers, the body was in a black body bag and was strapped down to the gurney with two thick canvass straps. The name under the photograph was Kathy Anderson and the reporter was saying something about her having come to New York from Washington to look for rental property and to start a new life with her fiancé who was to be joining her soon. The words came and went, drifting through the air like a thick mist for her to catch and hold onto mere snippets. The coroner had said there was evidence that it was no accident, and certainly not natural causes. Next on the screen was another gurney and a picture of a young man who was a member of staff at the hotel. His name went past on the bottom of the screen on the tickertape. Police were appealing for witnesses.

She continued to stare at the screen long

after the images had gone and had been replaced with a weather forecast. She wasn't watching, and she wasn't listening. She was simply staring into blankness. She knew what she had briefly seen in the coffee house, and she now knew why it had caught her attention. She realized how much the girl had looked like her, especially in that particular photograph, which had most probably been taken whilst the girl was in college. She also knew that it seemed a bit too much of a coincidence for a girl to look like her and be murdered on her first night in New York. And she also knew that if she had not got off in Newark, it might well have been her on that gurney and not some girl named Kathy Anderson, full of hopes and dreams and the excitement of a new life awaiting her.

## SIXTEEN

He had watched the television intently. The report had been concise and well documented. There was enough information there to be of interest, yet still there was the desire left with the viewer to want more. They would watch the evening news to find out if there had been any further developments and they would talk to their friends and acquaintances to exchange hypothesized opinions on what could have possibly happened to such a pretty young woman setting out on one of life's big adventures. To come to a city in search of a home, having secured a new job and to await your fiancé as he sorted out their final arrangements in what would soon become their previous life.

It was an innocent, somewhat idealized concept. Full of romance and self-discovery. How many people always say that they'd like to start over again, but fail to do anything about it? This young couple did and then look what happened.

Seeing the news story filled him with a sense of pride. It must have been similar to that of an artist's exhibition or a writer's book launch. That satisfying sense of relief of your work finally coming to fruition, to the attention of others. However, there was an all-encompassing emptiness to this news report. It was *his* exhibition. It was *his* time. The woman had been difficult to kill. She had struggled wildly, desperately. It had taken great effort to make her still, to take the life from her. And yet there was no recognition for his part. It had taken two. For him to kill, and for her to die. She had her recognition and she had her fifteen minutes of fame, but what about him? What about everything he had done?

He was starting to become angry at the notion. It saddened him that he never had the recognition he deserved and lived such a desperately empty life. He enjoyed his work, which went without saying, but he could never celebrate his accomplishments. There were no friends in his life and no respite from his work. He worked to live and lived to work.

He stood up and clutched the pain in his head with both hands. The pain was upon him once more and so was the red cloud, the red mist that came each and every time he started to feel this way.

So much effort, so much professionalism,

so much dedication to his work. And for what? For a hundred thousand dollars a few times a year.

The pain was starting to subside. It always came quickly and went the same way. It was like a rapid pulse of an electric shock, then gone, as if someone had merely turned off the switch. As if on cue his eyes had started to flicker. The anger was passing, but would be followed by the monotonous beating of the migraine that always ensued. The headaches were getting worse now. Dull and sickening. They seemed to take his life and put it on pause. He felt out of control. And only the weak lost control.

But it was the dreams that were worse. They took away any hope of a pure thought and held him inside his world of evil and despair. There was no good left in him now, not even within the hidden depths of his subconscious mind.

## SEVENTEEN

The boy stared out across the lake, shielding his eyes from the glare of the sun with a cupped hand. The lake was smooth and calm, and glistened like a bed of jewels on top of a polished mirror. He wished he had worn his sunglasses. He could barely see across to the other shore less than half a mile away. His clothing was bulky, the temperature was dropping daily now as fall beckoned winter. It was surprising how much colder it felt in the shadow of the tree.

He had chosen a spot on the bank, which lay under the canopy of a large spruce. The ground beneath it was a combination of soft, dry earth and sand, and nothing grew within the radius of the tree's canopy. The tree cast a cool, dark shadow across the water and offered brief respite to the intense ache behind his eyes. The glare was gone, cast aside by the carpet of shadow, and he could make out a patch of weed just a few yards from the bank.

He placed the tackle box down on the soft earth and started to put the rod together, slipping the two halves into place and twisting gently to align the eyes. The tiny reel was already attached and he set about carefully pulling the line through the thin metal eyes of the rod, ever watchful of snagging or tangling the line. His father had shown him the basic set up for light freshwater fishing and had taught him how to crimp the lead beads and tie the hook with a blood knot, but this was his first time fishing alone and away from the watchful supervision of his father. The process was time consuming, but after several fruitless attempts, he raised the rod, finally satisfied with the result. He fixed a bloodworm onto the hook, wiped the slime onto the leg of his pants and walked to the bank.

His cast was raw and jerky and part of the worm flew off into the reeds, but for the best part, the hook, and at least part of the bait, were where he had intended it to be. He sat down on the ground with his legs up to his chest and the rod resting on his lap with the tip just a few inches from the glassy surface of the water. He was Tom Sauer, he was Huckleberry Finn. He was just an innocent boy enjoying the great outdoors and a glorious Saturday.

He reached into the tackle box beside him and took out a plastic bottle of orange soda. Carefully, he balanced the rod in his lap and started to unscrew the bottle cap. The contents of the bottle fizzed and built up, threatening to spill from the cap. He quickly tightened the cap to save the contents, then felt the rod jolt in his hands. The tip sprung down and hit the water three times in quick succession. He dropped the bottle and caught hold of the rod with both hands. The tip of the rod bounced down again then went still. He waited, poised for the strike. He needed to get the hook embedded deeply into the fish's mouth, not just have it bite and pull at the bait and make off with a free lunch. The rod jolted again and he started to count silently, mouthing the numbers, just as his father had taught him. One... Two... Three! He struck quickly and firmly on the third bite, then screamed with delight as the line carved its way through the glassy water in smooth, labored arcs. The fish was running and it was now imperative the boy keep the line tight and avoid slackness otherwise the hook would simply pull out of the fish's mouth in the struggle. He watched the line and felt the continuous pressure on the rod. He didn't want to prolong the fight for his own gratification, simply land the creature and present it to his mother for her to cook. It would be his first fish on his own, and he so wanted his father's approval over the dinner table as they ate his catch. He had had a fish on the line before, but his father came to his aid and landed it for him. Like fathers do.

The fish was big and strong. At least a four pounder. It was working its way back to the bank and the thick mass of reeds and the potential safety awaiting it. The boy knew this and was working the reel and walking the other way to keep the taught line from slackening off. He felt the line suddenly go slack as the fish swam with him. There was a brief moment of uncertainty in the boy's eyes, then the tip of the rod straightened and the line went still in the water. He wound the handle of the reel furiously, but to no avail. The line was coming in and the fish had gone. Suddenly there was a terrific pull on the line and the rod almost bent double. There was a flicker of excitement in the boy's eyes, then the realization that he had caught the hook in a heavy mass of weed. He knew what to do in order to prevent the line from snapping and straightened the rod until the line was entirely outstretched from the reel. He checked his footing, then slowly walked backwards and took in the slack line with the reel. The weed was extremely heavy and it was a long, steady process, but he heaved and pulled and finally got the weed to the bank where he could safely untangle the hook. He wound in the slack line as he walked back towards the edge of the water, then stopped abruptly in his tracks.

The mass of weed had indeed been thick and heavy. But it was the bloated corpse that it had enveloped which had helped considerably to increase its weight. The corpse's face looked lifelessly up at the boy. A gaping, ragged bullet hole in its forehead.

## EIGHTEEN

Rob Stone sipped a mouthful of coffee and grimaced. It was warm but had sat on top of the machine hot plate for too long. It had gone bitter and tasted, albeit mildly, of tobacco. He placed the cup down on the desk and looked around the office. On the wall behind the vacant chair was a photograph from the academy with fresh-faced recruits grinning into the camera for the official end of training photograph. He tried hard to spot Captain Dolbeck but guessed that the photograph was at least twenty years old and that Dolbeck had not aged well. There was a stocky-looking guy in the second row which looked like a probable, but then again Dolbeck was a hell of a lot bigger than he had been twenty years ago and he knew that deskbound officers pile on the pounds after they hit forty. Dolbeck could have been anyone in the photograph.

He turned his eyes to the commendations and newspaper cuttings on the far wall. Captain

Dolbeck had obviously been around the block in the early part of his career and was still proud of those achievements. They were dated though, Stone noticed, indicating fewer glory days in the latter half of his career.

The door suddenly opened behind him and Stone looked around. Captain Dolbeck walked in, his head buried in the pages of an opened file. He was a big man, at least two-sixty, and most of it around his waist. His shoulders were fairly narrow and Stone changed his mind about Dolbeck being the stocky guy in the photograph.

"Got it right here," the captain paused. "Came through two days ago, just plain disappeared. Seems he had a woman on the side a couple of years ago. Got back with his wife and made another go of it, but when he didn't come home that night she just assumed he'd reverted to his old ways and gone off with some woman. She didn't even make the call until the next day."

Stone took the file from him and studied it. It was a desk report of incoming and outgoing calls and a list of everything that had been reported to the Montpelier Police Department two days previous.

"So he's been missing for three days, not two?" Stone studied the list a while longer, then dropped it onto the desk. "Is he actually listed as a missing person then?"

Dolbeck shrugged. "Kind of a grey area. Since the guy spent a while playing around behind his wife's back, we can't rule out that he's not just off having himself some fun."

"The guy's not some travelling salesman, he's a County Coroner. A professional. Surely that lends some weight?"

"Well, sort of," the police captain paused. "I mean, we're kind of worried now, responsible guy and all."

"So what happens now?" Stone asked.

The police captain spread his hands. "We've got twenty two missing people on our books. That's the ones we haven't given up hope for. A lot of them are children and teenagers. They get the priority. Next come the women, you know, wives and girlfriends who've run away to avoid a pair of fists. They're lying low, but they're still our priority, whether they want to be found or not." He put his arms above his head and stretched, straining the buttons on his shirt as he did so. "To be honest, with a grown male we don't do too much. If it looks real suspicious, like an assault or signs of a struggle, we look into it. Start an investigation. If the circumstances are not suspicious we post the details on the national database and wait for a lead to turn up. We can't go wasting our budget if the guy's just sinking his dick into some broad." He shook his head despairingly. "Had some damned tramp in here a few days ago, seems his friend went missing. The desk sergeant asks for the missing guy's address, but he's told the guy was sleeping rough or sometimes used an old ramshackle cabin in the woods. How in Hell's name can you waste your time, money and officers looking for some hobo who has most probably drunk his way through a gallon of hooch and is sleeping it off in some barn somewhere? People just come in here and waste our time every day."

Stone remained silent. There was something he couldn't get out of his head and he was losing concentration because of it.

"You OK?" Dolbeck stared at him.

"Sure, just thinking about something." He stood up, buttoned his jacket. "Thank you, Captain." He held out his hand. "You've been a great help."

"He'll turn up," Dolbeck said. "The coroner. Not the homeless guy."

Stone nodded. But he managed to stop himself from telling the police captain not to count on it.

As he stepped out into the low Vermont sun Stone felt the chill in the air. He reached for his sunglasses in his inside jacket pocket and slipped them on against the crystalline glare. A few leaves were falling and the sides of the roads were building up with crunchy mounds of yellow, red and brown.

Across the street from him a few kids were rushing through the fallen leaves and laughing. Stone watched them play. Something had troubled him in Captain Dolbeck's office and he needed clarity of mind to remember what it was. Approximately two hours after the county coroner had covered the remains of Professor Leipzig on the slab and forwarded his verdict to Sheriff Harper in down in Deal, nobody saw him again. He had disappeared. Sheriff Harper had concerns about the verdict and now those concerns could not be met.

As Stone walked across the quiet Montpelier street Sheriff Harper's words echoed in his ears. *"Because the guy was travelling in the other direction... There's no way he'd drive through that barrier and onto the road below. Not a damn way in the world..."*

## NINETEEN

The line was not connecting and Isobel had no alternative number on which she could reach Elizabeth Delaney. She had been calling all morning and now she was trying through the afternoon. She had been tempted to call the New York division of the bureau, but had not wanted to face an inquisition at the switchboard just to get through. She had no idea of how the system worked within the FBI and what questions would be asked of her, and she was not aware whether the division would know anything about her and the specific situation. She knew that Delaney was going to discuss the matter with David Stein, but what their next move was to be was beyond her reasoning.

She felt scared and very much alone. The murder of the young girl from Washington had shaken her to the core and she desperately needed to speak to Delaney and let her know the connection. It couldn't have been merely a coincidence. The odds were just too damn high. She pressed the redial button on her cell phone and waited. The screen came up with a message that the line was still busy and she threw the phone at the bed in frustration.

She paced the room and contemplated going out. It was true she had earlier felt more comfortable being anonymous within a crowd, but that was before the news report. She knew it was serious now, knew with every fiber of her being that she was in grave danger.

She picked up the cellphone and tried Delaney again, breathing a sigh of relief when she heard her friend's voice. However, it was short lived as she realized it was an answer phone message. She left a curt message saying that she was worried and for her to call her back when she could.

She understood that the FBI agent would be busy, but she was feeling out of the loop. She needed some control put back into the situation. She dropped her cell phone back onto the bed and picked up the remote control. There was nothing much on, so she just flicked through the channels and stared blankly at the screen. Her concentration wasn't really up to it, but she was glad of the distraction nevertheless.

The tiny cell phone beeped out a short, somewhat irritating tune and she picked it up. There was a message telling her that she had received a text message and she scrolled through the options to get to it.

*Isobel – can't get to you for a while - meetings all day. Will meet you tonight at a bar called Sullivan's between W 50 & W 51 on 9th Ave. Meet me @ 7 – it will be crowded and safe —E*

## TWENTY

Rob Stone had dropped the hire car back at the airport and was aboard a 737 to Dulles. He would arrive back in Washington DC at three-forty-five and get to his next objective by four-thirty. The aircraft was running at half capacity and he carried no luggage. Security was tougher these days, since nine-eleven, but he would show his credentials and be given priority. He expected to walk straight along the concourse and right out the door at arrivals.

He sifted through the thickening file in front of him and made the occasional note in the margin. He had removed his suit jacket and loosened his tie. To the cabin crew and his fellow passengers he looked like just another young businessman who most probably spent a lot of his downtime at the gym. He was clean cut and smart looking but in an ex-military kind of way. His glossy black hair was shaved down to an even half-inch all over but a little shorter at the back and sides. He wore an old Rolex diver's wristwatch and no other jewelry. The watch had belonged to his late father and was over twenty years old, but looked barely any different to its modern counterpart. His forearms bore a couple of light scars and the veins stood out as he turned the pages of the file. He looked serious, but the glint in his eye, as he asked the flight attendant for a drink, was kind and showed that there was an underlying sense of humor in there somewhere.

His briefing had been short and had come from the very top. The director had chosen him for the task. And now there were three people in the loop. Himself, the director of the Secret Service and the President of the United States. His investigation was in to a disbanded CIA assassination program. He was the second person to start this investigation, the first had been killed in the process. His investigation landed him to the door of the bioresearch facility. Here, his brief changed. He was to investigate the bioresearch facility's security. From this brief he was to surmise the likelihood of the outbreak of a major pandemic and to re-evaluate the facility's security procedures. He was to investigate the facility's contact with the combined military and intelligence services and proportion control of the project. Any development was to be shared equally with the intelligence community for the continued development and benefit of the country, and not one specific agency.

However, there had seemed to be an anomaly within the facility's fraternization and one particular agency was receiving more information and applying more technical support towards the project than any other. That agency was the CIA. He had started with this anomaly and it had led him away from the CIA as an agency and towards two people in particular. What were the chances of a connection between the assassination program, a particular CIA employee and the bioresearch facility? He couldn't ignore the facts, but with every day of the investigation the neck of the funnel was tightening. It was now time to take the hunt to the door.

As he predicted, Stone left the airport quickly and was at his car twenty minutes after disembarking the plane.

The car was a black '68 Mustang GT-390 and had been maintained to possibly better than its original condition. That was because the Ford line pumped so many units out that this iconic car was finished in a hurry to meet with supply and demand. This car, however, was pristine in every way and benefited from many modern extras, painstakingly fitted by its owner. Modern magnetic front and rear dampers and servo-assisted ABS brakes from Brembo to assist not only the handling but stopping. Holly carbs and a Garrett supercharger, and the gearbox from a '69 Shelby Cobra to cope with the extra horsepower and performance.

The gearbox was slick and smoothly changed down through the cogs as Rob Stone swung off the road and into the bioresearch facility's entrance. He floored the throttle and corrected the wheel as the rear wheels dug into the tarmac and left a couple of thick black lines in the car's wake. He was lifted by the boyish display and enjoyed the sensation of becoming braced tightly into the seat. He neared the first security booth and lifted his right foot off the throttle. It was back to business now and he settled back into his role of the consummate professional, though he was always glad of a brief respite.

The V8 rumbled and popped on tick over and he flashed a current security pass at the guard. The guard looked at the car, Stone suspected schoolboy admiration, although he was plaintively aware that you either loved or loathed this sort of vehicle. He was under no illusion that his choice of vehicle had been immature at best. But it was a lesson taught to him by his father. You make the most of life and seize it. You enjoy what you have. His father never uttered those words, nor any to that effect. He simply punched the clock his entire life and dropped down dead four days after his retirement. The watch had been a gift to his father from Stone's mother. He had coveted one all his life, and she marked his retirement by buying one for him, because she knew he never would. It had been a secondhand purchase from a quality jeweler and she had paid in installments for the entire year before picking it up the day before his final shift.

"Robert Stone, United States Secret Service."

The guard studied the pass and then handed it back to him. "And your business, Sir?"

"I'm here to see Doctor McCray."

"Do you have an appointment?"

"No. But he'll see me." He reached into his jacket pocket and retrieved a folded piece of paper and passed it to the guard. "He has no choice."

The guard studied the paper for a long while, then folded it back in half and handed it over. "Go right in, Agent Stone. I'll call ahead and get things rolling." He lifted the red and yellow striped barrier and stood back to allow him through. "You have a nice day, Sir."

Stone drove through the entrance and over the succession of speed humps and parked outside a set of smoked glass doors. A security guard appeared on cue and stood to the side of the

149

doors. The thumb of his left hand was looped through his utility belt. The right hand was resting on the butt of a 9mm Berretta. He was chewing gum and wore mirrored sunglasses.

"Good afternoon, Sir. I'm here to take you up to Doctor McCray's office."

Stone nodded curtly. "Thanks, lead on."

The floor was hard and loud under foot. It was a heavily glazed marble and the sound of the two of them walking the corridor echoed around the plain whitewashed walls. Above them row upon row of florescent tubes flickered and gave off a bright, clinically unnatural illumination. The walls were plain, but for the occasional copy of an architectural pencil drawing of the facility and monochrome photographs of the entire complex at varying stages of construction. These were housed inside highly polished chromium frames and were at least four feet square in size.

A short ride in the lift to the fifth floor and another walk the length of an identical corridor and the two men stood outside a smoked glass office door. The guard opened the door and allowed Stone to enter first.

A plump and severe looking woman of what Stone would have called indeterminable age stood up from behind her desk and smiled. The smile was thin and somewhat cruel and did not fit the voice which was warm and full of charm. "Hello, you must be Agent Stone." She beamed at him, her eyes brighter than the look given by her thin lips. "I'm Agnes Dempsey, Doctor McCray's personal assistant."

Stone nodded, turned to thank the guard, but the man had already left and they could both hear the footsteps getting lighter as he neared the lift. He looked back at the woman and extended his right hand. He already knew who she was of course, from his research. "Pleased to meet you. Please, call me Rob." He shook hands with her and was surprised by the firmness of her grip. "Doctor McCray is expecting me?"

"He is now," she paused, making sure she smiled. It countered her sardonic tone almost perfectly. "You were lucky to catch him, he wasn't due in the office at all today."

Stone smiled. "Somehow I knew he'd be in. Put it down to a lucky guess."

The door to the inner office suddenly opened and a smartly dressed man in his mid to late forties stepped in. Stone knew he was forty-six, knew his birth date and knew how many siblings he had. Stone knew more about Dr. McCray than the man's mother did or ever would.

"Agent Robert Stone." He held out his hand and shook McCray's hand firmly. The doctor's palm was warm and clammy. "So glad you could see me at such short notice."

"I'm sure," McCray paused. "Do you mind if I ask to see this letter I've heard about?" He held his hand out expectantly.

"Certainly not." Stone took out the letter and dropped it into McCray's outstretched hand. He then brushed past, moving the man an inch or two and walked into his office. "Let's get underway, I don't have much time."

McCray looked stunned, took his eyes off the letter and followed, glancing backwards towards his PA. "Err, coffee please Agnes, for two." He was visibly shaken at the Secret Service agent's actions. He stepped into his office and stared at Stone, who was sitting in his chair.

The chair was a reclining leather swivel design, and Stone was easing it gently from left to right. It was a subtle motion, but McCray couldn't take his eyes off the movement. Stone beckoned him in with his hand and pointed to the straight-legged chair intended for subordinates.

"Please Doctor McCray, do take a seat."

The man was stunned. He ran a hand through his thick greying hair and sat down somewhat hesitantly.

"I trust the letter was in order?" He held his hand out across the desk and smiled a thank you as the doctor placed it obediently in his hand. "Now, let me think ... Where do we start? Ah, yes... ARES."

McCray looked blankly at him. "I'm not sure that's the business of the Secret Service. Aren't you supposed to guard the president?"

Stone looked at him coldly. "What makes you think I'm not guarding him right now?"

"I don't understand."

"Of course you don't." Stone kept up the stare. "You've read the letter, you know how far my authority extends." He leant back in McCray's expensive leather chair and stared up at the ceiling. He placed his feet on the corner of the desk, crossing his ankles, then rubbed his chin thoughtfully and looked back at McCray. His stare was not as cold this time, but his eyes were serious and didn't seem to invite questions. "ARES was developed under the late Professor Leipzig as a concept weapon to be used as the first line of attack, solely as a covert 'softener'. Release it and tens, no hundreds of thousands of troops and civilians are killed or rendered incapacitated. The country in question begs for surrender and they beg for the antidote. Correct?"

McCray nodded awkwardly.

"How do you sleep at night? No, don't answer that, it's just a rhetorical question." He smiled briefly, and then looked stern and cold once more. "So you develop APHRODITE as the counter to the evil of ARES. Now this is something worth developing because it has other attributes, other significant uses. Strains of APHRODITE have had a dramatic effect on flu and the common cold. Other strains are looking good as regards to HIV and AIDS. Maybe even cancer. This is what the late Professor Leipzig was to announce at the combined military and intelligence conference. He was going to announce the wonders of APHRODITE and he was going to suggest major funding and development programs towards worthwhile research. Only, the professor takes a wrong turn on a Vermont mountain road and his subordinate, Isobel Bartlett takes the helm and doesn't manage to plead such a sound and convincing case," he smiled. "Thought it lacked passion, myself. Maybe we should put it down to nerves and grief. Maybe she doesn't do much public speaking."

"You were there?"

"Of course."

"I don't recognize your name from the manifest."

"You wouldn't."

"Who the hell *are* you?"

"Agent Robert Stone of the United States Secret Service. Just like the letter suggests, and just like the President's signature validates." He kept his feet on the desk and smiled at Agnes Dempsey, who had just entered carrying a tray of cups and jugs of cream and sugar. She looked horrified at seeing the secret service agent in McCray's chair, but quickly regained her composure as she placed the tray carefully down on the desk. McCray thanked her and she looked at him with concern then turned and walked back out of the office.

Stone took his feet off the desk, sat forward and reached over tipping a little cream and sugar into one of the cups of coffee, he stirred quickly with the spoon, then took the cup and drank an inch off the top. He made no effort to help McCray, who had to reach almost twice as far to pick up the remaining cup. Stone leant back in the man's chair and pondered for a moment.

"Got to be straight with you. I'm not liking Leipzig's death. Not buying it as an accident."

"The coroner seemed to be happy with the verdict," McCray paused. "What does the coroner say on the matter?"

Stone watched him carefully. He held the man's eyes, and then smiled as McCray looked away awkwardly. "You know, that's the strangest thing, I can't get hold of the coroner because he seems to have simply *disappeared.*" He watched McCray for a long moment, maybe even a whole minute, as the man remained silent and sipped from his cup of coffee. Stone took another mouthful of coffee and placed the cup down on the leather-topped desk. Drips of coffee ran down the side of the cup and pooled at the bottom. It would leave a ring. Stone didn't take any notice, but McCray's eyes stayed on the spilt coffee. "What do you think to that?"

"I'm sorry, are you accusing me of something?" McCray feigned indignation.

"Why would I do that?" Stone asked.

"You just seem to be insinuating, that's all."

Stone shrugged. "Hell, after what I've just said, all I could have insinuated was your involvement in the murder of Professor Leipzig and the disappearance of the Montpelier coroner." He chuckled light-heartedly, and then looked coldly at him. "Now that wouldn't be the case, would it?"

"Of course not!"

Stone didn't comment. He studied an apparent spot on his fingernail, then looked back at the doctor. "How safe is ARES?"

"What do you mean?"

"I mean, could someone simply pick it up and walk out the door?"

"Of course not."

"Why?"

McCray sighed. "Because it doesn't even exist anymore. We destroyed it, or Leipzig destroyed it just before he died. He split the genetic and technical information over two high-yield computer flash drives. The same for APHRODITE. Then two drives were stored in his own safe cabinet, one for half of ARES and one for half of APHRODITE, and two drives were stored in my own personal safe."

Stone looked thoughtful for a moment then smiled. "Take me to Leipzig's safe, and bring whatever you need to let me in."

The walk down to the technical support area was much the same as the walk up to McCray's offices within the administration department, except that these offices were smaller and had plain old chipboard table tops as opposed to leather-clad mahogany. Stone guessed the budget got smaller the further down you went. All money here was spent on production and not on fancy offices for executives. They entered Leipzig's office and McCray went over to the cabinet and opened a series of locks with a set of master keys. Stone looked around the office, trying to get a feel for the dead professor. He felt nothing. There was nothing human about the office, nothing by which he could judge the man or understand him. There were no family photographs – Stone knew that the professor had no wife or children, but it was unusual for the man's office to be bereft of any memorabilia or photographs of any kind. Stone assumed the man lived for science and that nothing else mattered.

McCray turned around. He looked crestfallen. "They're ... they're gone."

157

"Who else has access? Apart from yourself and the late Professor Leipzig?"

"Isobel Bartlett."

"The woman who gave the speech?" Stone was already making his way out of the door. "Where is she?"

McCray didn't have time to relock the cabinet and fussed with the keys as he caught up with Stone. "She's off for the weekend, back in on Monday morning."

Stone led the pace. It was fast and purposeful. McCray was trotting alongside to keep up. They were back at the lift. Stone pressed the button for the eighth floor and stood back as the doors closed.

"I want all the CCTV footage from her last shift and I want the log for the entrance and exit of all personnel. And I want to know who saw her last and when. Get them to work backwards from end of her shift. Exclude the time she was making her speech, for now. It will give us a narrower window to look through first."

They exited the lift and walked back down the corridor towards McCray's office. The echo from their footsteps was loud and obtrusive. Stone had to raise his voice over it to be heard.

"I want the footage within five minutes," he paused. "But first, I want to take a look in your safe."

"My safe?"

"Sure, got a problem with that?"

McCray looked ashen. "No...I..."

"Good." Stone breezed past McCray's PA, took off his jacket and dropped it on McCray's desk. It covered some paperwork and knocked a pen out of its holder. Stone didn't put it back. "Your safe. Now. You OK? You don't look so good."

"I'm fine."

"Really? I wouldn't be feeling fine if I'd just lost the newest, most deadly super virus made in a long while."

"'No, I mean I'm fine with you looking in my safe."

"Of course. Why wouldn't you be?"

McCray didn't answer. Instead, he stepped behind his desk and opened a wall cupboard. Inside the space was a false panel. He slid it across to reveal an iron door with a combination dial. Stone looked at it and shook his head. He could have had it open inside five minutes. McCray turned the dial to co-ordinate the four-figure combination and stood back as he opened the door.

"They're gone!" He looked back at Stone with a look of disbelief. "Someone's taken them..."

Stone nodded expectantly, then looked around the office and turned back to McCray.

"You got CCTV in here?"

"No."

Stone looked at him coldly, the glimmer of a grin starting to set on the comers of his mouth. "Now there's a surprise."

## TWENTY ONE

Stone blipped the throttle between the gear change and the highly tuned V8 roared loudly as the car surged forwards. He was heading for Isobel Bartlett's home in Westchester, but he already knew what he would find.

The CCTV footage showed her going into Professor Leipzig's office at four-ten, leaving five minutes later. The camera showed her slipping a shiny object into her bag which further forensic analysis would no doubt show to be the drives. She then made her way towards Dr. McCray's office without hesitation. It showed her walking down the passageway to McCray's door, then exiting soon after. McCray's office had no CCTV, nor did Agnes Dempsey's reception. No other persons appeared on the footage. A court prosecution would announce an open and shut case. He had with him a copy of the surveillance on DVD. What he wanted to do as soon as he got the opportunity was have the DVD footage analyzed by the Secret Service computer fraud division. He had a suspicion the experts would show it had been edited.

Stone had spent the past few months looking for anomalies. That was the basis of this investigation. After a while there were patterns and from patterns came the overall design. He recognized an anomaly when he saw one. It was slight and it would have remained undetected by most, but he recognized it and if his intuition was correct it would become another piece of the jigsaw.

He knew Isobel Bartlett's apartment would be empty and he knew she would have taken off soon after arriving home yesterday evening. Call it a hunch, or just plain common sense, but you don't steal highly sensitive government property and hang around the house at the weekend. There had been a look of sheer intensity on the young woman's face, and Stone knew what the face of fear and duress looked like. It had been there, as clear as crystal on the face of Isobel Bartlett.

He found a place to park outside the apartment building and brought the Mustang to a halt inside a wide parking bay. He got out and locked the door with the key. He took in his surroundings as he walked. It was in his instinct now, honed through years of training and operating in close protection. He took in the people in the street, the parked cars and entrances to the nearby buildings. If it moved, he saw it and if it didn't move he'd be ready if it did. Every part of his route, wherever he was, was mapped out in his head as he went. He would see exits, cover from attack, possible ambush sites. There would be points at which retreat was further than advance and vice versa and thus creating another reaction to a scenario, his years in the Secret Service, protecting the most powerful man in the world had drilled these skills into him. As a consequence, he never switched off. As an advantage, he was rarely ever caught out.

Isobel Bartlett's apartment was 4a. He pressed the buzzer and waited, but he already knew there would be no reply. He looked at the name above. Mrs. Coleridge. He pressed the button and waited.

"Hello?" The voice was old and frail.

"Hello, UPS. Need to get a package to 4a. Can you let me in to deliver? The items are perishable, some kind of organic farm market box. I need to get a signature from someone."

There was a click and the lock opened. He stepped on in and climbed the stairs to apartment 4a. The stairwell was clean and the doors to the apartments were painted in various colors, all recently and in a high gloss finish. He stopped outside the door to Isobel Bartlett's apartment and glanced around. He looked back at the door and shrugged to himself.

The door splintered open on his first kick, swung inwards quickly, and then rebounded back. He nudged the door open and stepped inside. The Sig Sauer P229 was already in his hand and he guided the .357 pistol around the room, looking only through the sights. The weapon and his arm were an extension to his eyes and nothing passed him by without first crossing the path of the short, stubby barrel. He went from room to room, then satisfied it was clear, he hitched up the tail of his jacket and slipped the heavy pistol back into the soft hide holster.

He looked at the entire apartment with a different set of eyes. He had searched out any potential threat with his combat eyes, now it was the eyes of the investigator that went to work.

She had packed quickly, that much was obvious. Although he had no idea of how much she had taken with her. It was the little things he observed like the unopened mail on the couch and the empty coffee cup on the table, yet to make it to the sink. The rest of the apartment was clean and tidy, so he had no reason to assume that she was a slob. The cup was out of character to the profile he was building. An anomaly.

He walked into the bathroom and checked what had been left. There was no toothbrush, toothpaste, shampoo or shower gel. Yet bath salts and various lotions remained. So she had packed just the mere essentials. In the bedroom it was the same story. Most of her cosmetics remained, but there was no night creams or cleansing lotions and there was a full bag of make-up. She had taken what she needed and nothing else. A quick glance in the wardrobe revealed plenty of clothes, but also a few empty hangers indicating that a selection of clothes, though not many, had been taken also.

He checked the kitchen and lounge and looked at the various photographs that were either large prints in frames on the walls, or four by six prints in clever little carousel-type holders. There were photographs of a couple in their sixties, which he took to be her parents, and there was another woman in her mid-twenties, which judging by the resemblance, was her sister. He didn't know, but made a mental note to check her file. There was one photograph of a young man in a *Redskins* jersey. He looked sporty and shared no features with Isobel so he guessed that he was probably a current, or past boyfriend. A photograph on the mantel confirmed it, as the two were posing for the camera in an intimate embrace. The two photographs looked a few years old, so Stone decided that it was in fact a previous partner, though still special to her to be out on display.

He turned around and looked over the room again. There was a neat little table in the comer with a telephone and a couple of directories on top. A little red address book was open and face down on the top of the pile. He turned over and looked at the entry: *Elizabeth Delaney (parent's address).* There was a phone number, but he didn't recognize the area code. He slipped the book into his pocket and picket up the receiver and pressed the redial button. The phone rang for a few moments, and then switched to one of those pre-recorded ring tones. After another few moments, the phone switched to a recorded answer phone message: *Delaney here, you know the drill...* The voice was no-nonsense and a little forced, like the person behind it was putting up an act.

Stone put the receiver back down and glanced around the room again. It was a short search but he had what he wanted.

## TWENTY TWO

*Sullivan's* was a trendy bar designed with the intention of a crossover between old town Irish grass roots and cosmopolitan chic. At least that was what was printed on the back of the laminated cocktail menu. Whether or not it was the fact that the likes of *Murphy's* or *Guinness* had made it into the cocktail menu as part of that cosmopolitan chic, Isobel didn't know. She had ordered a simple white rum and coke and had taken a secluded table in the furthest corner of the bar. She was now leafing through the extensive traditional grass roots Irish cocktail menu merely for a distraction. At the same time she was wondering what exactly it was that made Sullivan's so cosmopolitan chic. Perhaps it was the chromium finishing around the edges of the tables and bar counter, or perhaps it was the frameless prints of contemporary modern art on the walls. Either way, she thought the crossover was lame. Perhaps other people thought the same, maybe that was why the bar was so quiet.

Another glance at her watch told her that it was eight thirty. Five minutes later than when she had last looked and eight minutes later than the time before that. She picked up her cell phone and hit redial. It connected and played the same curt message. She tried Delaney's home number and was again greeted by the answer phone message, even curter than the first. Delaney had time to change her message, but not to answer her phone evidently. Isobel took a sip of her drink and realized that she was starting to cloud over. It was her fourth and she decided to make this one last longer than the previous three. She had not yet eaten and the combined effect of stress, tiredness and an empty stomach was going to take its toll if she didn't slow down. Besides, there seemed to be an awful lot of ice and not a lot of coke, and the glass wasn't all that tall either. They were easy to get through and the service was a little too quick for her liking. She had barely taken the glass from her lips and the waitress was asking if she cared for another. She didn't want to sit at a table without a drink in front of her, so had dutifully obliged. She kept catching the eye of the two bar stewards, who seemed to be talking about her. Either fancying their chances or making fun of her misfortune, sitting there for a whole hour and a half, all alone. They most probably had her down as an easy touch at the end of their shift. Most likely had bets and odds laid down.

Yet another glance at her watch told her that time was either dragging or that her battery was dying. Hardly two minutes had passed since she had last looked. It was becoming ridiculous, no matter how busy Delaney had been; she should have let her know by now. She picked up the glass, swallowed the rest of her drink and stood up. She felt a little unsteady. Delaney knew where she was staying and she could come to her, or call her when she was available. She was damned if she was going to wait alone looking like some lost cause that had been stood up for a date. She counted the chits and dropped a two twenties and a five down. She wasn't going to leave a tip worth a damn for the two aging *Cocktail* wannabes behind the bar.

The outside air cooled her down and cleared her head. There was a slight chill, a sign that fall was upon the city, but still not too harsh. She walked the two blocks and enjoyed the sights of the city by night. It was a good area, an area of theatres and bars and decent looking restaurants. The people were light on the street and the taxicabs carried passengers towards a night out of fun and entertainment. A few bars were still accommodating the after work drinkers, but most had taken off to eat or go home. Another half hour and the bars and clubs would start becoming busy for the start of the weekend and she could see various establishments further down the street becoming the destination for streams of yellow cabs. These were obviously the more popular bars and not dubious crossovers between Irish grass roots and cosmopolitan chic. She wanted to go and explore the city by night and eat in some of the excellent looking restaurants but she knew that she couldn't.

She felt vulnerable and she felt alone. She had hoped that Elizabeth Delaney would show more urgency, and she was starting to fear that the FBI agent was not taking her seriously. Or at least, was not being strictly on the level with her.

She shivered as she walked. It wasn't very far, but she was starting to regret having not brought a coat with her. She could see the hotel now, its sign bringing her to warmth and comfort like a ship to safe anchorage. She was tired and she was irksome. She needed to get a good night's sleep and look at things differently in the morning. She needed to get Delaney to communicate with her and she needed to know the extent of this man David Stein's input and what conclusions he had drawn.

There was a black and white squad car opposite the entrance to the hotel, its lights were off, but she could hear the chatter of the dispatch coming from the radio inside. She climbed the steps and walked into the foyer. She had a key card to the room, so didn't bother going to the reception desk, but stopped in her tracks as the duty manager stepped out from the desk and made a direct line for her.

"Ms. Bartlett," he paused. His face was ashen, a look of concern. "If you wouldn't mind waiting down here for a moment..."

"What's the problem?" She glanced around, there were a few people sitting around the foyer. They looked like travelers at an airport, just waiting because they had no other choice.

The manager sighed. "I'm afraid there has been a break in. Your room has been broken in to," he paused. "I'm ever so sorry, and on behalf of the hotel, I would like to extend my sincerest apologies. Of course, anything taken will be covered by our insurance..." He looked at her apologetically, but she made no comment. She was simply stunned and felt ill. The four rum and cokes weren't helping much. "I have taken the liberty of re-booking you a suite, free of charge of course. As soon as the police have finished with your room, I'll have your things moved over at once."

"The police? Oh, of course." She looked around for somewhere to sit, she felt as if she were about to fall. She glanced up and caught sight of a tall male police officer, carrying a clipboard. He walked straight towards her, glanced at the duty manager as if for confirmation, and then smiled.

"Ms. Bartlett, Isobel Bartlett?"

"Yes." The unsteady feeling had passed. She looked at the police officer, unsure whether to tell them what had been happening.

"If you'll come with me, we need an inventory of what has been taken."

She nodded dutifully and followed him to the lift. She said nothing as they rode up together, but looked at him as the lift stopped on the fifth floor.

"It's safe, right?"

"Sure, my partner's up here. She's keeping a guard on the door until you're moved." He beckoned her forwards and waited for her to leave the lift first. "After you, ma'am."

She stepped out in front of him and walked somewhat tentatively down the carpeted corridor towards her room. She had a hunch about what she'd find and the ramifications if it were so would be too much to bear.

She neared the room and looked at the door which was ajar. It had been splintered open and as she stepped into the room, she could see that it had crashed back into the wall, chipping and flaking the plaster. It must have been kicked hard, hellishly powerful, because the locks looked strong and the door was thick and heavy. A woman police officer smiled as she entered, then looked back at her clipboard as Isobel took in the scene.

There were piles of clothing that had been scattered across the room, and her bags were far from where she had left them, but even at a glance she could tell that nothing had been taken. She had been travelling light and really hadn't brought much with her. It was the attention that had been paid to the dresser, which sent a shiver down her spine. It had been moved, dumped aside and the carpet was torn up a good three feet around the area. She had told Elizabeth Delaney where she had hidden the flash drives, but for some inexplicable reason, she had decided to lie. And now there was all the confirmation she would ever need. She could trust no one.

She had never felt so alone.

## TWENTY THREE

She hadn't slept that night. Not even for a few minutes. Her mind had raced and her anger had raged. How could she have been so let down? How could she have been betrayed so? What had Delaney been thinking? She couldn't have possibly been involved in stealing ARES and APHRODITE so what had happened today? Had she contacted McCray directly, tried to get in on some sort of finder's fee? Or was she going to take it for herself and make McCray an offer? And was McCray even involved? Too many questions, too many possible answers.

She had left the Amsterdam Court Hotel as soon as the police had completed their report and left the building. The duty manager had attempted to persuade her to stay, but his pleas fell upon deaf ears. Isobel wanted out completely. There had been no charge for her room and her credit card had been reimbursed in full. The duty manager had called a cab for her and helped her with the door of the cab personally. The cab had taken her to a small hotel called The Albany on west 71st and Columbus. It had been thoroughly recommended by the taxi driver and the staff had been extremely accommodating as she checked in. The night manager had called for a porter to carry her largest bag and show her to the room and the night porter had willingly performed his duty offering no end of nighttime services, such as shoe polishing, room order service and personal early-morning wakeup calls – complete with her choice of newspaper and freshly brewed coffee. She figured the guy did pretty well on gratuities. Or maybe he had a thing going where all the services offered only existed on his shifts and the money went straight in his pocket.

She had unpacked, showered and ordered a club sandwich from the night porter's direct line. After she had eaten she lay on the bed to relax. Only she couldn't. There was so much to think about, and so many questions to be asked. However, it wasn't the questions that had played on her mind all night long, but the answers. Each answer opened a new question and each new question in tum needed to be answered.

She didn't know why she had lied to her friend, but she had. At the time it had felt like survival. An instinctive act of self-preservation. Why? She had felt a twinge of anxiety when she had told Elizabeth Delaney her story. The motive behind the two unknown voices back in the facility had been solely for money. To steal both the virus and anti-virus and create a sensation of mass hysteria. Whether their plans were in the long-term, or whether they were willing to act immediately, she had no idea. Long-term, they would have to invest in a legitimate pharmaceutical company and use APHRODITE as a basis for control. And it sounded like they had achieved this already Morgan-Klein. She had heard of them, naturally. She was knowledgeable of the sector and knew that Morgan-Klein was a mid-sized pharmaceutical company with eyes on the highest ranking within the pharmaceutical world. They would manufacture APHRODITE in response to an outbreak of ARES. Whoever was behind this would have access to stocks and stock options. Their portfolio would grow exponentially. But was Morgan-Klein involved directly? Possibly not, but an executive at the highest order would be. Had to be.

Morgan-Klein was a legitimate, legislated and regulated company. Who within the organization would get involved? Had there been coercion? Sure, deals happen, just look at GM food issues and government research. Monopolies operate the farming and producing sectors, fixing prices on production and providing the public with little choice in their consumption. But for them to approach a company and get a deal accepted first time only, that was too big a chance for them to take. Failure at the first hurdle was not an option. Secondly, they would need to have funds to invest in stock. Stock options were possible for the contribution of APHRODITE, but would not hold much water in an investigation. And dropping the miracle cure for a new super-virus into a pharmaceutical company's lap was always going to initiate an investigation of some kind. But the risks had obviously been worth it. ARES and APHRODITE were worth billions in the wrong hands. So there was a reason for betrayal right there. She had lied to Delaney about the location of the flash drives and she had subsequently been betrayed. She had been lured off to a bar on the premise of being helped by a friend and kept out of the hotel for over an hour whilst her room had been taken apart. Nothing had been stolen and that had puzzled the two officers of the NYPD. But their job sheets were full and they'd barely begun their shift. They had handed out an itinerary sheet for her to list, sign and return to the precinct if she could think of anything that had been taken, after she calmed down from the initial shock and then they had left without hesitation.

But in all her solitary questioning, the loudest, most persistent question of all kept rearing its head and screaming at her. Why? Sure, millions or billions of dollars for the ransom of APHRODITE would be worth as much to Delaney as the faceless men in the bioresearch facility. But there was something missing. Something that had kept nagging at her all through the night. They already had the other half of ARES and APHRODITE. And Elizabeth Delaney didn't. So why was she unharmed, and why was she able to leave the hotel and relocate?

## TWENTY FOUR

There was a bitter chill in the sea air. The sun was coming up over the distant buildings and casting a bright gold shaft of light across the bay. It glistened on the electric blue water, clear and crystalline under a seamless sky.

The wake from distant boats and ships was lapping at the pier, ending their journey from the middle of the icy waters of the East River. The surge left huge clumps of seaweed and kelp high out of the water then pushed it back, long tendrils wrapping at the struts of the pier, and then gracefully washing back towards the depths beyond. He watched the swaying motion of the kelp, hypnotic in its action; felt the salty air in his nostrils as he waited. The cold air lay heavy on his chest, ached at the back of his throat. He breathed out a steady stream of breath, watching the vapor coil and swirl in the cold air, disintegrating slowly and sporadically into nothing. Emptiness.

The cop looked like he should have retired

ten years ago. He was either really good at what he did, or really lucky. There were not many men left on the streets at his age. Maybe he had no choice, maybe the retirement plan had never worked out. He looked ready for a rest. He carried a good fifty pounds too much around his waist and was probably only a couple of pounds away from a coronary. He wore his breakfast down his hound's-tooth shirt and carried a carton of steaming coffee in each hand. He walked towards the edge of the pier and where David Stein was staring hypnotically at the wash of the wake and the gentle dance of the kelp.

"Cold as a witch's tit. Hot summer followed by a short, cold fall. Going to be a bitch of a winter in the city, I reckon." The cop passed him a steaming plastic carton and nodded back towards the entrance of the warehouse's loading bay. "Guys are pretty much done in there. Thought you might need this."

"What does it look like in there?" Stein sipped some coffee and grimaced. It was sweet and creamy, but the cop wasn't to have known his preference. "What happened?"

The cop shrugged. "Tortured for a while, I'd say. Not sexually, just..."

"Sadistically," said Stein

The old cop shook his head, looking out across the water. "Functionally," he paused.

"Spent a tour in Vietnam, most of a tour at least. Rangers, attached to Delta for the last few months." His eyes were cold, hard. They stared at the water. To Stein they looked like lifeless holes in the man's head. "We knew we were out of there, knew the war was done. We weren't winning shit anymore. Not with the leash congress had on us. We needed to play rough. Just like our boys with ISIS or Al Qaeda or the Taliban. But they can't either. Nobody has the stomach for dirty wars. Except the soldiers. They know what needs doing," he paused, taking a sip of coffee. "With the war pretty much a done deal, we spent our time locating MIA's and extracting them. *Son Tay* prison was our last job. Mean anything to you?"

Stein shook his head.

"Fuck, that figures. Nobody knows shit anymore." His eyes were unmoving, challenging the water to a staring contest. For all the world, Stein reckoned the man would win. "Saw some pretty bad shit over there. Torture and stuff. They were good at it too. Once they started they got what they needed to know. Some people said they enjoyed it, I say they just perfected it. Minimum effort, maximum effect. Just plain *functional*."

Stein nodded. "So what did they do to her?"

"I'd say it was one person, no more. You get a couple or a group torturing someone and they start a damn frenzy. Like sharks, feeding I guess.

No, this was practical and functional. Tied the victim up and went to work. A little cutting, a little burning and whole lot of hurt."

David Stein shuddered.

"You okay?"

"Sure, just..."

The cop nodded. "I know. It's tough." He took his eyes off the water and looked at him. He was human again. The eyes held some life in them once more. "The end was quick, just keep telling yourself that. She was executed, real quick and real clean."

Stein looked at the entrance to the warehouse. They were bringing Elizabeth Delaney's body out on a gurney. She was wrapped in a black rubber body bag and looked so small next to the men from the city coroner's office. He turned his back on the cop and walked across the loading bay towards her. His eyes weren't like the cop's. They were sore and carried tears. He would not see her again, lay with her in her bed, all the things he wished he could do right now. Simply touch her, see the sparkle in her eyes, the smirk on her tough, pretty face. Just to touch her hand and tell her that she mattered, and that he cared for her. All the things he had never said.

He watched them load the gurney into the back of the station wagon, close the door. She was gone now. Nothing was left of her except what he could remember. Someone had taken everything. All she had, and all she ever would have. She was gone.

## TWENTY FIVE

The hotel room was cheap and in desperate need of refurbishment. The papered walls were drab and faded and peeling at the corners and joins. The paper was wood-chip effect and had apparently once been fashionable. Stone doubted it very much as he toweled himself dry after an intermittent, hot and cold shower. He had read somewhere, he thought on a plane, that it was the new healthy thing to do, to shower oneself with warm water then take a blast of icy cold water to tighten the muscles and stimulate the blood and enhance the senses, but it hadn't been through choice. The shower either scalded or froze, or lost pressure altogether. He preferred his showers hot and to have plenty of time in it. However, he had arrived in the city late and had worried about secure parking for the Mustang and this cheap hotel off West 125th and Broadway was all he could find if he was ever going to get his head down for a reasonable rest. He didn't know exactly why he ended up there, but as he drove through the night he simply got to the stage of needing to stop, wherever he was. Besides, the call he'd made earlier to Elizabeth Delaney's parents had put him onto Manhattan and Broadway was central enough. He was close enough to the FBI offices and central enough to conduct his investigation, and although he had positioned himself centrally to do so, there was the underlying feeling of uncertainty that accompanies all investigations. Things have a habit of coming together all at once, and then almost as quickly, because you have to follow another lead, it seems as if you are starting all over again. He still had no idea where Isobel Bartlett was, or indeed if she were in New York at all, but he also had Elizabeth Delaney as a lead and she would be easier to find. He even had an address for her from the FBI database.

Once he had ascertained Elizabeth Delaney's identification, he had simply used the FBI database to get Delaney's address and work details. As a resource for his investigation into the bioresearch facility he had a direct pass into all intelligence and crime fighting databases. He simply had to log on to the internet and use specific passwords on what was termed the Inner-Net. These were unpublicized sites hidden from other browsers and internet traffic. With the right searches and the right passwords, he could get where he needed to go. He soon had the complete FBI file on Delaney and took the fact that both Delaney and Isobel Bartlett attended the same college as the basis for their acquaintance. Once he had Elizabeth Delaney, he was sure he would soon have Isobel Bartlett.

He got dressed quickly, choosing to look formal and officious for his trip to the bureau. When he had finished dressing, he looked every inch the Secret Service agent. Black was the theme, from shoes to suit and to tie. Only his shirt was white, and it was crisp, clean and well starched.

There were a selection of complimentary instant coffee sachets on the dresser and he had earlier chanced using the tired-looking kettle and made a cup of coffee with powdered cream. It tasted terrible and insipid and suited his surroundings perfectly but he needed the caffeine hit and the hotel offered nothing in the way of breakfasting facilities. Not even a bar or a lounge in which to buy a decent cup of coffee.

He packed his bag quickly and efficiently. He was used to living out of a bag or suitcase, used to a life continuously on the move. He'd paid for the room in advance, so just dropped the key into the key deposit box on top of the reception desk. There was no one on duty, nobody to be seen anywhere. He stepped out of the foyer and directly onto the quiet street. The air was crisp and cold. The pollution level was low and the air was easy to breathe. His car was parked around the corner in a fairly secure parking zone affiliated to the hotel and a couple of other buildings in the street. There were no gates or attendants, but plenty of signs informing that it was private property and that fines would be both swift and heavy.

The Mustang was dull and grubby, dirtied and smeared by the journey from Washington. The roads had been damp and greasy and the car would benefit from a short stop-off at a car wash. But that would have to come another time, after the investigation had been completed. Rob Stone's life was a continuous period of sporadic compromise. His life was quite literally on hold until he completed the mission that had been tasked to him.

The V8 lumbered somewhat lazily into life then ticked over raucously as he hit the de-misters and allowed the screen to clear. The engine raced energetically, and then started to steady itself as it warmed and settled into an unhurried tick-over. He blipped the throttle a couple of times, and the echo thundered off the surrounding buildings. Satisfied that the engine had warmed sufficiently, he wound the window down to aid the demisters, then selected first and crawled out of the car park.

Broadway was calm, but it was a Sunday and still early. He got his speed up to thirty and settled into the traffic. The lights were forgiving and he managed to catch most on green, racing the occasional amber and chancing he'd get through before red. At Worth on Broadway he readied himself for the turning and checked it down past Thompson Street. He turned onto Federal Plaza and looked out for a parking space. The road was almost empty and he got into an hour bay across from 32 & 34 Federal. Three doors up from 26 Federal Plaza, home to the FBI's New York office.

There are fifty-six FBI field offices in the United States and all of them look the same. Smoked-glass windows and marbled flooring in the foyer with the official emblem etched into the stonework like some kind of proud mosaic. You are met by at least two guards, who are United States Marshals. The same is true of other institutions such as the Federal Reserve and the Secret Service.

Stone was used to these buildings, because they mirrored the Secret Service exactly. They too, had field offices around the country and operated in more or less the same way as the offices of the Bureau, albeit on a smaller level.

He took out his leather wallet and flashed his Secret Service ID at the first marshal, who studied it briefly before passing it to his partner.

"How can we help, Sir?" The second marshal asked, passing the wallet back to him. He checked his log, then looked back at him. "You don't seem to have an appointment, Sir."

Stone took out the folded envelope from his jacket pocket and passed it to him. "I don't have an appointment, no. But this will make allowances for that. And I need to see the Field Office Director, Warren Oats if remember rightly."

The marshal read the letter and slipped it back into the envelope. There was no change in expression on his face. "FOD's not in his office at present, Sir. What with it being the weekend, and all. Duty Liaison Agent is best we can do at such short notice. I'll go and give him a call, tell him you're on your way." The marshal walked to the nearby desk and picked up a red telephone receiver.

The other marshal stepped forwards and guided Stone towards an electronic walk-through metal detector. "This way Sir, if you will."

"I'm carrying."

"All right Sir," he paused and picked up a deep tray. "Make it safe and place it in here please."

Stone took the compact-looking Sig Sauer P229 out from his hip holster and released the magazine. He jacked the slide, ejecting the chambered .357 round, and then dropped the weapon, magazine and stubby .357 sig cartridge in the tray. He reached into his inside jacket pocket and took out a spare magazine and added it to the tray. Then, he delved into his trouser pocket and retrieved a lock knife with a three inch folding blade and dropped it in the tray.

"That's it," he said and stepped through the metal detector.

The marshal took the tray and put it in a locked drawer behind the desk. The second marshal returned from making his telephone call and nodded curtly.

"Agent Sanchez will be with you shortly," he paused and pointed to a small waiting area just ahead. "Take a seat."

Stone did not want to make himself too comfortable, so preferred to stand. He walked over to the waiting area and studied the pictures on the wall. They were of various highly decorated agents within the New York field office. Underneath were inscriptions of their names and a brief synopsis of their achievements. To the left of the pictures was a brass plaque with a list of the names of agents and specific dates. He looked up at the plaque, found the date he wanted then looked at the name: *Andrew Robert Stone.* He felt a lump forming in his throat. The inscription at the top of the plaque read for the entire list of names. It read: *For the few who gave so much, for so many.* Beneath this, the inscription simply read: *Killed in the line of duty.*

"Agent Stone?"

He turned round and was greeted by a smart man in his early thirties. He was tall and thin, and his hair was greased back. Like an Italian waiter.

"Yes." Stone extended his right hand and looked the man in the eye. "And you are...?"

"Special Agent Sanchez, Duty Liaison," he paused. "How can I help?"

"I need to follow up a lead in an investigation I'm conducting," he paused, looked around for a moment. "You got an office we can use?"

Sanchez seemed to think for a moment, weighing up whether it was important enough to warrant an office to talk to this guy.

"Put it this way, agent Sanchez..." He took out the folded envelope and handed it to him. "I want an office, a decent cup of coffee and your complete co-operation in this matter."

The agent read the letter, and then passed it back to him. "Of course, I think we can manage that, Agent Stone."

The coffee was hot and strong, and the cream was fresh. The sugar was Jamaican, and it was dark and soft and deliciously sweet. Stone drank it, ever more appreciatively for the memory of the foul tasting coffee he'd had in his hotel room.

He waited patiently, sipping his coffee and occasionally glancing around the room at the other personnel, who were busying themselves at their workstations. There was only a skeleton crew working today, five or six in all. The office was approximately one hundred feet by sixty and made up of about twenty workstations and a small square seating area with a whiteboard. Stone presumed this was for group meetings or briefings. The office area was well lit and devoid of the merest glimpse of natural light. The smoked glass, the focal point of the exterior of the building was unseen from within, blocked from view by a wall of thick blast curtains, which had been fitted throughout the fifty-six field offices and every federal building after the tragic Oklahoma bombing. They could take direct hits from RPG's.

Stone had told Sanchez why he was there and that Elizabeth Delaney was a person of interest to his investigation. Agent Sanchez had left to make some calls and returned twenty minutes later looking perplexed. He sat down in the chair opposite him. He sipped a mouthful of coffee from his cup, placed it back down on the desk and looked up at him. "Sorry about that, just with you mentioning Elizabeth Delaney, I felt I should talk to someone else."

"Not quite sure what you mean."

Sanchez looked past him for a moment, and then stood up. "Agent Stone, this is Special Agent Stein." He gestured the man towards them and waited for the new arrival to walk around the workstation. "I'm sure that in light of things, Agent Stein will be of more use to you than I can be." He nodded curtly at them both, then walked away.

Stone stood up and looked at Stein. The man was in his early forties, about six-one and weighed around one-seventy. He looked lean and fit, like a quarterback. He was dressed in faded jeans and wore a sweatshirt under a leather jacket.

"I'm sorry, Agent Stone. Sanchez thought I should talk to you. I was taking some time off today. How can I be of help?"

Stone shrugged. "Beats the hell out of me. I thought Agent Sanchez was helping me, but he suddenly took off like a scalded cat while I was talking. Thanks for coming in by the way. You live close?"

"Two blocks." Stein walked around the desk and sat down heavily in the chair opposite Stone. "You mentioned Special Agent Delaney. Elizabeth Delaney. I'm involved in an investigation involving her, I guess he thought I'd be a more suitable person to talk to."

"What investigation?"

Stein sighed. "How about you giving a

little and letting us know what you want? Sanchez wasn't exactly clear, but he said you had a letter from the president, granting you access to all areas. How about we start there?" He smiled. "If you don't mind."

Stone sighed. He knew the drill. He was on the agent's turf and Stein wasn't giving anything up without a fight. "OK, here's the shortened version," he paused. "I was sanctioned to investigate a government research agency creating a certain *product* for military research. The order came from as high as it gets, and I was given *carte blanche.* No stone unturned, no lead left unfollowed. Your agent, Elizabeth Delaney, has been linked to a person involved in my investigation. The person concerned is called Isobel Bartlett, a senior technician at the facility. And she has been caught on camera taking this *product* from the facility. This *product* is highly dangerous and could cause massive casualties and fatalities if not secured."

"That *is* short. Care to elaborate a little?"

"No."

"Didn't think so. Worth a shot though, right?"

Stone shrugged impassively.

"All right, Agent Stone." Stein smirked. "I can see you play real hardball. In short, Agent Delaney isn't going to be of any help to you. She was killed sometime yesterday."

"I'm sorry."

"Sure you are. Next, I know of this Bartlett woman. She called Liz while I was at her apartment. Wanted to come and see her right away, seemed to be in a real bad situation. I figured her partner was beating up on her, or sleeping with somebody else."

"Were you and Elizabeth Delaney..." Stone said flatly. He looked down at the wedding ring on Stein's finger. "...Close?"

"That's none of your business and sure as hell isn't going to help your investigation. Right now, I want to find this Bartlett woman and ask her some pretty searching questions."

Stone nodded. "What happened to Agent Delaney?"

Stein grimaced. He took out a packet of Lucky Strikes and lit one with a cheap plastic lighter. He inhaled deeply and breathed out a thick plume of smoke. He didn't seem to mind that smoking was forbidden in the building. Maybe it was just because it was Sunday. Or maybe he'd just lost the love of his life and couldn't openly grieve because he was married. "She was found tortured and killed in a warehouse on pier seventeen. That's right near Brooklyn Bridge. Busy area, so quite a risky place. She had been cut and burnt, in all the right places for someone to extract information."

"How did she die?"

"Early days yet, but it was definitely a pistol shot to the back of the head. Medium caliber at close range, according to the coroner."

"I'm sorry." Stone said, quietly. He doubted that their affair was a secret inside the bureau. These things seldom are. "What have you got to go on?"

"Agent Stone, this is where our investigations cross paths and carry on in different directions. Like I said, I want to talk to this Bartlett woman."

"She's not your suspect."

"How do you know?"

"Doesn't figure. Doesn't even come close. Isobel Bartlett is five-five, one hundred pounds, maybe one-ten. She is a scientist, spends her days looking through microscopes and sitting at a desk. The only physical thing in her file is occasional horseback riding and a little swimming. Delaney was one-twenty, five-eight and a martial arts expert. She was trained in combat and an active field agent with the FBI. Isobel Bartlett wouldn't be capable of overpowering her. Not a chance in hell."

"It only takes a gun."

"Sure," Stone paused. "But trust me, Bartlett isn't your killer."

Stein took another drag on the cigarette, and

then stubbed it out in an ashtray on Sanchez's desk. The ashtray was designed to look like a no-smoking sign. Stone figured it was a stab at irony, given that there was no smoking aloud in the building.

"Let's assume you're right. What then?"

"I don't follow."

Stein clasped his hands, linking his fingers, and rested them in a giant ball on the desk. "I need to know Bartlett's association with Elizabeth Delaney, and so do you. I'm looking for the murderer of my friend and colleague and I need to question Isobel Bartlett. You don't give a shit about a dead FBI agent, you just want your *product* back."

"Go on..."

"I've got a way to get to Bartlett. It's a long shot, and she'll probably run like hell, but it's all I've got. But it's a hell of a lot more than *you've* got."

"Like I said, go on."

"Agent Delaney's cell phone was at the crime scene. There was a message in her out box, just a simple couple of lines arranging a meeting with Isobel Bartlett at a bar on Ninth Avenue, between West Fiftieth and West Fifty-First. Some flashy gin joint by all accounts, yet to follow it up."

"Delaney arranged a meet with Isobel Bartlett?"

"No. I've reason to believe the killer arranged a meet, using her phone. He used Delaney as either a distraction, or bait. You see, Delaney spoke briefly to me about Isobel Bartlett. About ARES and APHRODITE, about some professor that was killed ..."

"Jesus Christ!"

Stein held up a hand. "It's OK. Nobody else knows. She wanted to keep it real tight until we could get underneath this whole thing. Trouble is, I was up to my neck in meetings and briefings and Delaney took the reins on her own. Wanted to get stuck right in. She started checks on the bioresearch facility in Washington and called the coroner's office in Montpelier, Vermont."

"And?"

"And, nothing. I left her on a lone crusade and didn't hear from her after that. But I know one thing, she had no time for that stupid text messaging, and she would never have signed off using a letter 'E'. Delaney was a tough-ass, she would use the letter 'D'. Everybody called her Delaney, hell, even in her answer phone message she uses her surname."

Stone looked thoughtful. "So the killer used Delaney to get Bartlett into a bar and out into the open. Either they wanted Bartlett, or wanted Bartlett out of the way. We need to check out this bar on ninth, and we need to make a call to the local precinct and find out if there was any related incident in the vicinity. You've obviously got Bartlett's number on Delaney's cell phone. If we can get a call through to her and a satellite fix, we've got her. At least find the phone cell she's in."

"And involve the whole bureau? The very thing Delaney wanted to avoid at all costs?"

"What then?"

"Delaney told her she was going to involve me. She'll either trust me or she won't. If can get in touch with her, maybe we can arrange a meet?"

"Great."

Stein held up a hand. "OK, that's what I can do. Now, it seems to me that you still have jack and shit, and I'm holding one or two more aces."

Stone stared at him. It was cold and hard and told the FBI agent not to go any further. "I don't like to be taken for a ride," he said, coldly.

"Not taking you anywhere, Agent Stone. And certainly not in the vicinity of Isobel Bartlett. Hell, if I involved the whole bureau, went official you'd get nowhere near her at all. Not for a while at least. And certainly not until it was probably too late for your investigation. With a letter from the President or not, things can soon get delayed."

Stone suddenly realized that he had approached this investigation with the full weight of the President behind him, but he guessed that some people just don't get pushed around. He suddenly started to like Special Agent Stein. The man commanded respect.

"I think I sense a deal coming, even though, like you said, I've got jack and shit to deal with." He smiled, relaxed a little and sat further back in his seat. "You obviously know Isobel Bartlett's reasons for taking the drives. Hey, that's a Hell of a lot more than I do. Keep going."

"First we check out this gin-joint, *Sullivan's*. Then we check with police headquarters and check their log for last night and the vicinity near the bar."

"Funny, sounds rather like my idea," Stone paused. "What then?"

"At the moment, we can't afford to involve the FBI, not officially at least. If we can arrange to meet Isobel Bartlett, bring her in somewhere neutral. I want a thorough debrief, an off-limits interview with her to aid my investigation into Delaney's murder."

"And that's the deal?" Stone asked, looking at the agent dubiously. "You locate her, bring her in for me, and all you want is an interview?"

"Yeah."

Stone sensed there was a catch. He still had nothing to deal with. All he had was a letter. A well-read, much admired letter that hadn't cut him a great deal of slack with this man from the FBI.

"Well, I'm indebted to you." Stone said sincerely.

Stein shook his head. "No. I'm indebted to your brother. He was a Hell of an agent. I owe him my life."

## TWENTY SIX

Isobel Bartlett had showered and taken full advantage of the night porter's extra services, ordering an extra-large latte and a Danish for breakfast. Both were from the *Starbucks* across the street. She had given the night porter a twenty and hadn't seen any change. The night porter had thrown in a complimentary New York Times, and she figured that he had made about five dollars from the transaction. She calculated the number of rooms and multiplied that by the number of days he most probably worked a week and decided that the guy probably made more in a year than she did, given the fact that he certainly wouldn't be declaring his extra earnings to the IRS.

She sat back on the bed, supported upright by the pillows, as she unfolded the paper and took a mouthful of the Danish. The frosting was wet and sweet and oozed as she took a satisfying bite. She looked comfortable, taking the day slowly, contemplating her options.

He saw everything as he watched through the Leupold sniper scope, from the hotel room across the street. He was well back inside the room, with only a few inches separating the curtains. He had made sure that there was no backlit illumination and that he could focus on her room only. The clarity of the image was crystal clear and he could read the headlines of the print on the pages of the newspaper. On the front cover of the paper was a photograph of the president conducting a speech to an audience of Marines and Navy service men and women in California. He held the crosshairs of the sight on the man's right eye and mouthed a near-silent *boom*. The shot would have hit. The .223 bullet would have scythed through the air, tearing a path through the sky at twelve hundred feet a second, spinning towards its target with deadly accuracy. The bullet would have hit the president's eye, pushed the power vacuum, the displaced air in front of the bullet, through the brain and out through the back of his head. The brain and bone and matter would have been sprayed across most of the room, and the body would have been clinically dead before he had finished the pull-through on the match quality trigger.

He smiled to himself. The president would have been killed outright. It would have been the ultimate masterpiece, like Van Gogh's *Sunflowers,* or Michael Angelo's *David.* One day, he would achieve his own masterpiece. A kill so public and important on the world stage that it would be talked about for decades. After his masterpiece he would retire. He had no desire to kill this particular president, no more than his desire to experience the thrill of the ultimate kill. He had no particular political persuasion, no care for politics. He couldn't even remember if he had ever voted. Like so much of his life, he couldn't remember many things.

He watched as Isobel Bartlett turned the pages of the newspaper and scanned the headlines. She was attractive, in a plain, if not unpretentious sort of way. She wore no makeup, just a little colorless lip-gloss, which shined understatedly in the light. Her hair was pulled back in a ponytail and her skin was clear of imperfections. She looked wholesome and cute, the sort of girl he would have liked to take home to meet his mother and announce an engagement or something. Only, he had no recollection of ever having known his mother, couldn't picture her or remember the tone of her voice. There was nothing of her in his memories. However, he did dream about a woman he assumed was his mother, but it was the sort of dream that faded and died the moment he tried to recollect.

The thought made him sad. He put the

assault rifle down on the table in front of him and sat back in the chair. There was nothing in his memories, not in the way other people would remember. He would watch television, but would seldom be interested unless it was a classic film with old fashioned, classic actors like Steve McQueen, James Coburn or Clint Eastwood, or the older black and white films starring the likes of James Stewart, Audey Murphy or Randolph Scott.

Other people had friends or memories of good times, or something. But he had nothing. Nothing, but the knowledge of how to live from day-to-day, or how to kill. He could not remember where he had gained this knowledge, or when he had learned it. He remembered his time in the army and he remembered training hard physically in California and Florida, but the why and the how were blurred. He remembered a dojo and karate. And he remembered learning to surf and a pretty girl who had held his hand on the beach, where later they had made love by a fire fuelled by driftwood. He could not recall her name, nor whether he had seen her again. His contracts came via e-mail or text or Facebook messaging, but he could not remember having ever subscribed to an internet server, or having ever bought the laptop from which he worked.

He could feel the throbbing starting in his head. It was distant and it was faint, but he knew it would soon build and pulse and make him sick. It always did when he started to question his existence, his own mortality. He got up quickly from the chair and walked across the room where he picked up the plastic bottle of painkillers from the bedside table. They were prescription and extremely potent, capable of settling the strongest of migraines, just so long as he could swallow a couple in time. He fiddled with the bottle and the childproof cap, shaking the contents inside like a set of castanets, frantic to get to the tablets inside. He could feel the sensation of flickering from the periphery of his sight. He knew the flickering would grow to a frightening crescendo, from which the only escape was to sleep in complete darkness and shut himself off from the outside world.

He couldn't risk it. He could not risk being disabled whilst his quarry was across the street. He needed to stay with her, be ready to move at a moment's notice and the urgency of the situation made him struggle harder with the cap of the bottle. The cap suddenly gave way, relinquishing the contents over the bed and onto the floor. He grabbed at a couple and swallowed them down without water. He walked to the laptop on the table and watched the screen. The software was simple and easy to follow and had been custom-written for the task.

The screen showed a detailed city map and two colored markers. One was the location of the laptop the other was the location of the satellite transceivers that he had secreted into the lining of Isobel Bartlett's overnight bag and her jacket after he had lured her out of her hotel room under the premise of meeting Elizabeth Delaney.

The target was still in place or at least her luggage and jacket were and that was good enough for him. His head ached a little less now and he breathed a sigh of relief as he realized that he had caught the sensation in time.

He was grateful of the prescription tablets, but like everything else in his life, he had no idea where they had come from.

## TWENTY SEVEN

"Sure, Saturday night specials. You get them in every week. They just sit there waiting to get picked up by some guy. Usually unhappily married women after no string sex. We see it all the time. A woman comes in, buys a drink and waits it out. Sooner or later she either gets the come on from a guy, or they try their luck with one of us at the end of the evening." He smiled and placed the glass he'd been wiping dry with a cloth on the mirrored shelf behind him. "You'd be surprised just how many women come on to us bar tenders at the end of the night. Hell, it's just another tip, when all's said and done." He picked up another glass from the wash crate and polished it with the soft cloth. "They come over as desperate really, but hey, I'm out of there before first light. Kind of saves on the awkwardness in the morning."

Stone looked at the bartender impassively. "And was she a sure thing, desperate?"

"Sure, just the same as all the rest."

"And you made it with her at the end of your shift?"

"No."

"So she was a sure thing and looked desperate for a man," Stone paused and smiled coldly. "But not desperate enough to get laid with the likes of you or your buddy. Even if it meant a drink on the house."

"Yes. I mean no ..." The bar tender frowned. "Hey!"

"So she came on to you, but you blew her out?"

"No."

"So she left with someone else," Stone said. "Got a better offer."

"No. She left one her own."

Stone smirked. "Like I said, a better offer." He perched himself on the barstool and picked up a handful of pistachio nuts. He picked at one and started to open it wider to pull out the kernel. "So she was a sure thing, a desperate-looking woman who was out for some Saturday night action, but failed to either get hit on, or hit on anyone else in the bar. She didn't even attempt to chat to you two gigolos behind the bar, choosing instead to simply leave, while it was still early, on a Saturday night." Stone popped a couple nuts into his mouth and chewed slowly keeping his eyes on the bar tender's face all the while. "So maybe she was just having a quiet drink and waiting for someone. Maybe the person she was meeting simply got held up and she decided not to wait and waste her time any longer. How about that? How about when I ask you a simple question, like *do you remember a woman in her early thirties coming into the bar last night?* You give me a straight answer and don't elaborate a crock of shit?"

The bar tender glanced sideways at him and nodded. "Sure, whatever ..."

"So you remember a woman in her early thirties ..." David Stein interjected. "Around five foot-five, a hundred to one hundred and ten pounds. Black hair and light olive skin?"

"Sure," he replied somewhat sullen.

David Stein took out a pocketbook and a stubby pencil. "Right, shoot. Now let's start with what she was wearing."

\*\*\*

He could hear the background noise of the television and the occasional passive sound of a cough or a sigh. The aural clarity was clear and suffered no delay, just like listening to a telephone conversation. Each time there was a cough or a piece of background noise, he could see the movements or actions through the sniper scope.

Isobel Bartlett seemed to be in a quandary. Lost in her actions. Her cell phone was beside her, but neither rang, nor was it used. She simply sat back on the bed, her legs crossed and her arms cuddling her knees. She looked sweet and innocent like a child. She was suffering, unsure of what she should do next. As far as she was concerned her friend had let her down and she was now alone in the big city. He recognized her emotional state, but had no empathy. Her vulnerability was not his concern.

Her pain was mental, not physical like the female FBI agent's pain had been. When she had begged for him to release her from that pain, he had obliged ending it instantly with a single 9mm bullet, but only after she had told him all he had needed to know and only after she had tearfully written the text message on her cell phone. She had been hesitant, as if she had known it would be the last thing she would ever do. She had deliberated for so long on how to sign off, and he had watched as she had finally decided upon a single letter 'E'. He had pulled the trigger the moment she had pressed the send option. He had watched the life leave her body, as he had done so many times before. There had been the odd twitch and shudder of the limbs, which sometimes followed the massive trauma of a head shot and of course a great deal of blood and matter had been lain to waste across a vast distance. She had cried for him to stop hurting her and he had obliged.

From across the street he watched Isobel Bartlett. She looked pained by her situation. Maybe she would welcome release. All he needed was a reply to his e-mail and he would oblige. End her pain and misery for an eternity.

*** 

The police headquarters were on Grand and Broadway. The desk sergeant was a man in his early fifties named O'Reilly. He was a big guy, who was balding and weighed about two hundred and forty pounds. Most of it was pure donut. "Yeah, break in and entry," he paused, reading the notes from the handwritten log. "The Amsterdam Court Hotel on West Fiftieth. Got the details right here. You want the full report?"

Stein nodded. "Please, if it's not too much trouble."

"Never too much trouble helping out the FBI," he said. The tone was apparently neutral but both men could detect an undercurrent of sarcasm. The desk sergeant pressed an intercom button and waited for the reply. "Yeah Hank, I need report WAB1267. Yeah, right away." He looked up at the two men and nodded. "Be down here in ten." He ushered them towards a row of seats along the wall, then looked past them and at the growing line behind. "Yeah, next..."

***

She was crying. He could hear her on the receiver. It wasn't a full-blown wail, more of a gentle sob. He tightened his finger on the trigger, willing the e-mail to come through and grant him permission to end her pain. They were taking their time, deliberating over the information that he had provided. They wanted the information on those drives, and they wanted him to retrieve them. It made him angry. Their indecisiveness. He was paid to kill, not be some kind of errand boy. He tightened his finger a little more on the match quality trigger. It only needed a gentle two-pound pull, nothing really in terms of trigger pressure. He figured he had about one and a quarter on it, and that gave him a thrill, a sensation of all-encompassing supremacy. Would it, or wouldn't it? Had he guessed the poundage correctly? Would the rifle unexpectedly kick back into his shoulder and would the 5.56mm bullet hammer into the target's forehead at twelve hundred feet a second and carry straight on through the wall? It would too, because rather than standard military ammunition the weapon was loaded with

Swedish match grade .223 caliber varmint rounds. More powerful than mass produced military rounds, these had a slightly longer casing with more charge and were soft lead tipped hunting rounds designed to deform massively upon impact. He smiled at the thought of the God like supremacy he had at that exact moment. Her life was suspended in his hands. Her very existence was determined by whether he squeezed further or let go. Either action denoted the same amount of power. Should he be decisive and powerful, or should he be relenting and gracious? He released the pressure on the trigger and put the rifle back down onto the table. The act of sparing her life was somehow more rewarding at that moment. And the fact that she would never know how close it could have been filled him with a contended sense of all-powerful emotion.

The laptop's screen was still on the e-mail inbox. There had been no sound announcing an incoming message and no sign on the screen. He would have to wait for the order a little longer.

***

"And you offered her a room free of charge?"

The duty manager nodded. He was impeccably dressed in the hotel's burgundy uniform, which was basically a suit with a little sash of gold embroidery on the lapels. His brass-effect nameplate read: *Michael Fukkur, Duty Manager.* Stone guessed the guy had heard more than a few sniggers about his surname.

Stein looked at the register and matched the signature to a copy of the police report which she had signed. It was identical, or at least as identical as two separate signatures could ever be. "And she refused to stay?"

"Yes. She couldn't get out of the hotel quick enough," he paused. "Quite understandable really. I couldn't blame her, even if I did offer her a free upgrade to a luxury suite."

David Stein was scribbling notes into his pocketbook. He looked up impassively and asked, "What sort of frame of mind was she in when she left?"

The duty manager thought for a moment. "Shaken, that's for sure. But she wasn't hysterical or anything, more … disappointed. She looked like she had been really let down by someone."

David Stein didn't reply.

"And how did she leave?" Stone interjected. "Where did she go once she walked out through the door?"

"I called her a Yellow Cab, direct. The taxi got here in under ten minutes."

"You got a time on that?" Stein asked, glancing across at Stone for a moment.

He looked back at the duty manager. "That

would be *real* helpful."

The duty manager nodded. "Exactly ten-twenty. The night porter comes on shift at ten-thirty, but he's been getting later and later recently. I pulled him up on it earlier this week and he's been coming in on time ever since. Last night he was ten minutes early and I made a note of it for his appraisal. He walked into the foyer as she walked out and straight into the taxi."

\*\*\*

His impatience was mounting. He knew the importance of the two drives, and knew that she had hidden them in a place other than where she had told the female FBI agent. For some reason she had not trusted her friend. That much was for sure otherwise his search wouldn't have ended in vain. He also knew that he had no other choice in killing the FBI agent when he had. Normally, he would have kept her alive until all avenues had been ascertained. But the woman had been feisty to say the least and the warehouse at the pier was not as secluded as he had first hoped. There had been night watchmen at the entrances and busier looking warehouses, but the one he had chosen had been under renovation. Tools were nearby and work had recently been taking place. He knew that he would remain uninterrupted in his work but not for long, especially as the other warehouses looked to be in operation seven days a week. So he had used the FBI agent for information and a location on Bartlett. He had used her text message to get her out of the hotel and he had eliminated any possible threat by the FBI woman as soon as he was convinced that he knew all she had known.

He had waited throughout the day and watched her leave the hotel on time. He had waited a little longer to be sure and then gone inside. Nobody had been at reception and he had quickly checked the sign-in register at the desk. He had slipped upstairs and dodged a porter on his way and had Bartlett's door kicked open and her room torn apart within seconds. He searched everything as quickly as he could, and then placed a precision Swiss-made transponder, or homing device, inside the lining of her shoulder bag and a similarly sized voice-activated digital microphone in the lining of her jacket. Frustrated that he could not locate the drives either in the hiding place he'd been told or elsewhere, he had retreated back to his car and waited for the woman to return. Following her could not have been easier in the Yellow Cab and he had managed to procure a room in a cheap hotel across the back street from her street-side room.

Now, after informing his employers of the situation, he had sent an e-mail to determine whether Isobel Bartlett should be eliminated, therefore severing the link to the set of drives.

The laptop remained dormant. There had not yet been the message he was willing to come through. But it would come soon. He was sure of it.

\*\*\*

The old Mustang's V8 engine grumbled and popped as Stone changed down a gear and settled into the line of traffic. The streets were fairly quiet with pedestrians but the traffic was mounting and the progress was becoming increasingly slower as the morning wore on.

David Stein sat in the passenger seat. He was going through the transcripts of the notes he had taken. They were in some kind of shorthand but at a glance Stone didn't recognize it as anything standard. It was most likely his own abbreviation, his own personal code.

"So tell me what you know," Stone paused as he indicated and changed lanes. "Everything that Elizabeth Delaney told you about Isobel Bartlett."

David Stein sighed. The memory of Elizabeth Delaney was raw. The man had not yet had time to grieve. "I guess I don't know much. I was up to my neck in meetings and briefings yesterday, couldn't give her much time," he paused. He was obviously wishing that he had given her more of his time but like so many things in life, it was now too late. "She started by telling me that her friend was in a mess and coming to the city. I just figured that she was getting beat up on by some guy or that she had been cheated on... that kind of shit. That was on the Friday," he paused awkwardly. "When I was at her apartment."

Stone remained silent. He did not want to prompt. Prompting a conversation always seemed to load it towards your questioning, not release the information freely and discovering what was at the core. He switched lanes again, checking his mirror briefly.

"The next I heard was yesterday morning. She had had breakfast with Bartlett, but she didn't tell me where she was staying. She also told me that Bartlett had hidden a set of flash drives with important information on them, but again, she didn't tell me where."

"What did she say about the drives?"

"She said that Isobel had heard two men talking about taking the drives for blackmail or something, to make a profit out of them. She said that a virus called ARES and an anti-virus called APHRODITE was stored on them. Or half was stored on them, the other half was in the director's office."

Stone knew that they were not there and was still figuring out who had taken them. "And what did she tell Delaney about the other set?"

Stein shrugged. "I was busy. Delaney always gets..." he paused, looked sad. "...always got so damn impetuous, go off on a crusade. Most of the time it would draw a blank, that's why promotion or departmental moves kept passing her by. Don't get me wrong, she was a hell of a law enforcement officer and I'd have had her with me in a firefight or hard arrest every time. She just needed to take a breath sometimes. I didn't pay a huge amount of attention. After a few minutes, I had colleagues pointing at their watches and waving me towards a meeting. I said that I'd have a thorough talk with her later."

"Did she say if Isobel suspected that the other set of drives had been taken by these guys, the two she heard talking?"

Stein shook his head. "Not sure."

"I guess it's..." Stone stopped suddenly as his cell phone blurted out a short, shrill tune. He picked it up, answered abruptly and spoke for a couple of minutes, before thanking the caller and dropping the phone back into his pocket.

"Trouble?" David Stein asked, breaking the silence.

"For someone, yes. For me? Just another

thick fog to try and look through ..."

*\*\**

She needed to know for sure. The thoughts running through her head were clouding and she was seeing the possibility of good where she thought there was only bad, and bad where there should still have been a last bastion of good. She felt let down and betrayed, but her memory of events and feelings compelled to trust had clouded the fact. Delaney *couldn't* have betrayed her. *Couldn't* have tricked her out of the way and attempted to take the drives from her room. It just wasn't plausible. And where was Delaney now? Why had she not contacted her when she had found out that the drives were not where she had been told?

Like the person who has been cheated on and still lost in a void of denial she still tried to see some good and put everything else down to a clouding of facts. She needed to ask Delaney out straight, needed to hear what had happened. She needed to hear what she so desperately wanted to hear. She picked up the cell phone and dialed Delaney's number. The line rang for a moment, then changed tone and rang once more.

*\*\**

David Stein took his cell phone out of his pocket

and looked at the display. He turned to Stone, his face ashen. "It's her ... Isobel Bartlett. I re-directed all Delaney's calls to my phone ... I thought I should, you know ..."

Stone didn't know what the FBI man thought he should have done, but he figured it was the sort of thing that someone showing presence of mind after a death would do. He couldn't imagine being prepared to answer her calls on her behalf and greet the caller with the news. He looked at Stein and nodded. "Better answer it then."

The FBI agent pressed the answer button and spoke quietly. "Hello, this is Special Agent David Stein, of the FBI answering on behalf of Elizabeth Delaney ..." He looked back at Stone and shook his head. "She rang off."

"I'm not surprised, could you have been more formal?" He smirked, shaking his head. "Call her back, go to received calls and hit dial."

Stein fiddled with his cell phone, then held it to his ear. "Nothing ... she must have switched her phone off."

"Shit."

***

Isobel Bartlett had dropped the phone down on the bed beside her. She drew her legs up to her chest and rocked gently on the bed. She was tearful and scared and did not know whom she should trust.

The expression of indecision upon her face was agonizing.

He kept the cross hairs of the sniper scope on the center of her forehead. It would not be long now.

She would soon be at peace.

\*\*\*

David Stein tried several times to get a reply with each attempt yielding nothing. Isobel Bartlett had switched off her cell phone and there hadn't even been a messaging service on her line.

Stone swung the car in a wide arc and mounted the curb, pulling the Mustang to a halt inside the entrance to the Yellow Cab garage.

"Forget her," he paused, switching off the ignition. "We'll get to her soon enough. Let's go."

He opened his door and walked across the parking area towards the kiosk that acted as an office. Stein followed, he already had his pocketbook in hand ready to take notes.

"Can I help you?" A mechanic asked gruffly. He was covered in grease and his overalls were stained with oil and ripped at the knees.

"Yeah," Stone replied. He flicked open his leather wallet and flashed his ID. "Rob Stone, I'm an agent with the Secret Service, this is Special Agent Stein of the FBI. We need to speak with someone who can tell us about booked pick-ups last night."

The man nodded, then slipped a greasy pair of fingers into his mouth and whistled a shrill, loud call. "Yo! Louis! Out front!"

An overweight man in his late forties worked his way out from a myriad of parked cars and walked over. "Help you?" He was an Italian-New Yorker and his accent was heavy on the goodfella. "What you want?"

Stone flashed his ID and gold star. "Rob Stone, Secret Service. I need a look at your log for booked pick-ups. We want to speak with a woman that one of your cabs picked up last night from The Amsterdam Court Hotel, on West Fiftieth and Amsterdam. We need to talk to the driver."

"You got to be fuckin' kidding' me!" He frowned. "How the fuck should I know where she went?"

"I don't remember asking where she went," Stone paused. "I said I wanted to speak to the driver. The manager of the hotel called it in. That means there was a call from here to the driver and a specific driver was allocated the job. We want to know who the driver was and where we'll catch up with him."

"I got better things to do... get the fuck outta here!" He turned to walk away and Stone caught hold of him by the shoulder, digging his thumb deep into the side of the man's neck. He

224

dropped to his knees, his face screwed up in a silent scream.

Stone turned towards the mechanic, who seemed ready to intervene. "It'll be the last thing you do for yourself... from then on in, you'll be in a wheelchair. Think about it while you take a walk."

David Stein seemed to hover at Stone's shoulder, unsure whether to talk him down or look the other way.

"I suggest you take a look at the log in that office," Stone said to him. "While I talk to my new friend here ..."

Stein looked at the man on his knees for a moment then shrugged like it didn't really matter and walked over to the kiosk. He found the log and flicked back through the pages, then looked up. "Got it here! Guy's name is Rodriguez Fortes."

Stone released his grip a little. "This guy, Fortes, is he working today?"

"Fuck you!"

Stone buried his thumb deeper, easing it between two tendons and his carotid artery. The man screamed, and then contorted his face into a tight wince. "I'll have you arrested, hell, I could even find a way of shutting Yellow Cabs down for a week. Imagine that?"

"He's working out on Little Italy," the man

225

grunted. "Let the fuck go and I'll call him in."

Stone smiled. "OK, but I want you to remember two things. When I let you go, if you try and hit me, I'll break your arm."

"Sure, whatever," the man winced. "What else?"

Stone nodded towards David Stein, who was standing at the entrance of the kiosk. "He takes his coffee black and sour, I take mine sweet and with cream. Spit in either and I'll break both your legs..."

\*\*\*

Isobel Bartlett wanted to call Delaney's number again. It had either been re-directed, or David Stein had picked up her cell phone. But why would he? Why would Delaney be without her cell phone?

She got up off the bed and walked through to the bathroom. She ran the faucet and splashed some cold water on her face, rubbed it around her neck, then dabbed herself dry with the hand towel. She needed some fresh air, needed to get out onto the street and take a walk, get some air into her lungs and think things through. After that, she would contact the police and go through the whole story with them. She had no one she could trust and was back at where she had started. Only now, she was in a strange city and would have a lot more explaining to do.

\*\*\*

He watched her, taking his eye from the sniper scope every now and then to glance at the screen of the laptop. He watched her as she shuffled through the shoulder bag and checked her purse. She then swung her jacket over her shoulders and slipped her arms through. There was a small amount of static on the transceiver, but the equipment was the most expensive there was and of the highest quality available and the interference was short lived.

He lined up the sight on her temple and then traversed down for a shot to the neck. The precision-made scope held its crosshairs on the point of her carotid artery. He decided that shot to her neck would be most appropriate. After passing through the glass the bullet may be out of shape and off zero. With a shot to the neck the skin was soft, unlike the skull and there was a myriad of veins and arteries which would sever. The bullet may even hit the spine for an instant kill, or rupture her windpipe for a slower though still certain death. He doubted he'd have time for a follow up shot, as when she dropped she would do so out of view, but if there was time then that would seal the deal and a second bullet would not have to travel through the glass.

He glanced back at the screen of the laptop.

He was becoming impatient. He needed an answer to his inquiry and he needed it now. He watched as she slung the bag over her shoulder and then checked the room.

At that moment he made his decision. Whether she went for her overnight bag determined whether she would live or die...

\*\*\*

"So you remember the woman?" Stone asked. He was sure that the taxi driver was going to turn up a blank, the guy hadn't been too sure, but suddenly seemed to remember. Stone had asked him, but only gave a brief description, not wanting to prompt a blurred memory to the point of false recognition.

"Sure, I only had three call-ins for the whole evening. Everybody else, I take off the street." Rodriguez Fortes sipped some coffee from the plastic carton. "She was smart-looking, plain but real pretty. I picked her up from The Amsterdam Court Hotel, then dropped her off at a hotel on West 71$^{st}$ and Columbus."

"Which hotel?" Stein asked excitedly. "Can you remember the name?"

Fortes shrugged. "The... No, it's gone. It's real shitty on the outside though, but once you're inside its pretty good, I guess."

"Thanks, but we don't want to stay there,"

Stone paused. "We just want to know the name."

David Stein stepped closer to the taxi driver and put a gentle hand on the man's shoulder. "Listen, Bud, It'll be a real help if you could try and remember," he paused, whispering into the man's ear. "Don't mind my friend, he's just a little impatient, is all. We need to find this woman, and fast. Can you describe the hotel?"

"Hey, I said that I don't know the name, I didn't say I couldn't help." He took another sip of coffee, then placed it down on the hood of a nearby taxi and smiled. "If you want to know the quickest way across town, just follow my tail lights."

\*\*\*

The lock was an old-fashioned tumbler type, and not the more common key-card as used ever more increasingly in city hotels. There was no kicking this door in. He had wanted to unsettle Isobel Bartlett back inside the Amsterdam Court. He knew how to pick the lock and had a set of special tools for the task. It was a question of feel and gentle probing with the set of custom made titanium picklocks, but he was well practiced and had the lock open in a matter of seconds. He opened the door cautiously and stepped inside.

He tracked the room with his pistol, held firmly in his right hand. He knew she had left but could not bring the receiver with him, as it was far too bulky and connected to the laptop through the USB socket. As he had left his hotel and crossed the street he knew that there had been the possibility that she could have returned to the room whilst he had been in transit. He had decided that in this event he would simply kill her and retreat from the operation. She was the only link to the drives but he could not afford capture on his part.

Satisfied that the room was clear he started a careful and calculated search of the room starting high and working lower, checking all of the recesses and alcoves and under the edge of the carpet. He had an incredible short-term memory and worked hard at remembering where everything had been. He would stand back occasionally and study the room as if it were a photograph, then repeat the search only when he was happy that he had left nothing out of place and nowhere unchecked.

\*\*\*

The walk had done her good and she felt refreshed and in a more confident frame of mind. She had kept on West 71st and crossed over Columbus and Central Park West and had ventured into Central Park. The sky was a clear deep blue and utterly cloudless. The air had warmed and if she kept out of the shade there was no need for her jacket but once out of the bright sun's glare the temperature dropped considerably.

She watched the joggers uniformly skirting the park, the Sunday morning fathers and sons pitching and batting and the dog walkers who all seemed to be either throwing balls for their dogs or picking up their mess with plastic bags and depositing the package in the bins. It was a picture, a snapshot of normality and it had inspired, willed her to get over the situation and return to her own snapshot, her own little picture of normality.

She had paced the sidewalk back towards the hotel and she had entered the building with determination and a purpose. As she climbed the stairs she had formulated her plan and was going to return to Washington and contact the police. It would stand her in better stead than the NYPD and she would not feel so isolated and alone in her hometown. She had friends there and people she could possibly turn to.

She reached the top of the stairwell and caught up with an elderly couple, who climbed far slower than her. They were indecisive in their actions and stepped onto the next stairwell in front of her. She didn't want to hurry past them, and knew that they were oblivious to her, so instead settled into their pace and took the stairs one at a time as patiently as she could.

At the top of the stairwell the couple veered off to the right and Isobel turned left and walked along the empty corridor towards her room, fumbling to get the key out of her bag as she neared the door. She stopped for a second and felt a shiver run down her spine. It was eerily quiet, she reflected as she slipped the key into the lock. The stillness was most unnerving and she felt another shiver, this time more violent than the first as she unlocked the door and stepped inside.

## TWENTY EIGHT

Rodriguez Fortes drove erratically and without regard for his fellow motorists. Pedestrians were regarded even less, as were amber lights that were about to switch to red. He challenged the narrowest of gaps and made it through more by luck than by any degree of skill or judgment.

Rob Stone had to drive even harder and even faster than the taxi driver. Amber lights for Rodriguez Fortes were red for Stone. The gaps through which Fortes barely made it through narrowed further for Stone in the pursuing Mustang and the pedestrians were just that little bit further across the road. He worked the Mustang hard and grimaced as he continuously accelerated only to slam on the brakes for an obstruction. By the time they had reached West 71st trickles of perspiration ran down Stone's brow as he battled for control of the vehicle and kept up continuous concentration through the traffic. It

233

was an old car and not meant for driving like this. Stone owned it for vanity and release. In truth it was only fast in a straight line. The Mustang's V8 popped and rumbled as they slowed up and pulled to a halt in front of the entrance to an unremarkable hotel called *The Albany*.

Rob Stone got out and slammed the door. He nodded a quick thank you to Rodriguez Fortes who was standing by the taxi with a pointed finger towards the hotel's entrance, Stone then mounted the steps and walked briskly into the foyer. David Stein told the driver to go and followed Stone inside.

"I'm Agent Robert Stone, Secret Service." He flashed his ID wallet at the female receptionist. "I need to see your register."

She looked at him in bewilderment. "Is there any name you're looking for in particular?" She looked at her computer screen and brought up the current booking calendar. "It'll be far quicker this way."

"Thanks," he said appreciatively. "Isobel Bartlett."

The receptionist studied the screen for a moment and then looked up at him. "Room three fifteen."

"You have that many rooms?" Stein interjected.

"No. Fifteen to a floor, six floors. Three

just means level three." She looked back at Stone and pointed. "The stairwell is that way, or the elevator is just over there. She's in her room, or should be. She walked through the foyer about five minutes ago."

Stone ran the three flights of stairs and stopped when he reached the top. He turned back to face Stein right behind him. The FBI agent bent down and took a stubby revolver out of a concealed ankle holster gun in hand.

Stone looked at the snub-nosed revolver and frowned. It wasn't standard bureau issue, but then Stein hadn't been on duty today. It was most likely his off-duty piece. "What are you doing?"

Stein looked bewildered. "I've got a dead agent. Dead friend, even. I don't know this Bartlett woman, nothing other than what Delaney told me... and she's dead. I'm not going anywhere near her unarmed until I've got a few facts clarified."

"Wait here," he paused. "I'll go and confront her. I don't want you scaring her half to death with that."

"We had a deal, Agent Stone. I was to get to interview her. Don't welch out on me and start waving bits of paper at me now. It's still not too late for me to call in the bureau officially."

"I'm not welching out. What are you in high school? I just don't want to go in too heavy. It'll only scare her and make her clam up." He shook his head. "Wait here. Cover me with that, if you want. But let me go in first and tell her what's going on."

Stein thought for a moment, then nodded. He kept the revolver in his hand and leaned against the edge of an alcove, partially shrouded by a large potted rubber plant. He had a clear line of fire to the room at the end of the corridor. The revolver was small, but it was a .357 magnum with 158 grain loads. One shot stopped all. "Just remember our little deal, partner."

Stone smiled at the FBI agent and then walked quietly down the corridor and knocked on the door to room three-fifteen.

***

He was in a fury. A rage. His head was starting to pound and he could feel the flickering starting to return to his eyes. The blood pumped through his temples and erupted in a crescendo of malevolence, clouding his vision and interrupting his hearing. All he could hear was the sound of his own heartbeat, echoing through his ears.

He had glanced, purely by chance, out of the window and had seen the woman returning to the hotel. He had not had enough time to finish conducting his search and had been forced to leave before he was halfway through. He had managed to get down onto the second floor and wait for Isobel Bartlett to climb past the floor and onto the third. Once she was out of sight, and he heard her footfalls on the corridor above, he had run down the remaining stairs and out of the foyer. He had noticed the receptionist look up from her work but knew she had had no time to look closely enough to recognize him again if it were necessary for her to do so.

After arriving back in his hotel room he had quickly checked the screen of the laptop but still there was no message.

His head was starting to pound and it hindered his aim as he settled the sniper scope on the woman's forehead. He hated her. Hated her for leading him on this wild goose chase, hated her for coming back to her room before he could finish conducting his search. Had he found the drives she would already be dead. But now he was back at square one. Back in his room waiting for the order to kill her, or continue to follow her movements. He prayed for the order to kill, was willing it to come through.

He heard the knock on the door through the transceiver beside the laptop. It made him jump with a start. He watched her look of bewilderment, her expression of fear. He enjoyed watching her, enjoyed looking at her troubled face. He couldn't wait to squeeze on the trigger.

\*\*\*

"Open up, ma'am," Stone paused. He was standing by the door, his back to the wall, his hand outstretched to his side. He rapped on the heavy wooden door once more, waited for a moment. "My name is Robert Stone, I'm an agent with the Secret Service and I need to talk to you at once." He could hear movements inside the room and cursed himself for not checking out the layout of the room or the outside structure with the receptionist. She could be halfway down a fire escape by now and then he'd have no chance in catching up with her. Have to start all over. "I'm going to count to three, then I'm coming in! One... two ... three!"

He stepped backwards, squared himself to the door and pulled the Sig Sauer pistol out from its holster. David Stein was in the corridor now, inching his way towards him with his back to the wall.

The door opened cautiously. Stone stepped to one side keeping the pistol down by his side out of view from Bartlett behind the door. He holstered the weapon as he walked in. She hadn't noticed he was armed.

"Isobel Bartlett?" He asked, and she nodded meekly. "I have some questions for you regarding the theft of government property."

She nodded. Her demeanor was solemn but to Stone she looked like she had given into a fight. Resigned herself to her fate. "You'd best come in, then." She opened the door wider and stepped aside to allow him through.

Stone glanced down the corridor at Stein and then looked back to her. "I have a colleague with me, Special Agent David Stein of the FBI."

"David Stein?" She looked confused. "Then Elizabeth's here?"

"No ma'am," Stein said as he walked into the doorway. "I'll explain in a moment."

Stone walked inside and waited for Stein to follow. He glanced around the room and then looked across at Isobel Bartlett. The woman looked a wreck. Her eyes were sore looking and red, like she'd been crying for some time and her eye sockets were deep and dark.

"Take a seat, please Isobel." David Stein ushered her to a chair, then looked around for somewhere to sit. He perched himself on the edge of the bed and looked up at Stone who was leaning against the wall, his hands in his pockets. "You expected to see Elizabeth Delaney?"

She looked at him, unsure where it was leading. "No... I thought..."

"Thought what?" Stone interrupted.

"What's this about?" She asked, turning back towards David Stein.

"Don't play the innocent!" Stone snapped. "You were caught on CCTV at the facility. You contacted Delaney from the phone in your apartment..."

"You've been in my apartment?"

Stone ignored her protest. He glanced down at Stein and then looked back at her. "You arranged to meet Elizabeth Delaney, when was that?"

She hesitated, then looked at him defiantly. "I want a lawyer."

"Why? You're not under arrest."

"Then get the Hell out of my room!"

Stone smiled. "'Not under arrest yet, at least."

"Then go to Hell or arrest me! Either way I'll only talk with a lawyer present."

"Delaney. When did you meet her?'"

She stood up and slipped on her jacket, picked up her shoulder bag and stared at him. "I'll tell the cops. I've had enough of you lot."

"What lot?"

"Federal lot. Elizabeth Delaney was my friend and I couldn't even trust her in the end." She moved to pass between them, but Stein stood up and blocked her path. "Get the Hell out of my way!" she snapped.

"Sit down and shut up." Stein's voice was calm, yet firm. "Delaney's dead. You know anything about that?'"

She looked up at him, her face was ashen. "What?"

"Elizabeth Delaney. My friend, partner, lover..." He glared at her. "You were to meet her. That's the last we know."

"I had nothing to do..."

"Cut the crap! You arranged to meet her. You fed her a whole lot of shit about being on the run, not trusting anyone, now she's dead!"

She glanced up at Stone, but he remained impassive. "I know you! You're the NSA guy from the conference on Friday."

Stone smiled. "Small world."

David Stein looked at him. "NSA?"

"Cover," Stone said, continuing to stare at Bartlett.

"What the hell's going on?" She attempted to push past Stein once more but he stood firm and continued to block her path. "I'm going to the police."

Stone eased himself away from the wall and paced around the room. "Where are they? The flash drives. What have you done with them?"

"They're safe."

"Where?"

"Fuck you!"

"Really Isobel? You don't look the type to use profanity." He turned around and stared at her.

"At this moment in time, I want to believe in you. I want to believe that a lead I have been following for three months is still as strong as before you took the drives. I want to believe that you are good and true and that you acted out of decency and with fortitude. I want to believe that I was on the right track and that Professor Leipzig was murdered because he was an obstruction to the people behind this and that your old college friend, was killed whilst helping you." He continued to stare at her coldly. "I don't want to involve the police, and I don't want anyone but Agent Stein knowing what has happened. I don't want the people behind this getting to you. Or your family. I don't want the people involved getting away with this. And they will. Unless you start to co-operate and tell me what you know."

She seemed to be weighing up her options. She visibly relaxed, taking a breath. "OK," she paused. "But I don't know where to start."

"How about the beginning," Stein suggested.

\*\*\*

There was a discreet chime as the e-mail arrived. He looked at the screen, traced his finger across the mouse pad and clicked on the mail icon. He read carefully, not wanting to risk mistake. The orders were clear. His fee had been increased and he had been given the reference number for a new deposit to his offshore account.

He carried only the one bag and it was packed and ready. He quickly packed the laptop and the rest of the electronic equipment into a compact case and checked over the room for traces of his stay. It was immaculate and looked as if the room had been freshly remade. Satisfied that he was ready to leave he sat down at the table and picked up the customized M4 assault rifle. The weapon's soft rectangular carry case was open on the table. It looked like a suit carrier. He blinked several times to moisten his eyes and then took up aim at the figure in the window across the street. The weapon was light and compact and felt comfortable in his hands. He could hold the zero for hours, not shaking nor twitching as his muscles relaxed.

He moved the crosshairs of the sniper scope until they were lined up on the target. He had a clear shot at the center of the forehead. The target was still, and his aim was steady. The headache had gone and so had the hammering of his heartbeat. He was calm. He was controlled. And he held the zero completely.

His finger tensed on the custom trigger and he anticipated a pull of about a pound and a half. He rechecked his aim and breathed steadily out, losing all the breath from his lungs. He held steady. Held his breath, sound and relaxed. Almost trancelike as he watched the crosshairs line up for the last time. Then, slowly, surely, he squeezed the trigger.

## TWENTY NINE

There was no sound of a gunshot. Just the sound of the glass shattering and the bullet impacting into the very center of David Stein's forehead. His head snapped backwards and a thin mist of red puffed from the back of his head and splattered the wall behind. For an indeterminable moment in time he remained standing as he stared blankly at the ceiling, his legs shaking uncontrollably. The second bullet penetrated his chest with a solid thud, pierced his heart and passed through his back hitting the wall behind. He dropped lifelessly to the floor. Not flung backwards with the force of the bullet as depicted in movies but merely slumped inertly, the use of muscles and limbs and senses gone forever.

Time stood still for a moment for Isobel. She stared at Stein's body slumped lifelessly on the floor. She looked up at Stone who was moving towards her like a sprinter out of the blocks. He looked past her, his eyes on the baseball sized hole in the glass and the street beyond.

Stone's mind was working, his thoughts moving through the dense fog that had threatened to cloud his mind the moment Stein had been hit. Whereas Isobel was standing frozen, Stone's years of training for this scenario had suddenly and thankfully taken over. The hole was small, the second shot had found its way through without any loss in accuracy. The marksman was an expert, a supreme shot. There was no sound, the weapon had been a silenced one - there was no chance of detecting the sniper's location by hearing alone. All this had passed through his mind as he had taken his first step. As he had taken his second, his hand had reached behind his back and pulled the .357 pistol clear of its holster. He kept moving, powering his leg muscles and willing for the world to catch up and play at real-time. Isobel was still staring at him, her face was expressionless and her body hadn't moved from the spot where she'd been standing at the first shot. Stone reached her in three powerful strides and had his hand on the fabric of her jacket, just on top of her left shoulder. He heaved and twisted and pulled her towards him. In a split second, she had spun right around and was shielded by his body as he lined his weapon up one of the many windows across the street and they both fell to their knees.

There was little time to process the information, but he already knew that he was dealing with a professional marksman and could see the windows across the street. All but one had the drapes pulled wide open, and all but one of the windows was closed. He kept Isobel close to him and released a volley of fire at the window above and to the right of the direct line of sight of the room. He counted off the shots subliminally. He was moving now, getting them both clear of the window. The glass erupted in a maelstrom of splinters and shards and the wall on the other side of the room imploded debris of plaster and stucco as the sniper opened fire with an automatic cycle of return fire.

Stone marked the window, pushed Isobel hard onto her stomach and pinned her in place with his knee into the small of her back. There was a grunt of protest, but it was drowned out as he returned fire with a barrage of six shots. With both hands now free to use the weapon, he ejected the magazine and already had the spare in his left hand. It slipped quickly in place, nestled tightly in the pistol's thick butt, and he dropped the cocking lever, sending the slide plummeting forward with a sharp metallic click. The weapon was trained on the window and bouncing sharply in his hands as he fired another sustained burst of fire at the window. He was up and moving, rolling across the window bay and reaching for the scruff of Isobel's collar and the strap of her shoulder bag. He pulled hard and she slid across the shards of glass and into his grasp, just as the remaining pieces of window and frame were disintegrated in front of their eyes. Their path to the door was clear and the sniper would not be able to reach them as they made their escape. Stone heaved Isobel off the floor and they were running for the door, huddled together, as Stone half pulled, half pushed her into safety and away from the line of fire.

***

He swore loudly, stormed across the room and quickly broke the assault rifle down and dropped it into the custom carry bag. He had only expected to pick up one or two empty shells as he made his exit, but thanks to the idiot with the pistol, not to mention his own fury and the specially adapted magazine, the floor now glistened with over fifty brass cases. The gunfire from across the street would have attracted attention, and the government agent had the mark on him, knew his location. He had to get out now and he had to keep moving. He cursed again, slipping on the brass bullet cases like walking on ball bearings as he made his way to the door.

***

"Keep moving!" Stone yelled, pushing Isobel in front of him as they made their way down the stairwell. He had his weapon in his right hand, his left hand held her shoulder firmly.

She did not reply. She was running for her life and heaving for breath as she took the stairs two at a time. Her mind was a blank, she could not recall what had happened; rather saw the whole episode as a series of comic book snapshots. Stein staring at the ceiling, his eyes devoid of life, the thud of the second bullet hitting him and dropping him to the floor. Stone barging her to the floor, his eyes so full of hate and anger. The window disintegrating in front of them, the barrage of silent bullets impacting, some bouncing and ricocheting around the room.

Stone pushed her through the swing door at the bottom of the stairs. She took the full impact with her face and body. He kept her moving through the foyer. The receptionist looked up in bewilderment. She had the telephone receiver in her hand, was already calling the police. She froze as she saw them and then ducked for cover behind her desk, fearful of her own safety.

Stone and Isobel were out on the street and running down the sidewalk. People stopped and stared, some hunched down when they saw the pistol in his hand. |Others stared dumbly, blankly, lost in the confusion and curiosity of the moment. He kept the pistol aimed high, marking the window across the street as they ran.

Stone pushed her towards the Mustang, gripped her shoulder hard and put his foot into the back of her knee. She dropped down to her knees and he had her completely shielded between the car and his own body. He cursed loudly as he fumbled with the key and unlocked the passenger door, got the door open and damned near threw her into the seat. He kept the weapon trained on the fourth-floor window as he rounded the hood and got to the driver's door. His back was to the window now as he unlocked it but he already knew that the sniper had gone. There had been too many opportunities for a shot. But as he unlocked the door and dropped into the seat, he shuddered at the possibilities that had been open to the marksman as they had left the hotel. He had charged out of the front exit because that was where his vehicle was parked. He did not have central locking and had wasted valuable time at both doors and he had known all the long that the marksman could well have seen him arrive and would know which car to look out for. He would have to sharpen up, turn from investigator back to bodyguard.

The Mustang's V8 roared into life and Stone floored the throttle, biting the rear set of rubber into the tarmac and sending two plumes of thick smoke into the air as the rear of the vehicle twitched and slid from side to side down the road. He hammered the stick into second and the car gained traction and raced up towards eighty in a fraction over seven seconds, thanks to the painstaking time and money he had spent under the bonnet. He weaved in and around the cars and hit the brakes as he turned onto Central Park West. The traffic thickened and he had to return to more sensible speeds, keeping his eye on all his mirrors in an attempted to spot a tail.

He glanced across at her and then noticed the blood on her blouse. "Are you hit?" He reached across and patted her stomach, searching frantically for the wound. She did not respond. He snapped at her: "Isobel! Are you hit?"

She looked vacantly at him like she was drugged or drunk. "I ..." She stared down at the bloodstained material, and then started to scream.

Stone kept an eye on the traffic, driving with his left hand and feeling for the wound with his right. The blood was thick and did not seem to be pumping from one particular place. He tore at the blouse and ripped it at the buttons. Isobel was still screaming and shaking. Her eyes were wide and she was becoming hysterical. He looked at her stomach and saw that it was amassed with tiny incisions and he could see the glistening heads of tiny shards of glass.

"Isobel! You're OK. It's glass, not a gunshot wound," he paused to watch the road. "You're going to be alright." She did not respond, was frozen in panic and fear. He squeezed her knee tightly and shook her. "Isobel!"

***

The Mercedes E63 was a completely different animal to the raucous and wild customized Mustang. It was large, yet somehow discreet. It looked for the entire world like any other large luxury German sedan, but nestled under the hood was a 6.2 liter V8 with well over five hundred horsepower. Technically superior to any customized home-grown American classic. The power was seamless and graceful and gave everything at once to the committed driver. Traction control and all-wheel steer and the most technologically advanced engine management system in the world meant that although understated in looks it was more than a match for the Mustang.

He had reached the Mercedes and carefully stashed the sports bag and carry case in the trunk. There was no point in rushing; the Mustang would be long gone in a frenzy of smoking rubber and burning clutch. Instead, he set up the laptop on the passenger seat and plugged the power cable into the cigarette lighter. Next he put a dongle – a cell signal receiver – in the USB port. With the laptop booted up and the software initiated and now online, he studied the map on the screen and saw that the Mustang was making its way north on Central Park West and was two-point-seven miles ahead of him travelling at approximately thirty miles per hour.

He started the Mercedes and engaged drive. The car pulled effortlessly away from the curb and he smiled to himself as he saw the duo of flashing blues and twos making for *The Albany Hotel.*

He thought of the man in the room who had returned fire so quickly, who had taken Isobel Bartlett out of the line of fire. He was good, had reacted instinctively and professionally. The man was a worthy adversary. He would enjoy hunting him.

## THIRTY

The people moved quickly, almost comically, like a nineteen hundred silent movie as the picture wound onwards on fast forwards. Every so often he would stop the tape and pause the picture, study the people frozen on the screen and then wind it on again. He knew what he was looking for and had not made a mistake, the person would leap out at him from the screen.

It was the arrogance of the man that played on his mind the most, that and the air of coolness. It was somewhat unnerving how a man could exude such arrogance, such calmness in what he would describe as adversity. How he could flagrantly bounce around accusations in such a way that to rise to the merest of insinuations would announce only guilt. And all the time, he had smirked. Like he was teasing him, goading him into slipping up and walking right into the trap. The man had dared him.

He hit the play button again and let the DVD play on real-time. He could see what he thought was the back of him and then the side. And then he was gone. He watched, transfixed on the picture. Everybody else stepped into the frame, moved through the picture, turned his or her faces through every angle of portrait. The cameras picked out every guest, except for one. The man would almost be in frame, allowing a shoulder or elbow into view and then he would move. Not obviously, merely turn to talk to someone, sip from his glass or block his face with his arm as he scratched his head. But the anomaly was already set. You could avoid the camera's lens for so long and then after a while it became no accident. He checked off the names against the security pass log for the previous Friday.

His cell phone rang, jolting him from his vigil, his thoughts so rigid in concentration that his heart started to race as the ring tone played out its tune. He had dedicated the ringtone to one specific contact and already knew what the caller wanted.

"Yes?" he was abrupt, angered at the intrusion. He stopped the DVD with the remote.

"What the hell's going on?"

"What do you think? I'm trying to find out what's happened," he paused. "Anyway, I've told you not to call me at work."

"Get a grip, it's your cell phone. You're

holding it together, aren't you?"

"Of course. We need damage limitation and we need it real fucking quickly, that's all."

"We'll have it. It's just a matter of time, is all."

"If you say so."

"We need a meet, soon."

"Why?"

"Why the fuck do you think? Some bastard threw a joker in our hand, and now it isn't worth shit. I want to find out who. You know a diner on twenty-nine, near Rosslyn, place called *McBenn 's?* It's like a *Denny's* ..."

"I'll find it."

"Alright. Be there at six. And remember to watch your ass for a tail." The line went dead.

He placed the cell phone back down on the desk and picked up the remote. He pressed play and studied the picture once more. He would ascertain a name if he looked long enough, hard enough and if he couldn't find the man with the CCTV footage of the conference he would have to requisite the tapes for the rest of the building or even the parking lot. He needed to be sure. He needed to see how close the wolf had come to the door.

## THIRTY ONE

The silence had been uncomfortable in the car to say the least and Rob Stone was becoming concerned that Isobel Bartlett had gone into a vegetative state of shock. He had seen it before. The body shuts down after witnessing such trauma. All that is left is breathing. He had tried to ask her a few questions, start to explain what was happening but it had been to no avail. The woman had simply clammed up on him. David Stein's death had been tragic and completely unexpected and Stone could not help thinking that by tracking Bartlett down and involving the FBI agent he had been at least partially responsible for the man's death. Things had suddenly gone so horribly wrong. He glanced sideways at Isobel and didn't feel any differently about the situation.

Isobel was slumped in the seat, her blouse ripped loose but tucked across her body so that no part of her abdomen showed. The blood had started to clot and he could see that the bleeding had come from four or five wounds. He knew that he needed to get her some medical attention but was in a quandary as to what action to take. Somewhere, there was an unknown assassin who had stepped into the fray. Whether either of them were still a target or whether they had slipped the net was the question at the forefront of Stone's mind. In addition, he needed to contact the FBI headquarters and NYPD and explain what had happened back at *The Albany Hotel.* However, contacting the bureau and police would result in one thing and one thing only - he would have to give them access to Isobel Bartlett and he would lose valuable time. He might also deliver both himself and Isobel as a target once more.

They were heading north on twenty-two and had been travelling for around an hour and a half, at a fairly considerable pace. The sprawl of suburbia had long since given way to lush countryside and wooded areas with leaves of golden and red, and the horizon was marked with a thin vale of a golden sheen from the sun in the clear blue sky. They were nearing the three corners of New York State, Connecticut and Massachusetts and the sights of rivers and trees and waterfalls and long rolling hills was a welcome distraction from the hustle and bustle of the big city. Ahead of them he saw a cluster of buildings and looked out for a sign. As they approached, he slowed the Mustang down and indicated off the highway. There was a quiet looking diner and a small convenience store. The parking lot was quiet with only two SUV's and a tan colored sedan taking up space. As he pulled the car into the lot he caught a glimpse of a sign for a motel approximately a mile further up the highway.

"Isobel." Stone spoke softly, trying to gain her confidence. "I'm going to get a few things to clean you up. I need you to wait in the car."

She stared blankly ahead. There wasn't as much as a flicker from her eyes.

Stone pulled the car to a halt and got out. He jogged up the steps to the convenience store and looked around for the appropriate section. He found what he was looking for – tape, gauze, antiseptic ointment and a box of plastic band aids. As he turned to leave the aisle he picked up a box of maximum strength painkillers. At the counter he dropped the goods down then quickly went to a glass cabinet refrigerator and picked out two cans of full sugar soda and two glass bottles of mineral water. He paid the clerk without a word and rushed back outside to the car.

Isobel was still in her seat and he breathed a sigh of relief. He had half expected her to have taken off and in truth he wouldn't have blamed her.

He started the Mustang and put the box in first. There was little traffic on the road and he pulled out quickly onto the highway. He gunned the engine and within a minute he was turning back off the highway and into the drive of the motel.

\*\*\*

The Mercedes had crept to a gradual halt, its tires crunching on the loose chippings at the side of the road. There was no audible noise from the engine as the man brought the vehicle to a complete stop and studied the laptop's screen on the seat beside him. The red dot denoting the transponder hidden in the lining of Isobel Bartlett's shoulder bag and another in the lining of her coat had stopped flickering rhythmically, the sign that the target was no longer on the move.

He had pulled up on the crest of a bend less than a mile short of the target's location. He had waited somewhat impatiently at the side of the road and had tensed once more as he watched the red dot flicker slowly on the map and move off down the road. He had selected drive and had started to move off but had slowed to a halt again as he watched the red dot move off the road marking and stop in a dead area of green.

It frustrated him so, not knowing what the target was doing or how long they would be there.

He could feel the anger welling from within, the sudden rush of pulse at his temple, upon him and impeding his thoughts as an involuntary stutter impedes speech. He closed his eyes and took a deep breath. It helped to calm him, helped to put him at ease.

He thought back to the moment he had squeezed the trigger and had killed the man across the street. The second shot had come purely by instinct and he had been momentarily delighted at his handiwork. To have got two bullets through the same tiny hole in the glass and to have followed up the first shot before the corpse had hit the ground was testament to his skill as a marksman. The realization of which, made him feel invincible.

The e-mail had been short, concise and particular in its instructions. He was not to kill Isobel Bartlett until he had secured the location of the flash drives. His fee had been re-evaluated in his favor and he was to report his progress regularly and with immediate effect.

Hearing the conversation in the hotel room through the receiver had given him an invaluable advantage. He already knew of the man Robert Stone through his employers and knew that he may well come up against him in some way. But who was the FBI man? And why was he suddenly in the picture? Taking out the FBI agent had been a sudden improvisation. A new strategy and his alone. And he was both proud and pleased to have done so. He had moved the game on a level, increased the pace a little and provoked a reaction. He had undermined their security and would force them into making mistakes. He had also lessened the odds against him and equaled things out a little. All he needed now was patience. Patience to play the stalking cat to their cowering mouse. And that's exactly what they were. Like mice, they were small and insignificant and no match for his skill and power. And now they were scared. He would hunt them, amuse himself with them and then when the time was right he would kill them.

\*\*\*

The motel was a sixty dollar a night special with ample parking in front of the chalet rooms. It was aimed at working drivers like sales reps who wanted inexpensive rates and easy access to the interstate. Nobody would have stayed two nights. It provided a breakfast of donuts and Danish pastries from the diner down the road. Along with some jugs of juice and coffee from a machine in the reception. No frills.

Stone wasn't interested in donuts or coffee, or whether the rooms had cable. He paid up front and in full and took the key that the attendant had handed him. Inside the room he had dropped the paper bag of purchases on the nearest bed and ushered Isobel into the bathroom.

"Pass your blouse out through the door and take a shower," he paused. "I'll go get it washed while you get cleaned up, then I'll help sort those cuts out."

She didn't reply, but she did go inside the bathroom and shut the door. He heard her yelp and whimper inside and he assumed that she was taking her blouse off. Then the door opened slightly and she passed the bloodstained blouse out through the gap. He took it and was bemused by her silence but was at least thankful that she had done what he had instructed.

He made his way outside and followed the sign for the laundry. Inside there were two washers and two dryers as well as a drying rack and a heater. Next to the furthest-most dryer there was a vending machine for soap powder and fabric softener. He reached into his pocket for some quarters but hesitated when he noticed a newly washed halter-neck top on the drying rack. It looked to be a similar size to what Isobel would wear and quite possibly similar in taste. He looked down at the crimson stained blouse and balled it up and dropped it into the waste can. Without a glance he swiped the top and slipped it under his suit jacket and made his way back to the motel room.

Isobel was no longer in the bathroom, but was perched on the furthest bed wearing just jeans, her bra and a towel wrapped around her head. She was looking at her torso in the mirror and was attempting to get a shard of glass out of her stomach. She was wincing and sucking air through clenched teeth.

He dropped the newly acquired top on the bed. "Here, let me help." Stone paced towards her, but stopped as she recoiled.

"No," she said bluntly. "I'm fine." She fumbled with the shard, and it hurt badly. She winced.

"You know, I've got a small Swiss Army knife in my wallet. It's like a credit card design," he paused. "Not that you're interested in that, but it's got a pretty good set of tweezers on it." He walked closer and looked at her stomach. "It'll be a lot easier, and a sight less painful if you let me help." He took out his wallet and retrieved the card, thumbed out the tiny pair of tweezers. He passed them to her and she took them from him, snatching it from his clasp.

She pulled the makeshift turban from her head and dropped the towel on the bed. Her hair was wet, glossy and thick. "How about you explain what's going on," she snapped. "That'll help me a whole lot more."

He watched as she plucked the slither of

glass out and a trickle of blood seeped out and rolled over her olive skin. "I was hoping that you'd start off with what you know ..." He picked up a piece of gauze and dabbed the blood, cutting the flow short of her naval. "Why did you take the drives with the information on them?"

She removed another shard of glass with a flinch and looked up at him. "Who are you? And what about your friend?"

He thought of David Stein. *Friend.* He had only met the guy that morning, but he felt that he had lost exactly that. A good friend. Somebody we could have had a beer and a burger with after watching a game of football some time. He looked at her. She was vulnerable, yet resilient. "My name is Robert Stone, and I'm an agent with the Secret Service."

"You protect the president, right?"

"Amongst other things, yes." He looked down at the paper bag of purchases he had bought in the convenience store. He picked up a can of soda, pulled the tap and passed it to her. "Here, drink some," he paused as she took it from him. "The sugar hit will help." He tossed her the packet of painkillers and they landed on the bed beside the gauze pads.

"Thanks." She sipped a little of the sugary syrup drink, then placed the can on the floor. "You ever protect him, personally?" She asked, then looked down and opened the packet of painkillers and popped a couple into her mouth. She drank them down with the soda.

"I have done hope to again, someday. We don't just protect him though. Congressmen and woman, their families sometimes. Foreign dignitaries also." He opened a can for himself and drank half in the first few gulps. It was cool and sweet and refreshing. "And then there's the treasury. You commit a crime against Uncle Sam's dollar and we're all over your ass."

She picked up the ointment and slapped a little on a piece of gauze. "What do you do then?"

"I've worked in the treasury, against fraud and forgery. And I've worked as personal bodyguard to the president, within his close protection detail. Right before this assignment, I was working as an instructor. Teaching close protection to new recruits in the Secret Service."

"And what is *this* job?" She had finished with the gauze and was tearing lengths of tape to size.

Stone watched her, then tore some gauze into little squares and handed them to her. "I looked into the bioresearch facility after an investigation I was conducting kept turning up a few anomalies, as well as a couple of names. After my initial report I was assigned with conducting a security audit of the facility. From its employees and contracted workers through to its funding and directorship."

"And who tasked you with this assignment?"

Stone hesitated. He was gaining ground with her. It was important to gain her trust. He took the folded envelope from his inside pocket and passed it to her. "The president himself."

She read the letter, studied it for a while in silence, then slipped it back into the envelope and handed it back to him. "Pretty impressive," she paused. "But why you?"

"He trusts me. Trusts my family."

"Your family?"

"Yes."

"How do you mean?"

"It's a long story."

She smirked. "You going someplace?"

He looked at her abdomen, which now represented a patchwork quilt. The bleeding had stopped and she seemed to be unbothered by the wounds. Maybe it was the adrenaline, or perhaps the painkillers had started to kick in. Either way, she seemed far more controlled than she had been previously. He reached out and picked up the halter-top he had taken. He tossed it to her and she caught it, inspected it somewhat dubiously. "Yes," he said. "And so are you."

267

## THIRTY TWO

The woman was smiling. It was a smile that beamed brightly and served as a conduit from her soul to the outside world. There was warmth and love and happiness and pride. She looked down at him, towering over his tiny frame, though not imposing. Merely comforting and protective. The natural and definitive matriarch.

The table behind her was piled high with food, the result of much time spent attentively in the kitchen. There were French fancies – the little cupcakes with fondant icing and Chantilly cream in the middle. There were also pigs in blankets, mini quiches, sandwich fingers, Scotch eggs and great bowls of chips with various dips. Most of the kids had made a mess of the dips and the once pristinely white tablecloth was now a myriad of red and green and yellow puddles but the woman didn't seem to mind. The sandwiches were cut into delicate fingers and the fillings were falling out, as the children wasted no time in demolishing the buffet platter before them but she didn't seem to mind about that either.

She kept beaming her smile and ushered him towards the pile of colorfully wrapped presents. It was his birthday and he was the center of attention. The children were more interested in the food than in his presents and he felt sad, suddenly conscious of the sensation that his popularity had waned in favor of pigs in blankets and fancy cakes.

He stamped his feet in an act of frustration and shouted at his guests, but to no avail. Their attentions were towards the food and not a single child showed interest in the opening of his presents. He started to sob and a number of adults looked away in embarrassment for the boy's mother. There were parents too, they knew all too well how difficult a five-year old could be. It was the hollow feeling inside that he despised, like there were no surprises left, no enjoyment to be had for the remainder of the day. His mother put a hand around his shoulders and said something in his ear. He didn't know what, but he knew that she had been reassuring him.

The man looked up suddenly from where he had been staring blankly at the screen of the laptop, shaken back to the present and the objective. He wasn't sure what the memory had been or where it had come from but it was unlike any other. It hadn't been an enhanced daydream, willed to fruition by his desire to recall such things and it hadn't been a dream. He had simply remained wide-awake and lost himself in his own past. However, he *had* no memories of his past and he had no recognition of the woman in the memory. He was sure, even hopeful that the woman had been his own mother but with nothing to compare her with and no lateral memory to recall he wasn't sure if she was in fact merely a figment of his imagination.

He physically shook his head at the mere suggestion of the desire to will the memory into existence. That would have been a sign of weakness; to seek comfort in the blissful tranquility of his past.

He looked back down at the laptop's screen and noticed the little red dot start to flash intermittently and move steadily along the line indicating the road they had been travelling on.

He slipped the car's automatic shift into drive and eased off the gravel and back onto the tarmac road. There was no traffic in front or behind, so he kept his distance from the Mustang as he would not have the luxury of cover.

The sun was still bright in the sky, but the temperature had started to drop dramatically and the shadows from the trees were longer. The sky was a much darker blue now, with a tinge of red across to the west. He estimated that there was about an hour or so of sunlight and approximately another hour and a half of daylight left. He could afford to wait patiently for the dark. Darkness was his friend. It would keep him from view and it would provide him with a natural cloak of invisibility.

He did his best to forget the earlier episode of weakness; tried to rid himself of the memory altogether. But no matter how hard he tried, he couldn't help wanting to know who the woman had been, and above all, would he ever see her again?

## THIRTY THREE

He squeezed the maple syrup over the stack of shorts and meticulously levered each pancake off the other in an effort to douse each one in an equal layer of the sweet syrup. He placed the bottle back down on the table and picked up the shaker of powdered vanilla sugar.

"You can't be serious?"

Tom Hardy looked up startled by the intrusion. He dusted the stack with a blizzard of powdered sugar and smiled. "Absolutely," he paused to pick up his fork, and then looked at him once more. "Please, take a seat."

McCray eased himself along the bench seat and into the booth. "That looks like someone had an accident in the snow." He clicked his fingers at the nearby waitress and she came over and stood, somewhat impatiently with an order pad and pen. "Coffee, black. And can I get a piece of pecan pie?" She nodded curtly and wrote the order down as she walked back towards the counter. "No tip for her." He stared at the mess on Hardy's plate and shook his head. "Are you on first name terms with your orthodontist and cardiologist?"

"No, should I be?" Hardy's tone was impatient.

"Sorry, just saying..."

"Well don't." He shoveled another mouthful of pancakes and maple syrup away, then picked up his cup and drank some coffee as he chewed. He spoke with his mouthful. "We've got to start clearing this shit up and we've got to start now."

"I'm working on it."

"You're working on shit."

"I'm doing the best I can!"

"Keep your voice down, fool." Hardy looked around the diner and glared at him as the waitress neared. She dropped the plate down in front of McCray and filled his cup with coffee, straight to the top. Hardy waited for her to return to the counter before he continued. "If the bioresearch facility is under investigation, then they know something is wrong. That's obvious. And it's not going to take too long before they start looking in your direction. Again, I state the obvious."

McCray sipped some coffee. His hand was shaking. He spilt a little down his tie. "They already have," he paused. "The guy was a fucking asshole. Barged into my office, sat in my own fucking chair." He shook his head, said through gritted teeth. "Even got Agnes to make coffee. She was real fucking pissed with him when he left."

"Who was he?"

"Some guy called Stone. Robert Stone," McCray shook his head. "He said that he was from the Secret Service. Even had a letter granting him open access and unlimited cooperation. Signed by the fucking president, no less! What in Christ's name is the Secret Service doing investigating us?"

"I don't know." Hardy pushed the half-eaten portion of pancakes away from him and shook his head. "Anyway, it's not *us,* it's *you.*"

"Fuck you! We're in this together," McCray protested. "Anyway, you're the fucking spook, you *should* know. I thought you were going to take care of any shit like this."

"I will. We just have to know who the fuck he is and where he is. After that, I'll make him wish he hadn't been fucking born."

"Well, now you know his name and you know who he works for, so get on with it." McCray sipped some coffee, and then forked a mouthful of pecan pie. He chewed with his mouth open.

"I just can't see how they moved so fast," Hardy mused. "And why the Secret Service? They're just bullet catchers, for Christ's sake. And other than aspire to take a hit for the president or some dumb-fuck congressman, all they take care of is Treasury security and monetary acts of crime."

"Like what?"

"Like," Hardy took an extra-large forkful of pancakes, dripping the maple syrup on the edge of the table. He wiped the spillage clean with his napkin, and then looked back at McCray. "Forgery, or bearer bonds or major coups involving money yet to be released to public circulation. They come up with all the new banknote designs, security designs, that is. But that is an entirely different section of the Secret Service. Fuck knows what this asshole Stone is doing in our camp."

McCray pondered over his cup and then smiled at his companion. "What if this guy Stone wasn't on to my end of the operation? What if he was investigating you all along? That would explain how he arrived on the scene so soon. Perhaps he just got to bioresearch through keeping tabs on you."

Hardy looked at him and shrugged. "You think it hasn't happened before? Fuck, I've been CIA since I was twenty two years old. I'm almost sixty and still in the game. I've outlasted every other bastard who ever came along and tried to make a name for himself. Hell, if someone in Langley is trying to smear some shit on me then they had better be ready to take a bath in a ton of it. After that, they had better be ready to eat what's left. Leave this guy Stone to me and I'll have they guy behind the scenes pulling the little fuck's strings. I'll have his balls on rye with pastrami and mustard."

McCray looked at the coldness in Hardy's eyes. He felt a slight shiver run down his spine. In truth he had underestimated the man with his cheap suits and his five o'clock shadow and yesterday's breakfast down his shirt. Tom Hardy was a survivor in the least survivable organization on the planet. He sipped some coffee. There was a moment of silence, a little awkwardness with Hardy's threats still hanging in the air.

"What about the Bartlett problem?" McCray said, changing the subject.

"Under control, last I knew."

"Go on."

"My associate e-mailed me with the location, but as yet he hasn't secured the set of drives. When the time's right, he'll retrieve. By whatever means he has to. Then he'll eliminate her. Take her out of the equation altogether."

McCray looked at him dubiously. "And you can be sure of that?"

"Absolutely."

McCray scoffed at the notion. "And what if he fucks up? What if the police get hold of him?"

"That doesn't matter."

"Doesn't matter? What the fuck do you mean? If he is caught, arrested, he'll lead them back to us."

"Not a chance."

"I think you're deranged," McCray paused, shook his head. "I think you're a fucking oddball and I shouldn't have ever even thought about getting into this."

"Calm down," Hardy scowled at him. "It will be OK."

"I can't. I can't just calm down when you're being so damn flippant. What if your associate gets caught? What if he plain decides to take the drives for himself and blackmail us for them?"

"He won't. Relax." Hardy shook his head. "It just won't happen."

"And you're absolutely sure about that?"

"As sure as eggs is eggs."

McCray drank some coffee and sneered. "Fine. Just as long as you are absolutely sure that your *associate* is completely incapable of being caught." He put his cup back down and glared. "Who is he, Superman?"

"No. He's nobody. Nobody who ever

existed, anyway."

"I'm getting pissed off at this. I want to know who he is and why you're so being so fucking smug. He's human. He can fuck up just like everybody else."

Hardy laughed out loud. "You're so fucking naive, McCray. Especially for someone who works in bioresearch for the US government." He huddled forwards and spoke quietly. "You've got one hell of a lot to learn, that's for sure. Allow me to paint a little picture for you. Let you into a little secret. This man *isn't* human, not anymore at least. A human can't operate and do the things that this man is ordered to do. Sure, humans can kill and they can do it extremely efficiently. A serial killer loves to kill and is the most organized person within our entire race. Obsessive and organized? Definitely. Capable of operating and working under orders, to achieve a specific objective? No way. Not even a glimmer of a chance. It's been attempted, but all attempts that we are aware of failed. The serial killers were merely eliminated and disposed of. No use to us whatsoever." He picked up his cup and drank a little coffee, then placed the cup back down and stared at McCray coldly. "To kill is one thing. To continue killing is quite another. Soldiers are highly trained and kill when they have to. They operate under orders and attempt to achieve certain objectives. However, the theatre of war is different and the conditions under which they operate are different. Special Forces outfits produce highly capable, efficient killers, but they burn out quickly. They crack up after such a relatively short time. Like many soldiers who have experienced conflict, they tend to suffer Post Traumatic Stress Syndrome after a while and become utterly useless.

"About ten years ago I was part of a black ops project to create the perfect specialist skills operatives ..."

"You mean assassins," McCray interrupted. "Let's not put garnish on a stew. Say it how it is."

"OK," Hardy paused. "If you insist. The quest to create these assassins was called Operation Janus. After the Greek God with two faces. See, like you, we liked our Greek mythology over at Langley too."

"Roman."

"What?"

McCray smirked. "I'm pretty sure Janus was Roman. Transitional god. Hence the two faces. Please, continue."

"Dick," Hardy stared at him. "Anyway, operation Janus was revolutionary. It used genetic reshaping of cells, advanced drug therapy, plastic surgery and extremely successful methods of deep trance hypnosis. The result was, to an extent, the perfect assassin. An untraceable, unidentifiable killing machine. The training was both physical and suggestive through hypnosis and all memories of failure were erased from their minds. All they knew was success. Under interrogation, they could reveal nothing, would have no memory of their training or whom they worked for. There were even sleeper words installed in the chasms of their memory, which when used, would send them on a quest of self-termination. Suicide, if you will. We connected an installation trigger to a telephone message, which the operative would ring if ever arrested. You know, everyone is entitled to at least one phone call; it just happened that they would cut their wrists or hang themselves with a bed sheet after they had their call.

"They could be integrated into society and called upon when needed. The side effects of the treatment were negligible ... just headaches, but these were easily rectified by the application of painkillers. These painkillers were laced with a concoction of drugs which continued the passive hypnosis state, and were subsequently issued on a regular basis as part of the technical support given in the field."

"I can't believe what I'm hearing ..." McCray shook his head in bewilderment. "These assassins were still people. It's just that they were puppets and operating on remote control. They must have been like something out of the *Living Dead.* No life in them. Zombies. How the hell can you justify playing with people's lives like that?"

"That's rich, from the guy heading a project to create a super virus as a covert weapon of terror and attrition. A random killer of men, women and children." Hardy scoffed. "Anyway, it wasn't quite like that. They still led lives, just not the one they were born to, that's all."

"But what about Operation Janus?"

"Folded. A bleeding heart congressman found out and threatened to announce it, unless it was shut down. He could have shouted his mouth off afterwards, but we happened to have a few things on him, or at least set him up just in time to silence him. Sex with a minor. Managed to convince him it would border on pedophilia, which wouldn't have looked too good, seeing as he was a devout Christian and all."

"But what happened to the assassins?"

"Terminated." Hardy shook his head. "Poor souls never stood a chance. Just ex-military boys who volunteered for something they knew nothing about. All without family and very few friends. They were rounded up one at a time and subdued by pre- installed trigger sentences. They merely fell asleep, so that good old-fashioned hit man types could deal with them," he paused. "Hell, I think they rather enjoyed it. Kept them employed on the farm, so to speak."

"Jesus Christ! What about..."

"Yes. I managed to spare one," Hardy mused. "At the time, it was simply a matter of self-preservation. Hell, for a decade after the Cold War the redundancy axe was falling all over the place. I thought I could use my little secret to maximum effect. And I have. Each time something dirty is needed doing, they get on me to oversee it. *'Oh Hardy will get it sorted ... No questions asked ... He's the man to go to... '* Damned fucking right I am! I claim the funds as expenses, pay my boy off through his accounts, not that he sees any of the money, because he doesn't need to. He lives a hollow life, with an eggshell for a facade. His house is rented, he drives a flashy car, his clothes are new, his bank accounts are healthy, but they're not really his. What the fuck does he need money for? Hell, after each operation I just say a trigger word and shut him down. All he does then is eat, sleep and train for the next hit. He may think he went to California or Florida for a little R&R, but that's just what I tell him."

"And he's the one after Isobel Bartlett ..." McCray shook his head in disbelief at what he had just heard. "When will the job be done?"

Hardy sipped some coffee and smirked.

"When he gets it done," he paused. "One thing's for sure though ... He won't stop until it's finished."

McCray looked distant, his eyes not really focusing on anything in particular. He sipped a little coffee and looked up at Hardy. "Then Isobel Bartlett is as good as dead..."

## THIRTY FOUR

There were tears rolling gently down Isobel's cheeks. They trickled slowly at first and then as the flow met the already dampening skin they gained in pace until each rivulet ran quicker than the one before. She made no sound. No thwarted intake of breath, no nasal sound and certainly nothing like a sob. Stone had not been aware that she had been crying beside him and probably wouldn't have had he not glanced across at her for that brief moment.

There was no fast-moving anonymous interstate in the region, but skirting Green Mountain National Forest was Highway Seven and as roads go it was almost as good. They had gained in altitude, were gaining continuously and outside the air had cooled considerably. It was dusk and Stone flipped from sidelights to headlights. Most of the approaching vehicles had done the same. He glanced across at her again, then reached behind his seat and fumbled for a moment and came back with a wad of tissues.

"Here, take these," he said.

She accepted them and wiped her eyes with one of them. She bunched away the others, stuffing them into her pocket. "Thank you."

"Are you OK?"

"What do you think?" Her tone was sarcastic, sardonic. "We need to go to the police or something. What about David Stein?"

Stone knew what he *should* do. But he also knew that the FBI would see that the investigation of their fellow agent's killer would take priority over anything that he was working on. Their priorities would be conflicted and that would not be an acceptable compromise. He had a job to do and he was going to make damn sure that he continued to do it.

He looked at her momentarily, struggling to take his eyes off the road for long. "I will report what happened back there," he paused. "But for the time being, I'm more concerned for your safety."

"Bullshit!" she retorted venomously. "You're just concerned with finding the flash drives."

Stone shook his head. "Not true. If you can swear on your life that they're safe, I would rather they stay where they are. If what I hear is true about ARES, then I would rather they never turn up again. But decisions like that are not mine. Nor are they yours either." She didn't reply, simply looked ahead towards the oncoming traffic.

"Look, Isobel," he reasoned, "I need the full breakdown of what happened back at the bioresearch facility. And I need to know how they got to you so quickly."

"How the hell should I know that?"

"You contacted Delaney from your apartment, right?"

She looked thoughtful for a moment, and then nodded. "Yeah, I contacted her mother first, it was the only number I had for her."

"And she put you onto her?"

"Yes. It took a bit of persuading and she wouldn't let me know if she was still with the FBI, but she did give me her number in the end. We were good friends at college and we shared a house in our final year."

"And then you called Delaney?"

"Yes."

Stone pondered for a moment. "And you left soon afterwards. How did you travel to New York?"

"By train," Isobel paused. "Oh my god! I'd almost forgotten with all the shock. There was the girl!"

"What girl?" He frowned but kept his eyes on the road as he negotiated a bend. "What are you talking about?"

"Firstly, I was convinced that someone, a man, was watching me at the station back in Washington. Then, I was sure a woman was doing the same. Soon after that a girl with not dissimilar looks to myself rushed up to the edge of the platform. After a while I put it down to nerves, but the woman who I was sure was watching me at the station got off at Wilmington and I started to relax. My legs were stiffening so I decided to go for a walk down the line of carriages, but then I saw the same woman again. She looked up at me and seemed real pissed that I'd seen her. At Trenton, I got off the train, quite casually, but slipped back on just as it started to depart. The woman came running back onto the platform and made a call on her cell phone. By then, I was utterly convinced that I was being followed."

"So what did you do?" Stone asked. "And where does the girl on the platform come into this?"

"I'll get to her in a moment," Isobel paused. "I got off at Newark International and took a rather expensive cab into the city."

"What then?"

"I made contact with Elizabeth Delaney and arranged to meet for breakfast the next day," she paused, looked remorseful. "That was the first time I'd seen her in six years. And the last time that I will ever see her again... If I hadn't involved her she'd still be alive..." she wiped her eyes with a tissue and sniffed. Stone knew she was trying not to cry. "Later, I watched some TV, just flicked through and saw that the girl who had looked similar to me had been murdered. The footage showed a body bag on a gurney, but the news station also put out a picture of her. The report had said that she had come out to look for accommodation. That fitted in with her tearful goodbye to her boyfriend at the station in Washington. They were obviously going to spend a bit of time apart from one another. A hotel porter was also killed..."

Stone nodded. "And you're convinced that it was case of mistaken identity, that you were the one who should have been killed?"

"Well aren't you? Especially after today?"

"I don't know. It was David Stein who was shot, not you. You were just as clear a target."

"Yes, but my hotel room at The Amsterdam Court was ransacked. The killer never found the drives. He needs me alive, until he has them in his possession. Elizabeth Delaney sent me a text message to meet, he already had her when the message was sent. You know that!" She suddenly looked tearful at the thought.

"Well, it certainly seems viable," Stone paused. "Given the anomalies and connections."

"What does?"

"Sorry," he said. "I was just thinking out loud. The way it moved so fast, the way it all escalated so quickly. Tapping your phone line, scanning your cell phone. They were on to you before you left the facility and they had the counters initiated before you got home. You would have had surveillance on you before leaving your apartment for the train. That's quick. Quicker than anything the Secret Service could do. It indicates a highly professional input. CIA or NSA at least. Or at least a splinter cell, or highly financed ex-operatives. And to get a wet worker in so quickly."

"Wet worker?"

"An assassin," he paused. "We call it wet work. For obvious reasons."

Isobel grimaced. "But I don't get it. What are you saying? That the CIA are behind this?"

Stone shook his head. "Not exactly. The CIA aren't bad, but sometimes they have to do bad things. Occasionally they go way past their remit. Sometimes an agent goes too far. Can't see the wood for the trees... Look, it doesn't matter. Not just yet, anyway."

"You know something. Something you're not telling me." She looked at him accusingly.

"Please, level with me. I'm going out of my mind, I just want this to end."

"It's not as simple as that. I need to put things together properly, before I can draw a conclusion. But what happened at the bioresearch facility is merely the tip of the iceberg. I was on this investigation for months, before you took the drives. Several pieces of the jigsaw are missing and I have to find them and arrange them before I can start to put the whole picture together."

She looked at him, but decided against pressing the subject. "So where are we going now?"

"Montpelier, Vermont. I had a call this morning that I had somehow been expecting, giving me the news that I have been dreading."

"Which is?"

"I've got to go see a coroner."

## THIRTY FIVE

The motel was set approximately two hundred feet back from the road, situated within a well cultivated ring of privet. From the parking lot it looked as if you had driven into the center of a grand eighteenth century European maze and the goal, the reward for the accomplishment of reaching the middle was the delightful motel nestled inside.

He had parked outside on the side of the road and had moved quickly over the stretch of short grass to a vantage point between the dense hcdgcrow and the welcome sign and tariff at the entrance. From here he could watch the main entrance and from here he could see Isobel Bartlett and the government agent get out of the Mustang and go inside to the reception.

The parking lot was well lit, as too was the entrance to the reception and he was confident that from his position, crouched in the shadows, the back light would only add to the effect of darkness outside and he would be virtually invisible from the direction of the motel.

He could see Stone standing at the reception desk, conversing with the receptionist as she signed them in. Isobel Bartlett was standing at the window, well lit up from behind. Silhouetted and staring out into the darkness. She was looking directly at him, but from where she was, he knew that she would see nothing but the floodlit parking lot and not so far as to the cultivated gardens beyond. He enjoyed knowing that he was invisible to her, enjoyed the sensation of power. He raised his arm and pointed two fingers at her forehead. He sighted in as if aiming a large pistol and then mouthed a silent *boom.* The shot would have taken the top of her head off. He would have got off another shot before the agent moved. Hit him in the back of the head and watched him slump forwards onto the desk in front of the receptionist. He imagined it in frighteningly realistic images, could see everything in a movie format. He blinked tightly, clearing the fantastical images from his mind. Stone and Isobel were outside and back inside the Mustang. He heard the twin carbon steel exhaust pipes pop and gurgle as the big V8 engine fired up and he watched as the vehicle drove around fifty paces or so and parked outside a chalet to the right of the reception building. Stone swung round and reversed in to the space. Professionals never nose park their vehicles. The man noted this.

He watched them both get out and Stone carried a bag to the door. He remembered that Isobel had left her luggage back at *The Albany* and the memory of what had happened, the supremacy of those two shots, filled him with pride. Pride and confidence that he was on top form and would continue to have the advantage over his quarry. When the moment was right and when the objective was completed he would end their lives in a heartbeat.

They were already dead. They just didn't know it.

\*\*\*

"I need some clothes."

"We'll get you some tomorrow."

"And I've got no washing things. Nothing."

The room was a large family room with two king-sized beds and a fold out sofa-bed. Rob Stone dropped his sports bag onto the king-sized bed nearest to the door and flicked the television on with the remote. He sat down and searched for the news channel, and then dropped the remote onto the bed when he found it. "I'll get you everything you need in the morning," he said, with as much reassurance as he could muster. "Whatever you need, we'll get. It's on Uncle Sam." He got off the bed and stretched. "Look, they had a vending machine in reception. You wait here and I'll go and get you some wash things. The machine had razors, soap and toothpaste and brushes. I'll see what else they've got. Don't answer the door to anyone but me."

"Like I would." Her tone was sardonic, dry.

Stone pulled the blinds closed and the action didn't go unnoticed by Isobel. She shuddered at the thought of David Stein and what had happened back in New York, but it already felt an age away. She was exhausted, both physically and mentally and her mind was a blur. Stone smiled at her but it failed to lighten the mood. He opened the door, and looked back at her.

"I'll only be a few minutes," he said, again mustering all the reassurance he could.

The night air was cold and crisp and distinctly cleaner than it had been in New York. They were in the heart of Vermont and high in the mountain range the air couldn't get any purer. It carried a scent of pine needles and the odor of the forest vegetation. It reminded him of where he had been born and raised, far away from the large cities and everything that went with them.

He jogged up the short flight of steps and walked briskly into the reception foyer. A large man was checking in ahead of him, so he held back from the desk and allowed him some privacy. The walls of the foyer were donned with a variety of photographs, mostly of acrobatic skiing and snowboarding jumps, or fast turns with waves of clean, dry powdery snow. Stone assumed that this motel also served as a ski lodge, but only to those whose budget was lower than those who could afford to be in the mountains proper. Perhaps to the people who wanted a quick and easy route to the ski slopes but without the expense of being in the resorts paying resort prices. Simply call in, then drive a few miles further on to take the network of lifts to the slopes at the top and then spend the day enjoying the mountains.

The large man had finished checking in and was folding his wallet whilst holding the large tag of the key. He dropped it and bent down to pick it up, when he noticed Stone's feet just a pace away. He looked up and visibly flinched as he stared into Stone's face. He fumbled with his key and stood erect a full four or five inches taller than Stone. He seemed unable to make eye contact. He was impeccably attired in a smart, well-tailored business suit, crisp white shirt and a subtle floral print tie.

"Hello there," Stone smiled. He noticed the man's shoes. They were like black mirrors, boned to a shine. They reminded Stone of his time in the military. "Lovely evening," he added.

The man looked at him. Stone noticed a thin white scar running the whole length of his face. It seemed to shine in the spotlights above the desk.

"Yes. It is." The man seemed embarrassed. "And a lovely part of the country," he added, glancing back at the receptionist. "Good night."

She smiled and Stone nodded curtly and then stepped up to the desk. He placed a ten-dollar bill down on the counter and smiled at her. "I need some quarters and dollars please, for the machine." He nodded towards the vending machine in the corner of the foyer and glanced back but the man had already gone.

\*\*\*

Too close. Too close by far.

The man hurried towards his chalet door, looking over his shoulder as he went. He slipped the key into the lock and twisted. There was no play in the lock. He jiggled the key but was fearful of breaking it off in the lock. He dropped the sports bag and gun carry case onto the ground and the barrel of the stripped-down M4 assault rifle clattered on the concrete through the thin material. He slipped the key back out of the lock and tried again.

"You have to pull the door towards you."

The man jumped, startled by the voice. He tensed, let go of the key and slipped his hand onto the butt of his pistol and at the same time. He turned to the left, allowing the door to shield his right hand.

Stone stepped up to the threshold. "It happened with my door." He caught hold of the handle, pulled it towards him and twisted the key.

The man eased the pistol a little from the snug holster, wrapped his finger around the trigger.

"There you go!" Stone pushed the door in a little and held up the key. "Cheap locks, I reckon."

"Thanks," the man said, his voice devoid of all emotion. He released his grip on the pistol and took they key from him. He bent down and picked up the two bags in a hurry.

"Don't mention it," Stone replied. "Well, good night."

The man watched him walk along the path and to his chalet door. "Good night," he replied. And then he smiled and whispered, "Sweet dreams…"

## THIRTY SIX

"If you don't mind me asking, what were you investigating? In order to come up with a lead at the bioresearch facility?" Isobel was sprawled out on the queen-sized bed, a can of soda in one hand and pulling the tab with the other.

Stone was drinking coffee, freshly made from the packet of instants next to the kettle. It was loaded with sugar and powdered cream. He sipped it and grimaced. "I can't say, but it was always going to lead me there," he paused. "There was a major connection, that's all."

"A person?"

"Forget it," he chuckled. "I'm not going to crack."

She rolled carefully onto her side, ever tentative that the tiny wounds on her stomach would hurt her if she moved too quickly. She propped her head up on her elbow and looked at him with intrigue. "You said earlier, about the

President trusting you, trusting your family. What did you mean by that?"

Stone smiled. "I think I remember saying, it was a long story."

"Yes, but we really aren't going anywhere. At least not for a while." She took a sip of soda and looked dejected. "Come on, it will kill the time."

"I'll give you one thing, Isobel, you are persistent, if not subtle."

"It's what got me where I am today!" She scoffed. "For better or for worse."

"My older brother was an FBI agent. A good one," he relented. "He was highly commended, had all sorts of awards for bravery and all. But he got himself killed, as a result of his bravery or some would say stupidity. Prior to his death he stopped a major terrorist incident almost single handedly. I don't know the details myself. All I know is that because of that the president trusted him enough to give him a free rein." He looked away. It was hard to talk about his brother's death. "Anyway, he made a name for himself in certain circles."

"Which circles?"

"The ones that matter."

"And do you have the same name for yourself?" she asked. "In the same circles?"

"No."

"Why?"

"Because..."

"Because, what? Jesus, it's like getting blood out of a stone," she laughed. "Blood out of a stone... Agent Stone!"

"Funny."

"No, why? Why don't you have the same name in the same circles?"

"Because what I've achieved so far, I've done so in life. My brother made a mistake and ended up sacrificing himself because of it. He was brave, I'll certainly give him that, but he died because of it."

"What was he doing, when he died?"

"He was investigating something. Something big and something that someone wanted keeping quiet."

"And?"

"And he underestimated what he was up against."

"And you'll never do that?"

"No."

"Because you've learnt from his death, his mistake?"

"Yes."

"That sounds fairly arrogant. If you don't mind me saying?"

"I'm sure it does."

"So why won't you make the same mistake investigating this assignment, as your brother made with his?"

He stood up and put his cup down on the table, then picked up the remote for the television. He didn't like the conversation, wanted to get it over with. "Because I've got an advantage."

"Which is?"

"My brother died," he paused. "I know what I'm up against."

"But that was *his* assignment…"

"Yes. And now the same assignment is mine."

\*\*\*

The man was pleased with the clarity. He could hear every word of their conversation as clear as if they were in the same room. The screen of the laptop still showed Isobel Bartlett's location, and the transponder was working perfectly. He adjusted the volume on the receiver, keeping it low and ambient in the background. Just enough to catch the odd glimmer of conversation and enough to inform him that they were still there.

It sounded as if they were warming to each other, relaxing and becoming comfortable in one another's company. He was pleased. They would soon become over comfortable and that would soon lull them into making mistakes.

That would give him the advantage, and that would be their downfall.

He thought of the Secret Service agent and

smiled. What a silly profession he seemed to be in. A bullet catcher for men far from worth dying for. The protector of so-called democracy and freedom. By potentially giving their life so that others could continue to abuse their electoral power.

"Stone, Rob Stone," he said quietly. "Agent Robert Stone, of the Secret Service."

His brother had been in the FBI, he recalled. And he had been a very competent agent. But would the younger Stone prove to be better? He doubted it. He would dispatch him as efficiently as he had dispatched his brother. He thought back to the night, that cold, bleak night. It had been as dark as coal and raining heavily and he had used that to his advantage. The sound of the lashing rain had been loud and obtrusive and it had allowed him to get within two steps of the FBI agent, as he had searched the body of the cop for any sign of life. The rain had allowed him to get so close, granted him silence in his movements and he had been able to position the knife and clasp the agent tightly, hold him, clamp him from moving for the vital seconds it took to cut out his throat in just a few movements.

He had recalled watching, as he usually did, as the man had struggled to hold onto his life, kicking wildly, his hands clasping the open wound. The FBI agent knew he was dying, his eyes were so wide with terror. Then they had faded, accepting his fate. Death hadn't taken long. Not even two minutes for the unsuspecting agent to die in the pool of blood and rainwater, on that cold wintry night.

## THIRTY SEVEN

There were the deep reds and bright yellows of the leaves on the trees that only appeared in fall. A paradox that the most beautiful colors should come when summer is at all but an end. From a distance the foliage looked like the glowing embers of a forgotten fire, burning brilliantly though ever more moribund, in its last moments of existence before dying out completely.

The air was crisp and clean and autumnal. The change of season was in the air and with it the feeling of regret, of losing the impudence of summer, of having to face the dulling down of winter and the colder, darker months ahead. The sky was azure and the sun was opaque, lacking its brilliance as though exhausted from shining throughout the long hot summer.

The house was set back in a large clearing in the woods. The driveway cut through the trees from the quiet road approximately two hundred yards beyond. The trees cushioned and absorbed the occasional traffic, busier in the summer, less in the fall and scarce throughout the winter months. It was a back pass. A road connecting neighboring houses and beauty spots to the town, but finally arriving at a dead end roughly three-quarters of the way up the mountain to where a network of footpaths led to a scattering of hunting and fishing lodges on the fringe of the wilderness beyond. There was no other destination to be reached by the road and for six months of the year the road acted merely as a private drive for the residents dotted throughout the valley.

A tall maple towered alone and regal in the middle of a mounded knoll in the very center of the driveway. A swing hung from the lowest of the thick branches. It swayed gently, rhythmically in the breeze. Beneath it ground a deep channel in the dirt, worn through by the dragging feet of children outgrowing the seat's height. A child's bicycle, complete with stabilizers and red, white and blue ribbons trailing from the handlebars, sat propped against the wall of the house, abandoned by its rider in a hurry, most probably in favor of milk and cookies, or a much loved television show. It was a girl's bicycle and behind it, obscured from view, laid a boy's chopper-style bike with a battery-operated siren mounted in the middle of the tall handlebars. Less care had been taken with this bicycle, the tip of one of the handles had ground deep into the dirt and the front wheel was still spinning as its rider had left it in such wild and haphazard abandon.

He walked forward slowly. The property sounded quiet and deserted but he knew that the people were inside, knew that they would be waiting for his return. The day felt special, a day to be savored. He wanted to stand still and absorb the feeling, take it with him and hold it dear to him. He knew that his mother would be proud of him, had probably telephoned his aunts and uncles and cousins and told them of his achievements. He was a rarity in his family - the first they could think of who was actually attending college. Out of state and out of the small township at the end of the valley. From there the world would be his oyster. Although his family were far from poor, his father had worked at the lumberyard since the age of eighteen, as had his father before him. The mold had been broken, cracked from the cast and he was going to get the best education he could. And all thanks to his grades and partial scholarship and his father's hard work and overtime savings. He would make something of himself. Something of which the entire family could be proud.

His mother came out from the house, her arms behind her back fiddling with the strings of her apron. She was unaware that he was there and flinched when she saw him. Her face beamed brightly and she shouted something into the house. A little girl of about five years old came skipping out holding a half-eaten cookie the size of a tea saucer, followed by a boy of about nine. They smiled at him and waved excitedly and he grinned back, unable to contain the air of cool he had imagined and wanted to replicate on the bus home.

A tall, strong-looking man of about fifty walked out onto the porch. He was wiping his hands on a wash towel. He grinned and dropped the towel down onto a wicker chair. The family were smiling in unison, a picture of warmth and togetherness. He felt a tear at the corner of his eye and smiled back, as he walked across the dry earth driveway and towards his home.

He woke suddenly with a start. For a moment he was unsure what had happened, where he was and what he had been dreaming. Only now that he was back in the reality of the present day, he was sure that he had not been dreaming at all but had been merely remembering, recalling a past moment from his life.

He swung his legs over the edge of the bed and padded through to the bathroom and ran the faucet. He splashed a cupped handful of cold water over his face and rubbed it around his neck. It was icy and made him gasp momentarily, taking his breath away and refreshing him, un-clouding his mind all at once. He cupped his hand again and filled it like a vessel under the flow, then drank thirstily from it, supping the water down quickly. I t was thick and chalky and he could taste the fluoride in it. He spat out the remainder in his mouth, then rested both hands on the sink and stared long and hard into the mirror.

The memory had been as clear as crystal, like it had happened yesterday. The woman was the same woman as in his earlier memory, though older. And he was n o w sure that she had been real and he was convinced that she was indeed his mother. There was no doubt about it, which meant that the other people in this memory had been his family his brother, sister and father. For the first time, he felt emotion. It was raw and jagged and pulled at his soul like he had never imagined, nor ever previously experienced.

He walked back to the bedroom and looked at the screen of the laptop. I t showed nothing, had gone to standby. He ran his finger across the mouse pad and waited for the machine to come back to life. It took only a moment and when it did it showed the still, stationary red dot which indicated that the tracking device was immobile. He picked up the receiver and tested the transponder. He turned up the volume and could hear the faint sound of shared breathing, the fall and rise of two sets of lungs in close proximity.

Both Stone and Bartlett appeared to be sleeping. He only wished that his orders had been to eliminate, and not to follow. They would have stood next to no chance, sound asleep and off guard.

He turned the volume back down and walked back to the bed. A part of him wanted to relax and return to the dream, or the memory, or whatever it had been. The thought comforted him, made him feel warm and wanted. He sat down and swung his legs flat, rested his hands behind his head and closed his eyes. Only a part of him wanted the memory to return. And it was the part of him that had started to feel anxiety and curiosity at not knowing his past. The other part of him, the element that housed his survival instincts and desire for self-preservation wanted nothing more of it. Wanted the whole affair forgotten and put away back in the dark recesses of his mind. In essence, it was merely the part of him that was scared of what he may remember next.

## THIRTY EIGHT

The coffee was fresh out of a vending machine and hot. It came in a plastic cup. The cup defied the logic and probabilities of both physics and chemistry combined and seemed hotter itself than the liquid it held. The cup also possessed the ability to morph itself into any shape, except that of an original cup.

Stone looked across at Isobel, who was having the same problem with her plastic cup. It had morphed into a conical, semi-triangular receptacle and was threatening to spill the scalding liquid into her lap unless she sipped some immediately. He looked across the table at Captain Dolbeck who seemed to have conquered the quandary through attrition. Experience had taught the police captain that three cups were indeed better than one and as he sipped a mouthful of steaming coffee, he did so with both grace and confidence.

Stone put the cup on the desk in front of him, and as he did so he watched as the cup morphed once more to its original shape.

"You get used to it," Captain Dolbeck paused. "Those damn cups." He held the stack of cups high and smiled at Isobel. "Two cents worth of coffee and ten cents of plastic, all for two dollars and a taste like a mouthful of shit... if you'll excuse my profanity, ma'am."

She smiled and placed her cup alongside Stone's on the table.

Last night they had eaten a delivered pizza and dough balls in the room with sodas from the vending machine in reception. This morning they had risen early, breakfasted on complimentary coffee and a selection of donuts piled high from a cardboard takeout box in the foyer of the reception building. The drive had taken an hour with a short stop off at a clothes store at a retail park on the side of the highway where Stone had bought a sports-bag, a thick suede jacket and a selection of underwear and clothes for Isobel. As she picked out the underwear from the racks, he had felt uncomfortable. Watching her choose what she liked was teasing at his professionalism to the job in hand. She had asked his opinion, just casually, possibly simply for something to say but he had found himself wanting to comment and more than on a cellular level. He looked at her, studied her

311

figure, her looks, her glossy dark hair – could imagine himself being attracted to her, had he met her in a bar someplace. Maybe even make a move on her with drinks and some corny chat up lines. He wanted to keep his head clear of such thoughts, wanted her to choose the damn underwear and leave the store. When she had chosen what she needed, he bundled it off her and dropped it down on the counter without a word. His credit card was in his hand and there was no eye contact between them until they reached the parked Mustang. She had touched his arm and thanked him for the purchases. He shrugged it off quickly and had made a flippant comment that it was merely expenses and that he would get reimbursed. After that, they hadn't said much.

Now seated in Captain Dolbeck's office inside the police headquarters in Montpelier, they had said even less to each other as the police captain had brought them coffee in the ridiculously implausible plastic cups from the two-dollar vending machine in the hall.

"We got the body out of the lake on Saturday morning," Dolbeck said. He yawned and stretched, like he had had a rough night. Stone looked at him and believed he had, but then again, the man had looked the same a few of days before. Maybe the guy just looked rough. "A twelve year old boy found him, poor lad.

Floating face up in a bunch of weeds. The boy was fishing out on the lake over at Kennett's Ridge. Kid's hook and line tangled in the weeds and he heaved the bunch of weeds to the shore. Got a mighty big surprise when he went to check his line."

"What happened?" Stone asked. "Or is it too early to know just yet?"

"Well an autopsy will have to be done but the guy took a bullet straight to the forehead. Either a big-ass .44 or .45 magnum or something like a .50 Action Express. Having said that, it could well have been a double-tap from a medium caliber handgun, I'd say but don't quote me. The hole was real ragged, so I'd go with a quick one-two from something like a 9mm. Damn good shot, if that is the case. I mean exceptional. It took the whole back of his head off whatever it was. Just like a ripe watermelon. Just the face and a bit of the top of his head left. Just left it looking like an empty shell." Isobel cringed, grimaced at the thought of the vivid picture the police captain had painted. "You okay, lady?"

She nodded, picked up her cup and hurried a sip of coffee. "Fine, yes, just fine."

"I'll have to wait for the coroner of course, or assistant coroner. Hell, maybe the guy will be the chief coroner now. Guess he'll have to interview like anybody else. But he's a fine examiner. Anyway, the verdict should be an open and shut one. We can rule out suicide because the guy's hands were tied together with a length of wire. Real tight, and it cut real deep too. He must've struggled and panicked at the very end because it had cut through to the bone in some places. Like he was struggling for his life. Which he was, I guess..."

"You said the coroner had a history of infidelity," Stone ruminated. "Jealous husband maybe?"

"Well, you sure as shit don't want it to be, do you?" Dolbeck smiled.

Stone returned the smile. "Well, no. No it would be better for my investigation if it wasn't."

"Well, I wouldn't like to hazard a guess. The guy *did* have trouble keeping his pecker in his pants, that's for sure." He looked at Isobel. "Once again ma'am, sorry for any profanity." She shrugged like it didn't bother her either way and there was no need for an apology. He smiled and turned back towards Stone. "Affairs are quite common up here. Most get settled with a fist in the face. Or a few windows smashed on a guy's automobile. I haven't seen a murder for one, not cold blooded at least. Mind you, if you saw his wife, you'd have to ask yourself why this man played away from the marital bed. She's quite a looker, that's for sure. But hey, if she doesn't put out at night then the guy's got to go elsewhere, right? Either way, the guy did have a reputation for the ladies and he had an affair a short while ago, according to his wife. That's why she didn't file a missing person report until a couple of days ago and why we didn't move our asses as quick as we would have for someone without a history of doing such things." He sipped some coffee from the stack of three plastic cups and smiled. "I really wouldn't say it was a jealous husband though. I may be wrong and again, don't quote me, but this is upstate Vermont. If a guy's doing something he shouldn't be doing, the men around here are likely to kick his ass big style out in the back lot of a bar the old fashioned way. Then they're just as likely to shake the guy's hand, buy him a drink and moan about their wife to him all night long. Hell, shit happens from time to time, but tying the guy up and blowing the back of his head out is a bit too gangland California for these parts. Besides, most people have hunting rifles or shotguns up here. A handgun has little or no use to the folk around here."

Stone nodded. "Well, that helps me a little," he paused. "Do you mind if I take a look at the log for around the time professor Leipzig was killed. A few days both sides of it would be all I need."

"Sure," Captain Dolbeck said. He stood up and eased his substantial bulk around the desk.

"I'll just be a few minutes."

When he left the room Isobel looked at Stone and frowned. "What is all this about? And where does Professor Leipzig fit into this?"

"Just faceless pieces of the same jigsaw puzzle. Hopefully we'll get a picture if we look hard enough."

*"We?* Since when was it *we?"* She retorted. "I've just been dragged here, I'm not even part of this..."

"You took the damn drives, Isobel. What more of a part do you want? Hell, with what you did, you could sit in jail and rot before you got as much as a hearing. That's the way treason works."

"Treason!" She snapped. "I was *saving* people!"

Stone laughed cynically. "Certain people could make treason stick on you like glue. From now on, you're with me, helping me with this investigation."

"Since when?"

"Since treason still carries the death penalty," Stone said sardonically. "Since you became useful to me. Since I worked out a vital missing link in this puzzle, just a minute ago in this room ..." He stopped mid-sentence as Dolbeck walked back in.

The police captain was eating something, his cheeks full, like a chipmunk with a mouthful of nuts. Sugar glistened from the comers of the man's mouth and Stone concluded the he had swiped a jelly donut. "Here it is, right here. Lord only knows what use this will be to you. Professor Leipzig's accident was merely recorded, along with the· time and outcome. Casualties, location etc..."

Stone skipped the night of Leipzig's accident and looked at the rest of the log. He took a small leather-bound notebook out from his jacket pocket and started to write notes with a short stubby pencil. He flicked through the pages of the log and continued to write. The silence that accompanied his actions was deafening in its serene totality. Captain Dolbeck glanced somewhat awkwardly at Isobel, who simply smiled back amiably. After a few minutes, Stone stopped writing, closed the pages of the log and placed it down on the table. He took a sip of coffee from the flimsy plastic cup and smiled at the police captain.

"Thank you for your help," he paused, as he stood up. "We'll take up no more of your day."

## THIRTY NINE

The sun was bright and the sky was a pale blue with scattered drifts of cotton candy cloud. People who knew what they were talking about would probably have called it Cumulus and Strata Cumulus cloud, but to both Stone and Isobel alike, they would have described it like children's cotton candy. Besides, cotton candy seemed a far nicer way to describe the sporadic puffs of white passing gently through the crystalline blue sky.

The sun was in their eyes as Stone pulled off the highway and onto a slip road towards a small town signposted as South Chesterton (pop. 1032).

"I feel like I'm in the Deep South," Isobel commented. "Full of good 'old boys with pickup trucks and shotguns stowed in the gun rack behind the seat." She laughed. "Population one thousand and thirty two, Jesus. You can just imagine the mayor, who also runs the gas station, running down to the sign and changing the number each time a woman gives birth, or some old timer gives out."

Stone laughed with her. "Strange place, Vermont. Money all over the place. Ski resorts, hunting lodges for the wealthy city gents, farms and country businesses thriving, yet with little pockets of resistance dotted throughout."

"I'm sure that South Chesterton is quite lovely," she said. "But it sounds real hokey to me, at least it does from the sign."

They drove onwards and as they neared the town they were first greeted with a balustrade of tall, mature spruce either side of the road. They had obviously been planted by hand many years previous, no doubt with the unselfish foresight so often demonstrated by people who orchestrated such projects, but who would never live long enough to see them through to fruition. Whatever the reason behind the planting of the spruces, it certainly created a dramatic and beautiful effect as they neared the town, channeled towards the outskirts of the settlement by a tunnel of tall, monumental trees.

Stone had to shield his eyes from the glare of the sun as he drove. The effect of the vehicle's speed, coupled with the bright sunlight, led to a strobe-like effect as they were met with light-then-shade-then-light as they passed each thick trunk of the trees. He had read of similar plantings in France, ordered by Napoleon himself and suffered by the French almost two centuries later as cars passed those same trees. In many cases, every other tree had been felled to prevent the drivers of fast moving vehicles becoming entranced by the hypnotic effect. He figured that either the inhabitants of South Chesterton drove slower than the national limit, or that they just didn't give a damn about the potential for accidents occurred as a direct result of their beloved balustrade.

The sign once again gave the name of the town and the population in case anyone entering had forgotten, but Stone didn't recon anybody would. As he drove in past the neat rows of prefabricated houses, each with picket fences and tidy, well-kept lawns, he slowed his speed and started to look around for the town center.

"It doesn't look as hokey as it sounded," Isobel commented. " It looks as though there's a little money at least."

"And where there's a little money, you can always bet one thing…"

"What's that?"

"There's people with less."

Stone swung the car in front of a quiet looking diner, which was simply called *Annie's,* and was scripted, in a flowery, italic font. Blue writing on a brilliant white sign with a red border. "Very patriotic," Isobel said. "I'm sensing blueberry or apple pie on the menu. Maybe even Maryland chicken with corn and biscuits."

"And don't forget the gravy," Stone smiled. "Giblet gravy and a side of chidlings."

He switched off the engine and looked around the deserted town. Away in the distance he noticed an old man riding and even older bicycle. He was heading the other way.

"So what are we doing here?" Isobel unbuckled her seat belt and checked her face in the vanity mirror. "It's a little early for lunch."

"I want to ask about, find a few things out." He reached into his pocket and retrieved the notebook that he had used in Captain Dolbeck's office. He studied the pages for a moment, and then opened the door.

*Annie's* was clean and well presented with mainly pictures of local fishermen on the walls proudly showing off their various catches. Huge trout and catfish. A Sixties Whirlitzer played in the furthest-most comer, quietly sending out the dulcet tones of Elvis Presley singing *Love Me Tender.* Stone walked up to the counter, followed closely by Isobel. She nudged him and pointed towards a sign for blueberry pie. They both smiled as he pointed to the sign for extras that was chalked up on a blackboard, which included giblet gravy and creamed corn. He suddenly felt very cosmopolitan, and at the same time, very arrogant. He reeled himself back in and coughed for the waitress's attention.

"Good morning, Ma'am," he smiled, as she turned around. "Can I get an orange juice and a..." He looked to Isobel.

"A coffee, please."

"...And a coffee, thanks." The waitress nodded curtly and poured the coffee first. She placed it down next to Isobel, and left her a large pot of cream and a bowl of sugar. She poured Stone's orange juice from a large glass jug, straight from the chill- cabinet and put it in front of him. He dropped a five-dollar bill on the table and smiled. "Perhaps you could help us? We're looking for a man who lives in these parts. "

"Sure, I'll try. Go ahead." She said, taking the five and ringing it through the till. She dropped the change onto a tea plate and handed it over to him. "If he lives out here, I'll know him."

Stone smiled. "Joe Carver. Around seventy years of age..."

"Hobo Joe," she scoffed. "Yeah, I know him. Those two are more trouble than they're worth. Couple of old tramps."

"Who else?" Stone asked.

"Jeff... Don't know his surname. They live out in the woods, somewhere in the hills towards Hawk's Ridge. Always falling out, then getting drunk and becoming the best of pals again. They don't come into town much anymore, on account of the beating they both got when they ruffled a few feathers down at *The Lockup."*

"The Lockup?" Isobel asked. "What's that?"

"Honey, you don't want to go there. The place is a bar down on Canyon Drive. The building was a jail back around the civil war. Hence the name. It's out of town, but the young and the dumb come from all around on account that they don't mind who they serve. Kids and college students mainly. And those barred from other places... Stick to the *Woodsman Lodge* across the way." She pointed across the street at a log-paneled building. "That place is a bit classier, serves the weekend skiing set in the winter and the environmental lot through the summer months."

"So where can I find Hobo Joe?" Stone asked.

She looked at her wristwatch and frowned. "Round about now, I'd try the fishing hole on the edge of town. Just west of here past the general stores and on for about two miles." She looked thoughtful for a moment. "Yeah, that should be about right. He catches trout and catfish and sells them to the general store or the hotel out on Brenham's View. Just gets beer money, but that's good enough for him."

"And if he's not there?"

"Then he's out in the woods someplace,"

she paused. "And you ain't never going to find him out there."

"Thanks," Stone finished his orange juice and waited as Isobel hurried her coffee down. He dropped another couple of fives on the counter and smiled at the waitress. "You've been a great help."

"Thank you, honey," she smiled. "You have yourselves a nice day."

The Mustang was loud and ostentatious and Stone was very much aware of it as he ambled along the street and headed towards the opposite side of town. The car was suitable for city and suburban life, but out here in the country, in the mountains in particular, it was far from discreet. The exhaust rumbled loudly and he refrained from using too much throttle as he crawled along the street.

"So who's Hobo Joe?" Isobel leant back in her seat and watched the rows of neat houses pass by. "How does he fit into all this?"

"I'd rather not say, just a hunch at the moment," he paused. "But there was more to the log back at Captain Dolbeck's office than I had first realized on my previous visit."

"Such as?"

"A coincidence."

"And from that, you can make the right assumptions?"

"I don't like assumptions," Stone paused. "Besides, you know what they say about assumption being the mother of all disaster?"

She laughed. "So if not an assumption?"

"A hunch. And like I said about the early days of this investigation, it was anomalies that led me to the door of the bioresearch facility. Nothing more than two plus two."

"Adds up to four, last I tried."

Stone looked around, but kept heading straight out of town. He craned his neck to see through a bank of trees to his left and smiled. "That looks like the place," he said. "There's water through the trees, it must be the fishing hole." He swung the Mustang across the road and into a narrow lane. The lane widened quickly and became a large piece of flat ground. There were tire tracks ground into the dry earth and it was obvious that the place was a regular haunt for people, most probably the residents of South Chesterton.

"What a delightful setting," Isobel remarked, as they rounded a visual barrier of tall water reeds and they caught sight of the fishing hole.

Indeed it was a delightful setting. And far removed from the images that the name had conjured. It was a small lake really, but probably still around three acres in size, with a small waterfall over flat rocks at the narrowest edge and what looked like a fast moving brook at the opposite end. In the middle of the lake was a tiny wooded island about forty feet by sixty with a small clearing in the center. The lake looked shallow at the shore, from anywhere between mere inches to just a few feet deep, depending on the height of the bank and was the darkest of blues further out, indicating a considerable depth.

Stone switched off the Mustang's engine and the silence was almost eerie in comparison. He looked across at Isobel and smiled. "Let's take a walk."

The earth was soft yet dry and it was apparent that the clearing acted as a parking lot for the visitors but apart from the Mustang, it was completely deserted. They walked over to the water's edge and looked out across the smooth water of the lake. At four points, divided almost equally, there was a single white life-saving ring held high in view by a post. Each had a coil of orange buoy line gathered neatly and hooked to the post underneath.

"Imagine swimming here in the summer," Isobel sighed somewhat dreamily. "I bet it's wonderful. Swimming all afternoon and barbequing and drinking wine in the setting sun…"

"Sounds agreeable," Stone agreed. "Are you

a country girl at heart?"

"Oh yes. I used to live in Ohio as a child," she said. "Masses of wide open spaces and fields as far as the eye could see."

"I know."

"You've spent time in Ohio?" she asked.

"No. I just know you used to live out there."

She looked at him for a moment, puzzled, then flinched away as she realized what he had said. "Anything else you know about me that you'd care to share?" she snapped.

"I didn't mean to offend you," he apologized. "Sorry, I shouldn't have."

"'No, you shouldn't have." She walked away from him and paced along the shore, counter-clockwise to the lake.

"Hey, wait up!" He jogged quickly to catch her up and caught hold of her elbow. "I'm sorry, it's just my ..."

She spun around and glared at him. "Your what? Your job?" She snapped. "Well I don't have to like it. What else do you know about me?"

"It doesn't matter."

"The hell it doesn't!"

"Look, calm down and get it into perspective. You waltzed out of a government-contracted building with the next doomsday bug in your handbag and expect me to know nothing about you? You're lucky it's me on the case and not

327

some gung-ho Virginia farm boy from Langley. If it were, you'd be hauled in front of a judge, excluded bail and left to rot until everyone else had forgotten your damned name or that you ever existed."

"Oh, I'm supposed to be grateful?"

"No. Look, I'm sorry, I…" he paused, looked past her and smiled. She glanced over her shoulder, and then looked back at him.

"What?"

"I think we've found our tramp, that's what…"

"What?" She looked around and stared, but couldn't see anybody. She turned back to Stone, but he was already past her and walking towards the furthest most shore.

They walked silently along the bank and it wasn't until the last few strides that Isobel noticed the man squatting in the reeds, a large old fashioned fishing pole clasped in his hands.

"I was wondering when you'd find me," the man said as they approached. "That damn car will have frightened off the fish. Sounded like the baying hounds of Hell. Your exhaust pipes need a look at?"

Stone smiled. "No, they're meant to sound like that."

"Can't imagine why," the man scoffed.

"I race, occasionally. Classic races, drag

events, that sort of thing," Stone paused. "Are you into cars?"

"No, just know when one's too damn loud, is all."

"Would you be Joe Carver?"

"Maybe."

"Maybe yes, or maybe no?"

"Just maybe." He lifted the pole and the hook and bait came clear of the water. He then swung the pole out across the lake and the bait dropped around ten feet farther out. He kept the tip of the pole close to the water, squinting in the sun's glare, but keeping his eyes on the water the whole time. "You both police?"

"Sort of."

"How can you be sort of?"

"Same as you're a maybe," Stone chided. "My name's Rob Stone, this is my colleague, Isobel. I'm an agent with the Secret Service."

"And what business does the Secret Service have out at my fishing hole?" Carver reached into his fishing sack and retrieved a bottle of cheap label whisky. "Care for an aperitif?" he laughed. "I didn't know I'd have the company of a lady, otherwise I'd have had some Martini in, but at such short notice..."

Isobel smiled. "No thanks, a bit early for me."

"Ah! Never too early, never too on time and never too late." He swallowed a large mouthful from the neck of the bottle and gasped, satisfied.

"So if you're maybe Joe Carver, you'd maybe interested in talking about your missing friend?" Stone asked.

"What do you know about Jeff?" He looked concerned and made to get to his feet. "Is he OK?"

Stone shook his head. "I don't know, but I know one thing," he paused. "The police didn't take you seriously, but if you level with me, I will."

The man nodded. "Sure, whatever you say."

"Good. I take it you *are* Joe Carver?"

"Yeah man, that's me." He wiped his brow with the back of his hand and a silver bracelet slipped down from his sleeve.

Stone noticed it, looked at the bracelet curiously. "MIA?"

"Yeah."

"Missing in action," he said to Isobel. "Vietnam, obviously."

"Yeah," Carver smiled. "One of the lucky ones. They let me go. Kept two thousand of our boys and still have them." He raised his bottle. "God save their souls!" He took a long pull on the bottle and then stared out across the water for a moment, silent.

"Who were you with?"

Joe Carver laughed. "A shit-load of scared kids, that's who I was with, man." He looked at Stone. "What's it to you?"

"Just interested, that's all."

"Yeah, well I don't get interested in talking to kids who were too young to be there."

"Hell, it was your war, do what you want with it," Stone said.

Carver took another swig from the bottle and looked at his boots. They were army issue and worn to nothing. More holes than fabric and leather. "What would you know about war, Secret Service man? All dolled up in your Armani suit and expensive leather shoes. Why the fuck would you want to know about the hell of war?"

"Hey, like I said, it was your war, keep it with you."

"And what war was yours? What would you know about it anyhow?"

"Afghanistan. All that was on offer at the time."

"No shit," Carver smiled. "A brother in arms..."

"One tour. Nothing in comparison to yours, I'm sure. But we saw some shit..."

"Hey man, in war, there's no such thing as an easy ride. Battle is battle and only we know, right?" He smiled up at him and raised the bottle. "Here's to the lost and the fallen, and the one's still carrying it with them."

"No, not the one's still carrying it with them," Stone said. "If they try, they can leave it where it ended. On the battlefield. That's the best place for it."

Carver looked at him. "It's *that* easy, right?"

"No. It's real tough. But it can be done," he paused. "If you can get on the right track. There are people who can help, if you let them. You guys had nothing at the time, but there's a real infrastructure of help now. You could get some help if you wanted it."

Carver drank some more and grinned. "Well maybe I'll get a card off you later, Mister Counsellor." He laughed and jiggled the fishing pole a little, then let it go still once more.

Stone smiled. "So what about Jeff, what's the deal with him?"

Carver sighed. "He just plain disappeared. About a week ago now. Not a word, not so much as a note. It just doesn't add up."

"Why?" Stone asked. "He's homeless, right?"

"No way!" Carver snapped aggressively. "And nor am I. We live out in the woods a way. He has his own place, and I have mine. We may be out of the system and unregistered, but we have homes and don't stick our hands out for nothin' or nobody."

"What sort of homes do you have?" Isobel asked.

"Cabins. Prospector types. I started out here

with an A-frame survival shelter, built from branches and awning and crap that nobody wanted. Then slowly, bit-by-bit, I got to building a log cabin. It's warm and dry and it does for me. City slickers pay a hell of a lot more for a weekend in less."

"I'm sure it's lovely," she commented amiably.

"That it is." Carver smiled at her, then turned towards Stone. "Jeff and me just finished his, and then he ups and disappears into nowhere."

"I see," Stone said. "Tell me, does he have any family or other friends?"

"Nope. Not a soul. Accept for me. He's ex-army too. But he didn't see battle, on account he's twenty years younger than me. Just trained for it for twenty years. I guess that's worse in a way."

Stone looked out across the lake. He felt a chill in the air, but couldn't decide whether it was just him, or if the temperature had dropped a little. He shivered.

Carver stood up excitedly. "I thought that damn race car of yours had scared them off! But looks like I was wrong!" He held the rod firmly and staggered nearer to the bank of the lake. "Come to papa! Come and get your kisser on my lovely sharp hook!"

Isobel laughed. The sight of the old hobo, unsteady on his feet, numbed by almost a whole bottle of cheap whisky was somewhat amusing.

Stone stepped back out of the man's way and watched the water. Again, he felt the chill. It ran up his spine and tickled at the nape of his neck.

"That's it... See? Watch the pole, he's tugging it hard, just a little more and I can make the strike," Joe Carver was transfixed, possessed by the tip of the pole and the subtle movements it made. "That's it ... There she is... Nice and tasty, come take a bite ... Yes! She's on the hook!" He did a little war dance and pulled the rod upwards. "Look who's coming for supper..."

The bullet passed cleanly through his neck and cut him silent, mid-sentence. He spun around like a top and dropped to his knees and stared directly into Isobel's eyes. He looked puzzled, pleading and shocked. His eyes seemed to question her, ask her what was happening. The second shot took the top half of his head off in an explosion of crimson and pink and white.

For a moment, she stared disbelievingly into the sun, partially blinded by its glare and unable to comprehend what she had just witnessed. And then she felt the dull thud to her side and dropped heavily to the ground.

## FORTY

Simply registering at the local video library puts you onto a computer database. If that computer database has a modem, router and internet access, then the moment it logs onto the net, your information can be viewed by anyone with the means, knowledge or inclination to do so.

That is at the most basic level. Take into account the vast amounts of legitimate organizations or services that hold your information on file, and the limits are unbounded. Medical surgeries, banks, credit companies, hospitals, finance administrators, social networking sites and lawyer firms are to name but a few. Add to this any civil or federal law enforcement agencies, who subsequently share information and there is no fragment of your life that people cannot tap into.

Each credit card or bankcard transaction is logged by time and date, the amount spent and the location address. The same goes for any transaction done at a bank's counter, or even over the telephone to authorize a transfer in funds. No money can be debited or credited to another account without the same information being logged. And needless to say, the same is true for extra services your bank provides. Each new service is registered as a transaction whether money changes hands or not. This does not simply apply to banks in general. Indeed, any change or update of information is called an information transaction.

For the computer security expert, it does not take long to find what they are looking for, as long as they have the basic details to start with.

The apartment was cold and bare and unfurnished, except for a table and a single straight-backed wooden chair. It was a bolt-hole, one of many around the country on short-term leases. It was on the third floor of a tenement building, and had direct access to the fire escape outside the window. From the security aspect it was about perfect. There were two exits and no furniture or trappings where vital details could be lost or misplaced, so that when the occupant left, everything with them simply disappeared.

On the table was a laptop computer and a rectangular plastic box around ten inches by twelve and four inches deep. From the side of the box protruded a USB cable that linked directly into the computer. From the computer a cable fed out into the telephone socket in the wall. A power cable fed through a power break unit before trailing off to the sockets above the skirting board, right by the telephone socket. The additional box housed a hard drive with approximately one hundred times the processing power available to home PC's. It was a military design used in the application of housing the billions of codes needed for the launch of intercontinental ballistic missiles (ICBMs). For this application, however, it provided raw power.

At the table sat a gaunt looking man in his early forties wearing a pair of dark, seventies-style pilot sunglasses. His hair was black and thinning and a little greasy and he was holding onto his youth by sporting a ponytail. A neatly trimmed goatee hid his thin lips and weak chin and like so many ponytail wearers, he also displayed an earring in the lobe of his left ear. A cigarette hung loosely from the corner of his mouth and an empty Chinese takeout carton acted as an over-filling makeshift ashtray.

His fingers were long and dexterous and played across the keyboard with as much poise and grace and precision as that of a concert pianist. His eyes never once left the screen and he never once made a typing error. The reams of information spieled across the screen and the extra hard drive whirled and clicked and cracked beside him as it processed the information and threw up what he was looking for.

He paused occasionally to glance down at an open notebook beside him, but his fingers merely slowed momentarily and he kept typing throughout. His thumb glided across the mouse pad and sent the cursor where he wanted with precision, and the casual observer would not have even seen his fingers leave the keys to click the cursor in place.

As if stunned by an electric shock he suddenly ceased typing and his shoulders went slack. He leant back in the chair and took the cigarette out of his mouth and stubbed it out into the carton. He looked pleased with himself, almost triumphant. He had what he had been searching for. It had taken one hour and seven minutes but he had now pinpointed the last information transaction made in the name of Isobel Bartlett.

His next search started when he typed in: Robert Stone.

## FORTY ONE

She couldn't breathe. Couldn't force the air into her heaving lungs no matter how hard she tried. She wanted to scream. Wanted to cry. Wanted someone to tell he was going to be all right. She had banged her head as she had fallen and there was a solid thudding in her ears and she felt dazed, sure she would slip into unconsciousness and never wake from her sleep.

She felt rough hands on her, prodding her, holding her at the same time. She could see the tops of the trees in her periphery. She saw the cotton candy clouds passing slowly overhead. The sky was a crystalline blue, washed out. Like an artist brushing the paper of a water color painting with mostly water, and the merest hint of paint. It was unbelievably pale. She wasn't sure if the tone of her vision had paled significantly, like her senses were starting to fade out, heading her towards the unknown.

She managed a little air into her lungs and was grateful for a few more moments to reflect, to prepare herself for what may or may not lie ahead. And as she watched the clouds pass peacefully overhead she also reflected in the beauty of the day and that it was perhaps not the worst day on which to die.

Stone was on top of her now, looking into her eyes and feeling her stomach. He looked worried, shocked but at the same time there was a determined glint in his eye a look of power and purpose. He was focused.

"Isobel," he said quietly, yet there was an underlying tone of desperation in his voice. "Isobel, are you OK?"

She shook her head, tears in her eyes. "I... I've been hit..."

He looked shocked, puzzled. "Where?" He looked at her again, all the while keeping his head below the height of the reeds. "Tell me where!"

"My side," she said weakly. She laid her hand down flat across her waist and rolled her head almost incoherently. "Just here..."

For a fleeting moment Stone smiled, a look of relief upon his face. "No, you haven't... That's where my shoulder hit you when I took you down..."

The moment the second shot had been fired, the same moment that Joe Carver's head had disappeared in a puff of red mist, Stone had recovered his senses and had taken Isobel to the floor with all the power and force and speed he could muster. Like a blocker taking down a wide receiver on the twenty-yard line, around a hundred and ninety pounds of muscle had cannoned into her slightly built frame and taken her out of the line of fire.

"But... I'm sure I've been hit. .." She breathed heavily. She was winded to the core. "And my head..."

Stone rolled off her and kept his left arm across her shoulders, pinning her to the dirt. His eyes were scanning through the reeds, looking for a hint of movement. He had drawn the pistol from its holster and had it ready to aim. Isobel made to get up but he held her firm.

"Stay still! Move, and he'll fire," he said firmly. "Are you OK?"

She grimaced. "I guess... My head hurts like hell though."

Stone glanced across at the mess that was Joe Carver. He refrained from making a comparison to Carver's head. The man was infinitely worse off.

"I can't see anything," he said. "I have to be able to flush him out before we can move. I need to know where he is."

"Do you think it's the same gunman?" She

winced. "He couldn't have followed us from New York, could he?"

"I'm not sure. Seems too much of a coincidence not to be."

"What are we going to do? We can't stay here."

There was a sudden eruption of earth and reeds and small stones and Stone heaved her closer to him, rolled over and over and they reached the edge of a small embankment. He pulled and heaved again, and they rolled and slipped down the four feet or so to the bottom and into a muddy quagmire.

"That answers that," he said. He stood to a crouch and looked back towards the area of open ground where he had parked the mustang. "It's too far. He must be up in the woods and ..." He was cut short by a plume of mud that sprung up from the top of the bank just in front of his face. He dropped down again, and kept a hand on Isobel's shoulder to hold her still. He wiped the mud out of his face and the corner of his eyes with his sleeve. He looked down at her, his face grim. "The bastard is playing with us... I was a clear target. He took Joe Carver down with two well-aimed shots... And if it's the same guy as in New York, he wouldn't have missed me just then."

"What are we going to do?" She looked anxiously at him. "Can't you shoot back?"

"Too far," he commented flatly. "I can't see him. I can't hear him either, his gun has a suppressor. A silencer. But there's no cover for two hundred yards. He is well out of range for an accurate pistol shot. I might get him with a volley of shots, but I've got to be able to see the bastard first. Besides, it would just be a waste of precious ammo."

"How much have you got?"

"Twelve in this clip, four in the one left from the shootout at the hotel. Damn it! I've got a carton of fifty in the trunk of the Mustang. I can't afford to waste any by shooting wildly."

As he craned his neck to see if he could spot the sniper he thought back to his first patrol in Afghanistan. An old hand left his heavy M9 pistol and spare magazines in camp in favor of another half dozen clips for his M16 rifle. He saw Stone watching curiously and had said, "The day you need to use a pistol is the day you wish you had a rifle..." Stone finally knew what he had meant.

Another shower of dirt hit them, this time from further to their right. "The bastard's moving! He's creeping around on us, trying to out flank us..." He looked down at her, his face determined. "We've got to move, and move fast. Are you all right to run?"

"I'll have to be," she replied flatly. "Just

don't leave me..."

"Never."

He caught hold of her and heaved her to her feet. There was approximately twenty yards of quagmire, and then a little brook. After that it appeared to be just forest and dry, uneven ground.

They moved as quickly as they could through the marsh, sinking to their knees and becoming fleetingly stuck with every tread. Stone pushed Isobel ahead of him and attempted to cover the rear ground with the pistol. In reality, he knew it was in vain – the sniper was simply too skillful. However, he had moved once and maybe he was moving at the same time they were and unable to take a shot, or even see them heading away.

There were no more shots, because no more mud imploded from the ground. Maybe there were shots, maybe the bullets passed right past them and into the dense woods but Stone didn't know and nor did he care. There were enough trees behind them now, enough obstacles in the line of fire to deflect the bullets. They just had to keep moving, had to keep those obstacles between them and the man with the rifle.

***

He had watched the Secret Service man through the clear reticule of the sniper scope. He had held the cross hairs on his forehead for a split second and had then indulged himself with lining the sight up on the woman. He mouthed a bang through pursed lips as he did so, on both of them and had then got down to the business of lining up on his kill.

The old tramp had been prancing around and dancing like a fool. It had not been the easiest of shots and he had had to move across to his left a few feet to avoid the bullet passing straight through the old tramp and into Isobel Bartlett. When the man had finally slowed his prancing and concentrated on the fish in the water, he had squeezed the trigger and hit his aim-point to the mark. He had wanted the man to die on the ground and watch the two bystander's indecision through the clarity of the lens, but there was no hard and fast rules for how a person reacts to being shot and the follow-up shot had come a split second later purely by instinct.

What he hadn't bargained on was the sheer speed and velocity in which Stone had moved, and the speed in which they had disappeared completely from view.

He had been forced to move fast, gain higher ground to clear the reeds and head out further along the lake to try for another angle. He had seen the Secret Service man pop his head above the proverbial parapet but he didn't want to kill him just yet. He needed to flush them out, keep up the pace and panic them into making a futile mistake. Only then, only when he had the location of the drives, would he hunt them down and take his shot for real.

\*\*\*

Stone kept Isobel ahead of him, pushing her onwards when she fell back and lost pace. At the same time he guided her ordering her left or right to avoid obstructions like giant boulders or fallen trees. Better to go around and keep up the pace than to negotiate timely, possibly costly obstructions.

After a few minutes, the reached a short incline and Stone caught hold of her shoulder and held her back. "Wait up," he said quietly. "Get down behind this tree and take a breather."

He guided her towards a large fallen tree that had been propped up slightly from the ground at the canopy end by to smaller trees that had cushioned its fall. The fall leaves had dropped and drifted into large piles wherever there was something for them to build up against. He guided her behind the tree and pushed some of the pile of leaves towards her, hiding her from view.

"Wait here," he said. "Don't move a

muscle. Whatever you hear, just stay still."

He was gone before she could protest, moving fast across the forest floor and in a large semi-circle back in the direction they had ran. He ran for a few minutes covering around two hundred yards of dense ground before dropping to his stomach and nestling in tightly to the trunks of a clump of young trees.

His heart was beating wildly, hammering against the wall of his chest. He breathed long, deep breaths, desperately conscious of the need to be quiet. He listened intently, used his peripheral vision and kept his eyes moving, but his head perfectly still. It was one of the first rules of camouflage and concealment. No movement, and no unnatural shape. The .357 semi-auto pistol was in his hand and his palms were moist. He swapped the pistol over to his left hand and dabbed his right hand on his trousers in a bid to dry the perspiration.

The forest was silent. Somewhere a bird sang and something screeched, but it was a long way off and in the wrong direction. He remained still and listened for another twenty minutes, but there was nothing. Not a sound. And certainly nothing untoward to concern him. Which was what concerned him even more.

***

He squatted down on his haunches, the rifle resting steadily on both knees. The body of the old tramp lay face down and inert, crumpled and twisted in the most undignified fashion. The neck was bloody and the exit wound was clearly visible. Neat and tiny, and almost re-sealed. Nothing substantial had stood in the bullet's path, except for skin, arteries and sinew.

The bullet had travelled cleanly, spinning perfectly, at a fraction under the speed of sound. The charge was subsonic, to compliment the silencer, and the bullet had slowed the moment it had left the muzzle and had continued to slow as gravity had teased and pulled at it, forcing it to drop an inch in height for every two hundred feet travelled. With little resistance, it had sliced cleanly through the man's neck and dropped to the ground shortly after exiting. The second bullet had travelled just as cleanly, possibly a little straighter because the barrel was now hot and the metal would have expanded. It had hit just above the base of the neck, but with the soft brain matter inside and the hard shell of bone outside it had been like switching on a blender without the lid attached. Nothing left intact above the cadaver's eye line. And upon closer inspection, nothing was visible on the ground around it. It was like he had made part of the body in front of him disappear upon command.

He touched the back of the cadaver's neck, felt the heat on the tips of his cold fingers. It was still warm, still soft to the touch. It was relaxing, comforting as he touched what had once been a living, breathing person, but was not yet what people perceived to be a corpse. On a base level, the warmth said otherwise – like it was a metamorphosis, a transient state. Warm as in life, yet completely devoid of everything but death. He enjoyed being around the newly dead or dying. It brought him the peace he so desperately craved, and he never felt so alive than at times like these.

He stood upright and looked down into the quagmire below. There were footprints leading off into the forest beyond. The footprints were filling with water. Soon they would disappear, simply turn into tiny puddles and lose all shape. He could see the line they had taken, as they had run blindly, desperately into the unknown.

IIc chcckcd thc action of the rifle; saw the cartridge nestled into the well-oiled breech. He had fired nine shots in all. Two into the old tramp, four into the reeds and one near the Secret Service man's head to teach him a lesson and scare him into running. The next two had landed near them both and he had watched them take off wildly and with reckless abandon as a result.

He smiled to himself as he thought of them running for their lives into the dense forest. He had moved the game up a level. He was the marionette to their strings, was controlling the time and pace. He was invisible to them, and they were running scared once more. But he had teased them enough. He needed the woman alive. But the man was ready to be hunted.

## FORTY TWO

It was necessary for him to do it, had become a habit over the years. Possibly more of a tradition than a habit but either way he looked forward to it most when he visited New York. *Ess-A-Bagel's* New York bagels were quite simply, the best in town. He'd tried most of the renowned bagel stores and restaurants but this one in Manhattan was the best. He always ordered two. An onion bagel with a mixture of cream cheese and sour cream with fresh chives, topped with crispy-diced Canadian bacon, and a plain bagel with scrambled eggs and lox. He never usually ate salmon, let alone smoked, but on top of the creamy scrambled eggs that *Ess-A-Bagel* did so well, he could never resist.

Tom Hardy hadn't visited New York in a couple of years, but was determined that tradition didn't die out because of it. He ate his bagels and drank his coffee and delighted in every moment of it.

The gaunt-looking man with the ponytail

and earring slipped into the booth silently and cocked his head to one side. "Hungry?"

"What the fuck's it to you?" Hardy wiped his mouth with a paper napkin and reached for his cup. He drank down the mouthful of food and stared at the man in front of him. "Because I have a lot of food in front of me, you feel you have to comment? What do you want me to say? Gee... I hadn't noticed how much was on my plate, I couldn't possibly have really wanted all that!" He looked at him mockingly. "Well hey pal, guess what? You're going bald. And you're trying to take everyone's attention away from the fact by wearing that stupid ponytail and you think it makes you look ten years younger," Hardy smirked. "You know, lift a pony's tail up and you'll always find an asshole underneath. Hell, you could do with giving it a damn wash once in a while too. And what the fuck is with that gay earring? Didn't you hear? The nineties called, it wants its look back." Hardy put the cup down and took another bite from the bagel, the one with the eggs and lox. "Now, was that polite of me? Do you think I would have entered this damn meeting with that, if you hadn't commented on my food?"

The gaunt-looking man shrugged. "Hey man, I'm sorry," he paused, looked offended. "Gee, there was no need to bring my hair into it." He picked up the stainless steel sugar shaker and used it as a makeshift mirror. "I'm not really going bald, am I? It's just my high forehead. You see?"

"Yeah, and if your aunt had a dick she'd be your fucking uncle," Hardy scoffed. "There ain't no forehead that high. Anyway, you're fucking late."

"Traffic, man."

"'No excuse," Hardy stared at him. "I'm not going to regret this, am I? I'm not going to regret going to a disavowed CIA agent and hiring his services for more money than he could otherwise make in a fucking lifetime, am I? Tell me I'm not going to regret that, tell me I haven't made a mistake. I really want to hear I haven't made a fucking mistake."

"'No, man ... It's cool," he stammered. "Everything will be cool. Just take a damn chill-pill, will you…'"

"Fine. Tell me what you've got then."

"She set up a safety deposit box. Made the transaction at zero-nine fifty. Deposited items unknown at ten-twenty-two. And was logged leaving at ten-thirty- six."

"Where?"

"It's all in the report. Show me the money first."

"'I'll show you my foot up your fucking ass...'"

"Wow, too much! You really need to chill. .." The gaunt looking man took out a large folded envelope and pushed it across the table. "It's all there. Everything she's done in the past year and the last information transaction, which was her safety deposit box. There's everything I could get on this guy Stone too. But it isn't much. He's a bit of an anomaly. Doesn't have credit cards, none of his own at least. He has a small savings account, not much in it though. Spends a Hell of a lot on his car judging by his checking account. Doesn't have any credit, loans or even a mortgage. You'll see everything I could get in the file." He kept his hand on top of the envelope. "Now, show me the money."

Hardy snatched the envelope up and slipped it into his inside pocket. At the same time, he felt a dig in his ribs from behind, and caught a faint whiff of perfume.

"I wouldn't do that if I were you." The voice was calm and smooth and belonged to a woman. There was a hint of the orient about it. A sing-song tone, Thai or Vietnamese. "And that was most unfair about his hair, very uncalled for. Don't worry baby, I love your hair… Now, like he said, show him the money."

Hardy smiled. "Very clever," he paused. "This had better be right up to the minute."

The gaunt-looking man smiled. "Of course. Bang on the button," he paused, flashing a smile of crooked teeth. "That's Mindy by the way, my partner. And she's just dying for an excuse to slip that blade into your lung, so no tricks now."

Hardy picked up a thick package off the seat beside him. It was wrapped in brown packing paper fastened with string and was around the size of three house bricks. It was a mix of fifties and twenties. Used dollars. He passed it across the table, then looked back at his plate and took another bite of his bagel. When he looked back up, the man had gone. He turned around slowly, but there was nobody there and the only people behind him were an old couple struggling into the tight booth.

## FORTY THREE

The Central Intelligence Agency's New York field office had grown considerably in size as a direct result of the changes brought about since 9-11. In fact, all of the intelligence agencies and law enforcement organizations had been forced to evolve a great deal since that tragic day. And although the Central Intelligence Agency is strictly forbidden in operating and mounting missions taking part on US mainland soil as part of its mandate, the CIA's New York office in particular had grown substantially in both size and personnel levels in the time since Al-Qaeda had delivered their message to the entire civilized world. Ever since 9-11 the CIA has ignored its mandate and operated freely within the United States. To date its operational mandate has not been reviewed.

It was Tom Hardy's first visit to the new

premises and although the old field office was still operational, he knew that the newly acquired building was the beating heart of the CIA's presence in New York. He had studied the brief, talked with those involved in the fight against terrorism and had loosely agreed in principle that the battle towards eradicating terror should come from the very city in which it had so publicly and so unexpectedly raised its head.

He had arrived around an hour after his meeting with the disavowed agent. He had read and re-read the digitally compiled dossier on Isobel Bartlett on his way over in the taxi and had been quickly ushered through security and sign-in after his identity and position had been verified at the check-in desk. He was now seated in the duty liaison officer's private office and sipping sweet cappuccino from an oversized mug, which outrageously, had the Central Intelligence Agency's emblem emblazoned across it on both drinking sides. Just in case anyone forgot either who they worked for or who the cup belonged to. He looked up and smiled as the liaison officer returned with a sheaf of loosely gathered papers. "Not too much trouble, I trust?" Hardy asked.

"'No big thing, just don't get the requisition that often," he paused. "It's never happened to me at all, actually ... Are you sure you don't need a team with you on this?"

"Need to know," Hardy tapped his nose with his forefinger a couple of times and winked wryly. "You know how it is, after..."

"After what...?"

Tom Hardy looked up at a poster sized photograph of the Twin Towers on the wall to his right. The picture showed them in all their glory, a golden sunrise behind them. "After that day," he paused somberly. "Terrorism has changed the way we operate, changed the way we look at ourselves, as an intelligence agency, completely. Today it's validating the requisition to enter and search a safety deposit box. Tomorrow it's stopping another major terrorist incident. Tragedy, even."

"I understand. But believe me, Agent Hardy, this is so irregular. I really should contact Langley and get some kind of authorization on this matter."

"Sure, I understand," he paused. "Only, I thought after what I had heard back in Langley, that you would be OK with this."

He looked at Hardy for a moment, unsure. "What did you hear?" he asked, albeit somewhat tentatively.

"Oh, nothing. Look, I understand," Hardy nodded. "Go and call the farm, get approval. I just thought..."

"What?" The liaison officer looked intently at him, concerned. "What did you think?"

Hardy shrugged. "Well, it's just that in

certain circles, your name…" he paused, shaking his head resolutely. "Oh forget I said anything. Please, call Langley and get permission. I know it will take time. Hell, it may even be too late already, so there's no use worrying about another hour or two. Or day or two, knowing them. Virginia go slow time, eh? No, you'd best go to someone more senior, more qualified. Get permission. It's better to go by the book, even if it does continually seem to hamper us."

"What do you mean by hamper?"

He glanced back at the photograph. "Well, you know... Hell, we all *knew* about those damn rag heads hatching a plan to take out American targets on US soil," he paused. "Well, I'm sure you knew too, right? Hell, of course you did, *anybody* worth a damn did. And hey, you were out here, so it must have been hell on you, what with knowing that procedures had prevented us from sharing the intelligence we had ..." He shook his head, slammed his fist on the table. The cup of cappuccino spilt a little over the lip and onto the papers. "God damn fucking bureaucrats! If it wasn't for protocol and procedure and the damn necessity to cross every T and dot every last fucking I, we'd have stopped Al-Qaeda in their damn tracks. You know it, I know it." He looked at the liaison officer and held up both hands helplessly. "Sir, I apologize for my behavior. It just sickens me to the core that we are all so tied by procedure these days."

"Please, don't apologize, it's not necessary." The liaison officer looked at him intently. "And you think your lead is along the same lines? You think there's a possibility of another large-scale catastrophe?"

"Hell, all I know is that my lead was going to take me out to New York. Another terror attack planned, another screw-pot outfit looking for a major coup," he paused. "Go see Orville B Sullivan out at the New York office, they said..."

The liaison frowned. "Who said?"

He tapped his nose again. "Loose lips, sink ships. Anyway, where was I? Oh Yeah, go and see Orville B Sullivan. Real go to guy. He's making a name for himself. He's going places fast. Right to the top. Go see him and he'll move heaven and earth to get you what you need. Hell, time's at a premium and I need to move fast on this. You'll help me, right? You'll cut through the procedure crap and help avoid another catastrophe, right? I'll understand if you don't think you can, if you don't feel you can make such a *big* call. But if you can't make the decision, I need to know now. I need to know like ten minutes ago. And I need to speak to someone big enough, with enough balls who can..."

The liaison officer put his hand up to

silence him. "Agent Hardy, I think I've heard enough, and don't want to waste anymore of your time," he paused and handed him the sheaf of papers. "Now, tell me what it is you need and I'll make it happen..."

## FORTY FOUR

Stone kept up the rearguard, training his pistol through a wide arc of fire every few paces. He kept their direction unobvious, changing tack regularly as a sailboat navigates its course and like the navigators of old, he used the bearing of the sun to plot his course and keep direction. This was a skill he had honed during his time in Special Forces. He had wanted to head east, but before he could, he had to establish north and south. He had pointed the hour hand of his watch towards the sun, and then found the mid-way point between the hour hand and the twelve o'clock position. The line from the center of the watch pointed due south. From here, he could mentally recall his bearings every few minutes, re-tack his course and keep them from heading in the wrong direction.

They reached the top of a steep slope and Stone caught hold of Isobel's shoulder and steadied her. "Take a breath," he paused. "We've gained good ground, and if he's tracking us, he'll be a lot slower and besides, we've sent him on a merry little detour."

She rested her palms on her knees and breathed heavily. Stone slipped a hand under her ribs and eased her upright. "I can't get my breath," she protested.

"Keep standing up straight, you won't get enough air down you otherwise." He turned his back on her and used their elevation to get his bearings. "I reckon another mile, maybe a little less and we'll meet up with the road we came in on."

She looked at him, feigned a smile. "What the hell are we waiting for then?"

"Take it easy, tiger," he smiled. "Get a good breather and we'll make better time. We've made less than a mile to this point."

"You're kidding! We've been running for ages!" She looked despondent, crestfallen. "What about the gunman? Do you think he's close to us?"

Stone shook his head. "I'm not saying that he's not chasing us, but the path we took was far from straight and if he's following he's got to study the ground thoroughly. The forest is too dense to see further than seventy or eighty yards."

"Unless he's figured out our options. He knows where we took off from, and he might know by now where the road goes to. He knows we need to get

363

back to the car, or the town. He may even have a map and work out where we're going."

Stone looked thoughtful for a moment, then nodded. "Alright, in that case we had better hit the trail again. Put in a little more distance."

## FORTY FIVE

The sirens and flashing lights helped. The small, but efficient task force that Orville B Sullivan had assembled had only added to the effect and the bank had been entered with much swagger and flashing of ID wallets and the customers had been swiftly escorted outside.

The FBI would have been livid. The deployment of the CIA's recently devised counter-terrorist task force, in tandem operational control with Homeland Security, was not something they would have taken lightly. As ever, on US soil the FBI would and should have been notified first. The paperwork had been professionally compiled and was thoroughly complete. Even a high-court judge would have been fooled by its content and appearance and would have gladly signed his name to authorize the seizure of illicit contents. Which he indeed had, not twenty minutes previously on their way across town.

The bank's manager had been concerned for the personal safety of his staff and had been resolutely assured that there was in fact no immediate danger and that all personnel should temporarily occupy the break room and have an impromptu coffee break while the Task Force went about their necessary business.

Tom Hardy ushered the manager to one side and asked him to carefully read the order, signed and authorized by the judge and requested that he should have the bank's full co-operation in the matter. He reminded the manager that he was not Switzerland, merely a bank with safety deposit services and if the next 9-11 was to happen, he would not want to be the man the nation would turn to as having been able to halt another attack in its tracks. It may not have worked in Chicago or Los Angeles but this was New York, and New York was still raw. It always would be.

The manager had been only too pleased to help, apologized profusely for any impropriety which could have possibly taken part on the bank's premises and offered his full co-operation without premium. Ten minutes later and both the manager, Orville B Sullivan and Tom Hardy stood in the strong room, while the chief teller saw to recovering the safety deposit box, overriding the previously installed security system with the bank's own emergency default system.

The teller presented Hardy with the box and he thanked him, barely able to suppress the desire to smile. He did his best at appearing melancholy, like looking inside would only confirm his innermost fears, and walked off to the privacy booth to inspect the contents. He turned back to a perplexed Sullivan, and nodded his thanks. "You'll understand the need for security. Please, fetch me an evidence bag and I'll be right out."

Inside the box were the two flash drives. They looked tiny and insignificant in such a large container, yet what they contained could change the world dramatically. He picked them up, reached into his inside pocket and retrieved a clear plastic case containing four identical flash drives. He opened the case, tipped the drives out and replaced them with the two original drives from the facility and put them safely in his pocket. Next, he put two substitute drives back in the safety deposit box. He took a handkerchief from the pocket of his pants and wiped his brow hurriedly. He was perspiring and his heart beat rapidly. He took a deep, steadying breath and then opened the curtain and looked triumphantly at the CIA liaison officer.

"Eureka! These definitely look like what we've been looking for." He handed the safety deposit box back to the manager. "Please replace this. I've substituted the evidence. I will contact both you and your superiors about further action. We may need to conduct a sting in due course." He turned to Sullivan who had returned with the evidence bag. He held out the box with the two dummy drives inside. "Perhaps, you'll do the honors? This would not have been possible without you."

Sullivan beamed with pride as he put the two worthless disks into the plastic bag. He sealed it with the fastener and Hardy handed him a pen.

"Go on, make history. Evidence number A01, New York City," he said with a smile. "Now date it and write the name of the bank on the back. Sullivan grinned when he had finished and held the bag out for him. Hardy shook his head. "Please, initial it. I need a little anonymity with this case. Any commendations and I'll see that they come your way. Now, take them back to headquarters and lock them away. I'll have a tech team come over and inspect the data." He turned to the manager and held out his hand. The manager clasped it and Tom Hardy held his eye as they shook hands warmly. "You've been invaluable. I shall pass your name on to your superiors. Without your co-operation... well, need I say any more?"

The manager beamed a grin almost as ridiculous as Sullivan's and modestly said that there was nothing to be grateful for, and that he had merely acted in his bank's best interests.

As they made their way out of the strong room, Hardy turned to the manager and spoke quietly. "I have to call this in. Do you mind if use a computer with internet access? I need send a quick e-mail."

## FORTY SIX

"I've got to stop for a moment," Isobel panted breathily. She reached out and held herself against a large fir tree. Her legs were shaking. Her chest heaved as she breathed, her blouse was ripped and Stone caught a fleeting glimpse of bare flesh underneath. "I need a rest," she added.

Stone nodded and caught hold of her arm and led her to the other side of the tree. "Here, sit down and take a breather, you're out of sight right there, if he's behind us."

She rested her head back against the tree and closed her eyes. "My legs ache so much! How far to you think we've come?"

He looked up at the ridge of mountains and looked thoughtful for a moment. She thought he was using the question to catch his breath also, and didn't feel quite so guilty at holding them up. "Around three and a half to four miles," he replied. "Seems like fifteen with all the dense trees and obstacles we've met."

"And hills the height of skyscrapers!" she exclaimed.

"Yeah, it is a bit up and down out here, I'll give you that."

"Did you learn that stuff with your watch in the military?" She asked, then prompted him. "You said to Joe Carver that you were in the military, or at least told him where you saw action."

Stone smiled. He sighted the hour hand back on the sun and looked off to his left. "This is just Boy Scout stuff, that's all."

"Why do I detect you're just being modest? So is that it, you're just a regular Boy Scout, nothing more than that?" she smirked. And as quick as she lightened the mood, she looked as if she were about to break down and cry.

"What's wrong?"

Isobel looked down at the ground, shook her head slowly. "I just can't believe what happened back there. Or in New York. I've seen dead bodies before, but not people murdered. I was part of the Ebola task force sent out to Sierra Leone. A six week learning tour. It was thought good knowledge would come from it. I saw plenty of dead people and people in great distress. But I never saw somebody shot before. It was just awful." She wiped a tear away from her eye and looked up at him solemnly. "It's all my fault as well. If I hadn't have taken those damned drives, then Elizabeth, David Stein and Joe Carver would all still be alive. Oh god, and I had already forgotten about the poor girl who looked like me at the station! And that poor hotel porter…" She put her head down and started to sob. She was shaking, and her sobbing was becoming increasingly like a wail. She was like a child, hurt and wounded, insecure and scared.

Stone walked to her and crouched down. He took both her hands in his and rubbed them gently. "Hush now, don't cry. This situation is tough, but believe me, if you hadn't taken those drives with the information on them and they had got into the wrong hands, many more people might well have died in the future." He let go of her hands and pulled her towards him, he hugged her, comforted her, and held her close. "Isobel, you have been so brave, so decisive. Imagine if you hadn't taken them? Imagine what death and suffering could have occurred if you had been too scared to act? You did the right thing, I promise you that."

She stopped crying and wiped her eyes. She looked up at him and seemed so vulnerable in his arms. He wiped her wet cheek with his sleeve and smiled at her. She reached up and kissed him lightly on the edge of the mouth. It was a gesture of thanks, a token. Nothing more was meant, but as she did so, he kissed her back, returning her gesture with that of his own. They looked at each other for a moment, their heartbeats increasing in rhythm and pace. The look between them both became more intense, intoxicating even, and finally Stone could resist no more. He reached down and kissed her full on the lips, and to his relief, she responded. Their lips touched, sought each other, tentatively at first, and then with more hunger, and their tongues gradually started to probe and explore. It was a passionate kiss, with mutual meaning and adulation, but suddenly, Isobel pulled away and looked down at the ground.

"I can't do this," she said stiffly. "I can't do this out here with ..."

It wasn't necessary for her to finish the sentence. Stone knew exactly what she had meant. And when he thought about the circumstances, it even seemed ridiculous to him, that they should lose sight of the situation and get emotional. He caught hold of her arm and helped her to her feet.

"You're right," he said, but without any trace of malice or indignity. "Come on, let's get the hell out of here."

Even in the perilous situation they were in, there was the irony of everyday normality. And as they jogged and marched their way through the forest, with danger behind them and the unknown ahead, there was still the awkward silence and shared idiosyncrasies of their demeanor. It was almost humorous to think that a mere kiss could affect the shared bond brought about by the situation.

Thankfully, and almost instantly, they suddenly stumbled out of the forest and to the edge of a road which cut a snaking path through the forest and led deep into the mountains.

"Oh, thank god!" Isobel exclaimed loudly. She turned around and hugged Stone, but it was nothing more than friendly, a gesture brought about through the emotional relief that they had actually made it.

He returned her gesture with a sportsman's pat on the back, and smiled. "I knew we would, but I was getting worried after that last break. I couldn't have gone much further without another word from you." He grinned. "Come on, this way. I know this stretch of road."

"You do?"

"Yes. I've been here before," he smiled. "Perhaps this is just another coincidence?"

However, his words were lost on Isobel, who was looking down the road excitedly. "Look! There's a car. We can hitch a lift!" She stuck out her arm and made a thumbing sign. "This is a first, I've never done this before."

Stone looked up and smiled. A car was winding its way along the mountain road towards them, gaining ground quickly. It was a large silver colored sedan. Stone squinted in the sunlight, trying to make out the make and model. It was a big Mercedes, one of the new shapes. He could hear the engine. It was under heavy acceleration and sounded powerful. It certainly wasn't a common car for these parts, quite unusual really. There was a sudden and dramatic change in the engine's pitch. He put an arm around Isobel's shoulder and smiled at her. "Looks like we're in luck," he said. "It's slowing down."

## FORTY SEVEN

He had watched the corpse for a while and reflected upon the quality of the shot. He had no intention to go after Rob Stone and Isobel Bartlett in the forest, had no reason to. He had simply moved the game up a level and flushed them out once more. He felt sure that in doing so, he would force them into making a mistake and lead him to the flash drives.

After shooting the tramp he had removed the set of specially designed camouflage overalls and replaced the army issue jungle boots with his hand stitched Italian shoes. His appearance was slightly more ruffled than he would otherwise have wished, but necessity and practicality was the greater part of fashion today. After he had made the custom-built Colt M4 assault rifle safe and had re-loaded the magazine with ammunition, he had stowed it safely in its hidden rack in the trunk of the car.

He had then checked the transponder and transceiver hidden in the lining of Isobel Bartlett's coat and watched the devious course that they were taking through the forest. The map showed the green pattern that denoted forest, as well as depth and gradient. It also showed the road that they were heading towards some five miles to the east. Either it was dumb luck, or Stone was a more notable adversary than he had first anticipated. But either way, he would arrive at their destination fresh and ready to make the next move.

However, the move he was now to make was the move he had so waited for. The e-mail had come in from his paymaster and informed him that the level of the game had been raised to the highest stakes, and that he was to eliminate them both immediately. He had so wanted the message back in New York. Back where he could have ended it there and then with one precise squeeze of the trigger. Although, out here in the wilderness, he realized that there was now true sport ahead of him, and that nature could only add to the wealth of the experience. He was looking forward to the hunt.

He watched the laptop's display and estimated where the pair would join the deserted highway. He could see how close they were, didn't want to risk them being picked up by some well-meaning trucker hauling logs and accelerated accordingly.

The transponder showed them on the road, their movements still. He looked up and saw them ahead of him, casually waiting at the side of the road. He eased a custom built Colt 1911 model pistol and two spare magazines out of the glove box and placed it on the passenger seat. He had looked forward to using this piece for a while. The .45 bullets were hollow points and the charge was a heavy load. The pistol had its sights removed and a guttersnipe sighting channel had been made by a master gunsmith in Colorado. On the range, at close range it was a point and shoot competition winner.

He started to brake and changed down a gear, biting the rear wheels into the tarmac. They were so close now. He could see their faces clearly and he could see the expression of relief as they watched him drive towards them.

## FORTY EIGHT

Rob Stone watched as the big Mercedes slowed down and pulled in towards the side of the road. The sidings were made up of gravel chippings and the large tires crunched loudly as the car pulled off the road and slowed down. He could make out the outline, the silhouette of a man in the driver's seat. The sun visor obscured his face from view, but he could see clearly that the man was wearing a dark business suit. Which, along with the car, was a rarity in these parts. The man picked something off the passenger seat, most probably a cell phone or even something like a soda can in the way of any potential passenger.

He watched the car pull to a halt some twenty yards away. It surprised him that the owner of a car like that would give time to stop and offer a lift. It reminded him of his days as a teenager, hitching lifts into town to see a concert or go on a date with a girl. None of the drivers of luxury vehicles ever stopped. It was always the pickup truck, or the rusted old station wagon crammed with passengers and sticky children who would stop and offer room for *just one more.*

They walked towards the car and the driver opened his door slowly. Stone could see the man's face now, but something didn't seem right. Something was amiss. He had seen the man somewhere before. He tensed. What were the chances of bumping into someone you'd seen before, all the way out here? Coupled with that - at a time when they needed a lift the most. At a point on a deserted mountain road, picked up by a suited businessman whom he had seen. But he couldn't think where.

The man slid out of the seat and stood up. "You folks look like you could do with a lift..."

Stone knew the face, knew the voice. But from where? Where had he seen this man, and in what context? So much had happened in the past couple of days, so much. And then he had it. He knew he had seen the man last night. He had helped him into his chalet at the motel on the other side of the dramatic mountain ridge. What were the chances of that?

Isobel bounded forwards, but Stone caught her arm and stopped her. She looked annoyed, and the man visibly tensed.

"We've already met," Stone said. "Back at

the motel, last night."

The man seemed unsure. He smiled nervously. "Oh yeah, that's right. You helped me with the cheap lock. What are the chances of that?" he smiled. "You look as if you've seen hard times recently. What was it, engine trouble?" He moved out slightly from the open door of the Mercedes. "You can't have been out for a walk, you don't look well enough equipped."

The pistol was out and aimed at the man's chest. Stone shook his head. "'No, I think I've got all the equipment I need, right here." He spoke to Isobel, but didn't move his eyes even a fraction. "Get behind me, don't take your eyes off him."

"I don't understand," she said. "What's going on?"

"Yeah," the man added. "What's going on? I just stopped to give you a damned lift!"

"I don't like coincidences," Stone said coldly. "Put your hands where I can see them."

The man rested his left hand on the top of the doorframe and look in bewilderment at the pair of them. "Sir, please ... There's no need for the gun, if you want my car, then just take it. Hell, it's insured against carjacking."

"What's going on?" Isobel asked. She looked desperate, like their only chance of getting out of there and back to civilization was fading rapidly. "I don't understand."

Stone kept the pistol trained on him, watched the other man's eyes. "This man was at the motel last night. We've been shot at, hunted. And now he turns up and offers a lift just when we need it most? Too big a coincidence for me."

"But a man shooting at us is out there," she said, pointing behind them towards the mountainous forest. "This man is *here,* and he's offering us help!"

"There's someone shooting at you?" the man exclaimed. He looked around at the tree line across the road. "Don't waste time then! Get in!"

Stone shook his head. "But what if he never was hunting us? What if he shot at us and thought he'd head us off at this road?" He glanced at her for a second, wanted to believe it was true and that he had merely been paranoid. "We weren't shot at once we made a run for it…"he stopped, caught the movement with the corner of his eye. He looked back, but it was too late.

"You should have trusted your instincts," the man said. "They're usually right the first time around." He had the big Colt .45 aimed at them, his hand as steady as a rock. Stone kept his aim, kept his left hand on Isobel's shoulder. "The weapon is aimed at her throat, Agent Stone. One move from you and she gets a bullet. A bit high and she'll share looks with that old tramp out at the lake, a bit low and she'll take it in the chest. They're hollow points with hollow tails, made out of really soft lead. The hollow points are filled with mercury, sealed with wax. I estimate a hole of about three inches in diameter. Smaller than the hole in the coroner, but larger than the one I left in the FBI woman. Either way, the mercury seals the deal. No cure."

"She was my friend!" Isobel screamed venomously. "You bastard!"

"Most probably. I wouldn't know," he smiled. "All I know is that my weapon has you marked and the Secret Service man had better be an excellent marksman, because I'm shielded by bullet proof glass and a quarter of an inch of armored plating in the door. I'm rested, he's tired. I can see his hand shaking from here."

*How? How does he know so much about us?* Stone stopped himself from thinking, from going through the motions. He needed his wits about him, needed to be ready to act immediatcly. IIe had his weapon aimed at the man's mouth. Low resistance entry for a bullet, with the spine and brain stem behind. It was a money shot. However, his breathing was ragged after their incursion through the forest and now adrenaline was starting to kick in and surge through his veins. His hand was slightly unsteady, he couldn't swear to an accurate first shot and he knew he could only take one if he used just one hand. The other hand was holding

Isobel firm, but she was breathing hard and moving considerably.

"I heard your philosophy in the motel room, enjoyed your insight... personally I think indecision is the mother of all disaster, Agent Stone," the man smiled. "Not, as you say, assumption."

"I wouldn't know," Stone smirked. "It's you who assumes that I'm indecisive ..." He heaved Isobel backwards and at the same time, kicked the back of her knee, dropping her instantly and heavily to the floor. The man's pistol went off twice in quick succession and the world slowed in motion once more.

Stone dropped down onto one knee and saw the man's weapon coming around on him to aim. Stone fired two shots. The first hit the glass plumb center to the man's chest. The glass shattered, but remained in one piece. The second bullet hit higher, catching the doorframe and sparking like a rock upon flint. The man flinched, ducked, fired wildly and the bullets hit the road in front of them. Stone was already dragging Isobel out of the line of fire and firing at the man behind his automotive shield. The bullets impacted against the shattered glass, which now looked like a spider's web, albeit spun by a spider on LSD. The lines of fracture were haphazard and angled in every direction. Stone had tested this type of

Plexiglas before, whilst working as an instructor in the Secret Service and he knew that it could withstand more bullets than he had to offer. The man's head was shielded from view, but he still fired the pistol wildly in their direction. Stone had recognized the pistol was a 1911 model of some make or other, and knew it held seven rounds, eight if it had been chambered and the magazine reloaded. But that put too much pressure on the magazine springs and could cause a stoppage. Fine for the range, not fine for a gunfight. And a true marksman like this man would know that. He heaved Isobel to her feet and pushed her forcefully ahead of him. He directed a short burst of shots - he thought it was three, but the fog of combat was thickening – at a point under the open door. The man howled and sagged to the ground, but continued to fire his weapon at them as they sprinted across the road.

The man had managed a magazine change and was unveiling a lethal hail of fire towards them. The bullets hit the ground, some kicking up clumps of tarmac and others bouncing off and winging off into the fringe of trees ahead of them. Stone fired another two shots, but to his surprise, the weapon's slide kicked back and he knew it was empty. He ejected the magazine as he ran, pushed Isobel once more, and reloaded with the other magazine, but he knew that he only had another four shots at his disposal. He cursed himself at his error as he thought about the carton of .357 sig in the trunk of the Mustang.

Time wound on and started to play at real speed once more. The fog of combat was behind them, and they could not hear any more shots winging into the trees.

"Keep moving!" Stone barked. "Don't lose pace! The forest isn't thick enough yet!"

Isobel didn't reply. He wasn't even sure that she had heard him, but she kept running and that was good enough for him. He risked a glance over his shoulder and could see the fringe of trees at the edge of the road and the occasional slither of tarmac. But thankfully, he did not see the man. He ploughed onwards, kept pushing Isobel forwards and scanning the ground ahead of them for the best options to take. The forest started getting denser and the ground started to incline a little. There was still bush grass underfoot, and he knew that the terrain would soon give way to thick forest and mere dirt and pine needles on the ground. They had to keep going, had to get into the thick sanctuary of the forest.

The man was starting to recover from the shock of being shot. The wound was a graze, and hurt like a painful scald. The blood was thickening, and he knew it would soon clot. The bullet had hit the ground and bounced up catching his leg. The bullet would have been greatly deformed, after initial impact with the tarmac, and what had hit him would have been a twisted mass of copper and lead with razor sharp edges and enough heat to burn his skin. The gash was about four inches long and a quarter of an inch wide and almost as deep, and ran the whole width of his calf muscle.

He had hobbled to the rear of the car and opened the trunk. He quickly swallowed a handful of the prescription painkillers he used for his headaches and hurriedly got out of his clothes. He slipped the camouflaged overalls on and hastily fastened a utility waistcoat over the top. He pulled out a Glock 9mm pistol and slipped it into a holster built into the utility waistcoat. Then he took out the custom-made M4 assault rifle out of its rack. He filled the pouches of the waistcoat with four loaded thirty round magazines for the rifle and checked that they did not rattle. Next he took the Remington pump-action shotgun out and jacked the action. Click-click. He slung it over his shoulder and held the M4 loosely over his arm and slammed the trunk shut.

He checked his watch and looked up at the sun, and then out towards the forest in the direction his quarry had run. He cupped his hands to his mouth and started to shout, to resonate, echoing off into the forest and mountains beyond. "LISTEN UP AGENT STONE! I'M COMING FOR YOU!

I'M GOING TO HUNT YOU DOWN! AND I WILL KILL YOU! DO YOU HEAR ME? I'M COMING FOR YOU!"

He rested the M 4 assault rifle on the ground, and shouldered the pump action shotgun. He fired out into the woods in the direction they had fled, at a forty five degree angle, racking the slide and firing again until all five empty shell casings had spilt out onto the road. He could hear the BB shot falling into the trees. Each shot had echoed around the valley and off the two mountain ridges either side of him. They were like cannon fire and after he finished, the silence was eerie and total. "DO YOU HEAR? I'M COMING FOR YOU!" He picked up the assault rifle and walked purposefully into the thick fringe of trees... And the beginning of the hunt.

## FORTY NINE

The airline was not showing any movies on the flight as there was little enough time between JFK and Dulles. By the time the seatbelt sign had been switched off and the drinks cart had completed its journey down the aisles, followed by the snack trolley and hot face towels, there was only enough time to surf the six channels on offer. He caught a program about rednecks bidding for storage units and some guys running a pawn shop in Las Vegas. A little of a documentary about penguins in the Antarctic and some CNN headlines. He was bored of it all and took off the set of headphones and had another scotch and soda by way of compensation.

He decided to close his eyes and wait for the landing. He disliked flying at the best of times, but somehow today was worse. Behind him, in New York, lay a web of lies and deceit that would end his career and make him a wanted man. He didn't know how much time he had, before the rumblings became public, but he knew that time was short and he would have to move fast. He had the missing half of both ARES and APHRODITE in his hands and he would assume control of the operation and get it moving once more. McCray needed a little more motivation, needed to be put into the picture once and for all, and made to realize just how far they had come. They had moved outside the parameters of safety and security. There was no going back. They had what they needed and they needed to move with it. It would be out in the open soon, and if they didn't strike now then it may be too late. Another forty-eight hours and Tom Hardy knew that he would be a wanted man. And the CIA tends never to give up, nor lower the levels of resources or manpower when hunting one of their own. He needed the plan with ARES to come off, to reach fruition, to be a success. Needed his contact at Morgan-Klein to get APHRODITE manufactured and in enough quantities to stop ARES in its tracks.

As a CIA renegade, Tom Hardy knew that he would have few places left in the world in which to hide. And those places would cost a fortune, could bleed most wealthy criminals dry. But he was different, he could offer information and favors and contacts and money. He could buy his little slice of peace and quiet and sanctuary, and he could become a man of great worth to the right people. And besides, he enjoyed smoking enjoyed Cuban cigars and drinking mojitos and watching young women dance the Samba.

## FIFTY

The incline was more severe now and as they ran they could place their hands in front of them to gain better purchase on the sheer slope. Higher above them, the forest seemed to disappear from view and the sight as they looked up led to a feeling of confusion and uncertainty.

"I think there's some kind of plateau," Isobel panted breathily. "I think when we reach the top it will level out."

Stone nodded silently, not wanting to waste his energy in reply. It was obvious to him now. The slope was high and precipitous and the trees above were set back from the edge. He pushed on, heaved and stomped and continued to nudge Isobel in front, drive her onwards and keep her motivated.

The tufts of golden bush grass had long since given way to earth and pine needles and mulch as the forest had intensified in its density, but the slope they were now confronting was made up purely of loose gravel and shale. With each step they were faced with the infuriating prospect of sliding backwards half a pace or so and their calf muscles burned as if they had been set alight.

Isobel hesitated in front and came to a sudden rest. She fell forwards onto her outstretched arms, her hands sinking into the shale. She heaved for breath, unable to take in sufficient quantities of air, her shoulders rising and sinking with every breath. She felt light-headed, faint.

Stone pushed her forwards, but she collapsed onto her stomach. "Come on! Keep moving!" he shouted. "Isobel, we're sitting ducks on this slope! We have to reach the top!" Stone knew if they could gain the high ground advantage over the pursuing gunman, then even with just four bullets they may still have a chance.

There was a heavy thud approximately three feet or so to their right and a clump of thick sodden earthy clod flew up into the air and scattered loose debris on to their backs. A full second or more later there was a loud crack, which thudded and echoed all around them like distant thunder. Stone knew the man must have removed the weapon's suppressor, wanted them to hear the gunshots. Wanted them scared.

"He's on us! Isobel, move your fucking ass!" Stone heaved her, barged her buttocks with his shoulder and physically slid her a few feet further up the slope. She powered her legs in the thick shale and surged forward with new and revived vigor and determination. Stone clawed and scrabbled his way higher, and found time to barge her once more. They were now within sixty feet of the brow of the slope. "That's it, keep going, we're almost there now ..."

\*\*\*

He was breathing hard. They had three or four minutes on him, but with the density of the forest and the continuous gradient, that merely equated to three or four hundred meters. He had found them through his sniper scope, had seen them climbing the steep gradient where the trees thinned out. Actually, it was closer to five hundred and with the steep gradient taken into account, at approximately one foot of elevation for every ten foot travelled, that equated to a shot with the physical constraints and complexity of a seven hundred and fifty yard range. That was far too hopeful for the .223 cartridge and with the subsonic load accounted for it was virtually an impossible shot on the luxury setting of a level, wind-free range fired from a prone position, let alone standing with a tree trunk acting as a rest and the severe elevation needed to hit near the top of the slope. However, the first shot had neared them, and with a few minor adjustments, he may just get the bullet on target this time if he fired in groups and adjusted aim every three or four shots. He only had to hit them, not score range bulls eyes.

He held the cross hairs on the Isobel's back and then steadily raised the rifle until the acute center of the cross was approximately ten feet above her head. He felt the gentle breeze against the side of his face, and estimated the increase in wind pattern at their approximate height and then brought the rifle across three feet to her right and held it still. The sun was high and the base of the slope had warmed considerably in the sunlight. He allowed for the certain rising thermal, lowered the rifle a touch, and held it steady. He breathed progressively, eased the air from his lungs and held his breath when his lungs were empty. The trigger was light and smooth and the rifle recoiled a little as he fired three successive rounds. The bullets threw up clumps of clod and shale just above Isobel's head and she stopped moving in the lens, cleared her eyes with her sleeve. He had not allowed enough drop in elevation for the thermal moving up the slope. He took aim once more and calculated for the rise in warm air accordingly and fired three more shots.

\*\*\*

Stone had seen the bullets hit the ground. The trajectory had been so great that the bullets had hit the embankment on their edge, channeling through the shale and had bounced off to the right after hitting an area of stone. He had never witnessed a sight like it before and would never have thought it possible to actually see bullets land. However, he knew from the full three second pause between the impact and the sound of the gunshots that they were approaching the thousand yard point in distance.

"Go on Isobel!" He hollered. "Another few yards and we're in the clear!"

"I'm trying," she groaned. "I... can... hardly ... breath ..."

She was cut short, her footing slipped and she slid back down the slope at least three feet. The bullets impacted into the ground where her head had been and a thick wad of earth flew into the air and showered them with debris. The gunshots rang out and sung around the valley and mountain ridges, but its resonance was one of failure and not of victory. Stone shoulder barged her again and found renewed strength and determination and they scrambled for another ten seconds or so and crawled over the crest and rolled into safety, their lungs heaving and their hearts pounding so heavily, that they could hear nothing else in the world. Not even the wild volley of gunshots fired in a rage from the valley far below.

## FIFTY ONE

"How was your trip?"

"Fine," Tom Hardy paused and looked momentarily behind him to make sure that Agnes Dempsey had closed the door as she left. "A complete success. In a manner of speaking."

"You have the... merchandise?"

The CIA man laughed. He placed the freshly made cup of coffee down on the desk and smiled at him. "Merchandise?" he whispered mockingly. "Yes, I have the *merchandise*." He reached into his inside jacket pocket and retrieved the two flash drives. "Now, McCray, here's the deal... I've burned my bridges, damn near still crossing the fucking bridge as we speak. There's no going back for me. In forty-eight hours max, the CIA will have internal affairs on my ass. After that, my ass is screwed. Good and proper and a real tight fit. Homeland Security and the FBI will have me as most wanted."

"But..."

"Shut your mouth!" He glared at the man behind the desk, his eyes intense, cold and cruel. "Interrupt me again and I'll break your nose. Don't fucking doubt me for a moment. All of a sudden, I'm fresh out of patience." He waited for a protest, clenched his fist in case. He meant it, and what's more, McCray could see that he was deadly serious. "I've left this in your hands, listened to your advice from the start. Well, after seeing the way you operate, I can tell you one thing, you're a pussy. A gutless piece of shit, who couldn't get the balls together to make the move soon enough for fear of getting caught in your own damned department. Then, some stupid bitch takes the files from under your own fucking nose and beats you to it. I should have hired *her!* Well McCray, several people have died as a result of you not getting your shit together and thankfully, I've managed to sort this matter out." He turned the two flash drives over in his hand, and their shiny finish caught the light and glistened majestically, like the purest of gold. "I've sorted this unnecessary fiasco out, and as a result, I've fucked myself over. I'll be a marked man. A fucking fugitive and all because you didn't have the balls to have moved on this quicker."

"I ..." McCray protested, but the CIA operative moved so fast he didn't have time to shield his face. The punch connected with the tip of his nose and his top lip and he recoiled back into the chair with a yelp. The chair was on a swivel and castors and he swung around half a turn. He twisted the chair back, his hand cupping his nose and tears running down his cheeks.

"Don't say I didn't fucking warn you, McCray," he sneered viciously. "I'm telling you like it is. You don't interrupt me, ever again. Understand?" he paused, waiting for the man to nod. McCray took out a handkerchief and mopped the blood from his nostrils. He nodded reluctantly, more of a flinch, but it was good enough for Hardy. "Now, listen up. Interrupt me again and I'll break more than your nose. I may just throw my hand in and break your fucking neck. We need our little demonstration in place and we need it now. We need to have ARES manufactured immediately and set on an unsuspecting public. Which is your part. We need our demands channeled immediately afterwards and directed towards the people who can make decisions and get us our ransom money ... Which is my part." He dropped the drives on to the desk in front of him and slid them across towards McCray. "And we need Morgan-Klein to get APHRODITE manufactured immediately. Our investors need to start buying everything in Morgan-Klein, like yesterday. This is a two phase operation. We need cold, hard ransom money to disappear and we need real time investment in Morgan-Klein to live on. I trust you have the facilities in place to start making it? Please don't tell me you haven't sorted that out yet..."

"No, it's all in place," McCray paused, dabbing his nose carefully. The handkerchief was red and sodden. "I can be ready to move today."

"Good. I will make the call tomorrow morning, set the proverbial cat amongst the pigeons. By the time you've generated and cultured the virus and have it ready to release, they will have assumed it was just a hoax. That's when we make the strike; refresh their memories about what we meant, and what we want."

"Where do we release it?"

"You let me worry about that," Hardy paused. "The accounts are set and ready to receive transactions. After that, the money will be wired on a merry little journey, which the authorities will be unable to trace. Or at least, unable to trace before we've turned it into hard currency."

McCray nodded thoughtfully. "Where's Isobel Bartlett?"

"She's been taken care of," Hardy replied. "Her and that damn Secret Service agent, together."

"You have confirmation of that?"

Hardy glared at him. "There you go again. I don't think you understand me clearly yet. From now on in, you don't question my judgment, and you don't question my decisions, got it?"

McCray looked sullen. "Jesus, I was just trying to get a clear picture, that's all."

"Well, the picture's this... All you have to worry about from now on is getting the ARES formula into a lovely, deadly little super virus. If you ask me, I shouldn't have left you with so much to do. You clearly couldn't handle it. Now, I've got to watch my back as well as seeing to it that we reach the objective." He glanced at his watch, and then frowned at him. "What are you still doing here? Haven't you got a virus to make someplace?"

## FIFTY TWO

They heaved for breath, exhausted from the arduous climb up the side of the edifice. Isobel lay on her back, her breasts heaving, rising and falling dramatically with every labored breath. Stone preferred to lie on his stomach, his head resting between his outstretched arms. His breathing was as intense as Isobel's but he was fitter and his recovery time was quicker than hers. Although he was completely exhausted and thankful for the opportunity to rest. However, time was not on their side and he knew that they would have to keep moving if they were to survive.

He rolled over on to his side and looked at her. "Isobel," he said calmly. "We've got to get out of here. He lost a lot of time and distance taking those long shots but he'll be getting closer now."

"I know," she panted. "What do we do now?"

"We have to take a different route," he said. "We have to use the forest as cover and make sure we are never exposed like that again. But first, we have to move onwards."

"To where?"

"I know a place," he paused, sat up straight. "Over there ..." he pointed towards a ridge on their left. "The other side of that is a small town called Deal. I was there recently."

"How far?"

"About five or six miles or so," he replied. "If anything happens to me, keep that ridge in sight and don't stop walking until you get there. The sheriff is a good cop. He'll help. Mention my name."

She looked at him seriously, her face a picture of concern. "Don't say that," she said quietly. "Don't say anything will happen to you."

He looked at her and she reminded him of a child. Fragile and insecure. He wanted to put a comforting arm around her and tell her it would be all right, but at that moment he wasn't sure it would be.

\*\*\*

Curiosity killed the cat, apparently. But to those who know, curiosity had nothing to do with it. Arrogance was the key factor. Arrogance and stupidity. Cats were not as intelligent as people think. Sure, they are smart. They even had a fair stab at being bright or clever, especially when compared to the overt and open behavior of a dog. But what the cat possessed, which would always be its downfall, was the supreme arrogance and belief in its own importance. A cat will cross a road, and take its time. It will not believe that the car approaching will have the sheer audacity to hit it, nor does the cat think it should quicken its pace to compensate for the car's speed. The arrogance of the cat was what got it killed. Curiosity was just a kinder word for the cat's own stupidity.

Humans were different to cats. Sure, they were arrogant and stupid and many worse things combined. But above all, above everything else, they were curious. Curiosity led to the invention of everything man-made. Curiosity took man to the moon and to the bottom of the ocean's depths. Curiosity took man to the highest peaks and to the sound barrier. Arrogance and stupidity got him killed doing it.

He knew they would be curious. He knew that at some point, they would be unable to resist. At some point, a head would pop over the edge of the peak and present itself as a target. When someone is followed, they always look back. And that was always when they made their biggest mistake. That was when they got themselves caught. Or shot.

He had the trajectory acutely set and he had estimated the wind speed and thermal rise accordingly. Had Isobel not slipped a second after he had pulled the trigger, she would have been nailed by his shot, fallen to the very bottom of the precipice. He was clear on the diametric of the shot and knew that he would make it this time. All he needed was a head above the parapet.

***

"It's time to get going," Stone said. He got to his feet, but first checked that he was far enough away from the cliff edge. He looked down at Isobel and gave her a friendly nudge with the sole of his shoe. "Come on, we're out of time. The only thing going for us, is that he will be as tired as us when he reaches the top."

"Gee, you really know how to cheer a girl up."

"All part of the service," he said with a smile.

She got to her feet and stood shakily. "I've got cramp," she said. "It's not fully there yet, but it's on the verge of cramping."

"You'll walk it out."

"Ah, the voice of sympathy and understanding."

"That's just another service."

She scowled, but it was in jest. It helped to

lighten the mood. "We'd better check he's still on our tail," she said. "Take a quick look."

"I know," Stone replied. "But therein lies the quandary... Just like the soldiers of the First World War, sooner or later someone had to put his head over the top of the trench and see what the enemy was up to."

"And?"

"And they generally lost their head to a sniper," he said bluntly. "I'm quite attached to my head, I like it where it is."

"But how will we know if he's still after us? How will we know where he is?"

Stone walked forwards, caught hold of her shoulder and led her away from the cliff edge and towards the bank of trees at the other end of the plateau. "Oh, he'll be after us. I know that for a fact," he said. "As for where he is, I already know that. He'll be at the bottom of the cliff with the rifle aimed high and all the variables taken into account. He won't follow us up the way we came, he'd be too concerned of me firing on him from above as he climbed. He's a professional, and he wouldn't miss again. He'll be waiting for us to check on him and I'm certainly not going to give him the satisfaction of that."

They walked on for twenty minutes in silence. Their pace was quick but it felt like a comfortable amble compared with the sprint up the steep incline. Stone kept them on course with the distant mountain ridge, which ran parallel with the road below them in the cleft of the valley. The terrain was easier now, but the forest was dense and occasionally they would come up against vast rock falls and the remains of ancient glaciers, long since reduced to rubble. These crossings of rock procured them no cover and it was with quick feet and a heavy heart that they broached these obstructions, ever fearful for their safety.

After crossing one particularly wide piece of rocky ground, Stone called a halt and sat down on a rock, just behind a thin vale of trees. "This is far enough," he said. "We have to know if he is still following us."

"What was it you said about the soldiers in the First World War? Sticking their head up and getting them shot off. Seems reasonable enough not to take a look to me."

"I know, but there's more to it than that. This guy killed Delaney in New York. He shot David Stein dead and he killed Joe Carver," he said.

"And the girl in New York," Isobel interjected. "And the hotel porter."

"Exactly," agreed Stone. "He stops at nothing. So he isn't going to stop after we reach Deal. And he isn't going to stop if we make it back to DC. This guy is hunting us. You heard him shout it from the bottom of the valley. We ran because we had no cover. We kept running because we needed to reach cover."

"Hell, I was running because I was shit scared," Isobel interrupted. "Cover had damn all to do with it from my point of view."

Stone shrugged. "Well, I was running for cover and safety." He pointed to the distant ridge, and then swung his arm in a wide arc. "And now, I have it. In spades. I have cover, I have the invisibility that cover can bring the experienced soldier and I have the advantage of surprise."

"How do you figure that?"

"Because we ran. We ran for our lives. He's hunting us like scared game. And now the rules of engagement have changed," Stone smiled but his eyes were hard and cold. "Because now we're going to stop running and take the fight to him."

## FIFTY THREE

The pain was acute. It seared like a burn and pulsed with his heartbeat and had continued to bleed with the exertion put upon his leg. He took the bottle of pills out of his pocket, twisted off the lid and tipped two capsules into the palm of his hand. There were only two more left in the bottle, and he knew that the pain would outlast the painkillers. He swallowed the two capsules down and they stuck momentarily in his throat. He would have swallowed them with water, but he had none. It had been the one thing that he had overlooked. But he knew that his quarry had none either, so there was no advantageous factor over him. He got the bitter tablets down his throat with a shudder and continued to climb.

He had chosen a different route, foregoing the obvious hazards of following them to the top of the cliff. It would have been too easy to have been ambushed, too easy for the Secret Service agent to put a bullet in his head as he reached the top. Instead, he had moved approximately five hundred yards to his left and negotiated a slighter gradient, a less demanding route. The result was a viable compromise; he had wasted a little time, but would have undoubtedly arrived at the peak with reserves of energy and not burned out and ready to quit.

He had doubled back and picked up the trail from the top of the cliff, using the crystal clarity of the magnification of his sniper scope to survey the possible ambush sites around him. Stone's shoes were rubber soled with minimum tread and a thick heel, resulting in a difficult track to follow. However, Isobel Bartlett wore a slightly raised heel and although far from narrow, the increased elevation in the heel created a deeper track, as the pressure was acutely localized and left a significantly easier imprint to follow. The rest was simply a case dead reckoning. He knew that the only viable option left open to them was to head for the town of Deal. And he too, knew the area well. He had been there recently and seen the various sights. He had pushed a Chevy Tahoe off a precipice and watched it burn with the body inside, not one week before.

## FIFTY FOUR

Stone had found them some water amongst a rock fall. It was the result of rain running from the higher rocky ground, which had filtered down through the gravel and collected in a shallow pool at the bottom. The mineral-rich gravel had filtered out the impurities and it tasted sweet and thin, softened by nature. They drank thirstily and could feel their energy levels rising as the water enriched them to the core, rehydrating their kidneys and liver. The affect was instantaneous. It was like refueling a vehicle. They were revitalized and ready to continue.

Once they had drank their fill, they walked onwards, covering another two hundred yards or so, when Stone stopped and walked towards a clump of trees, almost entirely suspended in perpetual darkness from the canopy of trees above.

To the base of the tree was a clump of white spherical objects ranging in size from that of a little league softball to around the size of a soccer ball. He kicked one over, picked it up and carried it back to where Isobel had been watching somewhat incongruously from the more open ground at the perimeter of the rock fall.

"What on earth?" she exclaimed, staring at the ball with much curiosity.

"It's a puffball," Stone said. He took the medium sized folding knife from his pocket and whipped open the blade. He sliced off a large piece and handed it over to her. He did the same with another piece and dropped the remainder on the ground. "Smells like a wet dog, but tastes a little better..."

"Only a little?" she smiled.

Stone took a bite and chewed slowly. He hadn't realized just how hungry he had been. The fungus was smooth, a little chewy in its raw state but well worth eating, especially as there didn't seem to be a drive-thru anywhere nearby.

"It tastes like Shitake mushroom." Isobel said matter-of-factly. "You could pay ten dollars a pound in a deli for this stuff."

"If say so," Stone commented flatly with his mouth full. He walked back to the clump of dark trees and skirted around the trunk. The ground was damp and moist and the fall leaves had started to rot into a dank mulch. He found what he had been looking for and chiseled away at the trunk for a few moments. He walked back to Isobel with his hands cupped. "Here, try these." The fungus was a brilliant white color and perfectly mushroom shaped. She bit hesitantly into it, then put the whole thing in her mouth and chewed. She nodded approval. "Oyster fungi," Stone smiled. "Same as in the grocers."

"This is great," she said. "I was so hungry after having that water. How do you know all this stuff? The military, right?"

"Yeah, I've done a few survival courses in my time, that's fair to say. The forest is wealthy in food resources, but what we've just eaten has little carbohydrate, and therefore little in the way of calorific value. But it will suppress your appetite and keep you going for a while at least. And it's good to soak up all that water in your stomach." He sliced off two more manageable pieces of the puffball and threw the remainder into the trees. "Here, put these in your bag for later. We'd better get going again."

They marched onwards for another twenty minutes, then Stone stopped again. "This ought to do it," he said.

They had reached a narrow gulch within the plateau. Below them was steep ground with sporadic growth in trees. The slope seemed to go on forever, out of sight. Above them, the slope inclined heavily, reaching upwards and out of sight. The wooded plateau was approximately one hundred yards wide, no more. And ahead of them, the flat ground narrowed even further.

"What are we doing now?" Isobel asked hesitantly.

Stone watched the ground behind him for a moment, and then looked back at her. "We're going to walk on for another fifty to sixty paces or so making as much sign of our presence as we can. Go on, scuff the ground. If a twig or a thin branch is in your way, snap it."

"Why?"

"Because I want him to find us and I want him to become over confident in tracking us." He looked at the doubt on her face and grinned. "Just trust me."

They walked onwards and made their presence more noticeable. After about sixty or seventy yards, Stone stopped at a crop of young, springy trees. Saplings. They were around twelve feet tall and looked about three years old. "Isobel, I want you to walk a hundred yards further on and collect sticks like these." He snapped a twig off of a branch and gave it to her. It was approximately ten inches long and fairly straight. "As well as these, about ten in all, I want you to get two more, a little thicker and twice as long. And hurry."

415

She nodded curtly, although a little hesitantly and walked away.

Stone worked fast. He snapped off some thin branches and worked them into size. Then he took out his folding knife and with its razor edge, he whittled at the thin end of each one until he had a sharp tip. He placed them on the ground and took off his suit jacket. He had long since loosened his tie, but he removed that as well and dropped it on the ground beside him. He cut away at the lining of his jacket and removed a piece of silk around two feet square in size. He sliced this into strips and placed them beside the sharpened twigs. Next, he found a suitable branch belonging to one of the young trees and tested it for both strength and pliability. He took the knife and cut a thicker piece of branch and shaped it to his requirements. It resembled a sharp peg around nine inches long. He turned it on its end and split it in half lengthways. He then cut another strip from the lining of his jacket and sliced it into thin strips. He tied each strip together using a double reef knot until he had a length of makeshift cordage approximately six feet in length. He picked up the spikes and held them between his teeth, as he tied them singularly onto the branch with the strips of silk lining. When he had completed this, he tied his necktie in a loop, hooked it around the thin end of the branch and tied the cordage to the loop.

He fed this back and around the trunk of a young tree and then doubled it back on itself. Time was ticking by, and he kept checking in all directions for the gunman. He took the two split pegs and pressed them into the ground about a foot apart. He then tied two slipknots in the cordage at a similar distance. He eased the length of cordage towards him, using the tree trunk as a block and tackle, and eased the slipknot around the first peg. He secured it, then tentatively repeated the process with the second, making the necessary fine adjustments with the angle of the pegs. He hesitantly released his grip on the cordage and the pegs held the sprung branch firm.

Isobel looked up expectantly as Stone jogged near. He slowed up and nodded approvingly at the bundle of sticks that she had collected.

"Great," he said. "Keep hold of them and follow me."

They jogged across the flat ground another two hundred paces and as before, they made good use of the mulch and fallen leaves to alert their presence. They rounded a corner with a rock fall on one side and a sheer drop on the other. It was a natural funnel before the plateau widened out on both sides. Stone stopped running and looked around the ground.

"Here's as good a spot as any." He looked down the slope, and then above them, high up the mountain and nodded. "Perfect." He dropped to his knees, removed his tattered jacket and started to dig with the blade of the knife. Once the soil was loose, he extracted it with his bare hands and mounded the earth into a tidy pile. He loosened enough earth with the blade of the knife, and then handed it to Isobel, handle first. "Here, take this. Sharpen both ends of the sticks. Hurry now, I don't think we have much time." He turned back to the hole and continued to excavate a perfectly round hole about two feet across and a foot or so deep. He used one of the sharpened sticks to dig with, then scooped the soil out with his bare hands. He then took the sticks that Isobel had sharpened, and one-by-one, stuck them firmly in place two inches apart. Each spike was nestled at a downward angle, stuck in the walls of the hole, spiraled around until the pattern of sticks met. The points of the spikes almost touched. He looked up at Isobel and held out his hand. "Take off your jacket and give me your blouse," he ordered.

"What?"

"You heard, just do it," he snapped. "Hurry!"

She did as he asked. The air was getting colder and she shivered as she stood there in just her thin, lacy bra. Stone looked up, and then looked away again. She put her jacket back on and zipped it right up to the neck. Stone took the sheer blouse and folded it carefully. He took the two longer sticks and laid them on top of the hole in the form of a cross. He laid the folded blouse on top, and then carefully held the edges of material in place with a scattering of earth. He smoothed out the rest of the pile, and then gently sprinkled leaves over the blouse. When he had finished, the construction was completely untraceable. He stood up and nodded, satisfied with their efforts.

"What now?" Isobel asked. She shivered, stood closer to him.

"Now?" he said. "Now we find a good place to hide, and we wait."

## FIFTY FIVE

Tom Hardy stared blankly at the table. The remnants of an early dinner, prime Virginian ham and eggs lay on the plate in front of him. The plate had been too hot and the broken yolks had started to dry hard. There was grease on the plate too, and the remnants of the once delicious meal now looked as uninviting and unappetizing as one could possibly imagine.

He was staring into space, his cell phone held loosely to his ear, his brow perspiring profusely.

"Are you there, Hardy?" The voice was one of concern, broaching on panic. "Can you hear me?"

Tom Hardy looked up from the plate. He picked up the napkin and dabbed the sweat from his beaded brow. He left a little dry egg yolk on his cheek. He felt light- headed, faint. He sipped a mouthful of water and looked around the diner. He was sure onlookers would think he was having a coronary. He attempted to pull himself together as best he could, but he felt flummoxed. "Yeah," he replied. He coughed, cleared his throat. "What the fuck do you mean?"

"I mean the flash drives are blank," McCray said sardonically down the phone line. "Whatever the fuck you have here, it isn't the next super virus, nor is it the next miracle cure."

"Now listen, McCray ..." Hardy growled into the cell phone. "Don't even think about fucking me over. Don't even think that you can go it alone. I will fucking break you. Now once again, for the record. In case you made a silly mistake. Are the drives OK? Were you mistaken? Last chance."

"I 'm not stupid, Hardy. I have a fucking Masters and a PHD. I know when a USB stick contains the formulae for a virus, and I know when I'm listening to music downloads and looking at somebody's photo album."

"What?" Hardy was perplexed, his heart had started to race and he could feel the palpitations fluttering inside his chest.

"I mean the drives looked the same as the others. The only make we use at the facility. Only the bitch must have swiped a few for personal use," McCray explained curtly. "I slipped the drive into my computer and all that's on it is Isobel Bartlett's personal photos and some music."

Hardy shook his head in desperation. "What about the other flash drive?" he asked.

"Same. And essays for a paper she's writing. Nothing to do with ARES or APHRODITE."

"Oh fuck!" Hardy loosened his tie. "All right. Stay put. Go to work as normal and don't change a fucking thing in your life. Got that?"

"Yeah."

"Good. I'll be in touch and we'll have to work out a plan for damage limitation. Now, there is a slim possibility that I can get to my *associate* before he gets to Isobel Bartlett. I just need to get off the phone and make a quick e-mail." He hung up the call and got up from his seat and walked towards the door in a trance.

"Sir!" the waitress called after him. "Sir, you haven't paid your check!"

Her words fell upon deaf ears as Hardy walked out the door and towards his car in the parking lot. A couple of large men in mechanics overalls got off their stools at the counter and followed him outside. Hardy reached the car and opened the door.

"Hey, numb-nuts!" One of the guys called. "Little lady in there's saying you haven't paid your tab."

"Yeah," the other guy chipped in. "Got a

fancy car and all, but you can't make your damn bill?"

Hardy was aware that the two men were shouting at him, but he couldn't think why and at that moment, he simply didn't care. He knew that he could send an e-mail to his associate's web enabled smartphone and if he could do that in time, he would still have a shot at obtaining the drives. He sat down in his seat and thumbed the screen of his iPhone.

"Got a fancy damn car, and a fancy damn cell phone, but he can't make the fucking check?" one of the guys said loudly. "How about we get asswipe here to take a look at his priorities? That nice girl in there works for tips, pal."

"Yeah," the other guy sneered. "And I bet he has good medical insurance. How about giving him the chance to claim on his policy?"

The larger of the two men caught hold of the door of the car and pulled it open. Hardy glanced up. He had a decent signal and was halfway through his email.

The larger man punched him square to the ear and Hardy squealed loudly. It was an agonizing blow, to which he cupped his ear and grit his teeth. One of the guys grabbed at the iPhone and Hardy struggled to keep possession.

"Wait, I have to send an urgent ...!" He didn't finish the sentence, as both men set upon him with raining fists. The cell phone dropped out of the car and onto the ground. Hardy was pulled from the vehicle and kicked a couple of times, then witnessed the final humiliation as one of the guys stamped a work boot onto the screen and wires, silicon chips, the battery and other components spilled out onto the ground and scattered in all directions.

"That will teach you, corporate dick."

"Yeah, and maybe you won't run out on your bill again."

The two men whooped and patted backs and high-fived their way back inside the diner and were greeted by a smiling waitress who poured them both coffee and offered them a free dessert.

Hardy pushed himself up and sat back against the rear wing of his BMW. He cupped his throbbing ear with his hand and dabbed a handkerchief against his bloodied lips. His ribs ached and his heart had sunk. He knew it was too late, knew he was finished. He had grown confident, too confident by half. He had unleashed an unfailing, unrelenting assassin on the only person to know the true identity of the drives, and in doing so, had cut his own lifeline prematurely. He had not only signed his own death warrant, he had rolled it up and delivered into the bargain.

## FIFTY SIX

He had followed their tracks, grown used to the anomalies in contradiction of nature and compensated accordingly. Isobel's tracks bore the most success and in focusing upon her disturbance upon the ground, he had anticipated their route exactly. They were heading towards Deal. That much was obvious. They h a d chosen a simple and certainly the easiest route, skirting the mountain and using the relative flatness of the plateau to make the quickest progress across the terrain. He could speed his own progress, anticipate their path more and more and take a good look for confirmation less often. He estimated they had a seven hundred yard lead on him and he was sure that he was gaining ground all the time.

At a point near the most recent outcrop of rocks he noticed the tiny scattering of debris. It was white and flaky and looked like tufts of cotton candy. He looked around and noticed the large growth of fungi in the darkest stretch of wood. They had taken time to eat and rest. The fools! He was sure that he was ever closer now, ever gaining on them. They had become complacent and that made them ever more predictable.

The trail became increasingly easier to follow, progressively more noticeable. Part of this he put down to his acute skills, honing themselves in the theatre of practice. The other part, he put down to their amateur complacency. He kept the rifle held loosely in both hands, able to bring it to action in a split second. He was ready for them, but somehow he knew that the kill would not be as entertaining or fulfilling as the hunt. They were scared and they were too gutless to fight. He would have thought more of the Secret Service man, but then again bodyguards were reactive, not proactive. They were trained to protect, by whatever means and that usually meant standing their ground momentarily to react to the threat and then retreating to safety with their charge. The VIP was the most important thing and running from any conflict generally meant keeping them safe from harm.

This Secret Service agent was not proving to be a worthy adversary and he would let him know just what a letdown he had been before he killed him.

He stepped through a thin vale of trees, pushed some branches aside then saw the flash of the branch and felt the searing pain to his waist. He screamed vehemently, resonating an agonizing holler through the forest. Part of the scream was audible in the echo around the valley.

The branch had swung back with considerable speed, but he had been quick in his reactions, partially blocking it with his arm. Two spikes had impaled his forearm, piercing completely through the flesh to the other side; another two had spiked his stomach and groin but were mercifully shallow wounds because of the angle of his arm holding the branch out from him. He panted for breath, tried to process the information in his mind and comprehend what had happened. He was in shock, nearing nausea, but still he fought against the situation, and started to walk backwards. The spikes left his abdomen and groin, but he was held fast by the spikes imbedded in his forearm. He dropped the rifle to the ground and took a large combat sheath knife from his utility vest. He sliced through the bindings and dropped to the ground, the two spikes still stuck in his arm. The pain was insurmountable. He quickly reached for the bottle and took the last of the remaining pills. They were fearsomely strong and he already had a dose in his system. He chewed on them, clenching his teeth and enduring the pain by controlling his breathing. He wrenched the first spike out of his arm, then grit his teeth together firmly and pulled at the second. It held fast, but he forced and wriggled it and it lost purchase and slipped easily out. He was verging on blacking out, but hurriedly undid his utility vest, allowing it to hang open and tore at the shirt under his overalls. It wouldn't budge, so he cut at it with the knife and tugged out a considerable length. He wrapped it hastily around the wounds and tied the knot as best he could with one hand. It was tight, acted like a makeshift tourniquet as well as a dressing.

He was past care now, didn't worry unduly about the wound. All he wanted was to stem the blood flow long enough to see them both dead. After that, he didn't care, didn't even want to think that far ahead. All that mattered was killing the two targets and declaring victory over their dead bodies. He grit his teeth together tightly, fought through the pain and rose unsteadily to his feet. He picked up the rifle and moved tentatively forwards. They had been clever and they had made a strike back at him. But he was still the hunter and they were still the prey.

\*\*\*

The scream had been eerily loud and had reverberated throughout the tranquility of the forest. Isobel had flinched as the sound of the man's screams had enveloped them with the grisly echo. The silence that followed seemed a cruel and deathly respite. There was no way of knowing whether the man had fled, was on his way towards them, or was left impaled and dying, bleeding to death on the spikes.

In hindsight, which was a wonderfully ineffectual gift, Stone realized that visual confirmation was perhaps more desirable than he had first imagined. Now, he felt useless. He knew that the fight was still out there, but now he would have to break cover to confirm the condition of their enemy. He waited for perhaps twenty minutes, an agonizingly long time in the realm of the unknown, then turned to Isobel, his face full of concern. "I have got to go and check," he said. "It's no use us waiting here any longer. I have to confirm that we got him, or that he's still out there hunting for us."

"But you heard the scream," she whispered in protest. "They would have heard the scream in New Hampshire!"

Stone shook his head. "I have to know if he's alive or if he's dead. I have to know if he's still on our trail. Besides, if we did get him, and he's badly injured, I need to arrest him and get him medical help."

"Medical help?" She looked at him as if he were crazy. "He's killed people. He's even tried to kill us."

"What do you want me to do? Execute him, while he's impaled and vulnerable on the spikes?"

He paused. "I'll kill if I have to, have always been prepared to. But I won't kill a prisoner. Call it a soldier's code, a kind of base-level karma. What goes around comes around." He rose steadily and carefully from their makeshift hide, and looked down at her. "Just stay where you are and wait for me."

She looked worried, fearful. "But what if...?"

He looked at her mockingly. "Thanks for the vote of confidence! Just give me an hour. If I don't return by then, head for that ridge and run like hell. Deal is about three miles from here."

"An hour!" she exclaimed. "But the first trap is only a hundred meters or so over there." She pointed into the dark thickness of the pine forest.

"But I don't know what I will find." He turned around and walked cautiously down the incline and onto the thinly wooded plateau. He drew his pistol from its holster as he walked, and sighted it in front of himself as he disappeared from view. Four shots, he told himself. Make them count.

The forest was eerily quiet and the light was dimmer now that the sun had reached the top of the furthest most ridge and light would soon be at a premium. He detoured from their previous route, skirting the pitfall trap and arrived back at the setting of the first trap from behind. At first he had thought he had missed the spot completely, but then his heart sunk as he saw the severed strips of suit lining, and two spikes discarded upon the ground. He approached cautiously and studied the two spikes. They were bloodied and there were droplets of blood on the ground, captured on the surfaces of the fallen leaves. So the gunman hadn't faked the scream and he hadn't been on to the trap. He had been compromised, surprised and would no doubt be feeling a lot less powerful and invincible now that he had spilt some of his own blood on the ground.

Rob Stone looked around, in a quandary what to do next. He had struck a blow to their enemy, but surely getting to Deal safely was better than continuing to hunt the man down and perhaps lose control of the situation. His bodyguard instincts were starting to take over, to shout in his ear that there was more to life than fighting and winning. And that survival was the ultimate goal, and that he could leave now and live to fight another day. But as tempting as that sounded, he knew that the fight would have to be played out here and he knew that it would most probably end in death someone.

He looked down at the blood on the ground and studied the leaves for a moment. His eyes blurred as he attempted to take in such detail, then he saw the next drop of blood. And the next. And the next. Soon, he had the trail and was following it completely and easily. But instead of continuing on its path, or fleeing, the trail deliberately skirted the thinner forest and went up the incline. Stone started to follow, and then his heart beat ever more rapidly. Suddenly, reaching Isobel was his priority, not taking his time to hunt this man down. That would be a slow process and he may walk into an ambush, as the gunman had done so himself. Besides, he did not like the route and direction that the man had taken.

He moved fast down the plateau, keeping the pistol in front of him as he ran. As he neared, he slowed down and walked. Isobel was standing in front of a tree well away from where he had left her. He was angry at first, she should have kept hidden and stayed in one spot. He waved, but she did not respond. He frowned. And then noticed the expression of terror upon her face. Then, as he got nearer, he noticed that her hands were out of sight behind her back and that a strip of cord or leather was wrapped around her neck, securing her tightly to the tree. It looked as if she so much as flinched she would start to strangulate.

He moved his body in a wide arc, keeping the pistol in front of him. He searched the forest, but saw nothing. He knew he had lost, knew that everything had suddenly become hopeless. Above all else, he knew he was the target in a crystal clear rifle sight. The crosshairs centered on him.

"Put the weapon down, or I drill a bullet in her forehead!"

Stone tried to compensate for the echo, tried to get a fix on the location, but it was useless. He felt impotent. There was a gunshot to his left and a chunk of bark split off the trunk of the tree just above Isobel's head. Isobel let out a shrill scream.

"Do it!"

Stone dropped the pistol onto the ground, about four feet away from him.

There was another gunshot, another chunk of bark blown from the tree and another scream from Isobel. "Pick it up, and throw it as far as you can!"

Stone did as he was told, and turned towards the sound of the voice. He was tempted to start negotiating, but he was right out of candy. He knew he had nothing to offer and he knew that the gunman was holding the cards. All of them aces.

There was a rustling of branches and dried leaves and the man stepped out from the canopy of trees and entered the relative open of the clearing. Stone noticed the makeshift bandage around the man's arm and then he noticed the man favoring his left leg. So he *had* hit him back down on the road. Two-zip. But then he realized that the guy was about to score a homerun.

"I didn't think you were a worthy adversary," the man said loudly. "But then there was that trap. I compliment you on you ingenuity." He raised his arm displaying the bloodied bandage and limped forwards. "But I'd say I've evened things up now, wouldn't you?"

Stone remained silent. He glanced across at Isobel. She merely stared blankly ahead. She had been crying. God only knew what he had done or said to her as he had strung her up.

The man walked forwards and stopped just short of Stone. "Put your hands on top of your head," he ordered harshly. "Do it!"

Stone did as he was ordered. The man stepped forwards cautiously and jabbed the muzzle of the rifle into his stomach. Stone dropped instantly to the floor, his hands clutching the searing pain in his abdomen. He was winded and struggled to catch his breath.

"Good, I think I have your attention," he sneered. "Now, get up. On your knees. You're going to do some begging."

Stone rolled onto his side and felt an uncomfortable dig in his right leg. He gasped through the pain of his stomach and suddenly realized that what dug into his thigh had been the bulky handle of his folding lock knife. He rolled onto his stomach, shielding his right arm from view and made a deliberate farce of getting onto his knees. By the time he did so, he had the knife held tightly in the palm of his hand. The knife had a retro-fitted thumb stud on the blade, enabling it to be opened with only the use of one hand. The knife had sentimental value to Stone, but he had brought it up to date with both a thumb stud and a clip point. It was also razor sharp. Honed on a diamond whetstone. He pressed the stud with his thumb and rolled it in a tight arc, opening the blade slowly behind his back.

"You're going to beg," the man said cruelly. "I wish I could say I'd made your brother beg, but that would be a lie..."

Stone looked up at him, his eyes cold and cruel. "What do you know about my brother?"

The man took a couple of paces backwards and held the rifle up so that the muzzle pointed towards Stone's chest. "Ah, *now* it's clear. Your brother was investigating me, when he died. Or should I say, when I killed him."

"My brother was investigating a disbanded government program. What the hell did you have to do with it?" Stone clenched his teeth, put his left hand outstretched to hold him steady on his knees. "So you're one of *them,* are you? Yeah, that would make a whole lot of sense."

The man looked puzzled. "What do you mean? He was investigating me."

"Is that what that fucking psychopath Tom

435

Hardy told you? Because if you *are* one of them, you won't have a fucking clue what's been going on. You won't even know who the fuck Tom Hardy really is anyway."

"Who?" He frowned, held the rifle higher, like he was going to shoot and then relaxed his grip once more. "He was investigating me..."

"Sure," Stone spat at him. "Oh yeah, you're one of them all right. Brainwashed and head-fucked into knowing nothing. You don't know who Tom Hardy is? Well, where do you think your vital painkillers come from? Who do you think gets you all the things in your apartment, or the car you drive?"

"I get them..."

"You get shit, pal," snapped Stone. "Who's your mother? What does she do, where does she live? You don't know shit. Where's the family home? You don't even know your own name. Go on, tell me your name, or your best friend's name from high school, or the girl who popped your cherry..."

"I..."

"You don't know shit." Stone said flatly. "You are the only one that's left. The only piece left of the entire Janus Project. A project that took people and turned them into killers by using hypnosis and drugs and all sorts of genetically engineered hormone crap. Then you were used as a government tool. Wet work. Assassinations ... Women ... Children of powerful men that the filthy shadows of the government don't want to dirty their hands with. The CIA has plenty of those shadow departments and are only too pleased to use them to effect. And then a well-connected and honest senator finds out and threatens to shut down the operation and blow the whistle to the press. Janus is shut down almost overnight and all the subsequent operatives, the living experiments, are disposed of. All accept you. Tom Hardy's own little project. That's what my brother was investigating, and that's what I have been investigating."

"And I killed your brother," the man smiled. "I sliced his throat open and watch his life blood wash down the drain with the rainwater. He looked up at me as he struggled on the ground. Knew he was going to die."

Stone looked at him coldly. "What, you want me to scream and shout? Big deal. I know how my brother died, I've accepted it. You know, I didn't even think you would still exist. I assumed that Hardy had gotten into some shit and that you were a fabrication and accusation from former Janus personnel who wanted Hardy shut down. But I can see it's true. You really are a clueless machine with no emotion. You really should have been terminated along with the rest of the project.

Tell me, have you seen your mother in the dreams?" The man stared at him, non-committal. "Sure you have ... Around forty, blonde hair, a kind face. What do you remember? The cruel kids at your birthday party and the loving mother comforting you? Or your graduation from high school and the loving family greeting you home? I've read the brief, studied all of the files. I know all the memories they implanted, impregnated into your mind. The cool surf chick in LA, who pleasured you on the beach? Well, any memory you had was shared with the other freaks, the other experiments on the Janus project. They couldn't possibly waste time creating individual memories and legends for everyone..."

"No! Shut up!" The man screamed at him, dropped the rifle loosely by his side. He stared down at the ground for a moment, real and solemn emotion in his expression.

A moment of distraction was all Stone needed. He was up and rushing him, the blade of the knife scything towards the man's side, ready to gut him in one slash, his other hand going for the muzzle of the rifle. He got the muzzle, but the man let go of his grip on the rifle and snapped his fist out with a sharp jab, simultaneously sweeping his other arm in a wide arc which caught Stone's wrist and knocked the knife out of his grasp. Almost at once Stone was met by a short, sharp front kick into his abdomen. The wind rushed out of his lungs and he dropped onto his knees, let the rifle drop on the ground. As the man started to rain blows down, Stone jabbed him in the groin with two successive hard punches. Both men hit the ground. Two hundred and fifty plus pounds was slower getting up than one-ninety and Stone realized two things. The guy was very good at unarmed combat and he also had a considerable size and strength advantage.

Both men were in their fighting stances and both men kept moving. Both were light on their feet and were moving slowly in a counterclockwise rotation. The man edged forwards, his eyes on Stone's. Neither man looked anywhere but into the other's eyes. All other vision was by the periphery. Stone tried to guess the man's strengths and weaknesses. He didn't seem to have any. Stone hedged that he would have a speed advantage, but this was quickly dismissed when the man bounded out leading with a front kick and a combination of punches and strikes, each one narrowly missing Stone, who in reaction dodged to his left and snapped out a roundhouse kick. It hammered home, but lacked any real stopping power against the man's muscled torso. The man merely turned and kept coming. Stone dodged again and this time punched the man on the side of the head and followed it with a back fist across his neck. Neither of the strikes noticeably slowed the man down, and the two men merely squared off again having swapped positions.

Stone's heart pounded and he fought for breath. He knew he couldn't go on indefinitely and decided to go in hard and fast and make the man's eyes his target. He rushed forward and aimed a faked kick at the man's stomach. As the man reached out to block, Stone jumped high and into his space snapping out his fingers and aiming at the man's face. A finger found its mark and the man reeled backwards. Stone jabbed and swung a combination of blows at the man's face and then dropped low and punched the groin again. The man reeled backwards and groaned, but fought back hard and what started out looking like two experts parrying, ended up looking like two drunk hobos trading wild blows. The blows were vicious too and both men were bloodied and cut. Before he knew what had happened Stone felt the vice grip of the man bear hugging him. His arms were clamped against his sides and he was lifted clean off the ground and rushed backwards. Stone managed a vicious and powerful head-butt onto the bridge of the man's nose, smashing it flat. Blood and mucous poured out of the man's nostrils, and he stumbled a few feet until he crashed Stone's back up against a pine tree. The wind knocked out of him, his sight blurred by both tears and blood, Stone dropped to the ground. He reached up and caught hold of the

Glock pistol in the man's utility vest holster. He got the weapon free and brought the muzzle up under the man's chin, but it was hit out of his hand with a striking blow that threatened to break Stone's wrist. The stubby black pistol flew off into the trees. The man kicked Stone savagely in the face, and he fell down onto a bed of pine needles and twigs. The man then turned and limped towards the M4 rifle which lay strewn on the forest floor.

Through the tears and blood Stone saw the glint of the blade poking through the pine needles. He reached out and picked up his folding knife from where it lay. He got to his knees, saw the man bend down and pick up the assault rifle. The man brushed debris from the action, blew into the receiver to get any grit out and then looked back at Stone.

Stone raised the knife, flipped it over so that he held the tip of the blade between his thumb and first two fingers, and threw it as hard as he could at the man in front of him.

Stone knew the principles of knife throwing, if only as a curious child who played in the woods. He knew that from three, six and nine feet he should hold the blade, providing that the knife had an evenly distributed handle to blade weight ratio. The knife in question did, and in turn, it spun handle over blade all the way through the air until the blade thudded into the man's chest.

The man stood stock still, the rifle still in

his hand. He looked down curiously, stared transfixed at the polished rosewood handle protruding from his body. The brass studs in the handle glinted in the sunlight, glistening like gold in a jeweler's window. He clawed at the handle, clasped it and tried to pull it clear.

Stone got unsteadily to his feet, but quickly regained some composure and lunged towards the man and hammered the palm of his hand onto the end of the knife's handle, driving it deeper and forcing the man backwards. Stone, his hands by his sides, was spent. Battered, bloodied and bruised. It was all he could do to stand. He watched the man take three steps backwards, then recover his balance. The man raised the rifle in his right hand, aimed it shakily at Stone like he was wielding a pistol and cracked a smile through bloodied lips. The knife with its three inch blade stuck firm. All the way up to the hilt. But the man was solid muscle and must have had a fifty four inch chest. There had to be a good cushion of meat for the blade to slice through before doing serious damage to arteries or organs. It had bought some time at least.

The man wobbled a little, took another step backwards and tried to regain balance. His foot broke through the leaves and debris and the thin material it concealed. The drop was only a foot or so, but every inch of it ran over the sharpened spikes. It wasn't the drop that did the damage, but the man's reaction. He tried to pull his leg out quickly and each sharpened stick dug deeply into his flesh. He screamed in agony and like a trapped animal fought frantically to escape, only tightening the grip and effectiveness of the trap and driving the spikes deeper. He fell down awkwardly onto one knee, the other twisting as the spikes gripped firmly deep into the flesh of his calf.

Stone approached cautiously, pulled the rifle out of the man's grip and looked down at him. The man stared up defiantly. Stone pulled the knife out of the man's chest and a gush of thick, dark blood followed. Stone wiped the blade carefully on the man's shoulder, cleaning the blood away on his ripped and tattered shirt. "This was my brother's knife," he said calmly. "He carried it all his life. Showed me how to throw it into trees when we were kids." He looked into the man's eyes as he folded the blade and slipped it back into his pocket. The man's breathing was labored, but he still looked defiantly at Stone.

"I enjoyed killing him," the man rasped.

Stone said nothing as he reversed the rifle and held the barrel in both hands like an axe. He raised it high above his head and in a motion of absolute power and brute force brought it crashing down on the man's skull. It was a devastating blow and the man sagged lifelessly, his skull crushed and bloody.

Stone looked at the man's motionless body, then turned his back on him and walked over to Isobel. He took the knife back out and sliced at her bindings and she fell forwards into his arms. She said nothing, didn't need to, and they held on to each other tightly and listened to the wonderful silence of the forest which had now enveloped them.

## FIFTY SEVEN

It was dark and cold when they walked into Deal. The town was deathly quiet and the only light shone from within the houses. There didn't appear to be any street lamps. They were tired and looked a sight in their ripped clothes and muddied and bloodied skin. The Sheriff's department was closed, but there was a direct dial telephone hanging up in a box outside and Stone called through to Sheriff Harper at his home number. He was short with the sheriff on the phone and requested that he come over to meet them immediately. Harper said he would be there in twenty minutes and that was the best he could do. One horse towns.

They walked across the street and went into Sally's Diner. They were served by a waitress, who barely gave them both a second glance and they took their hot coffees and two donuts each over to an enclosed booth. Stone had ordered them two club sandwiches that the waitress started to prepare.

Just one member of staff doing it all. The donuts barely touched the sides and nor did the clubs, which were both heavy on turkey breast and maple smoked bacon and came with a side of fries. They were halfway through their refill coffees when they saw Sheriff Harper draw up outside the Sheriff's Department in his cruiser.

He looked around for them, and then looked over towards the diner. He noticed Stone at the booth and jogged across the road and straight up the steps. "Evening, Jodie," he said to the waitress behind the counter as he entered the otherwise empty diner. "A coffee, please..." He made his way over towards them, and stared at their appearance with much interest and amusement. "Been taking in the sights? I hear the mountains are good for walking at this time of year."

"Funny man," Stone commented flatly. "Take a seat before you fall down laughing."

Sheriff Harper sat beside Isobel, held out his hand. "Please to meet you, Ma'am." He took her hand softly and shook it. "Sheriff Harper. Call me John."

"Isobel," she replied.

Stone coughed, and both Harper and Isobel turned their attention to him. "Good, now that the pleasantries are out of the way, let's get down to business. Sheriff, we have an incident to report. And no time to hang around and help you with your inquiries."

Harper leaned forward and put his hands on the table. "Sounds as if you're both in a bit of a pickle."

"It could have been worse. There's a town not too far from here called South Chesterton, you know it?"

Harper smiled. "We're not in Hicksville. We *do* know who our neighbors are," he paused. "About ten miles in all, other side of the valley. We play them at Sunday league softball. They suck."

"Does your jurisdiction run to there?"

"When it has to."

"Good, just see that it does on this occasion. There's a dead hobo, out by the fishing hole. Well, he wasn't actually homeless, he had a cabin in the woods. Lived off the grid though. His body can't have been discovered yet, otherwise you would have heard about it."

"I've heard of him. There's a few vets out here living in the woods. Iraq and Afghan now too, not just veterans of Vietnam. What happened?" Harper looked up, then suddenly held his hand to silence Stone, as the waitress drew near with an empty cup and a pot of steaming coffee. She poured the coffee to fill the cup, and then walked away, sensing that she was intruding. "Sorry about that, small town, big gossip."

Stone nodded. "The man, Joe Carver, was shot in the throat and head from across the lake with a rifle, an M4 assault rifle, actually."

"That's a very precise description, what else can you tell me?"

"The gunman is lying dead, in the forest about four or five miles or so away from here, up on a plateau. He was trying to kill us. His vehicle, a big silver Mercedes sedan is abandoned on the road about three or four miles below and to the West."

"Sounds like that plateau is up on Beaumont Ridge. Judging from the road below. Good deer and elk shooting up that way. Plenty of water runs down and pools up there. The deer like that. What about the man's weapon?"

"The rifle is hidden in a clump of bushes twenty feet in a direct line from his head. I've made it safe and his knife is beside it." Stone took the Glock 9mm he'd recovered from the forest out from his holster and slid it across the table to Harper. "This is his also, you'd better hang on to it. There is a Sig Sauer pistol up there too, it's mine, but I couldn't waste any more time searching for it." He looked at the sheriff intently. "Now, we are on a tight schedule, I can answer any questions you have, but I just can't spare the time involved in a formal investigation."

"State Police will get involved in this, that's a certainty. I have no other choice but to let them in on it," he paused. "Of course, I could just play dumb, until you get yourself back here and let me know what happened. Let nature take its course, so to speak. Once the body of the hobo has been reported, I can take my time with the investigation. I won't have to let State Police know until the body of your gunman turns up, that way there will be an obvious connection and I'll have no choice but to inform them. But until then, you'll have all the time you need. And at this time of year, not many people are going to start heading out to Beaumont Ridge."

"Why is that?" Isobel asked.

"Bears, Ma'am. Whole damn lot of them been sighted out there, and they're real hungry, trying to get fat stores for winter. They shouldn't be approached. Best to stay out of the area completely." Harper paused. "At least, that's the warning I will put out at first light tomorrow."

"Sheriff," Stone stood up and held out his hand, "I like your style."

Harper took them back to his house where they both showered and borrowed some clean clothes. Harper's pants were a little baggy on Stone's trim, muscled waist and Mrs. Harper was a good two sizes bigger that Isobel, but she was grateful for the clean jeans and sweatshirt that the sheriff's wife willingly provided for her. Stone swabbed his cuts with some antiseptic and patched himself up with some sutures and band aids.

They drove out to the fishing hole on the outskirts of South Chesterton and the police cruiser's headlights lit up the deserted parking lot, deserted except for the bright red Ford Mustang, illuminated in the darkness by the cruiser's bright beams.

Stone opened his door and looked at both Isobel and Sheriff Harper. "Both of you wait here," he paused, picking up the flashlight which was fixed to the console of the car with a special holder. "I wouldn't be surprised if that sick bastard tampered with my car as an insurance policy. Give me a few minutes to make a check." He stepped out of the cruiser and slammed the door behind him.

The Mustang was parked on a stretch of dry dirt, its rear end raised slightly because of the contour of the ground. He approached cautiously, tracing the beam of the flashlight around the ground all around the vehicle. He walked slowly and surely, until he had completely circled the vehicle. Next, he got closer, and visually searched the wheel arches and under carriage, the chassis and underneath the engine. He opened the trunk with his key, carefully ran his finger along the open space, and then opened it all the way, all the while checking for contact wires or tripping devices. He opened both doors equally as carefully; taking the same precautions, then popped the hood and shone the beam all around the engine bay. The car appeared to be clear, and he had made sure to observe the minute detail, such as greasy finger marks on the coachwork. It was as thorough a job as he could hope to achieve in the darkness and he knew that the likelihood of the car being booby-trapped was slim. The assassin had been a master marksman, would have prided himself on the precision method he favored.

Stone slipped the key into the Mustang's ignition and fired up the engine. Part of him flinched, the other part regained self-control and composure. He walked over to the cruiser and bent down to the Sheriff's window. "Thanks for everything you've done. Perhaps you could do one more thing?"

"Shoot."

"Get that Mercedes off the road and away from any opportunistic thieves. I want to order a thorough examination of it at a later date. See what forensics can come up with. Put some surgical gloves on when you move it."

"No problem," Sheriff Harper smiled. "Now get yourselves out of here. You've caused me enough trouble tonight. So much for an easy life."

It was an eight-hour drive to Washington. Flying down would have taken the time down to a mere fraction, but Stone had wanted the time in which to think, to make sense of the recent events. The roads were quiet and the car sat happily at sixty to seventy miles per hour and with such little revs running, the twin exhausts made hardly any noise. It was only at an idling tick-over, or at full throttle or under heavy engine breaking that the exhausts sucked the noise from the mighty V8 and resonated like the clap and rumble of thunder.

Isobel had slept for most of the way, or least she had pretended to in that manner one does when there is little conversation to be gleaned mutually. She was aware that Stone was heavy in thought, and after the first few attempts to converse were rebuked, she settled into the journey and the company of her own thoughts. After a while, both of them were so deeply in thought that the journey appeared to rush past and before long they were around the halfway mark. They had stopped for fuel and refreshments and a moment to stretch their cramped legs at an all-night service station. Stone noticed that Isobel was becoming increasingly withdrawn. He decided that she was coming down from the adrenaline rush that had taken hold of them and ploughed them on through their ordeal.

Since the moment the gunman had squeezed the trigger in New York, they had been constantly running, persistently heading towards an objective. Isobel herself had undoubtedly been under the strain for a longer period of time, as she had been running scared since the moment she had taken the flash drives from the bioresearch facility. She now looked thoroughly drained, exhausted.

They had drank full-sugar sodas and eaten some less than healthy glazed pastries that tasted a day or two old and bought some gummy candy and bottled water for the remainder of the journey. After they had stretched their legs around the deserted floodlit parking lot they had returned to the car and continued with their journey.

They had arrived back in Washington DC a little after four AM and reached Stone's apartment soon after. Stone decided that Isobel's apartment was out of the question and besides, the Secret Service agent preferred to be on home ground when he felt under threat. Although the assassin was out of the picture, lying dead and trapped somewhat in the darkness of the Vermont forest, they had no idea of how many people were after them, nor if they were still under immediate threat.

Stone had shown Isobel to his own bedroom, given a clean bathrobe to her as well as some fresh towels from the linen closet and had said that if she wanted anything, then she was simply to help herself or come and wake him up. He had closed the door on her at four-thirty. Before he had collapsed on the couch, he took a loaded Glock model 19 pistol out from the back drawer of his bookcase, checked the magazine and breach and tucked it under his pillow. He was asleep two minutes later and awake a minute after that when Isobel came creeping out of the bedroom, had lifted the sheet and cuddled up beside him on the couch. Her breathing was soft, and her actions and body language had demanded nothing more than the comfort of sharing their sleep. Stone felt her soft flesh on his back, felt her knees resting into the back of his own, tensed as she wrapped an arm around his waist. And relaxed as he sensed her fall asleep against his back. He closed his eyes, relished the warmth of her breath on his skin, and was asleep before he could even begin to wonder why she had joined him in such a way.

When Stone woke at eight forty five, he was aware that he was now lying alone on the couch. Had he dreamt her presence? He didn't think so. There was something innocent and comforting about her actions, as if she were a scared and lonely child seeking comfort from a parent or sibling after a bad nightmare, although her gentle touch and the way in which they had lain together suggested more.

He rolled onto his back and stretched, yawned, then sniffed the air. There was the aroma of frying bacon and toast under the grill. He swung his legs over the edge of the couch and rubbed the sleep from his blurry eyes. He felt cheated, his sleep having passed by in a blink.

He flinched suddenly as his cell phone let out a shrill tone and started to vibrate on the table. The table was topped with a plate of thick polished glass and the tiny device started to perform an intermittent pirouette. He watched it for a moment, wondering whether it would in fact complete the circle. He cut the performance short: "Stone here."

"Hi there, Sheriff Harper here, from Vermont."

"Go ahead, Sheriff."

"Got that fancy Mercedes all secured, back at my place."

"Good. Can you keep it there?"

"Shouldn't be a problem, for too long. Just one thing, though."

"What's that?"

"It's like god damn mission control in there. Laptop computer, wireless modem connection booster. Military grade, I reckon. Even a receiver for a bug, or tracking device, or some damn thing," Sheriff Harper paused. "And the trunk was kitted out like an armory. Sub-machine pistol, customized job with a silencer, a sawn-off pump-

455

action shotgun next to the car and a number of pistols and ammunition tucked here and there."

"The man was a professional assassin. I guess it's just the tools of his trade."

"Well, whatever it is, I don't like having it all in my possession without the paperwork, you can understand that?"

"I understand, Sheriff. How about hanging in there for another twenty-four hours, that's all I ask. If haven't got back to you by then, call it in."

"Ok," Harper replied hesitantly. "Anyway, no word's come from the fishing hole out at South Chesterton. We've had heavy rain this morning, ain't nobody going fishing today so I guess you'll be clear for a while."

"Thank you, Sheriff. And thanks for your call, I appreciate your position. Look, one more thing. Joe, the hobo guy. He was a veteran. I feel bad him being out there like that. If there's no next of kin or sufficient funds, I'd like to pick up the tab for his funeral. Please contact me closer to the time, thanks Sheriff." Stone cut the connection and stared thoughtfully into space. There was more on his mind now and he wondered what a difference Harper's call would have made. The sheriff would be in a tight spot if Stone could not come up with another lead soon.

Isobel appeared in the doorway of the lounge, a plate of food in each hand. "Hi," she said, a little awkwardness in her voice. "Hungry?"

Stone covered his shorts with part of the sheet. He smiled, "Sure," he said. "You've been up a while?"

Isobel sat down beside him and handed him a plate and a fork. "Yeah, about thirty minutes," she said. "I thought we might have a lot to do today." She took a mouthful of scrambled egg, chewed a few times and swallowed. "What do you think?"

Stone hurriedly took a mouthful. It was smooth and creamy and had a little dried basil and black pepper in it as he always thought it should have. There was a little pat of butter on top, and the heat was melting it. It looked glossy and rich. "Delicious," he said.

"Not the egg, stupid," she teased. "Whether we might have a lot to do today, that's what I was asking. Anyway, who was that on the phone? You look worried."

Stone felt dumb. He cut a piece of bacon off with the edge of his fork and scooped some scrambled egg onto it. He ate it, chewing thoughtfully. When he had finished the mouthful, he frowned. "That was Sheriff Harper, just reporting in, nothing to worry about," he said. "And to your first question, and not mistaking it for your cooking this time, I reckon our only way forward is to take the direct approach. Take the bull by the horns and give him the shock of his life."

"Who do you suspect?"

"Well, I know Tom Hardy is in this up to his eyeballs." Stone paused. "You spoke to him at the conference. Do you think it was the same man who you heard in the restroom, or McCray's office?"

"Possibly."

"I'd be willing to bet definitely. What about McCray?"

"What about him?"

"Did it sound like him?"

"The restroom echoed, distorted the voices. I guess I would never have suspected him, so never linked the dots."

"What about in McCray's office?"

"Hard to say, I was absolutely petrified. My heart was beating so loudly, I could barely hear a thing. I was convinced I was going to be caught. It would make a lot of sense though."

Stone shook his head. "Not good enough. Although I would have to agree, it *would* make a lot of sense. I met with him, rattled him, he certainly looked to have a guilty conscience."

"Who *is* this guy Hardy, exactly?"

Stone put his plate down and leaned back against the couch. "Well, that's a long story, where do I start? Tom Hardy has been CIA as long as most people can remember. He's certainly outlasted every hotshot, new initiative director, hostile accountant, crusading politician and departmental cuts. You name it, Hardy's outlasted it. You name the coup or scandal and he can be linked, albeit indirectly to its very core. He's a survivor. That much is true."

"What about the assassin, the connection? What the Hell kind of project *was* that?"

"Possibly one of the most evil concocted from Langley, possibly not. There's so much shit that has come out of their special projects departments, nobody probably raised so much as an eyebrow. I got onto this case because the President found out about the program and wanted to know more. My brother was tasked before me, he simply thought I'd be the one person he could trust. He wanted to be assured that nothing like that would ever happen under his own administration. After a lot of digging, I found out that one of the chief researchers and directors was Tom Hardy. Hardy lives a pretty good existence for a company man, so I dug a little deeper. Hardy's indirect involvement in just about everything dark within the agency made me highly suspicious. There were locked files that I managed to unlock. Prominent targets had been neatly taken out of the picture, assassinated, in plain terms and all trailing back to Tom Hardy in some way. A posting, a requisition, a meeting, something. All the jobs were so neat. I'm ex-special forces and I know how untidy even the pros can get, especially under pressure. I started to get more suspicious of the man and his involvement in anything and everything. You see, if he were hiring privateer assassins, then sooner or later there would be a mistake. Assassins are not as professional and well used as people imagine. Even during the days of the cold war the top assassins on both sides perhaps had a kill record of maybe five or six, the law of averages soon level them out. The record connected with Hardy was different. Success following success. And no clue as to whom he had been hiring. I dug deep into the Janus thing, found out a lot of things I would sooner have not and reported my findings back to the President. Certain people were convinced that he had used the disbanded Janus Project to cream money off the top of CIA slush funds. He wasn't using local hit-teams from around the world; he was using an asset, albeit a defunct asset, of the CIA and keeping the set-up fees supposedly destined for local hit-teams.

"When Hardy started becoming linked to bioresearch, that was enough. With the things you lot were researching, I wanted a leash put on Hardy immediately."

"And?"

"And, that was denied." Stoned frowned. "The powers that be wanted it to ride, to refrain from scaring Hardy off. Instead, I was tasked to investigate discreetly, which is an oxymoron in terms. Any investigation has to be at full throttle, otherwise you lose pace, and the initiative. And that can be fatal."

"Worst case scenario?"

"I don't know, how about a contract on the key person in your investigation?" He looked at her, reached out and brushed a lock of hair away from her face. "You were lucky. We both were."

She smiled, but gently pulled away from him. "So what now? You know, I was scared witless in that outer office, but it could well have been McCray."

"Still not good enough. Either it was or it wasn't." He paused. He started to feel indifferent; maybe he had dreamt her presence last night. He wasn't so sure now. "We have to get the red-handed clause on our side." He looked at her intently, his eyes locked into her own. "Isobel, you trust me, right?"

"Of course."

Stone smiled. "I was afraid you'd say that."

## FIFTY EIGHT

The bottle of Jack Daniels lay on its side, clear and empty and discarded somewhat impotently. It was of no use to him now. The glass bore the remnants, about an inch and a half and was still gripped tightly in his left hand. The room was dark and stale and a thin plume of cigar smoke wafted up from the still burning cigar in the ashtray. There was no clean air left in the room and the cigar smoke clung to everything inside, contaminating with its pungent callous odor.

The gun in his right hand was a nickel plated Colt M 1 91 1 .45 automatic with mother of pearl grips. It was big and heavy and the .45 slug was both large and powerful. It was becoming an increasingly obsolete weapon the shooting world and law enforcement agencies in particular, had long since passed it by in favor of less powerful, but higher magazine capacity 9mm pistols, or the compromise of the more modern .40 or .357 sig models with more power than the 9mm shell and a good capacity of ammunition. But Hardy had a soft spot for this weapon, if one can possess the particular emotion for such things. He had used one when he had served at the end of the Vietnam War. Had carried one on every continent bar Antarctica. He liked the power, the tension safety in the grip, the single stack magazine and thinness which meant it was easier to conceal than more modern wider pistols. He looked at the inscription on the side of the fore slide. T.H – Thank You – H.N.S. A gift from General H. Norman Schwarzkopf, Jr. for his services during and after Operation Desert Shield and Desert Storm. Hardy had been the supreme commander's eyes inside Kuwait. Hardy turned the pistol over in his hand. He liked the feel of it. Liked its simplicity, its heavy weight and especially its power. No double taps needed with a .45. One shot one kill. He liked the power most of all. After all, he would only get one go at blowing the top of his head off and he wanted to get it right. He wanted to pull the trigger and have the lights switched out in an instant with no transference of pain or shock. He didn't want some lightweight, faster than sound bullet deviating on impact and exiting from the wrong spot. He didn't want to lay there in the dank, odor-filled room dying in his own mess of blood and skull. He wanted the cannon that was the Colt .45 and he wanted it over in an instant.

He sipped some more bourbon, almost the remainder of the glass, and moved the .45 to rest in his lap. The drink he had chosen to dull his sorrows and increase his courage was an appropriate one. It was both smooth and strong and went down so easily. And now, after draining the bottle, but for one remaining mouthful, he was almost ready. He looked around the apartment. There wasn't a lot to show for a man in his late fifties, and the thought of what little he had to show for his existence willed him closer to slipping the muzzle of the pistol firmly under the soft, sagging flesh of his chin.

There was nobody left in his life. There were the ex-wives, now only one left with a monthly alimony check and her taste for the finest things that life could offer her on his salary. She had been living with another man for three years, but would continue taking a chunk of his CIA salary until she wed her lover, and fiscal cunning had ruled that out of her life. She was both happy and content to service one man and take money from the other. The thought made Hardy want to commit two counts of homicide before the one count of suicide. His children were grown and scattered around the world and had not spoken to him in years. They had never been close to their father, he had served too many embassies around the world and spent too little time at home and they had merely sided with their mothers and taken the college fund money without guilt or hesitation. He wanted to leave this world with a mystery surrounding him, and maybe a little guilt on the heads of the strangers who had once been his family. He had left them everything in his will. He had no time for pettiness and smiled at the thought that they would all assume they had all been disinherited. He had laundered and legitimized and invested a substantial sum of money that he had creamed from the CIA slush funds he had access to over the years and he was in fact a wealthy man. The only problem in being a wealthy man within the CIA was that everyone would know that there was an anomaly. So he had waited for his retirement. But that would still hold as many pitfalls, so his next option had been to disappear completely. And therein laid the predicament, because what he had accumulated from his slush funds was not enough to disappear from existence and fund him through to his twilight years in some damned third world country with a damn tin pot despot as its leader. And so it was that greed had taken him.

The last of the Jack Daniels went down as

smoothly as the many mouthfuls before and without further ado or ceremony he slipped the gun under his chin and made sure that the angle was acute to its purpose. He cocked the hammer of the Colt .45 back until it locked with a definite click and then closed his eyes and started to gently take up pressure on the trigger.

The sound of the ringing telephone made him flinch and he nearly took the top of his head off there and then. The ringing was incessant and annoyed him. He lowered the gun and aimed it steadily at the telephone mounted on the wall opposite him, near the doorway to the kitchen. He squeezed the trigger and missed. A large clump of plaster and stucco exploded out of the wall and left a hole of about an inch in diameter. He cursed loudly. The telephone continued to ring and he heaved himself out of the chair and staggered across the room.

"Yes?"

"Tom, is that you?"

"What the fuck do you want, McCray?"

"Jesus! What's with you? I just phoned to say get your ass down here now, Isobel Bartlett and that fucking Secret Service agent just turned up."

Hardy hesitated, stared at the hole he had just made with the pistol. "But…"

"What, you want to waste more time?"

McCray snapped. "Your *associate* obviously screwed up. I can see them on the monitor, right now as we speak. Get yourself the fuck down here and let's sort this thing out once and for all."

Hardy blinked firmly, tried to clear his head from the fug of alcohol. "Do they have the flash drives?"

"Beats the hell out of me, but *you* don't, so that probably answers that question. Doesn't it?" McCray paused. "Christ, what's wrong with you?"

Hardy swayed, propped himself against the wall to maintain balance. "We need a plan."

"Obviously, so I suggest you get one on the way. I'm going to be unobtainable until you show yourself. I'll get them shown to my office and I'll meet you downstairs. Just hurry." The line went dead.

Hardy dropped the receiver to the floor and tucked the pistol into the waistband of his pants. He staggered into the bathroom and ran the faucet. He splashed a good deal of water over his face and rubbed it around his neck. He then put his mouth to the tap and drank as much as he physically could. He felt a little better, but was painfully aware that he was drunk. He loosened his collar and looked into the mirror. "Come on man! Second chance! Do you know how close you were to checking out? Get with it!" His reflection disgusted him. He turned away on himself and walked out into the lounge. He had to get a few things together and the forming of a plan was already in his mind. All he needed now was the stability, the soberness to pull it off.

## FIFTY NINE

Isobel stared hard at the double glass doors from inside Stone's Mustang. She looked down at her trembling hands. She looked up again and could see the outline silhouettes of the two security guards through the dark distortion of the heavily smoked glass, could make out one of the men with his thumbs stuck through his belt. The gunfighter's pose of the Wild West. The other man was swaggering, pacing the floor slowly, stopping periodically to peer through the glass and watch the comings and goings of the outside world.

"I can't go in," Isobel announced emphatically. "No way. Those two will detain me straight away."

Stone shook his head. "Trust me. I can handle those two rent-a-cops." He opened his door and looked intently at her. "It's getting close. The time's coming for you to clear your name and point your finger at the guilty party. Are you up to it?"

"I guess…"

"You guess correct." He stepped out of the car and closed the door behind him.

Isobel opened her door somewhat tentatively and stepped out. She took in the surroundings around her, possibly for the first time, noticing the flowerbeds, the signs for visiting VIPs and the neat crazy-paved brick work of the paths leading to different doors and walkways. It amazed her how much she had previously failed to notice in her day-to-day working life, but how much she now saw through fresh eyes. It was as if it were her first visit, stepping into the unknown, the unfamiliar.

Stone led the way and stopped at the entrance. He pressed the intercom buzzer, but instead of any inquisition one of the guards merely strolled over and pressed the button to grant them access.

He nodded at Stone like he knew him from old. "Good morning, Sir," he said with a thin smile. He turned to Isobel and nodded. "Nice to see you, Ma'am. Are you feeling better now?"

"Yes," she answered, slightly puzzled, and then she remembered the last time she had been there, and the last time she had seen the guard. "Thanks for asking."

The second guard approached them. He was carrying a clipboard, which was old and worn and from it was dangling a long length of string with a pen tied to the end and held into place with the edge of the clip. "Do you have an appointment, Sir? I don't see you entered on the log."

"No, just calling in on spec," Stone replied breezily. "I take it that's OK?"

"Who did you wish to see, Sir?" the first guard asked.

"Doctor McCray, if he's available. I'm sure he will be, for us." Stone smiled politely, then added: "You remember me? I trust my credentials are satisfactory?"

Both men nodded like no amount of protocol was going to stand in his way and that nothing was going to be too much trouble. The guard with the clipboard turned on his heel and walked over to the telephone on the check-in desk. He picked it up and started to talk in a hushed tone. After a few moments he replaced the receiver and returned to them. "Doctor McCray is busy in another department at the moment, but he will be pleased to meet you in his office," he paused, passing the clipboard to his colleague. "I'm to show you up. If you'll follow me."

Their footsteps on the hard floor echoed around their heads, reverberated by the plain walls and featureless ceiling. The occasional pane or panel of smoked glass changed the tone of the echo every now and then and as they approached the end of the corridor the open doors to various offices and walkways forced the sound of the echo to be gradually muted.

The door to the outer office was gaping open and there was no sign of occupation within. The guard led the way inside, peered behind the door for sight of Agnes Dempsey, then shrugged when he didn't see her and walked into McCray's open office.

The guard glanced around, and then paced over to the two waiting chairs and pulled one further out from the desk for Isobel. "If you'd care to take a seat, Ma'am," he paused, waiting for her to sit down. "I'll go take a look for Doctor McCray's personal assistant, see if can get her to make some coffee while you wait." He walked out of the office, his gait full of swagger.

"That guy just needs a horse and a lasso," Stone commented dryly.

"Sshh," Isobel giggled. "I've got to work here. Or at least, if I still have a job at the end of this."

"You'll still have a job," Stone said quietly.

Ten minutes passed and there was still no sign of the coffee or the personal secretary. Stone got up from his seat and paced out to the office. He returned a few minutes later, his face blank. "There isn't a soul in the place," he paused. "It's like a ghost ship. Is that usual?"

"No," Isobel said flatly. "The other offices are all admin. They're usually busy right up to five o'clock. Maybe there's a training session going on someplace?"

"Yes. That will be it," McCray paused and Isobel visibly flinched at the sound of his voice. "Sorry to startle you, my dear. What a very pleasant surprise to see you." He walked around the desk and sat down in his leather chair. "What curious company you keep." He looked across the table at Stone and smirked. "I see you've chosen the correct chair, this time. And how are you keeping, Agent Stone?"

Stone smiled. "Oh, very well, when all's said and done."

"Tell me ..." McCray paused. "You've come back here to say that my drives are all safe and well."

"I was hoping you'd be able to shed a little light on that subject," Stone said matter-of-factly.

"What could you possibly mean?"

Isobel glared at him. "You know full well

472

what he means."

"My dear Isobel," McCray looked at her, aghast. "You are a wanted woman. You left bioresearch with government property in your possession. I could have you arrested on the spot."

"Now, we both know that isn't true," Stone chipped in. "Your security personnel were none the wiser when we arrived. They simply thought Isobel had been off a couple of days sick. And as for being wanted, I checked the National Crime List this morning and there's not a mention of Isobel Bartlett anywhere." Stone lied easily, but hoped that McCray wouldn't see through his bluff. "Now, how can that be? Surely she was reported right after you found out she had taken the files? Surely you went straight to the FBI? The fact that she wasn't speaks volumes for yourself."

"But Isobel *did* take the drives."

"No, she took the flash drives from Professor Leipzig's cabinet. One half of both ARES and APHRODITE. And she'll admit to that in a court of law. But she had nothing to do with the disappearance of the drives from *your* safe." Stone stared at him icily. "You took those drives and were then going to take the set from Leipzig's cabinet. She merely beat you to it. After hearing your conversation with Tom Hardy in the restroom, that is." McCray looked shaken. He was obviously unaware that Isobel could have identified him. "Ah," Stone mocked. "Sound familiar now? And what if I said that she was under your personal assistant's desk when you took the flash drives from your own safe? What if I said that she would be willing to recite that in a court of law as well?"

McCray smiled. "Well, let's just say you're right, Agent Stone. Let's just say, for the purpose of hypothesis, that you are quite correct and that Isobel had nothing to do with the second set of drives going missing. And that I was involved and that I intended to ransom APHRODITE off after releasing ARES all over, say, Europe. Or China. Or the West Coast. How would that affect the outlook on everything?"

"Hypothetically?"

McCray smiled. "No. Actually, you've got me. I intended, or still intend to make billions from this. Sure, I need both sets of drives, but I do have the next best thing," he smiled at Isobel. "I have the woman behind most of it. You'll know where to fill in the blanks, won't you? I bet you could come up with the product given enough time and resources…"

"Go to Hell!" Isobel snapped.

"Oh, most probably dear," McCray smirked. "But you know where the information is. And there are very effective methods for getting somebody to talk. So I'm told."

Stone took a mini digital recorder out from his jacket pocket and put it down on the desk opposite McCray. The recording light was flashing red. He then took out the Glock 9mm pistol and held it loosely, its muzzle aimed at the doctor's midriff. "I'd say that enough, Doctor McCray." Stone paused. "I'd say that the game was over, and that you're under arrest. We still have both vital drives and as good as a confession on tape."

"You've got nothing, Agent Stone. Nothing but overconfidence and a big gun pointed at the back of your neck." McCray smiled. "The old look behind you trick. I know it's a tad clichéd, but I can't resist. Its simplicity is its complexity."

Stone stared straight ahead, his pistol unwavering, but Isobel turned around and let out a gasp. She turned back to Stone, her face ashen.

"He's right," Isobel stammered.

Stone smiled. "Tom Hardy, I presume?"

"It's all over, Stone," McCray paused. "Put the gun down and give me my fucking virus."

"You'd expect us to bring the drives here?" Stone said quietly. "Anyway, last time I checked, this gun was still pointed at you."

"And that's where it will stay," Hardy said from behind, the heavy Colt .45 a mere two feet from Stone's neck. "Get a shot off and I'll take the top of your head clean off. And then I'll blow the bitch's head off her shoulders too. Put the gun down, Agent Stone. It's over."

"What's wrong Hardy? Can't find someone to do your dirty work all of a sudden? I thought you had a man for that sort of thing?" Stone lowered the pistol and then dropped it onto the desk in front of him with a clatter. "I retired him, Hardy. Now *your* game is over."

"Funny? I thought it looked like I was winning, or at least it does from this angle," Hardy sneered. He stepped around them and stood a few feet away, almost alongside McCray. He aimed the pistol at Stone. The hammer was cocked and Stone knew that the trigger was light. Hardy looked at Isobel and smiled. "Now, little lady, I'm going to count to three and then I 'm going to blow most of Agent Stone's head off with one squeeze of the trigger. Understand?" His eyes flickered momentarily and he flung his face into hers. "Fucking understand?" he bellowed. Isobel flinched, nodded. "Good. Now don't worry about anyone hearing, the staff have been given the rest of the day off. Nobody will hear a thing. One... Two ..."

"Please..." Isobel stammered. The pistol was unwavering, completely steady in the man's hand.

"Don't!"

"Three..."

"Alright!" Isobel screamed. "They never left!"

"No don't!" Stone shouted. "Don't tell them anything!"

"Oh very gallant." McCray sneered. He looked across at Isobel and glared. "Where are they?"

"Don't clam up on us now," Hardy sneered. "I can count again. And I mean it, I'll shoot him in the head."

Isobel slouched, crestfallen. "I took t h e two flash drives out of here, but they were blanks. They were my personal USBs. I wanted to be seen with a set of drives on camera. I didn't know where half the hidden cameras were, but I knew that they weren't in Leipzig's office ... in here ... or in the restrooms."

"Clever girl," McCray said wistfully. "Then where are the *real* drives?"

"Still in Leipzig's office," she conceded.

"Hidden in the lining of his chair."

"Where do you hide a needle?" Tom Hardy smiled. "In a haystack? No. In a box of fucking needles." He moved the gun in his hand and did a sort of makeshift round of applause. "You've given us the run around, that much is true."

"What now?" Isobel asked.

"You don't need to know that." McCray snapped. He looked over at Hardy, who kept his eyes on Stone and the gun reasonably steady, despite his blood-alcohol level. "I'll go and check. You keep them covered. Let's not burn our bridges just yet." He walked briskly out of the office and they heard his footfalls echoing hurriedly down the corridor.

Stone looked up at Hardy, his eyes cold and hard. "You're finished, Hardy. You're a dead man walking."

"Idle threats."

"The agency is on to you. And the government. Right up to the oval office. Why do you think I'm on the case? The President doesn't trust the CIA as far as he could piss up the walls of Langley." Stone chuckled. "They know all about Janus. They have your accounts under investigation, and your assets. They'll seize them when they don't hear from me. They'll even have the body and DNA of that Janus assassin I killed up in Vermont."

"You think I'm bothered?" Hardy wobbled slightly on his legs, he was still suffering under the effects of alcohol. Only his professionalism, experience and twenty years of alcoholism enabled him to cope with the drink in his system. He perched himself in McCray's chair. "After I've released ARES on the fucking country I'll be long-

478

gone."

"They never give up hunting one of their own," Stone paused. "They'll take you down eventually."

"We've all got to go some time," he smiled. "Thought I'd release ARES in Virginia. That should slow the boys at Langley down some."

"They'll catch up with you sooner or later. But maybe they won't take you down," Stone smiled. "Maybe a bullet's too good for you. Maybe they'll get a file on you so thick and so damning, they'll try and make a lesson out of you. Take you to court for Lord only knows what, sentence you to two hundred years with no chance of parole. That's what they do to people, for treason. You'll die old and scared and lonely in some bad-ass prison with your ass for rent and your head full of memories you'd have willingly killed your mother ten times over to forget."

Hardy smirked. "Shut your mouth, boy. I've been an agency man since before you were an itch in your mother's crotch. I've talked the talk, walked the fucking walk, fucked more whores around the world and pissed more napalm than you could ever imagine. I was taking Vietcong prisoners out into the jungle and popping a bullet in the back of their heads before breakfast and not losing my appetite, or so much as a minute's sleep at night. I was doing that at nineteen. By the time I was twenty I had killed little girls just to get their Vietcong daddy's to talk. I threatened to shoot a baby to get its mother to talk, and then when I suspected she was lying, I shot the little slit-eyed fucker in the head. Do you know what a forty-five bullet does to a baby's head at close range? Do you? Of course you don't. You couldn't even possibly imagine. So don't pretend you know what goes on in my memories and don't assume I have any trouble living with them or sleeping at night. Because I don't. I manage just fine."

McCray walked back into the room. He was out of breath and carried the two USB flash drives in his left hand. He waved them in front of both Isobel and Stone. "Very clever, Isobel," he said coldly. "And very fucking stupid. You've lost your bargaining chip, you're out of the game."

"What are you going to do with us?" Isobel said quietly.

McCray smiled. He reached across the desk and picked up Stone's pistol. There were numerous scratches on the frame but it was well oiled. McCray looked at the weapon, turned it over in his hand and then pointed it at Isobel. "You are going on a trip with Mr. Hardy. I've decided to make use of your skills in a positive way. You are going to manufacture ARES for us at our little temporary laboratory."

"Go take a hike!" Isobel snapped.

"You'll do it, or you'll take a bullet in the head!" McCray retorted. He looked at Stone and smiled. "You? Well, you're coming with me."

Stone glared up at him. "Have you got what it takes?" he asked coldly. Then he looked across at Hardy and smirked. "But then again, it doesn't take much to pull a trigger."

McCray smiled. "My dear man, I'm not going to shoot you. Not unless you give me good reason to on the way."

"On the way?" Isobel interrupted.

"Yes," McCray nodded. He turned back to Stone and smiled. "Shooting you will be far too messy. And besides, I'm not embarrassed to admit it, I've never actually used a gun before." He pointed it at Stone's head and held it steady. "But I imagine it doesn't make any difference at this range, does it?" Stone simply glared at the man, didn't comment. "No, I didn't think so. No, what I've got planned for you is quiet dull and uninteresting. You see, we have this room here, in a part of the facility that has been left only part developed. The funding was pulled for some reason or another and there is nobody staffing a whole fifth of the building. This room is lockable, airtight, even. You won't get out, and you certainly won't live longer than a few days without food or water or a regular air supply. But I'm not leaving you for a few days. You see,

481

after Mr. Hardy leaves with Isobel, I'm tidying a few loose ends and putting one or two files into the accounts department, and then I'm leaving for good. It may be weeks, or perhaps even months before you're discovered. Tell me, Agent Stone. Are you scared of the dark?" McCray smiled, somewhat sadistically. "Because you soon will be."

## SIXTY

McCray held the pistol firmly in his right hand and walked several paces behind Stone. Hardy had previously searched him whilst McCray had kept the gun trained on Isobel. Stone had been tempted to make a move on Hardy's pistol, but he couldn't run the risk, Isobel was directly in the line of fire and McCray's finger need only to twitch and Isobel would have been shot.

McCray gave curt instructions to Stone as they walked, telling him which walkway to take and which doorways to go through. Stone had planned to take McCray down in the elevator, make a move on the weapon where space would be at a premium, but McCray had been smart and they had taken two separate stairwells to the other floors and McCray had been able to keep at least five paces behind Stone at all times.

The part of the building they had now entered was clearly unfinished. The walls were stucco clad, but were yet to receive either a coat of plaster or paint, and the floor was still covered with building dust from the original construction. Trestles still held planks of wood off the floor for sawing and there were even food wrappers, empty soda cans and other pieces of trash piled up high in the corners where the contractors had taken lunch breaks.

"You see what I mean?" McCray said, his voice echoing around the sparse walls like a huge chasm. "Nobody to hear you scream for help. And nobody to come and save you."

"What makes you think I'll scream? And what makes you think I need saving?" Stone replied. He had slowed his pace a fraction, hoping that McCray would gain ground on him. "You haven't got the stomach to shoot me, you'd only be kept awake at night by the images of what you saw. And leaving me alive in a room isn't going to give you much sleep at night either. You'll never know if I managed to escape, never know when I'm going to turn up and surprise you."

"I'll sleep just fine."

"You'll never sleep again," Stone sneered. "You'll have to sleep the rest of your days with one eye open." He lessened his pace some more, but kept talking so as not to be too obvious. "The powers that be are on to Tom Hardy have him marked. Within a week of me going off the chart, they'll send someone else. And another. And then another. They'll have you marked as well. For as long as you're alive, they'll continue to hunt you down. If the US government can find Osama Bin Laden with all his support and his kind's hatred towards the west, you've got no chance. Technology and money make the world a small place."

"Then maybe I won't *be* alive," McCray snapped. "Maybe I'll just have to fake my own death."

Stone laughed. "Maybe Hardy will make it more convincing than you can possibly imagine."

"What?" He stopped walking and Stone stopped in front of him. "What are you talking about?"

Stone turned around slowly and faced him. There was no more than three paces between them now. "You don't know Hardy as well as I do. I've studied his file so deeply, I probably know more about the man than *he* does." He kept his eyes on McCray, didn't take his eyes away from the other man's face. McCray's eyes were big and brown and docile. Stone's were cold blue and hard, like glacier ice. "The man has killed before, plenty of times as a young CIA operative in

485

Vietnam. He was part of the whole Phoenix thing out there. The black-ops. It was an assassination program. Assassinations and interrogations. There were no survivors of the interrogations."

"What are you saying?"

"I'm just saying that he is probably one of the coldest bastards alive. Forget ISIS or Al Qaeda, Tom Hardy would think they were pussies. He won't find it a problem to remove you from the equation. Hell, he's killed a hundred times before, he wouldn't find it a problem again,"

Stone smiled. "Tell me, McCray ... Where are the drives? You left them in your office, right?" McCray said nothing. His hand was shaking slightly, but the weapon moved no more than a fraction of an inch and they were far too close for a shot to miss. "You know, I bet when you get back to your office, you won't find the flash drives where you left them. Come to think of it, I bet Hardy has the other set as well. Probably convinced you that it would be best if he had them for safe keeping."

"He could keep them for all I care, he'll never have a chance of deciphering what's on them," he snapped.

"No, he won't," Stone smirked. "But then again, he didn't have Isobel Bartlett. And now he does. I hear she had a lot to do with the development of both ARES and APHRODITE.

I gather she was pretty much a driving force behind the project, especially once they discovered how beneficial APHRODITE would be to the rest of the world. You spent a lot of time in your office, I understand," Stone watched the man intently, studied his expression and minute body movements. He knew he had struck a chord with him, but he had to dig deeper. "While Isobel knew all there was to know. That would come in very handy for someone like Hardy. Should anything happen to you, he gets the virus made regardless. Maybe he gets a new business partner."

"No." McCray shook his head disbelievingly, glared at him. "Hardy *needs* me..."

"Past tense, McCray. *Needed*," Stone said coldly. "Now he's got everything he needs. He's got both sets of drives, the person to make the virus complete and he's banking on having you taken out of the picture as well. Without so much as lifting a finger."

"How do you figure that?"

"Pretty obvious really, isn't it?" Stone tensed his legs and the muscles in his arms as he talked. He wanted to be free and loose when he made his move. "You're a scientist. You have no affinity with guns or killing. I'm ex-military, a bodyguard to the most powerful man

487

on Earth, and have killed in the line of duty. He was banking on me taking care of you. In the meantime, *he* would be making his getaway with Isobel."

"You're wrong!" McCray held the weapon higher, pointed it directly at Stone's forehead. "Turn around and keep moving! Do it!"

"No."

"Do it!"

"Make me."

"If you don't move I'll blow your fucking head off!"

"Try it," Stone stepped a pace closer. Less than six feet separated them. "Just try it. Did you check the weapon? Maybe you did, but I didn't see? I don't remember seeing you check the chamber for a round. Have you taken a look at the pistol's safety? Does it even have a safety? There's a safety built into the trigger, but the Glock safe action usually requires specialist training in law enforcement. You get certified Glock competent. I usually carry a Sig Sauer. Secret Service issue. Much nicer weapon. That was my brother's FBI piece. But hey, take a shot, if you pardon the pun. That is if there's even a round in the chamber..."

McCray looked indecisive for a moment, then glanced down at the weapon, twisting it slightly in his hand to get a better look for the safety catch. Stone charged forward and caught hold of the pistol with his left hand and hammered a punch into the side of McCray's jaw with his right. McCray reeled back but as he did, he kicked out and caught Stone in the groin with his right foot. It was a completely unskilled, lucky, yet agonizing blow and Stone gasped for air, but he managed to keep hold of the pistol. McCray found his footing and charged into Stone with a flurry of punches to his head and face. Stone dropped in a low crouch to avoid the blows and kicked a roundhouse to McCray's knee. The man dropped and Stone kicked again, this time hitting him in the side of the neck, forcing him down onto all fours. It was a wholly scrappy affair and Stone rolled backwards across the floor to give himself a little distance. When he came up in a crouch to face his opponent, McCray was on him again, like a ferocious wildcat. It caught Stone by surprise that a man with a manic temper who attacked and hit with all the control and forethought of a hysterical child had brushed his training and professionalism so precariously to one side. The pistol was still in his left hand, held by the barrel and unusable as McCray's punches were raining down on him like a tempestuous squall. Finally, he saw an opening through the barrage and punched McCray on the nose with a straight right jab. He followed up with another, harder right cross and then as McCray stood stunned and wobbling on his feet, he bludgeoned him across the temple as hard as he could with the butt of the pistol. McCray was lifeless and already falling to the ground when Stone sent another right, this time a powerful hook with a twist of hips and a dropped opposite knee to drive through the power. His knuckles hit directly on McCray's left temple and he watched as the man fell, pole-axed to the hard tiled floor, breaking his fall with the back of his head.

Stone stood over the man, breathing heavily and angry with himself that it had not been a more controlled and technically proficient fight. However, no two fights were ever the same and he consoled himself that the worst opponent of all was the man in a rage with little to lose and much to prove.

Stone lashed out with his foot and connected heavily with the man's ribs. There was no movement, so he bent down and checked his neck for a pulse with two fingers. There was nothing, not even a flicker. The man was dead. He looked around and saw an open doorway at the end of the corridor. He caught hold of McCray's ankles and dragged him backwards. The dust on the floor was swept away as the body wiped it inadvertently clean, pulled roughly and hastily by Stone towards the doorway.

Stone dropped the body heavily inside the

room and checked the pockets and removed a large bunch of keys, which he knew to be the master keys for the entire building.

The room was intended to be a storeroom of some kind and was fitted with a one way outside lock. The door opened inwards. There were electrical wires protruding from the ceiling but no light fittings. The ceiling and walls were lined with stainless steel. It looked like the inside of a meat locker. Stone remembered McCray's vicious jibe at being scared of the dark. It would certainly have been an unescapable cell. He felt more than a little satisfaction at having turned the situation around. Then he put the emotion to one side, not wanting to gloat over the corpse and without further hesitation he pulled the door closed and made his way back towards the corridor.

## SIXTY ONE

Her hands and feet were bound together tightly with thin cord. When she attempted to move, the cord cut into her, biting and rasping at her flesh. He fingers tingled with the lack of circulation, stemmed at her wrists and her feet had long since gone to sleep, numbed by the strangulation of blood.

The air was thin, fume-filled and had lost its purity hours ago. The heat had become stifling and had enveloped her, caught hold of her and refused to release its hostile grip. She was wet from sweat and the gag that bit into her mouth staunched her breath and made her nostrils fight to keep her breathing.

The car made a great deal of noise from the exhaust beneath her and thundered over the road surface with monotonous continuity. There was no respite, no relief whatsoever. She prayed for an end to it and started to welcome any conclusion.

Tom Hardy had been rough with her and had exited the building via a covert doorway in the part-developed area of the building. When they had reached his BMW she had struggled, looked around for help and started to scream. Hardy had savagely chopped the side of her neck with the edge of his hand and from that moment onwards she remembered nothing about how she ended up in the trunk. However, when she came around, in the acrid darkness of the trunk, she had been frightfully aware that his subsequent treatment of her had been harsh, business-like and with little benevolence. She had been trussed like a slab of meat and manhandled forcefully. She could feel bruises on her and imagined herself being dropped without leniency into her automotive cell. She could feel her clothes riding up uncomfortably, undone in places and she hoped upon hope that she had not been violated in the intimate sense. She weighed Hardy up as a ruthless and hard man with an agenda and put aside the notion of perverseness. At least it made her situation easier to deal with, to comprehend if she was sure nothing more untoward than physical abuse had happened while she had lain unconscious and never more vulnerable.

She tried to ascertain how long she had been unconscious, and therefore how long she had been travelling in the back of the car. It was a useless exercise and her watch was behind her back so if she remained bound with the cord she would never be able to verify her calculations. Maybe at their destination she would be able to establish the time and work out how far she was from Washington. She figured on the car travelling at sixty miles an hour or so, so every minute was a mile, and so on. There were four time zones running through the breadth of the country, she knew that. But where were they and how straight did they run? She remembered in elementary school that one ran through the Rockies and that it zigzagged so much that a person could theoretically run around in a tight circle and travel in and out of two different time zones every few paces. She cursed her knowledge of stupid facts, wished she had listened throughout geography and taken note of where the time zones actually were. But it didn't matter any way, and she knew it. Her meandering thoughts were merely compensation for her fear and uncertainty and an exercise in positive thinking. She was making the best out of a terrible situation and if by thinking back to her days at elementary school gave room for a little hope and inspiration, then a subconscious part of her mind was pleased to do so.

Maybe it was the tedium of the journey or

maybe it was the hypnotic rhythm of the passing road underneath, the drumming of the wheels, or the exhaust note droning monotonously at the steady speed but at times her senses were so dulled that she drifted off in fitful bouts of sleep. Or maybe it was the carbon monoxide. She cursed herself, cursed the fact that she could not estimate her journey time and was falling into the trap of letting down her guard, of drifting with events and becoming too passive. She was a fighter at heart and she wanted to resolve this situation through attrition. She would take it in her stride and when the time was right, she would be as strong and resourceful as she had started out to be.

The engine was working harder now and she was rolling to the sides more regularly. Her angle of lean was also more acute, nudging her towards the back of the car, where she banged her head of the taillight units and could hear the gas sloshing about under her in the fuel tank. It was a big car, with a large fuel capacity and good tank range. The gas sounded low, surely Hardy would be forced to pull in and refuel before long? And the angle of travel, the constant changing of direction. That would supposedly mean narrow country roads, maybe even mountain roads?

Isobel already knew the answer to her musings. Vermont had played such a prominent part in the operation so far. Professor Leipzig had been killed in Vermont, near the town of Deal. And Joe Carver, 'Hobo Joe' as he had been referred to, had been killed merely ten miles from Deal, at South Chesterton. And then the Montpelier coroner had turned up floating in the lake. What part did either of those two play, to have been killed so mercilessly? Vermont had been the key throughout; surely it would not be out of the question to expect their hideout, their secret laboratory to be out there as well? The journey time seemed about right and the twisting roads now seemed more obvious, more familiar to her as she rolled and lulled and cracked her head continuously on the inside of the trunk.

The car slowed considerably and pulled harshly off the road and bounced over a speed hump. Then came to an abrupt halt. A door opened then closed, and Isobel could hear something rattling, unscrewing above her head. The fuel cap. She heard the nozzle of the pump insert, rattle on the metal neck of the tank and then heard the pump start up and the fuel slosh into the tank. She could smell the vapors. The urge to vomit was strong. She suppressed the notion quickly. She was gagged and would undoubtedly drown in her own vomit if she lost control. It was a big tank and the refueling took a good three or four minutes. The nozzle withdrew, rattled on metal and then the cap was screwed up tight. All was silent now, until what had to be five minutes later, she heard the door open and felt the car shake on its suspension. The door slammed shut with a solid thud. The engine started, the car surged forwards and the monotonous tone, the hypnotic rhythm were upon her once more and uncertainty was her constant companion in the darkness of her cell. It must have been another hour, she hoped she had estimated correctly, when the car slowed again and bounced on a short stretch of rough ground. Gravel crunched noisily under the wheels and the car swung in a wide arc, spewing gravel and dirt in its wake. Isobel was slung harshly against the side of the trunk and she could hear the hard plastic of the taillight units cracking under the weight of her head, which now supported her entire body weight and what felt like half a G of inertia.

The engine died and the door opened. It slammed, shaking the car unexpectedly and she heard footsteps crunching on the gravel. The trunk opened and she was blinded by daylight and felt a rush of cold air. It was like nectar as she breathed, almost making her lightheaded. She did not see Hardy, but heard his feet crunching on the gravel as he walked away, becoming softer and quieter in the distance. Gradually, the footfalls fell silent and suddenly, overwhelmingly she realized that she had never felt more alone. She tried to move position, but she could not feel her limbs. She felt completely paralyzed.

Another hour passed. She was more certain of her calculation now, had counted subconsciously in silence. It had comforted her to keep her mind active. She was cold with the trunk lid open. She thought about Rob Stone and whether his fate felt as hopeless and desperate as her own, and she silently prayed that he was all right and unharmed. It had felt as if she had been caught in a whirlwind since she had first made her move and it suddenly dawned on her that ironically, the most she had thought about Stone and the help he had given her, was while they were apart and suffering the same fate. She liked him, felt close to him. Was it was simply because he had saved her life, and more than once? Normally, she would not have been attracted to such a man; god knows he was so different to the men in her previous relationships. But she had felt overwhelmingly close to him when they had arrived back in Washington and she had taken it upon herself to make the move of sharing his bed, if only for sleep and had been pleased, relieved, when her advances had not been rebuked. However, as she had fell in and out of sleep, she knew that her emotions were mixed. Were her feelings for him simply a subconscious act of benevolence and gratitude for saving her life? Or were they deeper, more intimate? They had kissed in the forest, briefly yet passionately and she had drawn away from him then. It had troubled her, this mixture of emotion, so she had left his bed and dressed before she had made a mistake.

She shook her head, annoyed with herself for drifting into thoughts of insignificance. Such thoughts were ridiculous. Her situation was desperate. Stone was in the same predicament, or maybe even already dead. The thought brought on a wave of adrenaline that surged through her body and left her cold. She attempted to ease herself over onto her back tried to flex her muscles, but the cord gripped her, chaffed and burned her skin. She fell back onto her side, helpless and desperately scared.

The crunch of the footsteps upon gravel gradually returned, growing louder and ever more determined. She felt a shiver rush up her spine and tingle at the tiny soft hairs at the nape of her neck. She had visions of the barrel of a pistol coughing out the shots, the silent shots she would never hear because the first had smashed into her skull and had left her dying. She thought of the images of both David Stein and of Joe Carver, of their shock and dismay and disbelief at being shot, of the life leaving their eyes and the silent scream which never left their mouths.

She thought of Elizabeth Delaney. Her

friend, whom she had doubted and believed had betrayed her, but had been on her knees, knowing that at any minute the gunman was going to shoot her in the back of the head and that her last moments on earth were spent knowing she was going to die.

The gravel crunched noisily and then ceased. "Pleasant journey?" Hardy grinned down at her.

The sunset was shining on one side of his face. The light was bright and golden. The other half of his face was silhouetted. She couldn't make out his features on the dark side. It gave him the menacing illusion of having half a face. Or two different faces. Like Janus, the two faced god, and namesake of the CIA assassination program. The thought made her catch her breath. He was smiling perversely, like he was getting pleasure from watching her pain and vulnerability. He leaned into the car and caught hold of her legs and pulled them out of the trunk. He then took hold of her, tucking his hands under her armpits and heaved her out of the trunk completely. She was unsteady on her legs and fell down on the gravel. He pulled her up and he held her upright, supporting a little of her weight. Then gradually less until she was standing on her own. Rough hands pulled and ripped at her gag, and it was a blessed relief to breathe through her mouth, although it felt as dry as sand and she was desperate for a drink. Hardy whipped out a knife and sliced at the bindings on her ankles and she felt a sudden rush of blood, of agonizing pins and needles rush up her calf muscles and into her thighs. She tried to move her feet, but the throbbing of blood was so painful that she had to force herself not to scream. She did not want to give the man the satisfaction.

She wanted to tell him what to do and where he could do it, but the pain was so acute and was showing no sign of clemency. At that moment, Hardy seemed the least of her worries.

She looked at her surroundings. They were standing in the center of a copse of trees with a rough track to one side and a large log cabin approximately fifty yards to the other. The ground had been graveled, to provide grip to vehicles when the snow and ice of winter melted. The trees were tall and provided a barrier, an enclave in which sat the log cabin.

"Where am I?" she asked.

"Somewhere safe," Hardy replied. "Somewhere we won't be disturbed, by anyone." He stepped aside and pushed her forwards in the direction of the cabin. "Now hurry yourself up," he sneered. "I have a surprise for you ..."

## SIXTY TWO

To gamble with money is one thing, but to gamble with a life is quite another. It's the most crucial of all gambles with the highest odds and the ultimate stake. Stone had never truly gambled with a life before. He had faced tough opposition, and difficult decisions, but he had never gambled on a life and had hoped he would never have to.

He had driven the Ford Mustang as hard as he dared, hitting the maximum on the rev limiter in almost every gear. After ten miles, he parked and left it to the mercy of the parking attendants at the airport.

He had bypassed Dulles and gone straight to Washington National, parking at the domestic side of the civil airport. It had taken him a while to find the particular service, but when he had the booking clerk had shown his surprise. Stone had shown him his ID and letter from the President and when that had been scrutinized in great detail, he had thrown the Secret Service issue platinum visa card down onto the desk and told the man to think of a price. The man had thought of a price, doubled it and had then swiped the card and shown him out to the hanger where the Bell Jet Ranger helicopter sat, fuelled and ready to fly.

Cruising speed had been one hundred and twenty miles per hour and the ground below had swept past easily. The skies were clear and they had had a clear and straight flight path to the municipal airport at Danbury, Connecticut where they refueled and Stone's company credit card had taken another hammering.

The journey had taken a little over five hours in all, including the fuel stop and the pilot had put down on the softball field at Deal a little after three-thirty pm. The pilot nodded a goodbye, as Stone crouched and ran and looked back to wave.

Sheriff Harper was leaning against the hood of his police cruiser, his right hand on the butt of his pistol and the left hand holding a thick cigar. He sucked at the end and blew out a thick plume of smoke. The helicopter lifted and pirouetted just above the ground and then lifted high and sped off above the bank of trees fringing the softball field. When the peace and serenity returned, he looked at Stone and grinned. "Got your message," he said with a smile, through a cloud of thick, pungent cigar smoke. "I'll give you something, you certainly know how to make an entrance."

Sheriff Harper drove them to his own house at a steady speed, but he didn't live far outside the town limits. They bumped and wallowed over a rutted driveway and stopped outside a Dutch barn which had once been painted red and white, but had long since flaked and peeled and was left looking bare and derelict.

The two men got out of the police cruiser and Harper opened one of the large double doors. Inside was the silver Mercedes.

"What do you make of that?" Sheriff Harper ran a hand over the bonnet and stood back to admire its lines. "One hell of an automobile. Fast as they come, but smooth as silk to drive. I didn't want to get out of it when I got it back here," he paused thoughtfully. "Damn seats are more comfy than my couch. Cost a sight more too. That leather is as good and soft as you get."

Stone was uninterested in the car. He had the door open and took out the laptop. The battery was critically low and he switched on the ignition and put the charger plug into the USB outlet. The laptop went through a quick start up procedure. Stone had thought long and hard about the laptop on the flight to Vermont. He would only get three chances at a log in password, maybe even the one. He suspected that Tom Hardy had supplied the computer and unless Hardy had gone down the route of random numbers and letters then Hardy will also have come up with the password.

It could have been anything, but Stone had to go merely by his own conviction and the one word that would be synonymous with Tom Hardy and the assassin he had used. Stone typed in JANUS. The computer suddenly finished booting up and rested on its wallpaper and start menu. Stone let out a deep breath and turned back to Sheriff Harper, who was now studying the silenced .45 Ingram machine pistol from the trunk.

"This is quite a piece of kit," the sheriff smiled. "I'd like to get one of these for varmints. It would make a hell of a mess on jack rabbits."

"Probably wouldn't even hit one with it. Scare the shit out of it though," Stone replied absentmindedly. "Look here, I'm in to his computer." He moved the internal mouse pad and opened the e-mail package. At a glance, he saw the received e-mails that had instructed the assassin all along. He scrolled through, noting the times and days of the mail and the e-mail address of the sender, then closed the program down. The tech guys in the service would be able to trace Tom Hardy through the correspondence. He opened up the tracking receiver program and switched on the tracking receiver, which was already connected via its USB cable. It was about the size of an old cell phone. "Is this how it was found?" Stone asked.

"More or less," Harper nodded. "It was all laying on the front seat of the car, connected together. Some cables may have slipped out when I moved them, but I was pretty careful."

"And it was all switched on?'"

"Yeah. But the battery died last night."

Stone nodded. He knew how short the battery life was, but thankfully they did not take long to recharge once the laptop was connected to the car's power supply. He had been lucky with the password, which had reinstated itself after the battery had died. Stone watched the screen, but there was nothing. He hoped he had made the right move, would never forgive himself if something happened to Isobel. He looked at the map, and adjusted the magnifying glass icon in the bottom right hand corner of the screen. The image played out and became less detailed, but covered a far greater distance. He turned to Sheriff Harper. "Do you know this area?"

"Sure, it's about a twenty mile radius around the town."

"That's a lot of ground," Stone said. He just hoped it was enough.

"You know about all this equipment?" Sheriff Harper asked. He put the submachine pistol back in the trunk and looked at the screen.

"A bit," Stone replied. "Secret Service vehicles are all fitted with trackers, just in case one gets hijacked. And the VIP's car is always kept on satellite navigation screens like this one, so we can watch and keep a constant track of it at all times," he paused. "But I've never seen one as advanced as this one. This is something else."

"The guy you killed was CIA?"

Stone shrugged. "Sort of, he was more of a CIA project," he paused. "And I'd better not say anything else."

"Sure, I understand." Harper stared at the screen, frowned, and then looked back at Stone. "Something moved. On the bottom left of the screen."

Stone looked down but there was nothing. "Maybe you imagined it?"

"'No way!" He stepped forward and looked at the screen intently. "Right there, on the very edge..."

Stone looked, but there was nothing. He studied the map, in particular the bottom left of the screen. There was still no movement. He walked over to the worktop and picked up the submachine pistol.

"What the hell are you doing?" Harper exclaimed.

"Taking a drive," Stone replied curtly. "Thanks for your help, but I've got to go check something out."

"You're taking the Mercedes?"

Stone nodded. "Seems appropriate."

## SIXTY THREE

The log cabin was built from vast round lengths of maple, planed smooth and laid dovetailed at the corners to hold the timber in place. The roof was constructed from dark wooden slat tiles and the windows were all double glazed with cedar surround frames. The door looked to be heavy oak, and was accessed via the open porch veranda, that was furnished with padded cane garden seats and an old-fashioned wooden swing chair, which was swaying gently in the cool fall breeze sweeping down from the mountains.

A ski rack was built into the side of the wall, nearest the door and it was obvious to Isobel that the cabin's primary use was that of a ski lodge, which was possibly turned around with an entirely different cliental and used as a hunting lodge in the spring and summer months.

Isobel climbed the steps, pushed roughly forwards by Hardy and waited on the open porch for him to open the door. As the door opened, she peered tentatively inside, but before she could take in her surroundings she was handled harshly through the doorway and into the large open plan living area.

"Sit," Hardy snapped at her, pointing to a large leather couch. Isobel did as she was ordered and flopped down into the deep red couch, her hands still bound behind her back. "Wait there. Move and I'll put a bullet in you."

Isobel edged forwards and tried her best to perch to the front of the couch, wriggling and straining with her tightly bound hands hampering her. She looked at the unlocked door, her mind full of thoughts of escape. It was tempting, but supposing she even managed to open the catch, where would she go? If she bolted out into the forest, her attempts at evading her captors would be useless with her hands bound so tightly. If she fell and wounded herself, she would be finished.

She looked behind her and saw that Hardy had disappeared. She turned back and surveyed the rest of the room, noticed the telephone on a writing desk by the window and wondered whether she would have time to lift the receiver and dial 9-11. If she simply left the receiver off the hook surely they would have time to trace the number and dispatch a squad car? They would have to give the caller the benefit of the doubt and send someone to close the call. She had no idea where she was, but if she could get to that receiver, maybe the people at the dispatch would hear any conversation between herself and her captors.

The thought was too much to put to rest and she heaved herself forwards and got to her feet. She looked behind her, listening intently for footsteps and then crept across the highly polished wooden floorboards to the writing desk. She turned her back to the desk and bent down, trying her best to stretch her hands out straight and reach the receiver. She managed to get it off the hook, and tensed as it clattered down onto the desk. She craned her neck, straining the muscles to near spasm and nudged her outstretched finger to the nine and pressed. She could hear the tone change as the first number was negotiated. The next bit was easier, and she pressed the one button twice in quick succession. She heard the ringing tone and the voice of someone answering. At the same time, she heard two distant voices gradually becoming louder as they approached. She bounded back across the room and slumped into the couch just as she heard the footsteps clip against the wooden floorboards of the corridor that led off the rear of the room.

Her heart was pounding fiercely and she felt flushed. Even her breathing was heavy and she just prayed that she would not force them to become suspicious. She looked up at Hardy and he stared back at her with contempt.

"My friend here has no doubt been looking forward to your company," he said, his tone sardonic. "I imagine he's been lonely and craving conversation." Isobel could sense someone behind her, could even catch sight of a figure in her periphery, but chose to keep her eyes firmly on Hardy's face. The person walked around the couch and into view and Isobel's heart raced and sent a flutter of panic into her throat. She caught her breath and reeled back into the couch, her eyes wide and fixated on the figure. "Of course..." Hardy feigned surprise. "You've already met."

Professor Leipzig looked down at her and smiled. His once kindly face somehow seemed hard and cruel and his eyes belonged to someone else, not the amiable man Isobel had once known and liked.

"Don't look so shocked, my dear," Professor Leipzig said quietly. "I hear you've been the proverbial fly in the ointment, my dear. Most disappointing, if I may say?"

"I... I..." Isobel stopped herself. She now understood perfectly. Leipzig had given way to money. The one common denominator that eventually finds every man his price.

"I'm so glad you could be here for the occasion," Leipzig smiled. He was lisping slightly. His voice was different. "I have almost everything set, but you see, towards the end, ARES was becoming a joint effort. You were as crucial to the project as I. Without the information on those flash drives, even I would be looking at weeks, maybe even months to culture a working virus. In fact, without the drives I may not have been able to recreate them at all. I'm so glad you're alive, my dear, it will speed up the process no end. Help fill in the blanks, so to speak."

"But... You're dead," she said. She had wanted to resist such a contrite and obvious comment, but the words simply fell out of her mouth. "But, the body?"

"Was someone else..." Leipzig smiled. He glanced at Hardy, and then looked back at her. "Mister Hardy saw to the finer details, or I gather his *associate* did. It was rather tricky, and a little uncomfortable..." Isobel frowned at him and he shrugged nonchalantly. "Dentistry, my dear." He beamed a smile at her, and ran a fingernail across his teeth. "We needed a body in the truck, but dental records were only going to prove that it wasn't me who died in the crash. So we merely came up with a way around the problem."

"Stone *knew* that was what we did," Tom Hardy smiled. "That's why that hobo, Joe Carver, had to be taken care of. He was the only person who missed that damned tramp. Kicked up a damned fuss. Went over to Montpelier to talk to the police."

"The missing homeless guy?" Isobel frowned. "You killed him and put him in the truck?"

"An oversight on my associate's part," Hardy shrugged. "The man was the right shape and weight, but he had to go and kill the only damned hobo with a close friend. But yeah, he was the patsy."

"And indistinguishable from myself, after we gave him my set of teeth, of course. Oh, and set him on fire." Leipzig smiled and chattered his teeth together. "These are better than the originals. And after such an intense fire, there were only dental records left to go on."

"But the coroner smelled a rat," Isobel said flatly.

"Ah, my dear, you are delightfully well informed," Leipzig smiled. "Agent Stone was a little too clever for his own good. I imagine he's thinking along those lines as we speak? Doctor McCray should be here soon and then the little reunion will be complete."

"The coroner sniffed around a little too much, so he was retired," Hardy said coldly. "Stone sniffed around, and now he has suffered the same fate."

"You can be sure of that, can you?" Isobel spat at him. "Besides, you both think you were so clever? It was killing the coroner that led us to Vermont and to Joe Carver. You've already left a trail to follow. If Rob Stone isn't going to be around to follow it, then it's only a matter of time before someone else will be!" She felt choked, hadn't meant to write Stone off, but she needed to unsettle them, keep them talking. She had no idea whether the telephone was still connected to the emergency call dispatch, but she had to suppose it was. If it was, it would record everything.

"So what?" Hardy sneered. "No one has a clue where we are and what we intend to do next. By the time anyone does, I'll be long gone. And ARES will be released on the public and the only anti-virus will be worth billions in ransom. Or legitimate sale. Depends how it plays out."

"Bastards!" Isobel screamed at them.

"Oh grow up, my dear... What do you think this is all about?" Leipzig stroked her shoulder and she recoiled from his touch, repulsed. "It's all about the money. Nothing else. We're not in this for the sake of mankind and humanity. Any chances of a Nobel Prize went out of the window the moment I started to work for the government. They want secrecy, not articles in *Time Magazine*."

Hardy smiled, bent down and caught hold

of her by the shoulders. He pulled her to her feet and pushed her harshly away from the couch. "Move," he ordered her abruptly. "It's time for you to go somewhere a little less comfortable."

\*\*\*

Stone had parked the big silver Mercedes off the road, approximately five hundred meters from the stationary red dot in the center of the laptop's screen. The map indicated nothing but green, indicating forest filling up every bit of the screen. It did not register the logging tracks or occasional private driveway.

He had travelled a little way down the bumpy track and had pulled off and parked behind a spinney, a natural barrier of small saplings and thorn bushes. The car was completely out of sight from the track and he checked on the screen of the laptop for the direction of the red dot. It was due east and ahead was only large trees of maple and spruce and cedar. The track would naturally lead him to the destination, but he wanted to remain covert at all times and chose to head straight, around eighty yards parallel to the track.

He had never felt so on edge. He had gambled with Isobel's life on a hunch. The more he had thought about it, the more it made sense. Isobel was being tracked digitally. That was how the assassin had been on to them so efficiently, how he had turned up when they had been met on the road by the assassin. Her coat and shoulder bag were the only items she had with her in Vermont that she had also had with her in New York. Stone had bought her new clothes and she had binned the old ones back at the motel. Now, there was the slight chance that the assassin's tracking receiver could still find Isobel. There had been no more digital pulse other than the one Sheriff Harper had sworn he'd seen. The battery would be low or dead by now, but Stone had taken the grid reference where Harper had pointed to. It was all he had now to go on.

He checked his pistol, which now carried a full fifteen rounds and then holstered it and reached for the silenced submachine pistol. The magazine was full, giving him a total of thirty rounds, but he would have to be careful; the weapon could spit them out at a rate of 13 bullets a second.

He stepped out of the car and looked cautiously around. He felt nervous, apprehensive. He breathed deeply to steady his nerves. He knew from experience that when it came down to engaging with the enemy, his apprehension would be replaced with a fearless, determined desire to complete the task. However, until he made an aggressive move, he would have to carry with him this burdening emotion he despised so much.

He was ready now. Armed and committed. With another couple of deep, calming breaths, he brought the weapon up in front of him and viewed everything through the crude V and pin sights as he headed across the open bush grass towards the thick belt of trees.

***

Isobel dropped heavily to the floor, partly landing on the bare single mattress that had been pushed into the comer of the room. She sat up, tucked her knees up to her stomach and looked at her surroundings. The floor was made from thick slate in what had been constructed as a sort of utility room. Part of the wall and floor in the nearest corner was covered in thick, clear plastic sheeting, taped into place with heavy industrial duct-tape. To the far side of the room there was a bank of domestic appliances; a washing machine, tumble dryer and large chest freezer. Closer to the door were shelving units stacked with dried and canned goods, and in the middle of the room there was a large meat hook suspended from the ceiling with a drain and angled guttering directly underneath. Alongside the wall, near the hook, was a large wooden butcher's block with a selection of knives, saws and cleavers hanging from the ceiling above it from double ended hooks. Stacked high all down one wall were large cardboard boxes of various dimensions with names she recognized as suppliers and makers of medical and laboratory equipment and supplies. This is where ARES would be reborn. She looked back at the suspended meat hook and the block and the drain. Fitting that they planned to create ARES in this room of death.

Leipzig smiled and swept a hand towards the somewhat macabre in-home abattoir. "For butchering deer and elk, or god knows what else they shoot in these parts," he said breezily. "The drain takes away the blood as the animal bleeds before butchery. This stops the meat from souring and gives it a better flavor. It's a myth that corpses don't bleed, a few well-placed cuts and gravity sees to the rest."

Isobel shuddered, turned away from the morbid scene in front of her. The room felt cold, but it was more than the fall chill from the mountains; it was a feeling of death and finality. Magnificent beasts, hunted and shot for human gratification, were hauled up on the hook and left to bleed, then skinned and butchered, dismembered. The room stank of industrial strength bleach and disinfectant, but Isobel could still smell death. She looked over at the area covered by plastic sheeting, frowned and then turned her eyes to the floor.

"Ah, so much bewilderment, so much

curiosity," Leipzig smiled. Isobel stared at him, unsure who the man was in front of her. Leipzig was like a hyperactive child, his eyes wide and searching, and his bodily movements quick and concise. He seemed excitable, like a child on Christmas morning with a world of presents under the tree. "Everything has a purpose in life, do you not think? Take this room for instance. The hook, the drain, the butcher's block; they are all components of a larger part. The larger part being the steaks on your plate or the roasting joints in your freezer. Without these components," he swept his hand past the butcher's block and knives "There *is* no meat to put on the table." He paced across the room and stood in the center of the plastic sheeting then started tapping it with the toe of his shoe. It was rhythmical, a sort of tune, but Isobel didn't even attempt to guess what it could be. "Can you guess what this could possibly be for? No? This is where the tramp that doubled for me died. It's been cleaned, but he died in this very room. That coroner also. He was a ladies man. He was lured here by some rather lurid texts, promising the sort of things that wives don't. Not his own wife, anyway. Seems that the woman he'd recently met on an internet dating site was in fact a middle aged man with the CIA." He smiled at Tom Hardy. "Hardy got him to come here, while his *associate* took care of him."

Isobel shook her head at him. "You're sick," she said vehemently. "What's happened to you?" He bore no resemblance to the mentor she once knew. He was clearly insane.

"Money," Hardy announced flatly. He walked over and stood beside the professor. "He's a genius, whose work was always going to be undervalued because of the people he worked for. The government can do that to a person. You give your all, twenty-four-seven, if you have to and for what?" He smiled at Leipzig, who nodded enthusiastically in agreement. "Whatever you do, it is never enough. They play with your budget, challenge your decisions and take all the credit. I know, because I've been there my whole adult life." Hardy reached into the open flap of his jacket and took out the big Colt .45 automatic. He pulled back the hammer and raised it to Leipzig's head and pulled the trigger. The gunshot was deafening inside the room, and Leipzig dropped to the floor like a wet cloth. Isobel had screamed, but couldn't hear it for the resonance of the gunshot, which echoed from the walls and floor and ceiling. Blood and bone and cerebral matter had sprayed all over the plastic sheeting and was running steadily down the wall in a mass of rivulets, channeling in the creases and folds of the plastic. Leipzig's body twitched and his toes rubbed the plastic sheeting as the nervous system shut down. It only lasted a few seconds but Isobel couldn't watch. She stared at Hardy, tears in her eyes.

Hardy calmly tucked the large pistol into the back of his waistband and turned back to Isobel, looking at her coldly. "Professor Leipzig has retired. You're now in charge of the ARES project. He'd lost it. I've never seen someone lose their mind so quickly. I'll make you a different deal to the one I had with Leipzig. The man was greedy and wanted far too big a percentage. The man is now dead. You, I shall give freedom and nothing else. Create what I need and I will let you live. That's the deal and it is not open to negotiation."

Isobel was shaking. Her eyes were wide and staring transfixed at the corpse lying crumpled on the floor. The blood had collected in a pool, dammed in by a large fold in the plastic. Soon it threatened to overflow and rush out onto the slate floor and into the channel towards the drain.

She turned her eyes away from the macabre scene and stared up at him. "Go to hell," she said coldly. She felt a warm rush come over her. It enveloped the chill and the coldness of the room, enlightened the ambiance of death and raised her spirits. She wasn't scared any more, didn't feel as if anybody could have a hold on her again. "You're a fool, Hardy," she paused, looked at the cadaver and sneered back at him. "You just shot your last bolt. Have you heard from McCray recently? No? Well that probably means that Stone overpowered him. So *that* business partner is out of the equation as well. And now you've got all the money for yourself. But really, you have nothing. Who is going to make the virus for you now? Because I certainly won't! How stupid do you think I am? You had a deal with both McCray and Leipzig for Christ's sake. You'll never let me go when I finish making the virus. So you can take the flash drives and do two things with them; either buy a school chemistry set and try and replicate them for yourself, which is never going to happen," she laughed. "Or bend over and stick them where the sun is never going to shine."

Hardy stepped forwards, took the pistol out and aimed it at her head. "You *will* make the virus. I know how to get people to do things and believe me, it will be done."

"Go get the drives and I'll stick them up your ass right now!" she screamed at him. "Go on! I don't care anymore, just kill me and get it over with!" She lunged forwards and pressed her forehead against the muzzle of the weapon. It was still hot against her cold skin. "Do it, I dare you!"

Hardy stared at her, his eyes flickering. The indecision was written all over his face. He glanced down at Leipzig's body, a shallow shade of regret behind his otherwise cold, lifeless eyes. He tightened his grip on the pistol and stared at her coldly, then flinched as he heard the heavy knock on the door. He looked at her and smiled. His entire face changing in front of her eyes. There was a degree of certainty and confidence back in his expression. "That will be the good doctor," he said somewhat smugly. "Which means that your friend Stone is either dead, or soon will be. It would also seem that it were *you* who has shot their last bolt." He bent down and glared at her, his face contorted in quiet rage. He twisted her head harshly, forcing her to look at the body on the floor. "Take a good look at the good professor while I'm out of the room. You may soon be joining him. But know this; if you don't cooperate then I will kill you. And my God, it will be slow and painful you little bitch." He pulled at the gag hanging around her neck and wriggled it over her chin and forced it viciously into her mouth.

Hardy closed the door behind him, tucking the big pistol into the back of his waistband as he walked across the large open floor space towards the front door. He opened the door expectantly, but his expression dropped when he looked into the face of the Vermont county Sheriff.

"Sheriff Harper, Sir," the lawman smiled amiably and showed his ID wallet for extra verification. He made great pains to fold it and replace it carefully in his breast pocket. "We have a report that a 9-11 call was made from this address. Can you tell me anything about that?"

Hardy stared blankly at him, genuinely bewildered. "Err ... no. No, I can't," he said incongruously. He glanced casually down at the sheriff s sidearm. It was unclipped from the holster's leather thumb break and the sheriff's hand rested somewhat casually on the butt. It was a passive gesture, but it also put the .40 Glock a little too close for comfort. There was no way that Hardy could reach for the rear draw quicker than the sheriff.

"Well, that's mighty strange." Sheriff Harper frowned and scratched his brow with his left hand. "You see, dispatch don't make mistakes like that and I have to follow up the call. We can get a trace on a call real quick these days, so I drove on up to see if everything's okay. Perhaps you, or someone else knocked over the telephone by accident. These things happen, I'm sure... Dispatch heard and recorded raised voices. They thought it might be a domestic disturbance. Is anyone else here with you? Your wife, maybe?"

"No."

"So you're on your own," Harper frowned. "Now that is a puzzle…"

"It is. Well, I'll just go and check the phone," Hardy said. He stepped back from the door but stopped as the sheriff stepped into the threshold, his hand a little tighter on the butt of the pistol.

"Whoa there, chief," Harper smiled. "How about I go check with you?"

"Certainly," Hardy smiled. "Come on in."

***

Stone reached the edge of the wooded copse, crouched down low and caught his breath. He had heard the muffled gunshot from a little over two hundred yards away. He had dropped to the ground, fearful that he was under fire, but had soon realized that it was a long way distant and a one off. But then he had started to worry. It was a soft thud of a sound and not the high-velocity crack of a large caliber hunting rifle which is what he'd have expected in these parts. And then he had realized that if it wasn't a hunting rifle, then it was obviously a pistol shot and that it may not have been fired from a great distance, but from inside the house.

He had ran the rest of the way, careful to keep to the rough course he had plotted from the screen of the laptop. However, when he had finally pushed through the thick undergrowth and reached the fringe of the trees, he had seen the sheriff's cruiser pull in and park alongside the BMW. There was still fifty yards of open ground between the cars and the log cabin and by Stone's estimation he figured that the tracking device was inside the car. What the hell was Sheriff Harper doing here? Was the man involved as well? No, he couldn't be. But nothing so far had been straightforward.

Stone crept forwards and reached the car, his eyes on the house at all times. A cursory glance through the passenger window told him that the tracking device that the assassin had placed on Isobel was in fact in her shoulder bag, as it was clearly in view on the passenger seat. He looked back at the house and saw Sheriff Harper step inside. He knew that there was little time and darted back to the edge of the trees and started to skirt the periphery of the property, keeping his eyes on the log cabin.

***

"You see..." Sheriff Harper sounded perplexed. "I can understand that the receiver could quite easily get knocked off the cradle, but what I don't understand is that it should call 9-11. That's a hell of a chance, don't you think?"

"Gee, I guess," Hardy did his best to sound dumb and innocent. "But this cabin is a rental, perhaps 9-11 is on the memory button, in case foreign visitors don't know the number?"

"And the voices?"

"The television."

"What show were you watching?"

"Nothing. Just surfing the channels."

Sheriff Harper stared at him and shrugged. "Maybe you're right. Mind if I take a look around?"

"I'd rather you didn't," Hardy said, a little too quickly. "I'm..."

"What?"

"In the middle of something, right now."

"What's that, if you don't mind me asking?"

Hardy hesitated and then smiled. "I'm working on a novel. I'm using this cabin to get away from interruptions."

"Oh, I 'm sorry about that," Harper said indifferently. "Perhaps you wouldn't get interrupted if you took more care with your phone. Or surfed the channels so much. Can't imagine someone writing with the TV on."

Hardy smiled, stepped forwards and placed a hand on Harper's shoulder. "I will do just that, from now on. Now, if there's nothing more I can help you with ..."

The sheriff smiled. "No, you carry on. I'll just take a look around, and I'll be on my way," he paused. "How much is one of these cabins to rent anyway?"

Hardy sighed. "Just under two thousand a week, with taxes and the agency fees. So I'd appreciate getting some use out of it."

"Two thousand bucks a week!" Harper

exclaimed. "You must be a successful writer. What was it you said you write?"

"I didn't."

"No. You didn't," Harper pulled away from him and ambled across the room. He did it casually, taking in the paintings and photographs that adorned the walls. "I like mysteries myself. Detective stories."

"You don't say."

Sheriff Harper smiled at him. "So you're famous, right?"

"No."

"But you've written a lot, to afford this place, right?"

"No. As I said, I'm *working* on a novel."

"Right," Harper moved closer to the door to the utility room. Hardy tensed. Harper saw the movement and looked back at him. "So what's it about, this novel?"

"I ..." Hardy hesitated, frowned. "Look, sheriff... I am sorry if I wasted your time ... But you are wasting mine now. I am paying a fortune for this place for a little peace and quiet and I would like to think that it wasn't being wasted. Can you please accept my apologies and leave me to get back to work?"

Harper smiled. "Of course," he paused, his hand hesitating on the door handle, "I'll just take a quick look though, just to satisfy my report."

Harper turned his back on him briefly, noticed a sudden movement in the periphery of his vision and looked back at Hardy.

The Colt .45 was aimed straight and steady, the hammer back and tension on the trigger. Hardy's face was behind it, his eyes cold and every bit as steady as the pistol. "You wouldn't fucking listen. Had to keep nosing around. Well Sheriff, how about unhitching that gun belt and kicking it to one side?"

Harper did as he was told, slowly and surely and careful not to make a sudden, unsolicited move. "You can't do this," he said quietly. "They'll send someone else when I don't call in."

"What, another half-assed sheriff? I think I'll manage." Hardy glared at him, kept the pistol steady. "Now, satisfy your curiosity and open the door."

Harper turned the handle steadily and pushed the door inwards. He peered inside, his shoulders seemed to sag, like he knew it was hopeless, that there was too much distance between them and that his only hope of survival nestled snugly in the holster on the floor. He looked back at him, his face ashen at what he had witnessed and the hopelessness of his predicament. He was scared and Hardy could see it clearly in the man's eyes. He looked at Isobel squatting on the mattress, at the bloody mess surrounding the body on the floor.

Hardy moved closer, kept the heavy pistol trained on him. He smiled, enjoyed seeing the expression of fear upon the man's face. "Go inside and join them." Harper reluctantly did so and Hardy started to follow a few paces behind.

There was an eruption gunfire and wood splinters and chunks of stucco disintegrated in a cloud of plaster dust. Hardy turned and faced the gunfire, opening up with a salvo of .45 that sounded like canon fire in the confines of the cabin.

Stone darted out from the hallway and took cover in the doorway of one of the bedrooms. He fired a short burst from the machine pistol and four bullet holes punched into the wall inches from Hardy's face. The CIA man returned fire, then dropped onto one knee as he fished a magazine out of his pocket and reloaded the Colt. He dropped the slide forward and fired a double tap at Stone, who had already started to move.

Stone knew that in close quarter battle there were two types of people. Those who moved and those who died. He crouched low as he ran and felt Hardy's bullets pass inches from his face. He fired the machine pistol again, but it recoiled twice then clicked empty. He had the Glock 9mm out of its holster and ready to fire as he got to the central open fire place in the middle of the lounge area. It was three feet high and provided a barrier of bricks to crouch behind. The metal conical canopy provided more cover. Just a two foot space for Hardy to shoot through. Stone knew the person with the most cover had the best chance. He fired three shots and Hardy let out a scream and dropped the Colt on the floor. He bent to retrieve it but Stone fired three more shots. They missed, but threw up splinters of polished floorboard in the man's face. Hardy, held his injured arm and retreated to the doorway of the utility room. He was bleeding badly. He caught hold of Sheriff Harper's gun belt and scrambled to his feet. Stone crouched on his knees, sighting on the man's back, but he disappeared from view before he could fire.

Hardy stepped into the room pulling the .40 Glock clear of its holster. He looked for both Sheriff Harper and Isobel, had the pistol held out in front of him, dropped the empty gun belt to the floor. Where were they? He felt a wave of adrenaline wash over him as his eyes searched the room desperately. The mattress was in front of him and Isobel was gone. He turned to look for the sheriff, realizing that both he and Isobel could only be behind the door and by the bank of shelving. The searing pain that followed surged through him like a firebrand. His upper body contorted and his legs gave way as he dropped the pistol and clawed and grasped at his neck.

Isobel kept both hands on the handle of the butcher's knife and plunged it deeper into his neck, twisting and sawing and pressing it deeper to gain better purchase. Most of the ten inch blade was buried deep inside him and a wave of blood surged out and over her hands with every pulse of his weakening heartbeat. She grit her teeth together tightly and hissed at him: "How does it feel to die you bastard?" she panted. She continued to push the blade deeper, grunted under the effort. Hardy was on his knees, but pinned in place by the knife. He could not pull forwards and away from the blade and neither could he push backwards because Isobel's knees prevented him from moving. The sheer size of the blade was skewering him in place.

Harper was behind her, his expression aghast. He had used the knife to cut her bindings free, but she had grabbed it from him as the door had opened. Now his hands were on her shoulders pulling her away. But she resisted, shrugging him away.

"You lock me in a fucking slaughterhouse and think I'll just sit tight and wait to die? How does it feel?" She screamed at him through clenched teeth. She continued to twist the knife and the blood flow slowed and almost stopped altogether. Hardy was motionless now. She stepped backwards a pace and his body slumped forwards, the weight pulling the blade clean out of his neck as he fell, leaving the knife in Isobel's grasp.

Rob Stone was in the doorway and he

slipped his weapon back into its holster and caught hold of Isobel's bloodied wrists. Her bindings hung loose from each wrist, sliced through. He whispered for her to let go and she suddenly seemed to snap back into herself and looked appalled at her blood-soaked hands. She gradually released her grip on the knife and it dropped onto the floor next to Tom Hardy's body. His blood flowed slowly along the sloped floor and channeled into the gutter, before swirling into the purpose built drain in the floor.

## SIXTY FOUR

The sun shone brightly onto the bay and the lapping waves broke the reflections shimmering like polished gems on the surface of the sea. The ocean was emerald green, and the sky above was azure between fast moving broken white clouds. The air was fresh and autumnal chill was starting to grip tighter and take hold, pulling the city into the fringe of winter.

The waitress brought the two cappuccinos and Danish pastries on a silver tray. She placed each item down beside them, smiled and left to clear another table. They sat with their backs to the coffee house and looked out over the bay. In the distance the Statue of Liberty stood tall and proud and true. She was the watchtower of the city, the guardian landmark of the United States. Stone lent back in his chair and watched a tour boat go past. The cameras were clicking on both port and starboard sides as the tourists were taken out to the bay to sail near Liberty Island to capture a piece of America for prosperity, then on towards Staten Island and back around Ellis Island and Governor's Island back to Manhattan. The people on board new nothing of super viruses or dishonest CIA officers or insane professors or relentless assassins. They occupied a different realm in reality. Stone took a sip of the hot coffee and placed the cup back down on the saucer.

They had been interviewed by the Vermont State Police, who in turn, were being aided by the FBI as various crimes in the same case had crossed state lines. Stone had used his authorization from the White House to deliver the salient facts and keep them from being detained for too long. The FBI case officer had spoken to the New York FBI field office and an interview for the next morning had been arranged. Elizabeth Delaney and David Stein's involvement had been accounted for, and highly commended by Stone, and he agreed that he would put their names forward for a posthumous award from Washington. The interview had taken almost two hours, far longer than Stone could have argued for, but for the sake of professional courtesy, he had not objected. Isobel had answered for her actions with the FBI and an interview had been set for the government select committee that was charged with the overseeing of bioresearch and all other research and development facilities under their control. Stone had volunteered his presence during her

interview, but she had declined it vehemently. She would argue her reasons for taking the drives, but would do so on her own. The select committee merely had to cover themselves in case of repercussions, and as long as the information on ARES and APHRODITE were safe and the FBI corroborated her story, then she would be back at work at bioresearch as soon as she was ready, after a two-week vacation. There had even been the murmurs of a promotion. Stone too, was granted a leave of absence and what started out as a flippant comment from Stone about disappearing together for a week or two was taken seriously and warmly by Isobel. Almost at once had come a wave of awkward silences as each other thought about the coming days, and nights ahead. It wasn't going to be all pleasurable though, as both decided mutually to attend both David Stein's and Elizabeth Delaney's funeral services later in the week. Isobel sipped the frothy cappuccino and wiped the whipped cream from her top lip with
the paper napkin. "What I don't understand is why you started to believe that Professor Leipzig was still alive," she mused. "When did you guess?"

"I never truly did know for sure," Stone said. "'But it was in my mind, just a musing, from the first time I met with Sheriff Harper. He took me up to the spot where the truck went off and pointed out that it could not have been an accident. After studying the site, I was in full agreement." He sipped some of his drink, and Isobel laughed. She reached forwards and dabbed some cream off the end of his nose. "Thanks," he said coyly. "The next thing was the coroner. I mean, what were the chances of that? He was the link to the verdict on Leipzig's death. That got me thinking, but still only along the lines that the death was no accident. However, while I was in Captain Dolbeck's office in Montpelier, he was talking about how busy he was and that some hobo had come in asking about his friend. I mean, how do you find a missing person when they're already homeless? What was the bigger question was: who was ever going to miss a homeless guy?"

"Joe Carver did," Isobel said blankly.

"Right."

"So that was their mistake?"

"One of them," Stone nodded. "But that report had a long list of missing persons; a strip dancer come suspected prostitute from Montpelier, a couple of young teenagers, a dentist from Montpelier and a hobo from South Chesterton, barely ten miles from Deal. And although I ignored the missing dentist at first, I just couldn't ignore the death of the coroner or the unexplained disappearance of the tramp. The coroner got curious, probably raised the wrong questions and was taken care of."

"So what about the dentist?"

"I've told Chief Dolbeck and he's confirmed that the dentist is still missing. He's ordering a search of the lake where the coroner was discovered," he paused. "Regardless, we've got the body of Leipzig to prove that he faked his own death and the false teeth will corroborate the fact. They match records held at the missing dentist's practice. It's hopefully only a matter of time before they find his body. He had a wife and two kids, so they really need some closure."

Isobel nodded somberly. "So what now?"

"Well, the FBI will be looking in to Morgan-Klein, the pharmaceutical company. There's an element there who were willing to deal with Hardy and McCray. In doing so, they would have been involved in the release of ARES and the deaths of thousands. Once they start going through Hardy's computers they'll uncover something, I'm sure. As for this end of the investigation, well the drives are safe with the FBI and you've got to answer to the select committee, which I know will be just fine. But after that?" He leaned forward across the table and kissed her on the mouth. She responded, shyly at first, then a little more intimately. They broke apart and looked at each other intently. Stone smiled, "I'm looking forward to a break. Some good food, different scenery, good company ..."

"Well, I can't cook and I can't help the

scenery, but I *can* provide the company." She smiled at him, reached over the table and took his hand in hers. "Thank you," she said warmly. "Thank you for being there and helping me."

Stone smiled. "You know, I don't think you really needed any help, you seemed to do just fine by yourself." He looked at her, but she looked away and released his hand from hers. She had been withdrawn since the incident in the log cabin, and he knew from experience that killing a man is easy enough, but living with it is hard for the ethical person. He reached across and took up her hand and cursed inwardly as his cell phone started to chime. He took it out of his pocket and pressed the answer key.

"Stone here."

"Agent Stone, this is Sheriff Harper."

"Hi Sheriff, what can I do for you?'" He was curt, wanted to get back to Isobel.

"I just thought you'd like to know, we headed up into the hills, up to Beaumont Ridge. Everything was like you said. We recovered the weapons and saw your handiwork with the traps. Big Red Anderson came up there with us. He's a local hunter and expert tracker. We used his dogs to follow your scent. Now he's a trapper, and he said that they were damn fine examples of mantraps. Best he'd ever seen."

"Thanks Sheriff," Stone paused. Isobel had

looked away and was studying the Statue of Liberty in the distance. "What's your point?"

"Well hold on there, Agent Stone. We found everything like you said. Except we didn't find anybody in the trap."

Stone tensed rigid. He pushed the cell phone closer to his ear and turned side on. "What the hell do you mean?" he asked, then watched as Isobel got up from her seat and walked over and leaned against the metal railings. He turned away from her and listened to the sheriff.

"Like I said, we got the rifle and the big bowie knife, found your handgun and all, and we found the traps. And plenty of blood on the spikes in the pitfall trap, so there's no doubt you got him."

"I know I got him sheriff! I threw my knife into his chest and bludgeoned him with the butt of a rifle. I watched him die! Now listen to me, you get up into those hills and start looking. Maybe he was taken by a bear?"

"You sure know nothing about bears, Agent Stone. Now we get a few big black bears up here. And they wouldn't hesitate taking a wounded or dead man in a trap. Kind of like a buffet to them. But they'd be drag marks and pieces of him all over the place. Bears are lazy, they eat their food where they find it or kill it. They don't go dragging it back to some cave. Hell, they usually just sleep where it's warm and keep on roaming around. Especially the big males. And it's a big male most likely to drag a guy weighing two hundred and fifty pounds or so out of a trap."

Stone watched Isobel lean over the railings and look down at the sea birds below. Children were feeding them with pieces of hotdog bread and potato chips. He looked down at the ground near his feet. It was blurry, like his eyes had trouble focusing. "So what are you saying, sheriff?"

"Well, I'm saying that we found nothing. Big Red got his dogs on some scent, but we lost it after a mile or so and had to give up on it. Hell, we'll go back out there if you want, but the guy's gone. Period. He must have been one tough son of a bitch. You knocked him out, but he must have come round again. Either way, he wasn't there. He walked out of there on his own two feet. Lord only knows where he is now. Big Red said he was favoring a leg, like he was wounded. The track depression was deeper on one side. No, he definitely walked out of their Agent Stone and he sure as Hell didn't get dragged out of there by some hairy assed bear."

Stone cut the connection and switched off the cell phone. He got up from the table and walked over towards Isobel. She looked up and smiled. He placed his hands on her shoulders and gripped firmly. She turned around and hugged him, resting her head heavily on his chest.

"I can't believe this is all over," she said dreamily.

Stone glanced around, watched the gathering of people at the quay waiting for the boat to return. He looked at a man on his own at the end of the walkway. He looked at the parked van on the private roadway delivering bread to a restaurant. Everywhere he looked he saw a possible threat, somewhere for an assassin to hide and take aim. As a bodyguard he knew more than most that a highly motivated individual willing to trade their life in order to kill was an impossible threat to counter.

He looked back at Isobel and forced a smile. "No," he said flatly. "I can't either."

## SIXTY FIVE

*Six months later...*

In his New York office at the Centre for Virus Control, a department within the World Health Organization (WHO) Fernando Rodriguez continued to work through his in tray and sort the paperwork accordingly. He had recently returned from the Ivory Coast where Ebola was spreading throughout the West African countries. Angola, Senegal and Liberia had all reported cases in the hundreds and a continental pandemic was being prepared for by both WHO, the United Nations and a task force of the wealthiest world governments.

Rodriguez was a leading authority in his field and had recently written a paper on the spread of Ebola and the resistance the virus displayed to drugs and treatment. In research he had shown a clear indication that Ebola had mutated between African countries, the strain in Liberia proving harder to treat than the strain in Sierra Leone. Although identical in structure, there was evidence that treatment was becoming more difficult as the virus spread. It was the publication of this paper that most of his correspondence was in reply to.

The package intrigued him. It had been opened, resealed and stamped with the security clearance seal that WHO employed as standard operating procedure. It was a thickly padded brown envelope addressed to him personally. He knew security procedures would dictate a check, so he was not offended in any way. A white extremist group had once tried to send Anthrax in a bid to shut WHO down. Lord only knew their intent. He slit the tape with a craft knife and tipped the contents onto the desk in front of him. The two shiny USB flash drives caught the light, glistening. A single folded sheet of paper dropped out of the envelope. He unfolded it and frowned as he read. He picked up the first USB and slipped it into his laptop's drive. As he clicked to open the file he looked down again at the sheet of handwritten paper. It simply read: *So you can do the right thing.*